The Fire (

By Angela Aaron

A Fantasy Romance

Previously released in 2012, this revised 2024 edition has a brand-new cover and updated content just waiting for you to dive into the romance and fantasy. This 2024 edition is the only edition currently available.

This book is the product of the author's imagination. Although some minor characters and locations are factual, the information has been fictionalized to fit the story.

This is an adult romance with mature situations. It is intended for readers over the age of 18.

Edited by Guardian Proof Reading Services
Formatting by Lauralynn Elliott @ The Forge Book Finishers
Cover by Angela Aaron

The Fire of Beltane
by Angela Aaron

When the past is real, when the impossible becomes possible and dreams come true ... literally.

When Aedan is denied his soul mate that fateful Beltane night, he is given the gift of immortality, permitting him to wait for her prophesied return. Reunited after twelve-hundred years, he is disheartened to learn his true love holds no memory of him.

Wishing for a distraction from the winter doldrums, Aislinn never expects to be caught up in a whirlwind of magic and danger with a man she has spent her whole life dreaming about. What he asks of her tests the very reality she holds dear.

Now, as Beltane approaches, and with time running out, Aedan and Aislinn must reach Ireland to pledge their love to one another. But in order to live out their destinies, they must overcome an ancient foe determined to see an end to their fated love.

Twelve-hundred years he waited for her; he could lose her in a single moment.

Mature content

Dedication

To Jules who was the first to recognize the magic of Aedan and Aislinn and suggest their story to be told. Your unwavering encouragement during the writing was my inspiration during the toughest of times.

My gracious thanks to Heather for the endless hours of revising and editing. I couldn't have accomplished this without you.

Big hugs and kisses for my son who supported me in all ways from the moment I expressed a desire to writer. Your approval meant everything.

An additional thank you must also be given to Jan McDonell for her patience and advice in helping with the rewrite.

Glossary

AIDIDH – ANCIENT NAME for Aedan

Aislinn - Ancient name for Ashlynn

Dal Riata - Refers to territory that is now Northern Ireland

Dal Riada - Refers to territory in Western Scotland that was once controlled by the Dal Riata of Ireland

Un'Neill - O'Neil- A Territorial clan west of the Dal Riata territory

Del n'Araide, the Lady Druidess' tribe on the west coast of Ireland, south of the Dal Riata, north of the Dal Fiatach

Dal Fiatach- Ancient tribe on the east coast of Ireland, situated beneath the Dal n'Araide tribe.

Erin, Erie, Hibernia - Ancient names for Ireland

Alba, Scotti, Scotia - Ancient name for Scotland

Ciniodh - Kenneth (Kenneth MacAlpin)

Donel – Donald (Donald MacAlpin)

Prologue

I reland, Early 9th Century
She stood silently staring at the wooded grove in the distance. Fires dotted the hillside. Beltane. Fires were lit this night. Sacred fires meant to warm and awaken the world from the weariness of winter, a time for renewal, a time to celebrate life and to honor the Goddess and God. This time was for unions, for fertility, for love. It was a time for people to celebrate passion and human desires.

But this night belonged to her.

She could feel the cool evening mist from where she stood and could smell the fresh mossy air stirring around her. Crimson and amethyst hues faded in the twilight. Her destiny beckoned.

Her skin prickled with fear, or possibly anticipation. She turned away from the window.

The drums sounded. She could hear them out in the night. The rhythm became the night and the night called.

He called.

She drank the draught meant to ease her, but instead, the spicy brew heightened all of her senses.

Warmth grew deep inside her, coiling tightly in the very depths of her, spreading its tendrils through her belly. *The drink*, she thought *or him?* The drums called to her. Their pounding claimed her in the same manner he would claim her. No, the drink did not dull her.

She moved through a dream, and yet everything seemed very clear. Time slowed, senses heightened. She ached. The feel of light fabric billowing against her skin as she emerged into the night breeze teased her, aroused her. Would his touch do the same?

As she neared the grove of trees, her breath caught in her throat. She'd always known of this time. She'd waited for him and this night most of her life. They were fated to be together. The crowds gathered around her, two tribes becoming one, two clans uniting for strength. This union offered hope, protection. This commitment witnessed and shared by all so both tribes recognized their alliance to the other. Years in the planning. But this night meant so much more. It was the end of waiting, the end of longing. In secret this night had been given to them.

He stood within the circle of stones waiting for her, wanting her, knowing her. She could sense him so strongly now, his anticipation, his arousal. Her heart quickened as she felt his essence pulsing through her veins.

Clearly instructed in tonight's expectations, he was not to be the Druidh warrior; she was not to be the princess. Tonight, they were man and woman. Tonight, they were to give themselves over to the powers of the magic. Tonight, they would be primal, and ancient and human. They would join in a sharing of souls, of hearts; the acceptance of a grand gift from the Lady of the old religion, a reward for their fealty and love.

She allowed fear to cloud her thoughts. A nervous shiver flowed through her; she could not look at him, yet she knew he wanted her to look. He wanted to make her feel nothing but him. She knew his desires with assurance. She could feel them inside her. She shivered again, but this time, not from fear.

The fires danced and licked at her, smoke and the mystery encircled her. *He* encircled her. Her skin burned. Sweat beaded on her skin, despite the chill of the night air. Every nerve ending tingled with life, despite drinking the potion to dull. She dared to look at him, one glance from under her lashes. He stood a short distance away, waiting for her in the center of the sacred stones, powerful, dark, mysterious, raw, and male. She could feel him watching her, caressing her with his gaze. The knot deep within her tightened even more and the fires burned hotter.

He reached for her, easily lifting her to stand with him. She raised her eyes to look at his face and accepted his warm smile. However, despite his reassurance, her nervousness continued. Her gaze shifted to the onlookers. She tried to hide the apprehension she felt but knew she failed when he leaned into her and touched her arm.

"Donnae be frightened," he whispered.

She smiled, but looked past him again to the people gathered outside the circle. His determination filled her then, willing her to forget them. He raised his hand to her face, instantly bringing her attention back to him. He traced his thumb over her lips. She looked deep into his eyes. They accepted her and held her. Tonight, she would become his.

"Ken that I want you. I have always wanted you," his words were soft, barely audible, and spoken a moment before his lips touched hers. She opened freely to his kiss. He pulled her to him, pressing her tight against him. He buried his face in her hair. She heard him inhale deeply as if learning her scent. She could feel his essence flowing into every pore of her body, feel his life thrumming through her veins, filling her, branding her.

He kissed her again more deeply, capturing a small moan that escaped her lips. Somewhere low in the distance the chanting began.

"Do ye feel the drums?" His hands moved over her face, her neck, as if committing to memory every inch of her. He searched and explored, using hands and lips until she became breathless and writhed in his arms. She felt the rhythm, his rhythm.

The flames rose within her body, consuming her. She pulsed with each drumbeat, each crackle of fire. The feelings, the tightening, burned in the very core of her. Lifting his proud face, she saw the power, the hunger. He would possess her more deeply than her body tonight. She understood the cost and yet she ached endlessly for his possession.

He unfastened her gown and slid the fabric down her body. She knew her surrender, knew she no longer controlled her fate and felt insignificant compared to the great powers moving through her this night. She gave herself over to him, to the passion surging through her veins, as she reveled in its wonder and its ancientness.

She watched him move around her. He circled her, stalked her, a man after his prey. His hands explored and she thrilled to the warmth of his touch. His fingers traced the ancient designs painted on her body. Magic designs, the Lady's sacred symbols. In touching them, he acknowledged and accepted their connection.

The intricate marks circled her breasts and swirled around her abdomen and back before reaching her most feminine place. He bowed over her, raining kisses down her face and neck. He kissed her breasts until she melted beneath him, arching toward him. His kisses trailed lower and he followed the path of the ancient designs until he tasted her.

His deep, dark eyes burned with passion, and something else. She couldn't look away. They captured her, held her and made her yearn for him in the deepest part of her. She wanted to know him, to feel him in the way a man takes a woman. She wanted knowledge of the mystery coursing through her veins. She yearned for her own surrender.

She let him lift her and carry her toward the flat surface of the center stone. A fabric covered the rough surface, woven with the same mystic symbols she bore on her flesh. Despite his large stature, he moved with grace and control as he lay her down. He looked at her and must have sensed her unease, for once again, his gaze spoke of the rightness of this. She dared to look at him again, kneeling over her, savagely beautiful, his dark eyes watching her intensely.

She could see the effort, the discipline he possessed to keep his body still. His muscles were taut, straining with effort. She felt him tremble as she cautiously caressed him, learned him.

He smelled of heather and the sea, and she knew his power equaled the mighty waves crashing over the shore. The marks he bore proclaimed him Druidh, one of an ancient order of mystery and authority. She raised her eyes to his again, feeling him hard and pulsing between them, silently demanding her readiness to accept him. *I will lose myself tonight,* she thought. *I will lose myself to him. I will leave part of me in him and never be whole again.*

She looked past him into the night, into the flames. She saw bodies, naked and coupling, honoring the Goddess this night, celebrating spring, moving in rhythm to the drums, to the chanting, to the sounds of the night. *Lustful. Hot.* She wanted to know the rhythm, wanted to belong to this night, this one perfect night.

The fire entered her as he entered her. Pain gave way to pleasure. Flames lifted and swept over her, lapped at her, danced around her and in her, and promised a fulfillment she'd never known. She opened to him, gave him her innocence, and he filled her so completely she didn't know where she ended and he began. Somewhere in the night, the primal rhythm of the stones, the trees, and him throbbed inside her, bringing her closer to the connection she so desperately longed for.

With each movement, he buried himself deeper, and yet she needed him deeper still. She wanted him to take her, to burn her, to leave his mark so she would always know him. She could feel her essence reaching for his, straining to unite. Closer she flew toward the fire and closer he came to taking her soul.

The sounds. He began slipping away. *Intrusions.* The drums. The drums were gone. *The screaming!* Frantically he thrust, straining toward completion... *Whoosh!* Searing pain. Blood. He ripped himself away from her, leaving her cold and bewildered. An agonized cry tore from his throat. He knew. The warrior knew. Instantly, even in the throes of pure passion, he knew the gravity of the situation. She took longer to comprehend. *Attacked.* They were being attacked. She watched an arrow pierce his arm, jerking him with its force. He tore the jagged tip from his flesh, his blood splattering across her skin. He grabbed her and wrapped her in the alter cloth and tossed her into the throng of people. Stunned, she followed him blindly as he pulled her behind one of the stones, frantically scanning the surrounding area for another place to hide her.

"Nae," she cried, denying what she saw happening.

"Ye have to get out of here. Ye have to get away."

Through the stone circle, her clansmen were falling, dying in their attempt to reach her. Bodies littered the ground. He abruptly pushed her down and covered her as an arrow sailed by them. He then rose and tugged her after him. They made their way a few yards further and paused behind the shelter of a tree.

"Stay here," he commanded, leaping around the tree, intent on running back toward the fighting.

She watched him grab a sword from one of the fallen fighters and plunge into the thick of the battle. He moved through the fight, as if one of the ancient Tuatha De Danan, otherworldly and untouchable. She stood frozen behind the tree, stunned, unfulfilled and shaking uncontrollably.

A voice yelled through the chaos, startling her. One of her clansmen came running toward her.

"I thought we lost ya, lass." Her kinsman's trained eye looked around for a means of escape. "We must leave. Now!"

Numb and unable to speak, she didn't react to the urgency of the command.

"Can ye move, lass?"

Still, she didn't move. Her eyes searched frantically for him within the fighting.

"We must go!" The command came again.

"Nae. Donnae take me away."

"'Tis too late, lass."

"Nae. I cannae leave him."

Her kin forced her away from the battle. She was dragged through the woods against her will. Desperate to break free, she fought with every ounce of might she possessed, but her strength wasn't enough. She begged, pleaded, cried. He was the other half of her soul and she would never be whole without him.

Carried away from the fight, she knew with certainty she would never see him again. Her heart shattered into a thousand pieces. If somehow she survived this night and whatever future awaited her, a part of her would forever remain in the wooded grove waiting for him.

Chapter One

UNITED STATES, PRESENT Day

Aislinn stretched languidly. "*Hmm.*" She smiled sleepily, prolonging her reverie as best she could. "What a dream," she sighed. She rolled over and pulled the covers around her. Her skin tingled and warmed in the aftermath of her vivid imaginings. She loved when her dreams made her feel languid and aroused. She loved the place between waking and sleep, and desperately wanted to remain there, and she would have, too, if it weren't for the sudden buzzing of the alarm clock jolting her awake. She hit the snooze button, trying to hold onto the feelings fast ebbing away with the stark reality of morning. She closed her eyes.

"*Ugh,* I have to stop reading romance novels before bed," she mused, but honestly knew she would never give them up. A weekend with junk food and a good steamy romance proved a very cathartic way to keep the occasional loneliness at bay.

The alarm sounded again. "Okay, okay. I get it. I'm not supposed to go back to my perfect dream." Aislinn silenced the annoying device. "No, I would much prefer to get up and go out in this freezing weather and go to work," she huffed sarcastically. However, in the next instant, she thought about all the endearing little smiles that would greet her in her classroom this morning, and that provided the motivation she needed.

Aislinn flung her legs over the edge of the bed and looked in the direction of her closet, chiding herself for not ironing something to wear the night before.

Hurriedly trying on at least ten different outfits, nine of which ended up in a heap on her floor, she finally settled for a pair of khaki slacks and the least wrinkled blouse she could find. Adding to the morning's confusion, her thick curly hair had picked today to exercise its independence. Her wild, red locks defied all attempts at being pulled back. Stray wisps stubbornly escaped the tie and fluttered around her face.

Breakfast didn't go any easier. After weeks of half-charred toast, the toaster picked this morning to finally stop working. Having no time to cook anything else, she chose instead to munch on a cold peanut butter sandwich while she put on her coat.

She knew she should be more organized with everyday mundane things. But, in her mind, the morning's craziness was a small price to pay for staying up late reading, as well as this morning's overlong indulgence in her hot dream.

A half hour later found Aislinn pulling her car into the deserted parking lot of the school where she worked as a visual arts teacher. She turned off the engine glancing wistfully out the window at the bright moon. A big full moon always held a particular fascination for her, and this morning was no different. Aislinn found herself drawn to the mysterious orb by some unnamed thing stirring within her. She was mesmerized by the movement of the clouds playing hide and seek with her magical moon and secretly wished she were the recipient of some of its magic.

Aislinn often felt it's intrigue was perhaps a throwback to her Irish ancestors and their connections to the earth and its rhythms. But whatever the reason for her curiosity, it was a beautiful sight at 6:30 a.m. on a subzero January morning. It was definitely an image enchanting enough to rekindle memories of the handsome warrior who, only an hour ago, filled her slumber.

Aislinn sighed as her thoughts returned to this morning's dream. It seemed more real today than the previous times she'd awakened from the same dream, over the years. She didn't find it unusual that the dream was reoccurring, and figured it was due to some scene that she had read long ago that had stuck with her. What *was* unusual was the clarity with which it occurred this morning. She still reeled from the passion and heartache of the two people, wishing as she always did, that she could learn how the story ended, or at the very least see the warrior's face. She regretted not knowing what he looked like. In all the years she'd dreamed this dream, not once was she granted even that. She would give anything to have remained in that wooded place this morning, with the beautiful naked warrior, but well, reality called.

She shook her head, pulling herself out of her musings. "I've got to get out more." She half-joked out loud. Exhaling a long breath, she fastened her coat and gathered up her belongings. The frigid air was sobering as she opened the car door. She instantly shivered from the cold. Tossing the moon a final glance, she hurried into the school.

Aislinn turned on her computer and chose a playlist from a folder of music she kept on her desktop. Listening to music in her classroom in the mornings before the students arrived wasn't out of the ordinary for Aislinn, as she was a great connoisseur of unique world music. Being the art teacher did allow her a bit of extravagance without too many sideways glances from the other staff, and they often came by to hear her latest finds.

She smiled to herself as the soft Celtic music filled the classroom. This morning's musical choice was a bit quieter than the upbeat music she usually played, but then, she hadn't quite shaken her reflective mood from earlier, so it suited her disposition well.

Must be the midwinter blues, she thought, knowing she always became a bit restless just before spring. The Midwest winters were long and cold and unfortunately without sun most of the time. Dragging herself out of bed on these dark, cold mornings always proved extremely difficult this time of the year. That's why she loved dreaming about strapping warrior hunks. It was all the excuse she needed to stay snuggled in her covers. She glanced out into the hallway, whimsically casting the thought- *how nice life would be if dreams could come true and the warrior magically appeared right outside, waiting for her.*

Yeah, right, she thought with cynicism, rolling her eyes, pulling herself back to reality. *Only three more months of cold weather and ridiculous daydreams.* She sighed and returned to the task of preparing her classroom for the day's activities.

Aislinn happened to look up as one of her colleagues approached her door.

"Good morning, Beth," Aislinn called out a greeting.

"Good morning," Beth replied, leaning in the doorway. "Boy was it cold this morning."

"Sure was. I'm ready for it to be over," Aislinn agreed, pausing in her task of placing water containers and brushes on the worktables around her room and stepping over to her friend.

"Me too." Beth nodded. "By the way, I finally found that cake recipe we talked about. I'll run a copy and drop it in your mailbox. You are going to love it," Beth offered.

"Sounds wonderful. I can't wait to try it."

Beth chuckled. "Are we still on for dinner Thursday?"

"Yup. I'll meet you at the restaurant," Aislinn confirmed.

"Hey, isn't this coming Saturday your field trip to the art museum? I heard the kids chatting about it last week."

Aislinn smiled. She couldn't hide the passion she held for art. She delighted in sharing her appreciation for the subject with her students and their parents, and each year planned a trip to the Art Institute for them.

"Yup," she said.

"Well, they are going to love it," Beth complemented. "For some, this will be the only time they'll take a trip to a big city."

Aislinn knew the truth of Beth's statement all too well. Teaching in a small rural town often meant less opportunity for some of her students. A visit to a world class museum would be the trip of a lifetime for them.

"I will be making a trip down on Wednesday, just to scout things out. Since their renovation last year, things have moved and I'd feel better making sure I know where everything is ahead of time."

"You're so dedicated, making the trip twice in one week."

"Ah, Chicago's not far really, and this way Saturday will go much smoother. Besides, you know I love that place."

"You are so inspiring." Beth smiled.

Aislinn felt her face grow warm at her friend's compliment.

Beth checked her watch. "I'd better scoot. I still need to copy a few things before the kiddos arrive."

Aislinn waved good-bye as Beth bustled off leaving Aislinn to continue preparing her classroom.

Chapter Two

AEDAN STROLLED THE park's ice-covered sidewalks trying to shake the disconcerted feeling that had settled over him as of late. He often took walks in the predawn hours of the morning, drawn by the desolate beauty of winter's frozen stillness. It was during these hours that the windy city was almost quiet. Almost.

In this hushed time between night and the first light of day, Aedan usually found he could shed the burden of centuries and keep his restlessness at bay. But not today.

He glanced up at the moon, looming large and bright in the coming dawn. At one time the moon had offered comfort and magic, but today, the moon served only as a reminder of his aloneness.

Ignoring the cold, Aedan continued to walk, the wind biting his face. At least the frosty sting on his skin reminded him he was alive. Aedan glanced at a bare tree and caught sight of a small flock of sparrows huddled together against the chill. He opened his hand and stared at the tiny flame he conjured in his palm. He lifted his gaze and glanced around before dropping the flame on a pile of snow on the ground. The flame instantly melted the snow to water.

"Take your drink before the cold claims it again." He watched as one by one the birds flew down to the small puddle.

Aedan turned up his collar and continued his walk. This was his life now. Walking aimlessly in the January cold, far from his home, his land, and his time. He was lost from his history and all that he was, endlessly waiting for something seemingly farther from him now than in all the years past.

The promise of once again finding his love, his soul mate, sustained him during years on blood-soaked battlefields, or when chilled to the bone, huddled in a damp, leaky hut. Still, he clung to hope as the last of his kin passed into history and he was left alone, to face the endless years.

Even as life became less tenuous through the ages, the prophecy of her arrival sustained him. A lesser man might have given in; a lesser man might have strayed to any of a thousand vices and temptations to alleviate the boredoms. A lesser man might have become reckless and wild, not caring who or what suffered for the sake of a thrill, but not Aedan There were times he gave in to his loneliness, needing the feel of a woman beneath him. But these were nameless trysts, fleeting moments of comfort, serving only to remind him for whom he waited.

He had long ago shed his ancient name, Aididh, and went instead by the modern *Aedan*. There was no place in this modern world for magic or ancient things. This life was artificial and disconnected, too far removed from his time and the natural order of things, yet he adapted and waited, trapped within his increasing sense of despair. He didn't belong here and yet couldn't leave. Twelve hundred years he'd waited, and with another Beltane arriving in a few months, he was still alone.

Now, time was rearing its ugly head, filling him with doubt and sadness. Hope was slipping away. She was slipping away. Perhaps this torment of waiting was nothing more than a foolish dream he'd suffered all these years.

Aedan again glanced at the moon overhead, a constant reminder of the heartache and failure on that full-moon night long ago ...

Ireland, Early 9th Century

He fought with the fury of a wounded animal. Filled with the rage of unfulfilled passion, the torment of incompleteness, the injustice of what would not be. He fought with the abandonment of someone with nothing to lose. He protected her with all he possessed so that her people could find her. But in doing so, lost her. He shouted into the night for her, slashing and hacking his way through the fighting, but she did not hear him over the din of the battle.

He watched as her kin reached her. He saw her anguished expression as she looked in his direction while she was being dragged away, kicking and reaching for him. Her soundless cries pierced his heart as the arrow had pierced his arm. An agonizing scream tore from his throat, the sound resonating through the stones, through the battle, through time.

Aedan slowly closed then opened his eyes as if doing so would blink the memory away. It didn't. The anguish of that night still haunted him.

So many lives were lost, lives of the very tribe he'd sworn to protect. The few who survived the unexpected attack, distrusted him. They questioned his ability to rule or to stop his scheming brother Brennis. They immediately dissolved the alliance that he and the Lady, Druidess of Erin, spent years negotiating and instead hastily secreted away his mate, wedding her to another from a southern tribe who had been part of an alternate plan should something go awry.

Should a hundred swords pierce his flesh, Aedan had never experienced such pain as when he watched his soulmate being taken away. Today, that heartache was still a wound deeper than any he'd suffered over the years.

Making his way from the park to the street, Aedan tugged his scarf tighter against the cold. He eventually made his way into a small twenty-four-hour coffee shop he often frequented on his morning forays. He slipped into a secluded booth in the back and removed his coat and gloves.

"Good morning" came the greeting from a waitress, placing a mug of steaming coffee in front of him. "Nice to see you again."

Aedan nodded.

The waitress placed a menu on the table beside him. "Just wave me down when you're ready to order."

He nodded again as the waitress bustled off.

Aedan picked up the menu, and as he did, spied a middle-aged couple sitting several booths away. The loving looks, the small gestures and smiles that passed between the man and his woman made Aedan's heart constrict in his chest. The obvious affection between them was heartwarming and at the same time, made Aedan sad. All these years, Aedan harbored such indescribable resentment that what he desired most continued to elude him. He lowered his eyes, unable to continue to watch the couple and turned his attention to the menu before him, absently scanning the words, but not really seeing them.

"And what has you so broody this early in the morning, a good-looking guy like you?" The waitress returned to Aeden's table, breaking him away from his thoughts. "I've never seen anyone study the menu quite so intently, unless of course, I've missed something profound about the hash browns."

Aedan put down the menu and flashed a forced smile at the waitress' humor.

"I'll just have the usual."

She wrote down his order, topped off his coffee, and left him alone once more. Aedan scanned the restaurant. The couple he'd watched earlier conversed between themselves. In another booth, two men were laughing about something in this morning's paper. Another man occupied a table near the center of the floor. Nothing out of the ordinary, yet the uneasy feeling in his gut he'd woken with persisted, so much so, he no longer had an appetite. Aedan slipped a large bill on the table and without explanation, rose and left the diner.

Chapter Three

THE DAY STARTED OFF with the usual uneasiness Aedan harbored as of late, but as the hours drew on, he just couldn't seem to shake the nagging sensation.

Hoping to dispel the unsettled feeling, Aedan worked out until his body screamed with pain. The disquiet remained. He walked for hours through the city, hoping the cold would ease it but again, nothing changed.

Looking for any distraction, he found himself heading in the direction of the Art Institute where he worked as a curator in the medieval/renaissance department. Most times, Aedan worked nights, especially when negotiating acquisitions overseas or rearranging displays after hours, but today he found himself climbing the front steps toward the entrance in the middle of the day.

He made a point to stop at the lion statue, one of a pair adorning each side of the main entrance. Out of habit, he ran his fingers over the cold bronze. Touching the sculptures reputed to bring good luck if one made a wish while stroking the lion. He let his fingers fall, then turned and went inside the museum.

"You're early today," came the welcome from the security guard at the entrance.

"I have a bit of extra work I thought I'd get started on," Aedan said, pausing to sign an employee log. He shrugged out of his coat, and hooked it over his arm, stuffing his gloves and scarf in the pocket. He clipped on his I.D. badge which he fished out of his other pocket.

"I'll take your coat. I'm heading downstairs to the employee area in a few minutes for my break," The guard offered.

"Thank you." Aedan handed over the garment. "Looks busy, today." Aedan took note of the exceptional amount of people entering the museum.

"It's Picasso. Draws 'em every time." The guard said, referencing the special exhibit currently at the institute.

Aedan smiled. "He always did."

Aedan entered the main hallway of the museum intent on going to the office area, but stopped rather abruptly as the hair on his arm bristled and his skin tingled as if being stroked by invisible fingers. He looked around, becoming fully alert, but noticed nothing out of the ordinary. He changed his mind about going to his office, and instead made his way into the museum proper.

Cautiously moving through the Asian works, Aedan scanned the crowd. Next he moved through the African and Middle Eastern exhibits. *Nothing.* Still, his skin crawled. He made his way through the lower level and the miniature displays, his whole body now buzzing with sensation.

Aedan's heart began to pound, his blood racing through his veins, and every nerve alert and responsive. He inhaled a deep breath, attempting to calm himself. His instinct warned him something unusual was happening, but not knowing what it could be, was disconcerting.

Returning to the stairs, he made his way through the sculpture garden and underneath Georgia's "Sky." He moved through the arms and armor hall, searching and scanning every face in every gallery. Damn, there were too many people for him to clearly access every place he traveled.

Agitation gnawed at him with each second that ticked by. Every pore of his being was flooded with adrenaline, yet he still couldn't identify the cause. Politely, he tolerated and quickly answered visitor questions and comments, as he passed through the galleries up to the second floor.

Aedan paused by "Sunday Afternoon on the Isle of the Grande Jette" and scanned the people who studied the large painting. *Again nothing.* He pulled off his badge and hastily shoved the plastic card deep in his pocket, wanting no further distractions. He swiftly roamed through the impressionists, renaissance and medieval paintings.

Anticipation compelled him to keep searching. The main stairs were just ahead and he paused in order to focus before descending the marble steps.

He was unaware of what made him look in the direction of the gift shop area, but as he did, the longing of a thousand years flooded through him. The sensation was so powerful, so encompassing, he froze on the stairs as the feeling besieged him.

A long moment passed before he regained his composure and realized what the feelings indicated. He closed his eyes savoring the elation that filled him. When he opened them again he no longer hesitated. He moved down the grand staircase, and when he reached the bottom took several long strides toward the gift shop. When he entered the store he saw her.

Aislinn.

His heart stopped and his breath caught in his throat. His gaze traveled the length of her afraid to believe the woman standing before him was truly her. However, her coppery hair and timeless features were exactly as he remembered. She stood at a display, flipping through a book on the museum's paintings. She scanned the pages of the book she held with interest, unaware he watched her. She was so breathtakingly lovely, he couldn't take his eyes from her.

Approaching cautiously, Aedan watched as a sudden bewildered expression crossed her face and the book she'd been reading slid from her hands landing with a thud on the floor. She gripped the display shelf to support herself, while her other hand went to her head.

In two strides, Aedan was at her side. "Aislinn, are you alright?" He took hold of her elbow to steady her.

"Did you feel that?" Her puzzled gaze snapped up to meet his. She furrowed her brow at her momentary dizziness, lifting her arm from his hand. She responded belatedly to his question. "I'm sorry. Yes. Thank you." She stepped away. "How did you know my..."

"Would ye like to sit?"

"No, no. I'm fine. I think I just need to eat something. I haven't eaten all day." Still, she looked bewildered.

"Are you sure? I can buy you a candy bar or something."

"No really. I'm fine."

Aedan reached down, picked up the book and held it out to her, studying her for any sign of recognition.

"I'm sorry." She swallowed hard. "I don't know what came over me." Rubbing the gooseflesh rising on her arms, Aislinn took another step back.

Aedan saw the difficulty she had in meeting his eyes as she took the book from his hand, puzzled as to the cause of her discomfort.

"Are ye sure you are alright?"

"I'm fine. I'll just grab a bite to eat at the café. Thank you for your help."

Aedan saw the confusion remain on her face as she gave hm a final cautious glance and turned away from him.

Clenching his fists, he forced himself to step back despite all his instincts screaming to hold on to her. He watched her stroll to the check-out counter and pay for the book. He recalled the bitter words spoken to him centuries ago. "You must unlock her memories."

Aedan couldn't help the reflections that slipped into his mind at that moment as he stood staring at the woman before him...

Ireland, 9th Century

Battle weary and covered in blood, Aididh tripped over bodies as he stumbled away from the fighting. He slumped against a tree, his strength fading. Barely able to keep his eyes open, the wound in his side having soaked his hand with crimson, he slid to the ground. He bore a mortal wound, his death wound, delivered by the sword of his brother, Brennis. He could feel his life diminishing; he could feel the mist closing in around him.

"Aididh." A soft voice called to him from the mist.

"Aislinn," he choked. He found the strength to open his eyes but realized it wasn't Aislinn who stood before him. "Lady, forgive me," he murmured one last time gazing upon the Lady of Erin.

"My sweet Aididh. Even while you lay dying, you call to her. All these years after losing her, your final thought is of her. She still fills your heart."

Aididh lowered his eyes, humbly. "I have failed ye, Lady. I am dying and our people still bleed."

"As ye bleed for me," she acknowledged.

Aididh closed his eyes, slipping deeper into darkness. "Ambushed. Betrayed. Brennis."

"Aididh, ye are my most loyal vassal, even though your fealty cost ye your heart and land, ye have loved and honored me." The Lady reached out and stroked Aididh's sweat-covered face, now ashen from death. He opened his eyes again, staring into the silver pools of the Lady's gaze, recalling when, at the age of eight, he bravely peered into her face for the first time.

"I ken your heart, Aididh. I ken the ache ye carry. Ye never stopped loving her."

"Living without her has been ..." Aididh gasped for breath, "Unbearable."

"And yet ye bore the burden."

"My only wish was to have known her. Even death willnae erase the pain." His eyes closed.

"I will ease your pain, Aididh." The Lady touched the wound on Aididh's side. She closed her eyes, whispering words from an old language.

As the warmth seeped from her hand into his wound, the numbness of death ebbed away, replaced with the scorching pain of the tear in his side. His eyes flew open with shock as he gasped.

He was alive.

"Please, let me die, let this torment end," Aididh pleaded.

"It is nae your time, Aididh. Erin still needs you. Aislinn will need you."

The lady touched his shoulder affectionately. "Aididh, your heartache makes ye reckless," the Lady reminded him.

Aididh looked away, ashamed.

"Ye have lost hope."

"Ye ask more than I am able to give. Ye bound my soul to Aislinn. When she was taken away, a piece of me died that day. Ye made her so much a part of me, 'tis nigh impossible to live without her," Aididh confessed.

"And she without you. Ye both suffer." The Lady looked away seeing something in the distance visible only to her. A troubled look crossed her face. Several still moments passed before she turned to Aididh and spoke again.

"Ye will ken Aislinn again, many years from now. Ye will live many lifetimes until then." She continued. "Ye will need strength and patience. She will nae know you. Ye must unlock her memories from a life long passed." The Lady paused. "I see great peril before you."

"To be with Aislinn I would face any demons."

"Ye will have to." The Lady stroked his face. He could feel her strength flowing into him.

Slender hands reached out and placed a medallion around Aididh's neck. "This stone carries the power of immortality. Your life is bound to this stone." The Lady ran her fingers over the medallion. "It took great sacrifice to grant you this. There is one who will seek the magic for evil and will stop at nothing to find ye and the stone. He must nae be allowed to find it."

A bright spark lit the darkness and a loud crack tore through the night. The Lady lifted half of the stone away. "To have what ye desire, both halves must unite. Upon finding her, ye must once again lie with Aislinn in the stone glen of your first union. I will give ye the words to bind you to her and to her time. Only then will ye obtain what you desire. Fail to do this on Beltane and ye are condemned to an eternity alone and broken."

Aididh raised a weakened arm gesturing to the other half of the stone the Lady held.

"The stone's power is in its wholeness. The other half will find you when it is time. Ye carry the magic now. Donnae let it fall into the wrong hands."

"But ..."

"I have said enough. I must leave ye and this place. My time is over, but Erin will need ye, yet. Be well, dear Aididh. Love her well ..."

Aedan absently fingered the amulet under his shirt as the memory faded away. His half of the stone hummed with renewed life, reacting to the nearness of the other half, residing somewhere close with Aislinn.

He knew without a doubt her sudden reaction was at his approach, but instead of his presence triggering her memory, she became unsteady and disoriented.

Swallowing the lump forming in his throat, Aedan fought the twisting deep in his gut. He'd waited hundreds of lifetimes for her and she had no idea who he was.

Aedan knew he couldn't just let her walk out the door, out of his life, not now, not ever. He frantically sought a way to approach her without frightening her or seeming overly zealous in his attempt to jog her memory. However, he overheard her say in a brief conversation with the cashier that she would be back this Saturday with a school group. He also noticed she wrote a check for her purchase. At the very least, he would have her address.

She thanked the clerk, and turning in his direction, cast a quick, wary glance his way before heading out of the gift shop.

Aedan knew that despite all he'd suffered at Aislinn's absence over the centuries, it would be nothing compared to what he would suffer over the next three days.

Chapter Four

IRELAND, PRESENT DAY

Brennis blinked, his eyes heavy with the fatigue of sleep. Many uncomfortable minutes passed before he could fully open them. Focusing on his dim surroundings proved difficult.

"We've been waiting for you."

He heard the words, but too many years of idle nothingness had left his brain fogged and unable to respond. Slowly he moved his head, the muscles in his neck painfully stiff. His arms and legs were heavy, weighed down by years of inactivity. But they remained whole and not withered, a testament to the success of the magic.

The cold slab beneath him was uncomfortable and made movement difficult, so he relinquished the idea for the moment.

"What century?" he managed to mouth more than speak, his voice raspy and faint.

"Twenty-first," the reply came.

No wonder rousing proved such a challenge.

Brennis attempted to swallow the spiced liquid offered to him, but succeeded only in downing a few drops before his parched throat agonizingly protested.

"Hurry with the oil," a sharp command sounded.

Oil? he thought, a moment before he possessed his answer. The hot liquid immediately warmed his skin where delicate fingers, several sets of them, he noted, worked the pungent oil into the rigid muscles of his body.

Little by little, movement returned, and his body reacquainted itself with life. *At least*, he thought with an arrogant smirk, *one part of him boasted no problem responding to the hands expertly kneading and massaging him.* He could not tell if the hands caressing him were female or male, but still, his body responded with enthusiasm. His cock stiffened immediately, unaffected by the dullness of sleep.

Fingers tightened around him, slipping and sliding up and down with perfect rhythm and pressure rewarding his arousal with the same generous attention the rest of him received. Hard and throbbing in a matter of moments, he closed his eyes, determined to take full advantage of the caresses expertly bringing him toward climax.

He envisioned the nimble fingers belonging to a certain red-haired beauty that had occupied his thoughts since childhood. His jaw clenched tightly remembering the way she passionately clung to his half-brother as Aedan took her. Damn, but that should have been him she gave her innocence to. He had been too late to prevent the union, but not too late to see it interrupted.

Aislinn. Her name was a dry whisper in between his current pleasure moans. Her beautiful emerald eyes and porcelain skin were the stuff of his dreams since meeting her. Oh, but that should have been his body her thighs were wrapped around that fateful night.

He allowed a wicked smile to cross his lips. He would find her and he would have her, of that he would make sure. This thought only increased the arousal presently claiming him. Minutes later, Brennis yielded to his pleasure.

Brennis flexed his sword hand again, opening and closing his fist, testing his grip. He stepped from the bath, water running in rivulets down his lean body, pleased a thousand plus years of enchanted sleep hadn't diminished his strength or determination.

One purpose continued to occupy his thoughts and actions. He flipped his head, tossing his lengthy blond hair away from his face.

"It is good to see there are no repercussions from such a long slumber."

Brennis swiftly spun around as his hand shot out and abruptly grabbed the man who had appeared behind him, around the throat. The man struggled and gasped for air, clawing at Brennis' arm. Assured his warning was perceived, Brennis released the attendant from his grip. The man crumbled to a heap on the floor, sucking in lungsful of air.

"Ye would bode well to nae sneak up on me again," Brennis' voice, although rough, was still filled with a menacing edge. Brennis bent and retrieved the drying cloth the attendant had dropped on the floor.

"Bravo my medieval friend," another voice resounded as a second male sauntered into the bathing room. "I see you are feeling yourself again."

Brennis approached this man curiously. "Welcome to the twenty-first century."

"Ye speak in falsehoods. We arenae friends," Brennis growled.

"Correct you are, but we will be." This second man sounded all too confident in his explanation. Brennis eyed him suspiciously. "Where do ye hail? I donnae recognize yer tongue."

"You are still in Ireland."

"Ireland?" Brennis tested the word.

"Erie. Erin. Hibernia."

Brennis' brow furrowed. "By what name are ye called?"

"Colin O'Connor at your service."

Brennis eyed him carefully, not deeming him a threat, but not missing the man's cunning manner. "I require sustenance," demanded Brennis.

"Ah, and you shall have it. First, here are your clothes. Dress and then I will take you to the dining area where we will eat." Colin handed Brennis a pile of folded garments. Brennis looked between the clothes he held and the ones Colin was wearing. "'Tis the manner of dress in this century?"

"Yes," Colin confirmed.

"Ye dress in black, much like the priests of my day," Brennis noted.

"You are correct again. We dress in black pants and shirt to set us apart from the populous."

"But ye are nae a priest."

"Right again. Actually, just the opposite, but we like to keep that a secret. We dress like this as to not raise any suspicions as to our real vocation."

"And what vocation is that?"

"The darker side of magic."

Brennis remained silent while he contemplated what he was being told. If this man spoke true, then he and others in this facility were the descendants of those dark priests entrusted with his care many years ago.

"What do ye ken of me?"

"I know much, but all in due time," Colin explained. "There are things you must become acquainted with first. This century is vastly different from yours, and we have much to discuss. I will be your tutor. I am familiar with your mission and interested in what you seek."

Brennis' initial instinct was to run this man through with his sword, but he didn't have his sword nearby, and if this Colin were correct, Brennis would need instruction to navigate this century. He stilled his hand for now, tempering his impatience, gritting his teeth sternly. He simply nodded his acceptance of Colin's explanation and began to dress in the garments he was provided.

After a hearty meal of beef and vegetables, Colin led Brennis out the rear of the dining hall to what appeared to be a farm. This wasn't too different from what Brennis was familiar with, however there were several strange items scattered about he had no knowledge of.

"We call this farm 'The Heritage.' The locals think it's a reclusive monastic retreat. But in fact, it's a working farm that provides our food and income."

Brennis pointed to a large machine.

"These are tractors. Machines that do a lot of the labor that men used to do," Colin explained, noting Brennis' curious glances at the various farm equipment. "I'm sure the animals are the same," Colin spoke, seeing Brennis' nod of agreement. "We support ourselves with produce and animals we sell at the market for our coin. This is how we support our community."

As much as some things didn't seem too dissimilar, there was much that was. When Brennis looked out over the landscape, he noted the fields dotting the hillsides and objects he assumed were dwellings. The lush green land of Erin was a welcome sight, however there was an unfamiliar rhythm about this time. Something unidentifiable kept him feeling uneasy and wary.

Brennis' thoughts were suddenly disrupted by the rumbling of an automobile passing down the dirt road in front of the farm. Brennis' head snapped up at the sound.

"What kind of wagon moves without the aid of horses?"

Colin chuckled. "Those are called cars. They are a kind of machine that work with a liquid fuel. I think you will like some of these modern inventions once you understand them."

Brennis took a deep breath. It was obvious that there was a great deal of knowledge to be acquired if he were going to survive in this time. With this realization also came another thought that filled him with fury. Aedan, having been alive to experience the changing world, would be very familiar and comfortable with the modern technology. This was his affliction and he never liked being at a disadvantage. Aedan would not best him in this, he swore. He would learn everything there was to learn to keep Aedan from having the upper hand.

"How long until Beltane?" Brennis suddenly asked, not outwardly showing his resolve.

"It's the beginning of January, so the remainder of this month, all of February, all of March and all of April. So just under four months," Colin answered.

"Then, I need ye to teach me everything there is to ken. I cannae allow me brother to use the modern way against me. I must be his equal," Brennis demanded.

"And you will be." Colin assured.

Chapter Five

UNITED STATES, PRESENT Day

There was something a bit peculiar about this day. Aislinn couldn't name it, but she felt it just the same. She thought perhaps the feeling was stemming from her students' enthusiasm about the field trip. She couldn't be more delighted at seeing the children so excited about visiting the Art Institute.

After a several hours ride, Aislinn and her entourage arrived at the group entrance of the museum. She thought to take one last head count before everyone scattered, and she stepped back to see her entire group better. It was then, as she counted, she absently backed up into a brick wall, or at least something resembling a brick wall- if brick walls were six foot four and solid muscle. The clipboard she'd been holding flew from her hand upon impact as she stumbled.

A very large arm shot out to steady her.

"I'm so very sorry I didn't see ..." She spun around. "You!" Her mouth gaped in surprise. She remembered the encounter in the gift shop several days before and the man who'd come to her aid. She brushed his arm aside as he reached for her.

Aislinn straightened herself eyeing the man before her. He stood tall, towering over her, making her feel very small. He kept his black hair pulled back with a tie, serving to exaggerate his oh so ruggedly handsome face, firm square jaw and very dark eyes.

He bore an ageless look about him, as if he belonged to a different time or place. He sported a gray and plum colored tie over a fitted deep plum dress shirt, tucked into gray pants, which, she noted fit him as if they were purposely tailored for him. *My God*, she thought in some strangely comical moment, *here stood a man who could actually wear the color plum and look hot!*

Gazing at his perfect features and the way his trousers molded flawlessly over his sculpted ass, she felt the unexpected intake of breath and half-jokingly thought she should have taken him up on his offer of help in the gift shop.

"Hello again," he greeted.

Aislinn took another step away from him, aware the parents and her students were watching the odd exchange.

"I'm Aedan MacKendrick." He jiggled the I.D. badge clipped to the pocket of his shirt. "I'm here to help if you need anything. I saw you signed in a museum tour and I thought I'd offer my services."

"You work here?" Aislinn questioned. *Of course, he did.* Aislinn cleared her throat. "Thank you, but I think we're fine."

Both Aislinn and Aedan reached to retrieve the fallen clipboard at the same time and as their hands touched, their movements froze and Aislinn found herself staring into the darkest brown eyes she'd ever seen. She couldn't seem to pull her gaze away. His eyes held a multitude of secrets she strangely wanted to know.

She wasn't the only one who experienced the odd sensation. Her students were acutely aware of the curious moment between their teacher and this man and acknowledged the awkward encounter with "*Whoo Hoo*...Ms. O'Neil" or "*Whoa*..." in their teasing tones. Aislinn reluctantly pulled her gaze away and shot an if-looks-could-kill glance at her students, who continued to giggle.

"Well, if I cannae help ye, may I tag along on your tour? I'm working on improving some of the museum's teacher resources and am very interested in learning what artwork ye and your students have come here to see." Aedan asked.

'Cannae?' 'Ye?' That accent! Scottish? Irish? Perhaps a little of both? Get a grip. Lots of people had accents. Aislinn pulled her thoughts back to the present.

Of all the tour groups arriving at the same time as hers, Aislinn wondered why he'd chosen her group. But in the same second she thought it must be because he recognized her. He did act a little familiar, and seemed rather determined to accompany them. *Darn*, she thought. She was looking forward to a nice relaxing day, and now she felt as if she had to don her professional persona to accommodate his request. So, with both parents and students' continued scrutiny, she remained polite and reluctantly agreed.

Mr. MacKendrick's presence was intense. Well, actually it was fighting the constant thrumming of her body when he was near, that was exhausting. At least that is the excuse Aislinn gave herself. It was either that or her hormones working overtime in response to his constant gaze and velvety-smooth voice.

She wasn't used to someone studying her the way he did, and although he politely hung toward the back of the group, his unyielding attention unnerved her.

At one point during the day, as Mr. MacKendrick waited alongside her on a bench, Aislinn couldn't help but notice the strange energy dancing in the air between them. She kept it to herself and instead just shot him a puzzled look and proceeded to put more space between them.

"Ms. O'Neil, do you specifically write your lessons for your students based on the artwork we have here at the museum?" Aedan asked, attempting conversation.

Aislinn ignored his question and asked one of her own. "How do you know my name?" *Hadn't he called her by name in the gift shop a couple of days ago, as well?* She'd driven herself crazy trying to remember the encounter replaying the incident over and over in her head, finally deciding she must have imagined it.

Aedan pointed to the clipboard she held, where she'd written her name in a black marker. He smiled at her.

"Oh." She took a deep breath. This man sure had a way of making her feel awkward, despite claiming he was just doing his job. Both times she'd met Mr. MacKendrick, he was nothing short of polite. Maybe his job *did* entail trying to enhance the museum's resources, she told herself. And truth be known, she knew her subject. Maybe he could tell. Perhaps he really *was* only interested in her art lessons and her jittery reaction was just her imagination running away with her.

Perhaps his appearance really *was* a coincidence. Maybe he truly thought her a valuable asset to his task. Maybe he figured she'd remember him from the gift shop and therefore would be more receptive to accommodating his request to join her. That was it, she told herself, despite knowing she would still have to find a way to ignore the fact he made every inch of her skin prickle.

Aislinn managed to get through the rest of the day, convincing herself to ignore him. *Sure, like I could ignore him*, she chided herself in a brief moment alone. The sheer volume of him made *that* impossible.

Later in the afternoon, when the buses arrived to load for the return trip, the self-confident look Mr. MacKendrick wore waivered. Aislinn saw something else flicker in those dark eyes. Fear, maybe, she wasn't sure exactly, but his expression notably changed.

He asked her if he might contact her if he had any more questions. Although his request was a fairly normal one, the way he waited for her answer suggested much depended on her reply. Aislinn got the uncanny feeling his request to contact her held the weight of an unnamed burden, a mystery she couldn't quite put a finger on. That one single question hanging in the air, was filled with a hundred more.

She looked at this man while he waited for her answer and realized, despite all attempts to the contrary, in one afternoon, he'd managed to get completely under her skin. She didn't understand why she suddenly felt averse to leaving the man who'd spent an entire day keeping her off-kilter.

With the tiniest breath, she finally answered "Yes," before turning and stepping onto the bus.

She dared to look at him through the window. He stood there, regal in stature, legs apart, his pose majestic. She could easily envision him standing on a lush green hill, his plaid snapping in the wind around him, his hair dancing around his face, looking as if he were one of her romance book heroes.

He gave a wave to the kids, but his eyes sought hers through the glass. He nodded at her as if he knew her exact thoughts. She didn't breathe again until the bus rounded the corner and obscured him from sight.

Chapter Six

TWO UNEVENTFUL WEEKS had passed since Aislinn's field trip to the art museum and life slipped back into its normal routine. Aislinn had almost put the thoughts of Mr. MacKendrick out of her mind. Almost. Men like Aedan MacKendrick were hard to forget. They were the stuff of fantasies. Safe, mundane fantasies. In reality, men like him were way out of her league. She had known a man like that once and it hadn't turned out well. It was that heartbreaking experience that set her on the course of concentrating on her career instead of her love life.

She liked the quiet, consistent life she had fallen into. It had been necessary in order to heal and reclaim herself. She was content - happy actually, once again enjoying the things that brought her joy. The last thing she wanted at this time was a disruption to her nice neat world.

But that was exactly what happened this morning in her classroom when, as she busily prepared her materials for the day, humming and swaying to her favorite music, she turned around and discovered her supervising principal escorting Aedan MacKendrick into her classroom.

She didn't hide the play of emotions she knew crossed her face as they approached her, in mid-conversation.

"I think you'll find Ms. O'Neil very capable of working with you and your project. She wrote and developed our entire art curriculum,

K through 12. I know she will be excited to participate with you and the Art Institute."

Aislinn's eyes widened, as she looked between her principal and Aedan. Shock, puzzlement, panic, and frustration were all there on her face she was sure, as she listened to what her principal was saying.

Aislinn forced herself to straighten and quickly composed herself, while inside she was reeling.

"This is Ms ..." Her principal began the introduction.

"Loreena McKennitt." Aedan spoke to Aislinn, interrupting the principal's sentence.

"No, this is Ms. O'Neil," her principal corrected.

"He means the music." Aislinn stepped over to click off her speaker.

"Yes, well, um...Aislinn, this is Mr. MacKendrick from the art museum in Chicago," her Principal began. "He's been explaining the institute's work in expanding their resources for educators. He has requested your assistance in helping develop their new online curriculum. I just knew you'd be interested in this."

Aedan reached out and offered his hand in greeting. Aislinn hesitantly shook it, pulling hers away a bit too quickly. Damn, but there she went again, unnerved by this man's presence.

"Apparently you left quite an impression on your visit a couple of weeks ago."

"I did?"

"Of course, you did," her principal confirmed. "I'm sure you will enjoy working with Mr. MacKendrick for the next several months. This will be an exciting opportunity for your career. I know how passionate you are about teaching art."

"Months?" was all Aislinn was able to mumble.

Aedan flashed a smile at her that had her swallowing further words in frustration. By God, he almost looked smug at her inability to articulate anything further.

The first morning bell rang, announcing the arrival of students.

"Yes. Mr. MacKendrick will explain everything." The principal turned to Aeden. "I will leave you in Ms. O'Neil's capable hands. Duty calls. Nice to meet you, Aedan. We'll be seeing you regularly, I'm sure." The principal shook Aedan's hand and quickly made an exit from the room amidst the voices and clatter of students entering the building.

Aislinn threw a glance at the clock, "Would you like some coffee? I know I would." She grabbed her mug off her desk and exited the room, not waiting for Aedan's answer, but hearing his chuckle at her hasty departure.

She returned a few moments later, carrying an extra cup of coffee which she handed to Mr. MacKendrick. She tossed packets of cream and sugar on her desk. "I didn't know if you like cream or sugar."

"Black. Thank you."

Aislinn proceeded to empty a cream into her coffee, all the while studying him from under her lashes. She took a deep breath, deciding to just be forthcoming and honest with him.

"Look, Mr. MacKendrick..."

"Aedan."

"Aedan," she repeated. "I don't like being caught off guard. It makes me feel on edge and..."

"My presence makes you feel on edge?"

She sipped her coffee. "Quite."

"I'm sorry. 'Tis nae my intent to upset you."

'Tis? Nae? That accent again! She pulled her thoughts to the present.

"I'm more of a planning kind of person, not so spontaneous, so your sudden appearance is daunting."

Aedan just nodded.

"Listen, I will do my best to provide the information you're looking for and to answer your questions the best I can so you can be on your way."

"I'm in nae hurry. I have many weeks in which to gather information."

Aislinn inwardly groaned. That is what she was afraid of.

"Still …" she began, but the remainder of her statement remained unfinished as the door to her room opened and her first class began entering and taking their seats.

"You can sit at my desk," she motioned to Aedan, setting down her coffee and turning toward her students.

It was going to be a very long day.

Chapter Seven

IRELAND, PRESENT DAY

"Och, but I grow weary of these history lessons!" Brennis spat, agitation lacing his voice. He snapped shut the large book in front of him and sprang to his feet going to the window of the small library housed within the walls of the false monastic building.

The political climate of today's Ireland and Scotland, as they were now called, was more different than he'd ever imagined. There was no place for him in this modern world. Long gone were clans and chiefs and territorial kings, replaced by governments and useless rulers.

Brennis watched as another strange horseless vehicle passed along the road nearby. He needed to rethink his strategy and purpose. Gaining land and title were no longer an option, and yet he suspected his brother thrived in this new world. Well, he would thrive as well ... better even. And once he got his hands on the two halves of the amulet and used the magic he was given, he could have it all then. Immortality would be his, Aislinn would be his, and then the possibilities were endless. His ambition hadn't changed, only the end game. It was now more personal. He vowed he would not allow Aedan the satisfaction of achieving the goal he'd long awaited.

Brennis began pacing the length of the library room. Colin O'Connor closed the large encyclopedia and slumped back in his chair.

"Whilst I sit here akin to a simple cleric, me brother makes plans for Beltane." Brennis covered the small library in a few strides, then turned and looked pointedly at Colin.

"Have you found me brother, yet?" he asked.

"We are close," Colin answered. "We are using every technology available to find him," Colin explained. "Locating him should be just a matter of days."

Brennis placed his hands on his hips glaring at Colin.

"We've tracked him to the United States. Remember, this is across the sea on the continent of North ..."

"Aye. I remember what ye explained. I am nae daft," Brennis impatiently interrupted. "And those machines, those computers as ye call them. They can locate him?"

"In a sense. We can use them to find certain records that will narrow down his exact location. But your brother is careful. He doesn't leave an easy trail. Aislinn, on the other hand is proving to be a bit easier."

Brennis nodded, smiling slightly at the mention of Aislinn's name. He'd first learned of her when he and Aedan were brought to be fostered by the Del n'Araide, the Lady Druidess' tribe at the start of their druid training. He was twelve and Aedan was ten. Up until then, He'd only heard about the brother across the sea who would one day come to control his lands. His clansmen spoke with discontent against his father's marriage to Alpin's sister and the agreement naming Aedan ruler.

He and Aedan couldn't have been more different. From an early age Brennis harbored aspirations for the chiefdom but Aedan had a different calling. His future was larger, and this was a threat to everything that would be his.

Aedan was well liked, kind, and fair, opposite of his nature. He was war rough, aggressive and usually succeeded with bullying and intimidation. Aedan was equally as powerful when it came to being a warrior and could be equally as menacing in the battlefield.

There was nothing gentle about Brennis. He had a cruel streak that Aedan didn't possess, which put Aedan in the favor of the Lady and clan chiefs. It was his violent nature that lead to him first meeting Aislinn. He was fourteen years old and was caught beating one of the war horses during training on one of the hottest days of the year. For his rash behavior he was escorted off to one of the cells to cool his temper and contemplate his action. Unbeknownst to him he'd been watched from a tower window above.

Suffering the stifling heat and stale air of the cell only served to increase his anger and frustration, which lent him additional time locked away. When he was near delirious from heat exhaustion and close to passing out, a young girl arrived in secret to his cell, bearing cool water and a portion of bread. At that moment, in his delirium he was sure he had died and was being visited by an angel. Her one simple act of compassion touched him deeper than he cared to admit. She told him her name was Aislinn and she was the lady's niece and that she had been watching him. She asked him why he had beaten the horse, and as he looked at her innocent, disapproving face waiting for an answer, for the first time in his life, he had been ashamed of his act. Right then and there, in his stupor, he vowed this girl, would one day be his.

He must have spoken his intent out loud, for she immediately put distance between herself and his cell bars, explaining her act of kindness was just that and there was no romantic intent. She merely wanted to offer him water being that he was Aedan's brother. He learned later she was promised to Aedan and he to her by the lady. Aedan would take the only tenderness Brennis had ever known. Any affectionate feelings he had felt turned bitter and vindictive upon hearing this.

It was clear then that Aedan had the favor of the lady and the tribe and was not only being trained in the druid arts, but being groomed as the leader. While *he* coveted a thirst for power, Aedan's ambitions were selfless, putting Ireland and the people above all else.

Once he was released from captivity, Brennis, finding no further use for the druid training, left and returned to his Dal Riata. Aedan was fine to let him "rule" in his stead while he completed his training.

It was during this period he began making alliances with the Un'Neills, because more and more of the Dal Riata saw the benefit of supporting Aedan and the other coastal tribes as the Norse raids increased. Aedan, with the lady's help, forged strong bonds with the Dal n'Araide and the Dal Fiatach, forming a formidable alliance, along with the promised support of his cousin Kenneth MacAlpin from Scotland.

Brennis had never forgotten his vow that he would have Aislinn, and although he'd pushed aside his affection for her, it didn't mean he wouldn't take her. Circumstances hadn't been in his favor then, but the tide had certainly changed. The opportunity to finally steal the one thing from Aedan that meant the most to him was oh so close. He could imagine the sweet feel of her as he plowed her belly, reveling in the knowledge he would finally have what Aedan couldn't.

Brennis' thoughts were interrupted by Colin standing and pushing in his chair.

"Come on. Let's go see what progress we've made." Colin walked toward the door, Brennis close on his heels. Colin led the impatient warrior to another room where two gentlemen, dressed in the same manner as Colin, sat at machines looking at what appeared to be a screen of sort.

Brennis watched as they typed a series of symbols and words and watched as images and what Brennis assumed was writing appeared instantly.

"We've narrowed down Aedan's location to Chicago."

"Let us go to this Chicago," Brennis bellowed.

"Whoa, easy Brennis. It's not that simple. Chicago is an ocean away. You need a birth certificate, identification, a passport, to be able to travel."

"I grow weary of excuses."

"Like I tried to explain earlier, it's more complicated than just mounting a horse and riding out like in your time. There is paperwork and ..."

"Enough!" Brennis bellowed.

"Once we confirm your brother's location. I can send men on an airplane to try and find him." Colin turned to Brennis who once again studied the computers the men were using. "Patience, my medieval friend. Patience."

Chapter Eight

UNITED STATES, PRESENT Day

Aislinn rolled over, waking from the familiar reoccurring dream. She smiled as a passionate tingle shivered down her spine. The warrior was so real. She'd known him for years. She could actually feel the powerful muscles beneath her fingertips. She knew the mystery of being among the mist and the stones, the drums and the magic. She couldn't exactly recall when she began dreaming this dream and was positive the fantasy was the result of some romance novel she'd read long ago. The book obviously left an impression on her by the countless times over the years she'd dreamed the same dream, or a version of the dream.

She didn't experience the dream every night. As a matter of fact, it had been a while since she'd recalled it. Only recently had her warrior once again become part of her nightly slumber.

Aislinn climbed from the bed and padded out to her living room, knowing she would not be able to go back to sleep. She curled up on the couch, wrapping herself in an old blanket her grandmother had given her.

She loved the blanket, handed down in her family for generations. It had traveled from Ireland with an ancestor long ago. She loved the hand stitched intricate knotwork designs, and remembered her grandmother insisting she use the throw and not just put it out of sight in a trunk. Pulling the fabric around her shoulders gave Aislinn a sense of comfort, reminiscent of her grandmother who'd passed several months ago.

She could talk about anything with her grandmother and often did. She missed her Gram's insight to life. Her grandmother would tell her on numerous occasions that everything happened for a reason and that all things were connected. Aislinn came to believe in the simple philosophy over these past couple of months, since her life had settled down into a very cozy place following the devasting break-up with Grant.

Gorgeous, suave Grant.

Aislinn's stomach tightened at the unpleasant memory. She couldn't believe her luck, when in college, the handsome upperclassman noticed her. This in itself should have been a red flag warning, because in her world, men such as Grant didn't notice average girls like her.

Never in her wildest dreams did she ever think someone with his sophistication and social status would be interested in her but he was, or so she was led to believe. She quickly became star-struck with all the attention he lavished on her. Aislinn cringed. Looking back, she must have seemed so gullible to him.

Several years into the relationship with Grant, she once again began having the dream. It was as if the dream mocked the lack of passion in her relationship with Grant. Too bad she hadn't realized it at the time.

Leaving Grant was the most difficult, yet the best decision she'd ever made. It was a turning point in her life and despite the chaos leaving Grant caused, she became the strong, independent woman she was now.

There were times she questioned the quiet, uneventful life she'd made for herself and her driving stubborn need to prove to every single person on the planet she didn't need anyone in her life to find success and happiness. But she was content. Her job provided rewarding challenges. She loved being a teacher and she loved her students and actively threw herself into her work.

There were times however, such as this morning, that her dream left her feeling lonely for an all-encompassing love. But once the stark reality of morning settled in and she considered the mess her life had been, she simply attributed the dream and her melancholy to being a hopeless romantic.

Her head and her heart often fought a battle over whether all-consuming, wild passion truly existed. Her head firmly argued on the side of logic, but her heart, ah, her heart craved desire, and hunger, and a man who wouldn't stop wanting her, just like the warrior in her dream. Aislinn decided, after Grant, living vicariously through fantasies proved much safer than experiencing the heartache of rejection and devastation again.

Aislinn was grateful there wasn't much set-up this morning for today's classes. She was dragging a little from rising earlier than normal. She plunked down at her desk after turning on a set of crayon shaped lava lamps on a small table behind her desk. She turned on her speaker and opened a play list on her phone. Closing her eyes, she rubbed her temples, allowing the soothing rhythms to relax her.

The unexpected arrival of Aedan MacKendrick kept her mind whirling. She couldn't help but compare Aedan with her ex-fiancée. Aedan possessed the same suave appeal as Grant, the same sophistication and worldliness as well, not to mention he oozed sex appeal.

She would not be fooled again, not that Aedan MacKendrick gave any indication he was interested in her in that way. Still, she was leery that something wasn't quite right. The way her body reacted to his nearness at the museum was strange, to say the least. Instantly her skin prickled, her heart raced, and everything around her became heightened. She didn't understand the odd reaction he elicited from her and was grateful it was only for one day. She had nearly pushed him from her mind the following weeks after the visit to the museum, but when she turned around yesterday and saw Mr. MacKendrick standing before her, those same reactions came rushing back. His presence was so daunting, and she was so damned distracted by him, she could swear her brain ceased to function. It was all she could do to get through her day. Finding a way to work with him was going to be a challenge, for sure.

Suddenly, the hair on the back of her neck bristled, drawing her away from her thoughts. Aislinn's eyes flew open. The very subject of her musings stood right before her. She hadn't even heard him enter the room.

"I didnae mean to startle you. You seemed so deep in thought." Aedan handed her a cup of coffee. "With cream, right?"

Aislinn nodded taking the coffee, surprised he'd notice how she drank it. "You're here early," she commented, trying her best not to notice how ruggedly perfect he looked.

He pulled over one of the student chairs, spun it around, and sat leaning over the back. "Do you always come to school this early? I'm just wondering what time I should arrive."

"I just happened to wake early today." She watched him sip his coffee and continued. "I kind of like the quiet before the hustle and bustle of the day. I'm not much of a morning person. So, the chance to gather my thoughts and get my plans together is nice."

Aedan nodded at her explanation.

A long moment of silence ensued until Aislinn spoke up. "There is something that has been bugging me that I'd like to ask you about. In the gift shop, at the museum, the Wednesday before I came with the students, I felt a bit faint and you picked up a book I dropped. How did you happen to know my name?"

Aislinn watched as he nearly choked on his coffee, but recovered quickly.

"I said your name?" he answered her question with a question.

"Well, I thought you did." Aislinn now doubted what she thought she'd heard. "Maybe you didn't. I could be mistaken."

"Aislinn 'tis a lovely name, though," Aedan offered. "I knew someone named Aislinn, once."

Aislinn noticed a distant look fill his eyes as if he were recalling a long-forgotten memory. He offered no further information.

"How odd we would have the same name."

"Aye," Aedan answered, but changed the subject. "You have a nice collection of Celtic music."

"Thank you. I'm glad you like it."

"With the name MacKendrick?"

Aislinn half chuckled. "I suppose."

It fell quiet for a few moments more while Aislinn sipped her hot coffee. "Thanks for the coffee."

"You're welcome."

"Mr. MacKendrick..."

"Aedan, please."

"Aedan. I'm not really clear as to why you are here, or what I can do to help you."

"Your principal explained my purpose."

"Yes, but what exactly do you want from me? I know there are a lot of art teachers more qualified to help you than I am. It just seems a bit odd you should come all the way here, to a rural school district to find the help you need when there are plenty of teachers in your own city."

"'Tis is exactly why I chose to come here. This is the heart and soul of the museum. Everyday people who come to learn about and enjoy art. And, I have to admit, I was impressed by your students' knowledge."

"So, we are not a bunch of country bumpkins?"

"I never thought that."

Aislinn sensed he spoke the truth. "I'm sorry. I didn't mean to sound defensive. Sometimes people from the city mistake rural living with a lack of sophistication or education."

"And ye assume I've always lived in Chicago?"

Aislinn drew a breath. Perhaps she, too, made an assumption based on his expensive suit and well-groomed appearance. And that accent... "Touché, Mr. MacKendrick. I guess I, too, should not assume." Aislinn continued to sip her coffee as he just smiled.

"And do you live close?" Aedan eventually asked.

"I live about a half hour south of here."

"Ah, where the hotel I'm staying at is located?"

"Most likely."

"And do you have family near?"

"No." She didn't elaborate and waited for him to speak of his family, but he wasn't forthcoming with information.

"May I buy you lunch today?" Aedan asked, suddenly changing the conversation.

"Thank you. No. I don't usually have time. I spend my lunch preparing for my afternoon classes."

"Then how about dinner tonight?" he suggested.

Aislinn became quiet, as her internal alarm began sounding. Best she make it clear from the start she was not interested in anything more than a professional relationship.

"Your choice," Aedan added. "Wherever you'd like. I'm sure ye ken all the good places."

"Thank you for the offer, but no."

"I would be honored to have you dine with me," he persisted.

The strangeness of his words struck Aislinn. *Honored*? Who talked like that?

"No. But again, thank you," she firmly answered.

Aislinn dared a glance at him as she rose from her chair. He was not angry at her rejection, nor surprised. She saw only patience and maybe a bit of resolve as he continued to watch her. She rubbed down the gooseflesh on her arms in an attempt to dispel the uneasiness growing inside her.

As she came around her desk, Aedan rose, blocking her exit. He suddenly and very unexpectantly tugged her into an embrace. His lips swiftly claimed hers. It took several long seconds for her brain to realize what was happening and in that time she found his kiss oddly familiar and oh those arms... instinctively, she melted against him, delighting in the taste of coffee and male. But as his lips continued their ambush of hers, reason returned and fear had her slamming her palms against his chest and shoving as hard as she could, pushing him back. Her hand connected with his cheek with a hard slap as she immediately put distance between them.

"I suppose I deserve that," Aedan said, taking a step back.

"What the hell do you think you are doing? Get away from me," she stammered, still quite stunned, not only by his impulsive action but by her surprising reaction as well.

"What were you thinking?"

"That I wanted to kiss you."

"You arrogant son-of-a-bitch. What would possess you to do that? This is not acceptable." Aislinn swiped at the flush rising on her cheeks.

"I didnae mean to frighten you," he apologized.

Any attraction she'd felt toward Mr. MacKendrick completely evaporated as she struggled with what had just happened and how best to deal with it.

"What you did was not professional and not appropriate by any means and I don't appreciate being put in this position.

"That's nae what I felt from you" he merely stated.

She knew all too well of her response to him and was trying her damnedest to put it from her mind. "Well, then you are sadly mistaken about my feelings. Try anything like this again and I won't hesitate to file a report or press charges."

Aislinn strode from the room in an attempt to temper the disquiet growing inside her. She knew her threat to report him was an empty one. She was just as guilty as he, when she melted willingly against him and accepted his kiss. How could she, in all good conscience, report him when she was, albeit for a short time, completely captivated by his kiss?

Aislinn found teaching difficult with Aedan watching her every move. His eyes followed her everywhere. Between his constant scrutiny and his jotting notes in his notebook, she felt extremely self-conscious. Despite her best efforts, Aedan was hard to ignore. Raw sexuality oozing from him in wave after continuous wave that never stopped washing over her. Try as she might, she was not impervious to his intense presence. Surely Michelangelo sculpted David in Mr. MacKendrick's image. He was perfect and at the same time intimidating.

She found herself sneaking glances of him throughout the day, trying to assess what he was thinking, all the while trying to act as casual and calm as possible. *Yeah, like that was possible*, she thought, remembering the feel of being held in his arms. She replayed the kiss over and over, pondering if perhaps if she *had* unintentionally given him a signal to kiss her.

Any other time Aislinn would've been very accommodating to visitors, however most visitors didn't grab her and kiss her. And it wasn't so much the fact he kissed her she found distressing, as it was that she swiftly realized she was not immune to him. There was something so completely natural about the way she felt in his arms, and this was alarming having just met him.

The kids thought Mr. "Mac" as they called him, was extremely cool. He was genuine and gracious with them, answering their questions and talking with them about some of the art they saw at the museum. The boys especially loved to talk with him about the institute's weapon collection. And truth be told, Aislinn couldn't help but be delighted to see several students excitedly asking him questions.

So, her plans for the day went awry, probably for the best since honestly, she found even thinking difficult with Aedan in such close proximity. *What was it about this man that kept her totally off-kilter?* she wondered. Never had anyone affected her like this, and frankly it was disconcerting. The whole situation was odd.

"Look, Mr. Mac...er Aedan," Aislinn began as she gathered up her things, grateful the exhausting day had finally ended. "I can't help but feel you are going to be disappointed."

Aedan paused in putting his notebook in his leather bag. "I understand my appearance is rather sudden, and ye were caught by surprise, but I'm nae disappointed," he admitted.

Aislinn purposely didn't meet his gaze and instead continued to pack up her belongings with the pretense of indifference.

"I just wish I had known about this. I feel totally unprepared. I'm not sure what kind of time you are expecting me to put into this project."

"We will go at your pace."

Aislinn looked at him, then. She had the uncanny feeling he spoke of more than the work. His words were enigmatic, his expression hard to read.

"Then lets plan on a week from Saturday. We can meet here," she offered, hoping they could do whatever needed to be done in one day.

"Perfect. I will keep observing you, getting a feel for your lessons. We can start mapping our plans when we get together."

Nodding her reluctant agreement, Aislinn wasn't sure she could take any more days of him watching her. She bid Aedan farewell and before heading out, she decided to drop by her friend, Beth's, room.

Aislinn caught her friend just about to leave as well, but filled her in on the peculiar events of the day, leaving out the kiss and her embarrassing response to it.

"Beth, doesn't this seem strange to you?" Aislinn followed her friend toward the door. "Why would he just show up here? At our district? All the way from Chicago, to work with me? I'm sure there are better choices than me. I'm finding this whole thing very bizarre."

"Aislinn, I think you are overthinking this. You worry too much. Don't you think you might unfairly be comparing him to Grant? Perhaps Mr. MacKendrick really *was* impressed by you. You're a good teacher. Maybe, just maybe, you really have the talent and education he is looking for, for this project. This might be a great opportunity. Besides, if he was the man I saw in the office earlier, the man is drop-dead gorgeous, Aislinn." Beth flashed a smile and raised her brows.

Aislinn just shook her head as the two women left the building and headed for the parking lot.

"So maybe his asking you to dinner was a little fast, but you should have gone out with him." Beth chided as they approached their cars.

Aislinn shook her head unable to explain her hesitancy.

"I'll call you later and we can talk more," Beth assured her. "Take a breath and relax."

Aislinn raised her brows in a skeptical gesture, mimicking her friend's earlier expression. She waved good-bye and turned in the direction of her car.

As she climbed inside and turned the key to start the motor, Aislinn suddenly remembered the morning several weeks ago when she'd taken the time to admire the moon. The little annoying voice in her head suddenly spoke up. *Be careful what you wish for.*

"Oh, shut up."

It was going to be a very long winter, indeed.

Chapter Nine

AEDAN ARRIVED AT THE classroom, once again sporting a cup of coffee he'd purchased for Aislinn as a goodwill gesture, hoping to alleviate some of the tension between them. A slight smile tugged at the corners of his mouth as he thought about the kiss yesterday. He hoped in kissing her so abruptly it would have jolted her into remembering him. There was something, he knew. Aislinn felt the connection between them before she pulled away. However, his overenthusiastic action only served to scare her and increase her skepticism of him, proved by her conspicuous absence from the room this morning.

All kissing her had accomplished was to create more distance between them and confirm it was going to take more than a kiss to unlock her memories. Still, it felt wonderful to hold her, however brief.

He leaned over her desk to set down the coffee and spied the oddly shaped flat stone hanging among her keys she'd tossed haphazardly on a stack of papers. The medallion under Aedan's shirt thrummed warmly by her stone's proximity. Her half of the stone bore the same ancient symbol as the one he wore. She obviously didn't know the stone's importance or the amulet would never have been a trinket on her key ring.

The lady told him his stone would seek the other half, and what she had foretold had come to pass. The events in his life leading him to this place and time were all part of the Lady's plan. Each decision, each choice Aedan made in his life was unwittingly influenced by the stone's need to find it's other half.

During the times he could not remain in Ireland due to his agelessness, Aedan moved to Scotland. When he deemed his return safe, he would reemerge as a son or nephew of the previous "Aedan."

The first years in Ireland, Aedan relentlessly searched for information about Aislinn and the man in the Dal Fiatach tribe she was forced to marry. She was kept well hidden from him. Many years passed until he finally verified a granddaughter. And thus began his vigil over the Lady's descendants.

For hundreds of years Aedan devotedly kept track of generation after generation of the Lady's female descendants. Many beautiful, vibrant women blessed the Lady's lineage, yet none had been the one he waited for.

Memories of the Lady were long forgotten, but each woman unknowingly carried the poise and strength of her ancestor. As time passed, many fled to the new land, to prosperity and a new life, desperate to escape the famine and loss of crops from Erin's once fertile fields. The lady's descendants were among those who left Erin's shores and Aedan followed the migration to the new land.

New York teamed with thousands of immigrants arriving every day. Finding Aislinn would be difficult, he knew, but a task he'd no choice but to undertake. He eventually followed a path westward.

Years passed and Aedan continued his search in Chicago. Eight years after the great fire, he received his first job at the Art Institute. He'd attended a special exhibit of old-world textiles at the newly opened museum and in talking to the curator, his knowledge and possession of some antiquities became obvious, and he was offered a job. Despite settling down into nineteenth century living, Aedan continued with his life quest, every so often disappearing for several years and then returning again, reinventing himself.

In the 1950's Aedan came across a document in one of the institute's archives on their textile holdings referencing a Chicago family some twenty years previous. They owned an ancient cloth from Ireland and were looking to have an appraisal. In the margins were pencil sketches of the design so familiar to him. Although no further information existed, Aedan at least knew he remained in the correct geographical area.

After so many years with no information about the whereabouts of the Lady's descendants, this was a reassuring boon. When impossible to hide his agelessness, Aedan left the Art Institute, however he remained in Chicago.

Seventy more years passed before Aedan reapplied for employment with the museum. He didn't need to work, he had substantial wealth collected over the years, but he needed to stave off the boredom of waiting. He felt Chicago was the right city, so he stayed and continued his search.

Aedan dismissed his reminiscences and reached across Aislinn's desk, picking up the key ring. He squeezed the stone between his fingers. The smooth surface vibrated with the life force within it. Despite searching for years, with so many disappointing results, the stone brought her to him exactly as the Lady had predicted.

She spoke of other things, too. Aislinn needing him, great peril, demons, and one who would stop at nothing to find the amulets. Surely, the centuries had lessened the threats. Surely, he alone survived and carried the knowledge of the magic. His future, no their future, depended on the stones and them uniting, and seeing the amulet dangling carelessly on her key ring concerned him.

In one decisive moment, Aedan pulled the stone free from the chain, leaving the clasp open, making it appear as if the trinket had simply broken off the ring. He slipped the stone into his pocket just a moment before Aislinn walked back into the room, followed by her first class. Aedan nodded in her direction, acknowledging her ability to avoid him this morning; inwardly he smiled at her tenacity.

He settled back in a chair, crossing his arms over his chest, his gaze following her as she moved through the classroom. She loved teaching and her enthusiasm was as contagious for him as it was for her students.

She cared very deeply for her students, and he was almost jealous of her affection toward them. He longed to be the recipient of her simple touch, proud smile, or encouraging words.

He could feel her doubt concerning him, and yes even the barrier she had erected, perceiving he was some depraved maniac, but there was curiosity inside her as well and this made him hopeful.

He loved watching her, and despite her confusion about him, she exuded confidence and poise. Aedan loved the little strand of hair that refused to stay behind her ear, and how she struggled to tame it. The burnt color of her hair reminded him of a deep, rich copper sunset, and he couldn't help but remember entwining his fingers in the thick mass of curls that Beltane night, pulling the locks aside to kiss her neck below her ear.

Her eyes were a rare lush green that Aedan knew darkened with passion. Christ, he'd never stopped thinking of their night together. How innocent she was then, shy and cautious. Now, he thought, this modern Aislinn would be passionate and a bit untamed. He liked this modern Aislinn, but then, he always knew he would.

With the school day over, Aedan slid into the SUV his bulk and height necessitated he drive. As he turned the key, he wondered what his brother Brennis would have made of this new world, the machines, the technology. The modern world was such a spectacle, so out of the comprehension of a medieval mind. Had he not seen the inventions first hand, not grown and experienced the changes as they happened, he would have never believed it himself. Even the most imaginative bard couldn't have created tales to equal the wonders and horrors Aedan had witnessed throughout the years.

It wasn't with fondness Aedan thought of his brother, acceptance maybe, possibly the indifference time purchased, but never fondness. He couldn't believe after all these years he still thought of him at all, but Brennis was cunning, and Aedan often wondered what became of him.

He expertly maneuvered his vehicle through the city traffic toward his hotel as easily as he once controlled his horse through battle, instinctive and with purpose. He waged a different battle now.

"To find Aislinn, I would face any demons."

"You will have to." The lady had said to him.

He much preferred meeting his combatant head on, on the battlefield with might and strength and a sharp sword. At least he knew what he was up against. This waiting and wondering if and in what manifestation this *thing* would appear gave him a disadvantage.

He didn't know if his adversary was time, or Aislinn's lack of memories, or if some evil would try to harm them. Aedan's nature was to consider all possibilities. He was not to be the hunted. With his sharp wit and skill, he was the hunter.

Now, every second since finding Aislinn, he remained vigilant, silently watching for the unnamed thing the lady had warned would threaten his future with her. Fiercely determined, Aedan would let nothing stand in the way of their union.

Since finding Aislinn that first day at the museum, her feelings and emotions flickered and danced around his heart. At first just a little, but each day they were together intensified his connection to her.

From an early age, Aedan knew he would be pledged to Aislinn. The Lady revealed as much to him upon meeting him at the age of eight. At this same time, he began feeling the profundity of the impending union, the bond designed to unite his soul and hers, the anticipation of a life mate. This was given to him by the Lady to hold and sustain him until such time as the actual union between he and Aislinn would occur.

But that union did not occur. Brennis, his men, and the Un'Neills shattered that dream when they'd broken up the ceremony. The cost of losing Aislinn was instantaneous. Her presence was the other half of his heart, and to find her essence gone left nothing but despair and emptiness shrouding him.

Once again, the sense of Aislinn filled him, and everything before this seemed inconsequential. Feeling her warmth, her emotions, was like reclaiming a part of him that made him whole.

Fate was unpredictable, Aedan thought, pulling his car into the hotel parking lot and shutting off the engine. For all of Brennis' schemes, his existence had become nothing more than a name in a very distant past and all the endless centuries weighing heavy on Aedan's heart were finally at an end.

Chapter Ten

IRELAND, 9th Century

"Cut off two more of his fingers," Brennis instructed his man, glancing at the Lady's druid priest tied to a bench before him. "Let's see if this will convince him to give up the spell or if he'd rather have stumps instead of hands."

Brennis' statement was followed by the muffled screams of the priest as another finger was severed from his hand. Blood shot everywhere as the method of removal was less than delicate.

The priest's head fell, weakened by the continued torture, having already sacrificed three digits for not revealing the sleep spell Brennis wanted. Brennis stepped over to the man, and yanked up his head by his hair. "Are ye ready to give me what I want?" Brennis asked calmly.

The man, trying his best to remain coherent eventually nodded, having endured extensive punishment previous to the latest finger detachment.

Brennis bent toward the priest. "I want the sleep spell and the immortal spell. Clear?" The man nodded, as a board with parchment and a quill pen were thrust at him. Brennis' man untied the priest's good hand and shoved the quill into his palm.

"The immortality magic willnae work on you with the sleep spell. Only the amulet will allow immortality," the priest choked. "And the immortality spell willnae work while you sleep. Only after you wake will it work. Only one spell, one time, unless you possess the amulet."

Brennis grumbled at this bit of news. So, he wouldn't be able to spell his men right away, nor himself without the amulet. He paced the length of the cave, angered by this new development. No matter. This was of small consequence to him as he didn't anticipate being under the sleep spell for long. As soon as he woke, he would go in search of his brother and the amulets. Satisfied with his assessment, he paused once again in front of the priest. "Write."

For the next few moments, and in between bouts of lucidity, the priest managed to write down the magic spells Brennis wanted. When completed, the priest sighed, remorseful and at the same time relieved thinking his ordeal was over. Brennis took the parchment and read, nodding in approval at what it said. "Good. Now kill him," Brennis coolly instructed, turning and strolling toward the exit of the cave where they had hidden the priest. As he entered the daylight, he was followed by the tortured death cries of the druid priest. Brennis smiled.

Ireland, present day

Brennis glanced at the younger man standing before him. He fidgeted nervously while waiting on Brennis. Brennis next threw a glance at Collin, the only other person in the small room before turning his attention to the rolled piece of parchment he held in his hands.

The immortality spell was to be the reward to his men who were his guardians until he woke. In return for his gift, he would demand their loyalty and thus build an inner circle of companions who would share his legacy and benefit from his magical power. Once he'd taken the amulet halves from his brother, the amulet would render him immortal. He would need more than just himself to pursue his ambitious plans for the future, and that is why the pledge to offer this spell to those who were his guardians was incentive enough for the men to care for him. Little did he realize that the promise of immortality would become the stuff of legends over the years, enough to entice generation after generation of eager followers, hopeful his time to awaken would be during their life time so that they might be the recipient of the magic.

"I feel honored that you were awakened during my time here. I am glad to serve you and offer my loyalty to you," the younger man spoke enthusiastically.

Brennis offered a nod as he unrolled the parchment and began reciting the ancient words. As he finished the spell that would render the young man immortal, he looked up at the first of his modern companions to see if there were any outward signs that the spell was successful. Brennis was greeted with a look of horror that crossed the young man's face a split second before he dropped dead to the floor.

Collin swiftly went to the fallen man to see if he could revive him, however after a few minutes moved away and shook his head.

Brennis slammed his hand down on the wooden table, his anger flaring. Och, but that old priest had played him a fool. He never intended to give Brennis the magic he wanted. Oh, he got the sleep spell from him, alright, but the spell for immortality was actually a death spell designed to kill off Brennis' men.

Brennis paced the small room. Without this spell, he had nothing to entice these men to his cause. And because he was still at their mercy, Brennis was feeling more vulnerable than ever and this was a feeling foreign to him. He stopped suddenly and spun around, pinning Collin with his stare. "I want to see the oldest manuscripts you have in this facility."

Collin scrambled to his feet, went to the door and spoke to someone on the other side before closing it again. "We will see they are brought to your room."

"Good," Brennis bellowed, grabbing his sword from where it rested close by and throwing open the door with the intent to exit. He paused and looked back at Collin. "See that this body is removed," he growled before turning and leaving.

Brennis exited the confines of the oppressive stone building. He'd had enough of the dark and dreary chambers. He needed to move and fight. What he wouldn't give for someone equal to his skill, who could swing a blade. Och, but so much was lost to this modern world, he thought, settling for moving through maneuvers, swinging and slicing the air with his sword as fury built inside him. His life, his land, everything he'd fought for, now lost, and yet the one person who he despised and who had taken everything from him, remained.

If Brennis had ruled the Dal Riata, his people would have seen glory even to this day. By right, this should have been his Chiefdom. He should have been the one to negotiate and gain the power and the rule of the coastal tribes, not Aedan and certainly not the Lady.

Having all the power of the land would have kept him from groveling to those damn Un'Neills for support. He could have squelched their attempts at the high kingship early on.

If anyone should have married the Lady's niece, it should have been he. He could have used her to gain the necessary power. He knew she and Aedan were connected by magic, somehow. *He* should have had that magic. He wanted it, even now, and he could still have it if he could just get the two halves of the amulet. Oh, sweet Aislinn. How he looked forward to having her, too, he mused.

Brennis smiled as he continued his duel with an invisible opponent. Taking his brother's woman would be sweet revenge indeed. *Perhaps*, Brennis thought shrewdly, he'd even make his brother watch as he plowed her before Aedan disappeared back to his wretched past, helpless to do naught but carry the vision of Brennis fucking his woman until the end of his days.

Once the stones were his, he'd obtain the magic, and easily dispose of Aislinn after her appeal wore off. Brennis' smile widened. He did take some comfort that Aedan did suffer all these long years without his woman.

His thoughts were interrupted by the arrival of Collin. "Just wanted to inform you that we have located the woman," he spoke. "We will need to talk about a few things regarding how you'd like to proceed. There are some minor issues to work out, but I'm sure we can come up with a solution."

Brennis lowered his sword arm. He was going to have to count on the help of these modern men more than he'd anticipated, at least for the time being.

"What issues?"

"Well, the fact they are in a totally different country quite a distance away, that you cannot access right now. But we can."

Brennis growled. *Always a problem,* he thought. This modern world was nothing but obstacles. Having Aedan so far from him might be a problem for now, but eventually Aedan would have to return to Erin for Beltane, and then he could stop him once and for all.

He destroyed Aedan once, no actually twice, he mused. Once upon breaking up his ceremony with his beloved Aislinn with the Un'Neills and again upon his return from Alba after conveying the news to his cousin. Brennis was confident he could stop Aedan again. The woman made him vulnerable and this was *his* advantage. Surely the years that had passed had weakened Aedan. He would be ill prepared for battle, since in this world it was a thing of the past.

Brennis chuckled. Aedan was so distraught over losing his woman, he never saw his ambush coming. He probably never knew he was the one who dealt his deathblow.

Brennis gazed up at the walls of the old building. He was going to have to find a way to convince these men that he would find the spell that was promised to them.

In a world he'd recently learned didn't hold to the truth of ancient magic, there were this small group of men who continued to covet the old knowledge. Maybe they would prove valuable after all. There was still much to learn, and they would be useful in his quest. But for now, he needed to get his hands on the stones and his brother.

"Have the old manuscripts been brought to my chamber?"

"I believe so." Collin nodded.

"Aye, you can be assured I will get that spell, if not from the old tomes, then from my brother. One way or another, I will get it." Brennis stepped past Collin.

"Of that I have no doubt," Collin assured him, turning as Brennis passed.

"Let us go speak of these *issues* you refer to. I am anxious to find my brother."

Collin fell into step behind Brennis as they returned to the building.

Chapter Eleven

UNITED STATES, PRESENT Day

Aislinn realized her awkward mistake the instant she heard the door to her classroom close. Her backside was sticking in the air as she bent halfway under her desk, searching for a trinket broken from her key chain. When she'd heard Aedan enter, she tried to right herself but managed only to clunk her head in the process.

"Damn," she muttered from under the desk. In her haste not to give him any further view of her rear, she extracted herself quickly, tugging and straightening her clothes.

"Lose something?"

Too late, she thought, seeing the hint of a smirk and twinkle of amusement in Aedan's eyes at the view she'd provided him. He cleared his throat and handed her a cup of coffee.

She took the cup from him. "As a matter of fact, I did lose something. You didn't happen to see a little stone with strange symbols on it, did you?" Aislinn plopped down in her chair, putting her purse in a desk drawer. She rubbed down the gooseflesh on her arms that seemed to always appear with Aedan's proximity. *What was it about this man that always has me reacting this way around him?*

"Nae. Was it something important?"

"Nah, just a little charm from my grandmother." Aislinn noted how Aedan's amused expression suddenly became tempered before he changed the subject.

"I brought a salad for us for lunch. It's in the lounge refrigerator," he said.

Aislinn sighed in resignation. Whether she liked it or not, she would have to work with Mr. MacKendrick. She had to admit, developing this program with the institute would be a great professional opportunity. And, this was a good time in her personal life for devoting her energy to such an endeavor.

She did think that Aedan had more than a professional relationship in mind especially after the kiss. But she put that idea to rest after threatening to report him. Her life had just settled down into a comfortable place and becoming involved with someone right now was the furthest thing from her mind.

"I'm sorry our kiss upset you," he spoke unexpectedly in response to her lack of conversation.

Did he just read my mind? Aislinn let out a breath, collecting her thoughts. *Be honest. Tell him how you really feel.* "Frankly, Mr. MacKendrick, I want you to know I'm uncomfortable working with you after what you did yesterday."

"I donnae want you to feel uncomfortable around me. I know what I did seemed aggressive and frightening. I cannae explain to you why I did it, but please understand there was intent behind my action. I donnae want you to be frightened of me. I would never hurt you. Just the opposite actually. I would protect you with my life."

"Still, You shouldn't have done it. It was inappropriate."

"Agreed. I'll admit it was a bit presumptuous of me, but I willnae apologize, in lieu of your response. However, I willnae kiss you again...unless you ask."

"For a moment, I thought you were being sincere," Aislinn snapped.

"I am being sincere. I meant what I said. Next time *you* have to ask."

God the arrogance of the man, she thought rolling her eyes as she sipped her coffee. *Next time?* Lord but his brazen manner sure kept her askew. She didn't know how to react to him.

"Don't hold your breath." *Oh my God, did I just say that? Did I just digress to snapping frustrated retorts at him?* She shot him a glance. The man actually had the nerve to chuckle at her. "Well, thank you for bringing lunch," was all she could think to say.

"I wanted to work out the details for this Sunday." Aedan pulled up a chair and sat across from her, his amusement replaced with seriousness. "Ye ken we are slated for a pretty big snow storm this weekend?"

"Yes, but we always get snow storms in the winter."

"But you live over a half hour from here," he reminded her.

Aislinn questioningly at him. "How do you know where I live?"

"You mentioned where you lived once to the kids."

Does he remember everything I say? "Aedan don't worry. We can meet here at nine. All my materials are here, so this makes the most sense." Aislinn rose from her chair. "Now, I have some of the kids' artwork to hang up in the hallway before class," she said. As Aislinn ended the conversation, and came around her desk, she purposely made a wide berth around Aedan.

As she scooped up a pile of drawings, she stopped suddenly, turning to pin Aedan's gaze. "And, what do you mean you kissed me on purpose and that you can't tell me why?" She inquired, recalling what Aedan had said a few moments ago.

Just as Aedan was about to respond, the door to her room burst open and a student, bundled up in a coat much too big, with bright red cheeks from the cold, stumbled in huffing and puffing.

"Ms. O'Neil, quick!

Aislinn hurried over to the panting child. "What's the matter, Alex?"

"It's Devin. He was playing around on the ice on the way into school, and he slipped on the sidewalk and he says he can't move his leg. He's crying."

Devin was a third grader, who just days before had participated in a very animated discussion with Aedan about several medieval weapons Devin had seen at the Art Institute. And since Devin was less than enthusiastic about doing art in her class, Aislinn let him spend the fifty minutes of art time engaged in conversation with Aedan. She was delighted to see Devin finally take an interest in something, and she admittedly appreciated Aedan's patience with him.

Aislinn dropped the papers, grabbed her coat, and offered a reassuring smile to calm Alex before heading out with him.

Aedan grabbed his own coat and followed. As Aislinn slipped and slid on the same icy walkway in an attempt to reach the cluster of students gathered around the crying child, Aedan took her elbow to keep her from falling. She was so focused on reaching the little boy she hadn't noticed Aedan's steadying hand on her arm.

Aedan released her upon reaching the child, and she knelt next to the little boy, immediately assessing the situation. She saw the odd angle of the child's leg and knew not to move him.

"Devin, it's Ms. O'Neil. I'm here to help. Can you tell me what happened?" Aislinn thought to distract him from the pain of his injury by talking to him. While she conversed, she also sent another student off to alert the principal while Aedan called an ambulance.

Aislinn took her coat off, wrapping the garment around Devin to keep him warm. She continued to talk calmly and soothingly, all the while wiping away his tears as he choked out a few words about what happened.

Aedan helped tuck her coat tighter around Devin to immobilize him the best they could, while Aislinn distracted him. After Devin had settled a little, Aedan slipped his own coat over Aislinn's shoulders. She acknowledged his thoughtfulness, mouthing "Thank you" and boldly scanned Aedan's eyes before returning her attention to Devin.

Within a few moments, an ambulance arrived, as did the boy's mother. She gratefully hugged Aislinn, thanking her for her help while the paramedics tended to Devin, placing him on a stretcher and then into the ambulance.

With Devin taken care of, Aislinn turned her attention to the worried students gathered around. She talked to them for a few minutes assuring them their classmate would be alright, and calmed their fears.

Noticing her teeth chattering, Aedan made the suggestion that they go inside. She agreed, realizing how cold she actually was. Aedan once again helped her along the icy path to the rear door of the building, but this time she noticed his assistance.

"*Brr.*" Aislinn rubbed her arms and stomped the snow off her shoes once inside. She started to take off Aedan's coat, but he stopped her.

"Leave it on for a few minutes, until you are warmed up," he suggested.

"Thanks. I've got to go to the office now to fill out some paperwork about the accident. Why don't you just wait in the classroom? I'll be back in a few minutes." Aislinn left Aedan at the door to her room and headed for the office.

Sitting at an extra desk beside the school secretary, Aislinn completed the necessary forms. Glancing at Aedan's jacket she cradled in her lap and finding the temptation too great, she lifted Aedan's leather coat discreetly to her face. She inhaled, once again smelling the unique scent of him she'd noticed when he had slipped it around her shoulders. She couldn't quite put her finger on it, but God, whatever the aroma was, she found it very stirring.

"Damn," she admonished herself. What did she go and do that for? She knew the scent would be forever imprinted on her brain now. She looked around somewhat guiltily making sure no one saw what she had done and then lifted the coat and inhaled again.

After leaving school for the day, Aislinn pulled up to the front of curb of Devin's house. She wanted to bring him a little something to make him feel better about his ordeal that morning. She learned Devin was in a full leg cast from ankle to hip, and was confined to a wheel chair for several weeks. He'd be out of school for a couple of days while he adjusted to the cast.

As she climbed out of the car, she noticed the vehicle parked in the driveway. The big, black SUV belonged to Aedan. The vehicle was equally as dark and mysterious as he was.

Devin's mother welcomed her in and led her toward the family room. What she saw when she approached stunned and surprised her. Devin sat in his wheel chair lifting, with some effort, a very real-looking sword. Aedan was leaning over him, offering assistance.

Aislinn stopped in her tracks. Never had Devin been this excited about anything in school. She would have never guessed his less than stellar academic performance by the eagerness he showed for the sword. She watched intently while Aedan explained the blade's parts and how to hold it. The continuous questions Devin asked Aedan as well as the genuine interest Aedan took in the boy flabbergasted Aislinn. Aedan really seemed to like Devin and Devin obviously had taken to Aedan. As she watched the interaction between the two of them, the thought crossed her mind that maybe, just maybe, Aedan was more than he appeared to be.

Aedan happened to glance up and see Aislinn watching them. He smiled warmly at her and then cleared his throat, signaling to Devin to look up. Aedan drew Devin's attention toward Aislinn strolling into the family room.

"What a surprise," Aislinn greeted Devin, but stole a quick glance at Aedan.

"Ms. O'Neil, isn't it cool? Mr. MacKendrick brought a sword to show me. A Scottish Claymore."

"I see. The weapon looks very real."

"It is. And it's very old," Devin said excitedly. "From medieval times."

Aedan lifted the sword from Devin's hand, throwing Aislinn a look much like a boy himself being caught with something he shouldn't be playing with.

"Mr. MacKendrick is just full of surprises." Aislinn's gaze fluttered to Aedan then back to Devin.

Aedan cleared his throat. "*Hmm*. Yes, well, I just thought Devin might want some cheering up."

Aislinn slipped the box of cupcakes and mylar balloon she'd brought onto the table.

"Mr. MacKendrick told me in the old days, you weren't considered a great warrior until you were wounded in battle," Devin explained.

"Is that so?" She shot another look at Aedan. "So does that count for broken legs, too?" she asked.

"Absolutely!" Devin squealed. "Right Mr. Mac? Hey, show Ms. O'Neil the scar on your arm from your battle." Devin pointed to Aedan's left forearm.

Aislinn watched Aedan quickly look at his arm then change the subject.

"Devin, look at the treat Ms. O'Neil brought." Aedan motioned toward the box of cupcakes on the table.

"Great. I love cupcakes."

"Would you like one? Your mother said it would be alright," Aislinn offered.

"Yeah," Devin said excitedly. "You can have one, too," he said to Aedan.

"Thank you. I'd like that."

Aislinn passed out the cupcakes, which were hastily devoured within seconds by the two males. But despite the sugary snack, Devin appeared weary. She caught the attention of Aedan and nodded toward Devin. "I think Devin is looking a bit tired. I think we should let him get some rest and regain his strength."

"I think you're right," Aedan agreed, much to the protests of Devin as he packed up his sword in a carrying case. "Warriors must know when it's time to rest as well, Devin." Aedan informed him. "Remember what I said. I will have those pictures for you when you come back to school."

"Cool."

Aedan tousled Devin's hair. "I'm glad to see you're doing so well."

Devin beamed. "Thanks for the cupcakes, Ms. O'Neil."

"You're welcome. We'll see you in a couple of days."

"Okay. Bye."

As Aislinn and Aedan departed, Devin's mother returned Aislinn's coat and thanked them both for stopping by to see her son.

"Well, aren't you full of surprises, Mr. MacKendrick," Aislinn said as they walked down the driveway.

"I just wanted to see how he fared," Aedan explained.

"This is the first time I've seen Devin show such an interest in something. How did you do it?" Aislinn inquired.

"Do what?"

"Spark his curiosity."

"I remembered he asked me about the armor and weapons at the museum."

Aislinn looked at Aedan curiously. "And you just happened to have a medieval claymore on you?"

"Yes."

Aislinn stopped and shook her head in disbelief before continuing toward her car. "Well, okay, then," came her somewhat cynical reply.

"Devin lacks confidence in his own ability. I simply encouraged him a bit with something I knew he liked."

"Thank you, Aedan. That was nice of you to take an interest in him." She kept her compliment simple to avoid admitting Aedan's kind gesture with the young Devin had touched her deeply.

"I enjoyed it."

Aislinn stopped outside her vehicle, realizing Aedan had walked her to her car. She climbed inside, and he shut the door for her. He knocked on the window for her to lower it.

"Aislinn, I noticed you cared enough to show up here as well." He winked at her. "Devin is lucky to have you as a teacher."

Aislinn gave him a nod, turning the key in the ignition, as she closed the window. As she watched Aedan walk toward the black SUV, that nagging little voice crept back inside her head. This time it was tinged with curiosity and a touch of admiration.

What an enigma you are, Mr. MacKendrick.

Chapter Twelve

AISLINN STOOD STARING at the sea of white flakes out of her living room picture window. The snow had begun to fall around midnight and hadn't let up since. Blowing winds, excessive drifting, and freezing temperatures accompanied the snowfall. According to the news, roads were a hazard and travel conditions would be challenging.

Most times Aislinn was pretty fearless when it came to driving in inclement weather but even she knew when it wouldn't be worth taking a chance.

Just great, Aislinn thought, knowing she would have to brave the less-than-ideal conditions. The winter storm would have to happen when she was supposed to meet Aedan at school. She knew he'd have no problem navigating the roads in the large SUV he drove, but her little old compact was another story. She wished she knew how to get a hold of him so she could postpone their meeting.

The quicker we meet, the sooner he'll be on his way. That thought popped into her head as she continued to gaze out her window. Although, she had to admit, the previous couple of days had passed pretty normally, that was, until yesterday afternoon. Up until then, there seemed some sort of unspoken understanding between her and Aedan. Although she suspected his interest in her continued, he kept his demeanor professional but there was still something about him that kept her a bit on guard.

That uneasy truce between them dissolved yesterday just after she'd finished putting the day's materials away and was preparing to leave. She hadn't heard Aedan step up behind her, and when she turned she almost smacked right into him, startling her.

"How about dinner tonight?" he'd asked, flashing his most charming smile.

Aislinn had remined quiet, as the little voice in her head dared her to say yes. "Aedan, I thought we were keeping this professional," she reminded him.

"Aislinn, I'd like the chance to get to know you."

"Thank you but maybe another time," she politely declined if for no other reason than to confirm her seriousness about keeping their relationship professional.

Aedan looked at her pointedly. "What are you afraid of?"

Aislinn was taken aback. His question hit too close to home. "I'm not afraid of anything," she responded becoming defensive.

"Then come out with me."

"I wish you'd stop asking me."

"Why?"

"I'm not interested in dating anyone right now."

"Why?" he asked again.

"That's none of your business." He was persistent, she'd have to give him that much. Darn, just when she'd begun feeling confident about working with him and quelling the butterflies in her stomach whenever he was near, now she'd have to guard herself once again. She had hoped he'd forgotten about the whole kiss thing. Apparently not.

Aislinn sighed, watching the thick blanket of snowfall knowing she'd have to fight the storm and meet Aedan, despite yesterday's dinner rejection making it awkward. She thought about just staying home, but if he arrived at the school and she wasn't there to open the building, well, she'd feel guilty about making him drive back in the storm.

Why didn't she think to make alternate plans when he mentioned it might snow? She could have at least gotten a phone number. Usually, she was more responsible than this. That man sure had a way of jumbling her thoughts.

She knew if she made it to school, she'd probably get stuck there overnight. It wouldn't be the first time she'd stayed there. She kept a change of clothes, extra personal supplies, a light blanket and some canned food in the closet for just this reason. Actually, several of the other teachers that lived a distance away did the same. That's where she got the idea from when she first took the job. She purposely ignored the thought that this time, if she stayed, she would not be alone.

Aislinn turned and bundled up in her coat, boots, hat, scarf and gloves. She grabbed her keys, threw her purse and a couple of books in her backpack and headed for her car.

After only a few miles from home, Aislinn seriously questioned her decision to drive in this weather. It was ludicrous to be out in conditions like this. She couldn't see two inches in front of her car. She maybe drove fifteen miles per hour while her fingers gripped the steering wheel so tightly they ached. The roads were a sheet of ice and she had no idea how she was managing to stay on them.

Damn him, she thought, blaming Aedan for everything from the weather, to her decision to drive in this storm to even her mish-mashed feelings. In the last few days her quiet little life had been turned inside out because of him.

He made her crazy. Mister dark and mysterious, who just showed up as if stepping out of a dream, all handsome and in control, exuding maleness and sensuality, making her question everything about her life.

Okay, Aislinn admitted, her hormones did do flip-flops every time Aedan was near, and she recognized the edgy self-conscious sensations as attraction for him. On one level it was nice to know she could still be attracted to someone, but in order to work with him and keep their relationship professional, she needed to get her feelings under control before she made an idiot of herself. She'd allowed her feelings to run away with her one other time with Grant, and look where that got her. She would not repeat that with Aedan.

Aislinn peered out the windshield, trying to see between swipes of the wipers. Why was she thinking of Aedan when she should be concentrating on the road? Because, she reminded herself, she hadn't stopped thinking about him since her accidental meeting with him at the museum.

Get a grip!

Aislinn was amazed when she saw there was actually someone else on the road beside her. A pickup truck pulled up behind her and moved out, attempting to pass her car. She hoped he would hurry and move past her. Her nerves were frazzled trying to navigate the storm and all she wanted to do was reach her destination in one piece. She would be perfectly fine staying in her room for the weekend. There was television, heat, water, computer, and music. She didn't need much else.

Whispering a silent prayer as she continued on, she promised if she got through this, she would never attempt anything as foolish as to go out in this kind of weather in her small car again.

She could barely see the truck pulling over much too close in front of her because of the cloud of snow it kicked up. Snow went flying across her windshield. She definitely didn't see, as much as she felt the truck's bumper hit the front of her car, but by the time she recognized what had happened, it was too late. The impact with the other vehicle had her car sliding, tumbling and rolling down an embankment. She was aware of her head hitting something and her last coherent thought was her seatbelt was digging into her neck, holding her in an awkward position. A dream-like sensation overcame her and at one point, she even thought there were people trying to help her, but the images faded in and out before the blackness shrouded her and then nothing.

Aedan regretted his decision to meet Aislinn in her classroom, having followed the weather reports about the storm for days before today. His decision not to call and cancel their meeting was another mistake, not wanting to reveal to her how he got her phone number. He should have just cancelled. When they both reached their destination, he would advise they stay in the school overnight until the weather passed. He smiled. He couldn't wait to see her face with that suggestion. He loved the way her emotions were so transparent. Maybe he'd even confess what thoughts filled his mind when he'd entered her room and found her bent over before him searching under her desk the other day. That most assuredly would get a series of reactions. He chuckled slightly.

Aislinn's quick thinking and determined actions when taking care of Devin impressed him, but then his woman would be like that. She carried the blood of her ancestors, strong and brave. He witnessed her compassion, too, not only by her comforting Devin and the other children, but also by the look she gave him when he covered her with his coat.

For that briefest of moments, he saw her unshielded heart and the possibilities within it. Despite the gravity of the situation, he couldn't help feeling warmed by the look she'd given him.

He couldn't help the possessiveness he felt at having Aislinn wrapped in his coat and thinking that now she wore his scent. This aroused him greatly. The need for her to recognize him by scent, sound, and touch was so strong. He grew impatient for her recollection of what they meant to each other.

But there was something holding her back from opening to him. Something that had caused her pain and kept her distant and this bothered him. Aedan gripped the steering wheel. He could easily use the magic to make her remember him. A few words and a touch and she would be his again. The temptation lasted only a fleeting moment, though. One of the first rules he learned about the ancient secrets was changing the will of others for personal gain went against the natural order and was forbidden. Magic came with a great responsibility; one he'd made a commitment to maintain regardless of personal sacrifice.

Aedan flipped on the wipers to dispel the snow settling on the windshield. He could feel anxiety he knew was coming from Aislinn. She too was obviously concerned about the weather. They were definitely going to stay at the school. He would do whatever it took to keep her safe.

As Aedan came within two miles of the exit, he suddenly felt something wasn't quite right. He could no longer feel Aislinn. The abrupt way he lost his sense of her was alarming.

He scanned the highway the best he could through the blinding snow. His intuition continued to batter him that something was wrong, yet he couldn't see anything. All his senses became alert as he slowed to a crawl, searching the road and ditches. He silently invoked the magic words to help him locate her, while he continued to search the highway. Long moments passed until...

There off in the distance, down in a gully a tiny red light, hardly visible. Fear brought panic surfacing within him. "Noo...!" he roared, knowing instantly it was Aislinn.

Aedan maneuvered his SUV to the side of the road and jumped out, giving no thought to anything except reaching Aislinn. He fought his way through the thick snow, following what oddly appeared to be footsteps to her car. "I'm nae losing ye again," he bellowed, using all his strength to reach her through the thigh deep snow as if it were nothing.

Her car was on its side, down the embankment half buried in a deep drift. Most of the front end was buried, as were the doors. Effortlessly, he dragged the piles of snow away from the door in his attempt to reach her. He could see her wedged between the door and the air bag, slumped over with her hair covering her face. The horror of that fateful night all those years ago came flooding back to him providing the adrenaline and strength he needed to continue.

Aedan eventually cleared enough snow which enabled him to climb on the car to reach the door, but no matter how hard he pulled, the mangled car prohibited the door from opening.

Without thinking, Aedan smashed his fist against the glass, shattering it on the first attempt. The snow blew in around Aislinn, who was hanging awkwardly by her seatbelt, as he felt for and found the lock to release the door. He yanked again with all his strength, but the door refused to budge.

Aedan closed his eyes and without thought spoke the ancient words. The door suddenly gave way. Aedan pushed it open and leaning into the car, began disentangling Aislinn from the seat belt. She moaned as she was moved. "'Tis me," he whispered, reaching over pulling her away from the air bag so that he might look at her. He moved her hair aside to see her face clearly. She'd hit her head presumably on the door or maybe even the steering wheel, he thought, seeing the awkward position of the airbag. Her forehead was bleeding, her eye was swollen and red and her neck held the red marks where the seatbelt had torn her flesh. He quickly ran his hands over her to feel for broken bones, grateful at not finding any.

"Aislinn, can you hear me? I'm going to get you out of here." Another moan escaped her, as if she were trying to respond. "I'm going to release the seat belt, but I have you. I willnae let you fall. You're going' to be alright."

Through the blackness, Aislinn thought she heard a familiar voice beckon to her. The soft brogue felt warm and reassuring. She tried to speak but couldn't seem to form the words, just as well, as the more she tried, the more the pain assaulted her. The voice which called to her faded once more and she slipped back into the painless oblivion.

When she finally opened her eyes, Aislinn was certain her head had been cleaved in two. She attempted to move but thought better of it as her brain seemed close to exploding.

"*Shh*. I'm here."

A moment passed before Aislinn registered that the deep voice coming from just behind her was Aedan's. She was seated on the floor between his legs, leaning back against him, his arms wrapped around her.

"This is going to be cold, but we need to keep the swelling down," he warned a second before placing a fistful of snow on her forehead and eye.

The abrupt contact made her wince.

"Ye have a nasty bump, and your eye is swollen and bruised."

Aislinn tried to move again, but a wave of nausea came over her. "I'm going to be sick." She closed her eyes, fighting the feeling climbing up from her stomach. She slumped against him as he brought a wastebasket to her side should she need it.

"Try nae to move and the nausea will subside."

"What happened?"

"Your car slid off the road and landed sideways in a ditch. Ye hit your head."

Aislinn remained quiet for a few moments until she remembered something. "A truck ran me off the road. A red one. He tried to pass me but pulled over too quickly and hit the front of my car."

"*Shh*. Just rest. You'll be fine if you rest. I've seen worse."

If Aislinn had been more alert than she was, she would have thought to ask him how he could have seen many head wounds. She instead slumped against him and sought the refuge of sleep.

She didn't know how long she slept, but she felt comfortable in her half-awake state. Every now and then, the scent of heather would tease her nostrils, and somewhere in the back of her mind, she recalled the scent being familiar. With the pain in her head, she didn't dwell on where she'd smelled heather before; that it was familiar was enough.

"Aislinn? You need to wake up for a moment. Have a drink of water."

A moan escaped Aislinn's lips. The pain started intruding into her quiet place.

"My head..."

"I ken, but ye have to wake for a few minutes," Aedan insisted, helping to lift her off him. He brought a cup to her lips. "Try to drink a little."

She took a small sip but couldn't bring herself to drink more.

"My head feels like it's been used as a punching bag." She sat up and shifted to lean against the wall. "My backpack? It was in the car."

Aedan nodded toward her bag sitting not too far from her.

"I retrieved it from the car along with your keys."

"I've got some Tylenol," she moaned.

As Aedan moved to get her bag, Aislinn noticed the lacerations and swollen bruises on his hand.

"Did you do that helping me?" He dropped the pack and withdrew his hand.

"'Tis nothing." He flexed his hand to show her the injury wasn't bad.

"I'm so sorry, Aedan." She fished for the pills, swallowing them, hoping for relief from the awful headache. "I've got to lie down before my stomach decides to turn inside out."

Aislinn leaned over and stretched out on the carpet. "I want to sleep for a few minutes, until the pills start to work." She closed her eyes as Aedan bunched up her coat and placed the garment under her head as a pillow. As she settled in, she heard Aedan quietly whisper words she didn't recognize while placing his leather coat over her. She snuggled against it, inhaling deeply. She thought she could smell a faint aroma of heather magically wrapping around her.

Somewhere in the haze of her mind, she knew the smell belonged to Aedan. She let the comforting scent flow over her, fill her, and draw her into a peaceful slumber.

Aedan turned off the television in the corner of Aislinn's classroom. It still wasn't possible to chance going out into the storm. More roads were closing and authorities were asking people to stay home. The snow continued to pile up faster than the plows could clear it away. People were stranded everywhere and Aedan didn't want to risk leaving with Aislinn and getting stuck. Here they were warm and comfortable.

He did what he could for her. He managed to stop the blood from the gash on her forehead with a small first aid kit found in the teacher's lounge, but she needed stitches. The skin around the wound was turning a nasty shade of blue. In addition, the white of her right eye was now completely red and swollen, and he suspected she may have bleeding there as well. He would wake her every few hours to check the concussion and to make sure she drank something.

All in all, she was lucky. He spoke the truth when he told her he'd seen worse injuries, but what he neglected to mention was the injured were battle hardened warriors, not a woman who'd never seen battle.

Sitting on the floor beside her, Aedan tucked his coat around her a bit tighter, making sure she rested well. He dusted a strand of hair off her face, lightly touching the bruise on her forehead. Something about the accident was bothering him. He could swear the marks leading to and around her car were footprints, yet there was no one else around. It was possible people in the truck she said hit her tried to help her, but then why would they leave and not try and get help? Heeding his gut instinct, he knew something was out of place about the accident.

He continued to watch her sleep. Despite her injuries he found her breathtaking. Today, she wore a vivid royal blue turtleneck sweater. Nestled next to the fiery color of her hair, it reminded Aedan of a Van Gogh painting. Her cheekbones sported just a hint of blush. The lines of her face were soft and feminine and Aedan gave into the urge to run his fingers over her skin. "How long?" he whispered to her sleeping form. "Until you know me and remember my touch?"

Aislinn opened her eyes. The room was dim except for the soft glow of the crayon lava lamp by her desk. Her slight movement had Aedan instantly waking. He helped her to sit up. She winced against the pain in her head.

"What time is it?" Aislinn asked, rubbing her head and throwing a glance at the darkness out the window.

"Around ten p.m. Ye've slept most of the day."

"I have to get up." She tried to stand, but pain assaulted her head. Aedan grabbed her arm to steady her.

"I have to use the restroom."

"I'll help."

"Ah...no." Aislinn shook her head. "I can do it."

"I mean I'll walk you to the door," he clarified.

Despite her proud boast, she clung onto his arm, still unsteady on her feet.

Aedan waited just outside the door, and the instant she emerged, took hold of her once again, leading her to a spot on the floor. She propped herself against the wall, leaning her head back and closing her eyes against the pain.

"Be right back. Donnae move," he instructed leaving the room.

Aedan returned a few moments later with a hand full of packed snow that he wrapped in paper towels and placed on her forehead. "Keep the cold on your head as much as ye can." He gave her extra towels to wipe the melting drops.

"Are you hungry or thirsty? I could scrounge in the refrigerator in the teacher's lounge to see if I can find something. Maybe I can find some tea or coffee?"

"No. I'm not hungry." She murmured, closing her eyes.

Aedan sat down beside her and pulled her against him. She settled into him without protest. He circled his arms around her, stroking her hair with a gentle touch that any other time she would have thought too intimate.

"I ken you are uncomfortable." Aedan whispered. Taking the ice from her hand and holding it in place. "I will do what I can to help."

"How did you find me?" Aislinn asked, eyes still closed, as sleep once again approached.

"I wasnae too far behind you. I saw tail lights off the road in the distance and pulled over to see if someone needed help. I recognized your car. We were close to the school so I brought you here."

"Thank you for your assistance. I know you hardly know me." Aislinn drifted toward sleep.

"I know you," he whispered near her ear.

Images of Aedan in some long-forgotten place briefly flashed through her mind. Only snippets and they disappeared as quickly as they had appeared. She briefly opened her eyes to gaze at him through the dim light and she thought she saw him nod ever so slightly. If she didn't know any better, she would swear he knew exactly what she had seen. She once again closed her eyes, convinced it was her mind playing tricks on her, in her need for sleep. She relaxed against him and drifted off and into her familiar dream.

Aislinn never felt such despair, such soul-deep pain. Her heart was torn in two. To know such a love and to have it instantly taken away was more than she could bear. She watched the battle wage on around her. She watched him steal one heart-wrenching glance at her before being swallowed up by the fighting. She ducked as arrows whizzed past her.

Only moments before she was experiencing such pure bliss, and now she was bereft, and trying to stay alive. She ached so deeply; the pain reached her very soul. The helpless look in his eyes with his final glance as the fighting engulfed him was like a knife piercing her heart. She knew she'd never see him again, and she didn't know how she would live without him. She tried to fight against those who were taking her away.

She kicked and screamed, calling out his name and reaching for him "Aididh!" She scanned the battle desperate for a glimpse of him. "Aididh! she cried over and over until her voice was hoarse and barely audible. 'Nae...' she sobbed as he became only a blur in the distance as she was dragged further and further away. When she could see him no more she collapsed from the torment that filled her and rendered her completely numb.

The devastation of losing the other half of her soul was a burden she could not bear. All the life drained from her then, and she became only a shell of her former self. She uttered only one final plea, "Find me Aididh."

"Aislinn. Wake up."

Aislinn abruptly opened her eyes and sat up. She thought better of moving when the room began spinning. Aedan placed steadying arms around her.

"Ye were dreaming. Are you alright?"

Aislinn swiped away the tears on her cheeks, and at the same time attempted to shake the intense feelings of the dream.

"Take a deep breath," Aedan instructed her, leaning slightly to reach for a glass of water he handed her. "Take a drink."

"Must be from the bump on my head. God it seemed so real," she muttered, taking a sip of water.

"What seemed real?"

"The battle, the arrows, the blood. I couldn't find him." She looked at Aedan and saw the odd look on his face. "Never mind. It was just a dream." She rubbed her head.

"Tell me about it," he prompted.

"It's just a dream."

"But it obviously upset you. You'll feel better if you talk about it." Aedan took the glass she'd been drinking from and set it aside. "Tell me."

Aislinn sighed. "I've always had very vivid dreams, ever since I was a little girl, but as I got older, there is one dream that I've had quite a few times. It's like a movie. Sometimes I dream the beginning part, sometimes I dream the middle, sometimes, the end, or what I think is the end. Tonight, I dreamed the end. I've dreamed it before, but never with such clarity and sadness. I could actually feel the gut-wrenching pain of one of the people, as if it were happening to me."

"What happens that's so sad?"

"I don't really know all the details. I can only guess how it all fits together. The dream takes place a long time ago, probably in the middle ages. There is some kind of ceremony between a man and a woman." Aislinn decided to leave out the intimate part. "The ceremony gets interrupted by men starting a battle. I can feel arrows shooting around my head. I think I'm the woman, but then at times, I'm seeing the action as if I'm a spectator." Aislinn shifted against Aedan.

"It's obvious the man and woman love each other because the battle tears them apart, and she wants to go to him but she's being taken away. I can feel her heart breaking. I can see the look in his eyes as he leaves her, but I can never really see him. He's always shrouded in a mist of sorts. I know they won't see each other again and it's very sad. At times, like tonight, the dream seems so very real," she paused shaking off the feelings. "It's so strange."

Aedan lowered his face next to hers. "Do you ever dream a happy ending?"

"The dream always ends there. It seems incomplete, or that I only know a part of it. It may even be a scene I read from a romance book long ago. I'm not sure." She looked at him scrunching her face with a twinge of embarrassment. "Yes, I read romance novels."

Aedan chuckled. "I promise I won't divulge your secret."

"I'm getting sleepy again, Aedan. You were right, I do feel better after talking about it." Aislinn yawned.

"I'm glad. Now sleep," he instructed as she closed her eyes. "Maybe you'll dream an ending."

Aedan held her as she slept peacefully. He was anything but peaceful thinking on Aislinn's dream. It wasn't a dream and he knew the ending. Those memories were as vivid today as they were twelve hundred years ago. He closed his eyes as the scene played over in his mind ...

Ireland, ninth century

Aididh stumbled blindly over the grotesquely twisted bodies littering the ground. He swiped the blood and grime from his eyes, blinking to clear the smoke stinging his vision. Aididh scanned the clearing, attempting to see through the smoke and early morning fog for any sign of movement, anyone left alive who could tell him where they'd taken Aislinn.

He was desperate in his search, focused on naught else but finding her. So, he continued on, turning and tossing aside bodies, trudging through the dead and dying, some foe, but most friends. "Where is she?" He found himself hollering to the lifeless stare of one of her clan before shoving the corpse away from him. "Where have ye taken her?" Aididh bellowed moving deeper into the carnage.

Enraged by the loss of Aislinn and the senseless death of so many, Aididh was nearly mad in his attempt to search every fallen man for someone who could tell him Aislinn's whereabouts.

As the hours wore on and the chance of finding anyone left alive became slim, Aididh suddenly heard the raspy gasps of someone struggling to draw breath. The sound seemed eerie amidst the chilling silence. At first he thought exhaustion was playing tricks on him, but he paused to listen and honed in on the gasps, unmistakable this time. He did not hesitate in moving in the direction of the labored breathing. Mindless of the bodies that separated him and the sound, Aididh tripped and picked his way in frantic deliberation to reach the source.

Off in the distance, leaning awkwardly against a battered cart sat a man Aididh recognized and who just the previous night drank to his health and impending union with his clan. Aididh was relieved the old chief still lived, but his relief was short lived when he noticed the gaping, bloody wound in the man's chest. He would not survive another day. Aididh knelt next to the man.

"Where is she?" he demanded. "What have ye done with Aislinn?"

The chief opened his eyes, having difficulty focusing on Aididh, but comprehending who spoke to him.

"Aididh," he addressed him. "She is gone."

"Gone? Where? Where is she, mon?" Aididh grabbed the tattered remains of the man's shirt to keep his waning attention focused on him. "Tell me."

"She is nae for you."

"Our union was fated by the lady." Aididh's heart constricted from the impending news of Aislinn.

"We had to make an alternate plan should something happen. We anticipated yer brother's betrayal."

The chief's voice was fractured by a fit of coughing. "She has been given to another this very morning. One of the Dal Fiatach who will now ally with us."

Aididh's anger was near exploding. "Speak true."

"I speak the truth, Aididh. Our ties with the Dal Riata are broken. We align with the Dal Fiatach this very day through her marriage. 'Tis..." the chief tried to gesture toward the death and destruction surrounding them. "'Tis proof 'tis too dangerous to align with the divided Dal Riata."

"These dead are Un'Neills. I recognize their markings."

"'Twas your own brother Brennis who courted the Un'Neills and encouraged this fight. And where are our men? Off with your cousin Ciniodh, fighting on Alba for a cause nae of our own. He asks for our men to fight his battles but does nae keep his promise to help us when we are in need. Nothing but broken promises from Ciniodh, and now your brother allying with the Un'Neills, trying to wrest your chiefdom from you. We have no choice but to align with the Dal Fiatach to protect our shores. You need to strengthen your own kingdom." The chief choked out his next words. "Nae. The Dal Riata cannae help. We donnae have the numbers to beat them back. Despite all the power you possess, all of your magic, you donnae see the traitors at your verra back."

"Where is Aislinn?" roared Aididh, ignoring the old man's accusations.

The old chief seemed to soften. "Yer a good man, Aididh, and it does grieve me 'tis come to this. I always liked you. But even you and your good heart cannae control a divided Riata. My job is to take care of my clan above all else, despite my personal feelings. I'm sorry Aididh, but she is now with the Dal Fiatach, married and bedded, even as the Fiatach and what is left of my clan pursue the Un'Neills north."

"Ye planned this all along? You planned on betraying our union?"

"I wasnae betraying our union- your unio." The man coughed and wheezed, finding talk more difficult and barely able to draw breath. "'Twas a plan only if aught dinnae go well. Donnae try to find her. She will be hidden. The Lady's power grows weaker." More coughing and a long painful inhalation of breath prevented further words.

"Aislinn was mine," Aididh spoke, the defeat obvious in his voice.

The pained look the old chief gave him reflected pity, even as he lay dying. "Nae, she is not. I wish 'twere different. I would have liked to fight alongside you as kin." The chief's eyes closed one final time, his voice weakened. "Bring our men home from Alba. Strengthen our coasts against the invaders. See to yer kingdom. The Riata needs to join..." His sentence went unfinished as his words died quietly in the exhalation of his final breath.

Aididh placed the man's sword across his lap, his hand grasping the hilt before standing and once again scanning the hopeless devastation.

Despite the heartache, Aididh didn't harbor any resentment against the old chief. Times were too unsettled, too unpredictable and he did the duty of a chief and prepared for all possible outcomes with alternate plans ready to implement on a moment's notice. And truth be known, he respected and liked the old man's cunning and stealth. He'd known him as a firm, strong leader, with his clan's interests always at heart. Now the fragile relationship he had with the chief was gone in the closing of an eye and a final breath.

Aididh looked to the heavens and let out a cry more tortured than any he'd released before. His scream filled the air with his anguish and suffering, for all he'd lost this day. The chief wasn't the cause of his heartache. 'Twas Brennis, and Aididh vowed to make him pay.

United States, present day

Aedan shuddered, holding Aislinn tighter while his memory dissipated. She wasn't the only one haunted with dreams of a life long ago. Hearing Aislinn recount her dream brought back all his heartache of that fateful night as well. Despite the years that had passed, the pain hadn't dulled.

Aedan sighed, what mattered now was that Aislinn was here and she felt wonderful in his arms. Never again would he lose her. Never again would she be taken from him.

He lowered his head to hers. She always smelled of a hint of roses. He'd never forgotten that aroma. When she told him of her dream, hope flared inside him. She still held some memories of their night together, despite thinking them a dream. He touched her face gently, moving aside her hair to check for any change in her injuries. They remained the same.

He let his eyes travel the length of her. Aislinn hadn't changed, curved and full and round in all the right places. She was a perfect match to his size and bulk. Her breasts were ample and lush and could drive a man crazy with the mere thought of touching them. Her waist, although not small was well proportioned to the rest of her. Her hips were perfect and beautiful, beckoning to give a man a hundred babes. Her legs were long and strong, and Aedan craved to feel them wrapped around him.

He remembered her eyes deepening to the green of the forest when she became aroused. He remembered the way she looked all flushed with passion and hungered to know that sight again. He longed for her to know him in all things, and once she did, she would love him, he knew, as they were a part of each other. Each carried a piece of the other in the deepest part of their souls and only together would they both be whole.

She was strong, and smart, and independent, yet he saw a vulnerable side to her she kept hidden. She tried to need no one, and he wanted more than anything for her to need him. He vowed to erase whatever hurt she carried in her heart so that their love was all she knew.

Aedan placed the lightest of kisses on her cheek. "Sleep. Heal. All will be well soon."

Chapter Thirteen

Ireland, Present Day

Brennis paced the small damp chamber, attempting to keep his anger under control. He pushed the hair away from his eyes, halting abruptly as the door to his chamber opened.

"You called for me?" Collin hesitantly stepped into the room.

Brennis instantly pierced him with his seething stare. "Is everyone in the God forsaken century inept?" He waved his fist in frustration. "How could your men be so careless?" What Brennis wouldn't give for his companions of old, instead of these modern men who had no warrior skills, and didn't know what to do nor how to get a task done.

Collin cowered back. "The snowstorm proved more intense than expected. They had no way of knowing her car would crash."

"Is she dead?" Brennis asked between gritted teeth not confessing her death would distress him more than he cared to admit.

"No," Collin simply answered.

Brennis turned away, his anger near a breaking point. "Tell me what happened. Every detail."

Collin relayed the information about finding Aislinn and following her when she left her house. They hadn't expected her to travel any distance so they tagged behind, expecting her to eventually stop.

"And what were you going to do when she stopped? Knock her out? Kidnap her?" Brennis pounded his fist on the wooden table.

"I guess it depended on where she stopped and if there were others around."

In two large strides Brennis approached Collin and grabbed him by the front of his shirt, lifting him so his feet barely touched the ground. "And then what? Casually ask her if by chance she had an old stone talisman?" Brennis released his grip on Collin, who sank onto the stone floor. "You fool. If she knows what the stone is, she's not going to carry it on her person. She's going to put it somewhere safe."

"But what if she doesn't know what it is?" Collin suggested, rising and brushing himself off.

"Aedan knows and he's nae going to let her or the stone out of his sight. My brother will always be close to her regardless if she knows what the stone is or nae."

"The men tried to get her out of the car, but the snow was too deep and the car too damaged," Collin explained.

Brennis seethed, once again approaching Collin and grabbing hold of Collin's arm, twisting the limb behind the man. "I donnae want to hear your excuses." Brennis spat, twisting Collin's arm tighter until he winced and cried out. "I told ye nae to harm her, but instead your men just left her, not knowing if she were injured. If she dies before Beltane this whole mission is for naught."

"You said yourself, Aedan would be close. Surely he would have found her," Collin choked.

"Your stupidity cost me the element of surprise. My brother is nae fool. He would have seen the tracks in the snow and known someone else had been there." Brennis tightened his hold on Collin so much that Collin actually screamed. "By now my brother will have figured out her accident was nae accident. He most assuredly will be even more vigilant. Any further attempts to locate the stone will be difficult."

"We will not fail again," Collin whispered. "I have another idea we can try."

"Let this be your last blunder. If there are more problems, be warned, I will personally see this is the last thing you do." Brennis tossed the man across the room where he landed with a thud against the far wall, before turning and storming from the chamber.

Chapter Fourteen

UNITED STATES, PRESENT Day

Light shone in the window when Aislinn woke. She could hear the wind howling outside and knew the storm continued to rage on. At least she was safe and warm, comfortable in Aedan's arms.

What? She sat up with surprise. *Aedan's arms?* Aislinn held her head when dizziness followed her quick movement. She tried to scramble to her feet, but Aedan was quick to help her up.

"Aislinn, donnae try to move so fast. You'll make yourself sick." She slid into a chair at one of the tables while she regained her balance.

"I'm alright. Just let me rest for a moment."

"I could make you some coffee or tea in the lounge if you'd like. After that, I'm afraid it's pretty meager fare."

Aislinn closed her eyes while her brain tried to unscramble itself.

"I have some things. Soup, I'm sure. In the bottom cabinet in the storage room. There's probably tea or cocoa, maybe even some granola bars. And there's a hotpot." He looked a curious question at her before going into the art supply room in the rear of her classroom.

"I've been caught here before," she called out an explanation. "I learned to keep a few items on hand just in case I stayed."

He brought out several cans of soup along with the other items. He plopped everything down on one of the tables. "Ye had a blanket in there, too." He handed it to her.

"I've worked so late before I've just stayed the night. I found keeping a few food things here and a change of clothes convenient. I'm sorry I didn't think of it sooner."

Aislinn attempted to rise again, gripping the table for support. Aedan instantly came to her side, slipping his arm protectively around her, but Aislinn stepped out of his hold. "I'm alright. I'm just going to use the restroom."

Once inside the bathroom and the door closed, she leaned against the cool tile wall, fighting the exhaustion from this one small movement. Her head screamed; her body felt so heavy yet all she could think about was how nice it felt to wake up in Aedan's arms.

She pushed aside the thought. It had to be her mind playing tricks on her. She didn't know him well enough to feel so comfortable. He was just being polite, she convinced herself, thinking on all he'd done to see to her comfort.

However, she recalled him saying he would always protect her when she confessed he made her nervous after stealing the kiss. That had her taking pause. That was a strange proclamation from someone whom she'd just met. Aedan obviously thought he had some connection with her. She would have to make it clear that although she appreciated his concern and care, it by no means meant there was anything between them. She was not looking for a relationship. Period.

She suddenly froze. *Oh God, you told him about the dream.*

I know you, he'd said.

Goosebumps rose on her arms. Did he say that or had she dreamed it? She didn't trust her thoughts right now. Everything seemed so jumbled. She couldn't be sure what she'd dreamed and what had actually happened between them. She decided it was best not to bring up the dream again. And what was up with his more pronounced accent? And why did it seem so natural? Lord, but did she need to rest. Her thoughts were all over the place.

When she finally came out, Aislinn declined any help from Aedan. She instead dug through her backpack, found her Tylenol and took two with a sip of water. She wrapped herself in the blanket and lay down to sleep again. If in fact she had told him about the dream, she'd revealed more than she ever intended. She would have to be more careful.

When Aislinn woke again, Aedan was sitting quietly watching the weather reports on the classroom TV.

"How long did I sleep?" Aislinn asked sitting up.

"Most of the day and part of the evening."

"What are they saying on the news?"

"There's no school tomorrow."

"Kind of knew that was coming." She closed her eyes letting her head sort itself.

Aedan rose, and went to a back counter area. He poured a cup of something from the hotpot and brought it to her, handing her the mug. "I heated up some soup. Try and eat something."

As Aislinn took the mug, she noticed his hand. She thought he'd bruised it yet there wasn't a mark on it. Had she imagined seeing his knuckles swollen and bloody? She shook her head, clearing her thoughts. The bump on her head had her so mixed up. Maybe she'd just thought he'd been hurt. Obviously, now, he wasn't. She seriously needed to see a doctor as soon as it was safe to leave.

She lifted the mug of soup. The aroma of the warm liquid was enticing. Her stomach rumbled as she sipped.

"I went out while you slept and dug my car out of the snow. I'm afraid it was probably a lesson in futility, though. The school grounds havenae been plowed and it would be more than difficult to get out until they are."

Aislinn nodded, and continued to drink her soup. "Did you eat something?"

"I will when ye've had your fill."

"Take what's left, Aedan. Please. I don't want any more. I'm not that hungry." He nodded, but still waited until she'd finished.

While he ate, she took two more painkillers, hoping for even the slightest relief from the incessant headache and jumbled thoughts.

While she waited for the medicine to begin taking effect, Aislinn went to the large window at the far side of the room, watching the snow fall, settling in the large piles outside the window. Her shoulders slumped. She resigned herself to being stuck in the building for a little longer.

How odd it was that they would get the blizzard of the century this weekend. If she hadn't known any better, if she believed in the mystical forces her grandmother professed existed, she would have sworn something conspired to keep her and Aedan in this building.

She glanced over as Aedan joined her at the window, standing alongside her for several silent moments. She felt small next to him, but surprisingly at ease. She looked up at him. He watched her with those intense dark eyes.

What was it about him? She'd known him only two weeks and yet she felt such a pull toward him she couldn't explain. As her eyes locked with his, she sensed they were searching for something she didn't quite understand. His gaze held such mystery, she found herself wanting to lose herself in them. His dark depths made her imagine impossible fantasies could be real.

Aislinn pulled her eyes away, taking a breath to steady herself. She was letting her thoughts run away. Needing to put distance between her and Aedan, she moved away from the window and lay down on her makeshift bed, pulling the blanket around her. There were several moments of silence between them before she spoke.

"Where were you born? I remember you saying you weren't always from Chicago."

"Scotland. However, I've spent a lot of time in Ireland as well."

"Ah, I thought I noticed bit of an accent."

"I can make me accent verra thick ta impress the ladies," Aedan teased, speaking with a heavy Scottish brogue." He winked at Aislinn. "But I try to keep it reined in most of the time. Still, a bit slips out now and then."

She smiled.

"I've lived here for a long time, though," he added.

"Is Aedan a Scottish name? I was thinking it was Irish."

"It is Irish. It's an ancient name meaning fire or one who is fire. I am named after an ancestor who was a great warrior. Me Mum was Scottish, me Da was Irish."

Aislinn nodded. "People from Europe have long family pedigrees. Many of us from the states whose ancestors came here don't know our family roots. Our ancestors wanted to forget where they came from and who they were. This is where they came to start over."

"Aislinn. Dream. A vision."

"What?"

"That's what your name means. A dream. It's a beautiful old name."

Aislinn rubbed the goose flesh appearing on her arms again, swallowing hard.

"Is your family back in Scotland?"

Aedan paused. "Nae anymore," he finally answered.

"I'm sorry," she apologized.

"'Tis alright. A long time has passed since then. My mother died when I was very young, my father shortly after. I donnae remember them. I was raised by my uncle. He's since died. How about you? Tell me about your family."

Aislinn recognized how quickly he turned the conversation back to her. He would offer no further information. Disappointment filled her. She found herself wanting to know more about him. She wanted to know about the man who just happened to have a medieval sword on his person and roused a little boy's interest in learning stories of great battles. She wanted to know more about the man who'd showed up so unexpectedly, claiming an interest in her work. She wanted to know more about the man she just couldn't get out of her head.

Aislinn sighed. "There really isn't much to tell. Pretty boring, actually. I told you my mother lives some distance. There's a bit of a strain between us because of ... er ... something that happened a year ago.

"A boyfriend?"

"A fiancé."

"What happened?" he inquired.

"To make a long story short, I called off a wedding and upset a lot of people- mostly my mother." Aislinn attempted to keep the bitterness out of her voice. "The only one who understood my decision was my grandmother. She was so wise. She kept reminding me to follow my heart. I didn't have to give her reasons why I couldn't go through with the wedding. She understood. She understood a lot of things. She had insight into things which had no explanation."

"Do you ever regret not marrying him?"

Aislinn didn't hesitate. "I could have had everything with Grant..."

Aedan finished her sentence, "Except love."

Aislinn threw a glance at Aedan. How quickly he assessed her. "My mother never forgave me for calling it off."

"But do *you* regret your decision to call it off?" he asked again.

"No."

Was that relief she saw cross Aedan's features?

"Can we change the subject?" Aislinn didn't want to go into her motives for breaking off with Grant, despite Aedan making her feel as if she could say anything to him. She'd already spoken more than she'd ever intended.

"I think I'm ready to rest a bit," she said, snuggling into her makeshift bed and closing her eyes.

As Aedan watched Aislinn sleep. He could feel her wanting to trust him, wanting to open to him but then she would withdraw from him just as quickly. He knew for all the toughness she exhibited, there was pain she kept hidden as well. He longed for the moment he would be able to breech that barrier and she would trust him with everything that hurt her.

He understood her hesitancy now. She'd been hurt not only by a man, but also by family. He knew Aislinn hadn't told him everything, but at least the little she revealed was a start.

Late on Monday, the storm began winding down. Aedan and Aislinn occupied the day making small talk and watching television. She didn't enter into any further conversations with him that were personal in nature.

Aedan continued to worry about her. She still didn't feel well, and Aedan knew she needed to get to a hospital. He was relieved when he finally heard drivers plowing around the school and made the decision then that they would leave. School had been cancelled for the following day, so no preparations were needed.

They arrived at the emergency room around dinner time. After explaining everything to the doctors, a C.A.T. scan and x-rays were ordered. An ophthalmology specialist was called in to examine her eye, as well.

Aedan waited for the test results restlessly pacing the waiting room. After several hours, they called Aedan into the room where Aislinn rested.

Aislinn sported stitches on her forehead, and held an ice pack against it to relieve the swelling. One eye was bandaged after receiving medicine for a small laceration on her eyeball.

The doctors told Aedan she was suffering from an acute concussion that could last ten to fourteen days. They reassured him she would be fine and would eventually heal, but needed to rest for at least a week if not two. They arranged to have Aislinn spend the night for observation.

Aedan thanked the doctors, before turning and pulling a chair beside Aislinn's bed.

She yawned sleepily from the medication given to her. "I'm sorry. If you want to go ..."

"I'm nae going anywhere," Aedan confirmed. "I'll be right here when ye wake."

As Aislinn drifted off to sleep she could swear she heard Aedan whisper, *I lost you once, I willnae lose you again.*

As Aedan kept watch over Aislinn as she slept, he found his thoughts drifting in and out of his past as he twirled a strand of her hair around his finger.

Ireland, ninth century

He was eight years old when the mysterious female visitor came to his uncle's keep. She was dressed in the most ethereal gown. It covered all parts of her except her face. He remembered how it shimmered iridescent as she floated past him, like the wings of a dragonfly.

She paused and turned back toward him, reaching one hand out to gently cup his chin. She tilted his small face to hers, and Aididh remembered her touch was as light as a feather. He often wondered afterward if she had really even touched him or if he had imagined it. Even though he somehow knew he was not worthy to look upon her, he dared lift his proud eyes to hers. The Lady's eyes were the palest blue he had ever seen, almost silver, and they reached deep into him.

"You will know love, my brave warrior," her voice spoke to his mind, without speaking out loud. She smiled a knowing smile at him, and he was compelled to avert his gaze.

He knew he had not looked into the face of a mere human. She had caressed his soul with her promise. And for someone without parents nor a true home she offered him everything he yearned for.

Aididh was too young to know his mother or father, he only knew about them from what he had been told. Aididh's mother purposely named him after a distant ancestor, Aididh mac Gabrian, King of the Dal Riata. Aididh mac Gabrian was a fearless warrior and a great leader of the Dal Riata people during his time, and she wanted these qualities in her son, despite the three hundred years that had passed between Aididh mac Gabrian's death and his own birth. It was a legacy he was expected to live, a way of life he was destined to preserve, a path carved out for him on the day he was born by a mother who pledged his life to Erin because of the man she had married and the name given to him.

Aididh's father was absent most times, off fighting the raiders on Alba's shores. He was killed in one of these skirmishes when Aididh was very young.

He knew then, that this was why the Lady had come. At the tender age of eight, he knew she had come for him. Many words were exchanged between his uncle Alpin and this Lady, and he and his cousins tried pressing their ears against the wooden door to hear what was being said.

Later, he learned that she had come for him, that he was to inherit the land and people of his father, and that his warrior skills would be needed in the fight to keep Erin free of outsiders. The arrangement that he would be taken to Erin to claim his father's land was part of the marriage contract between his mother and father orchestrated by his uncle, Alpin, upon his birth. In exchange for Aididh going to Erin, the Lady promised a future alliance with Erin's two largest tribes, which she convinced Alpin was in his son, Ciniodh's, best interest.

More passed between Aididh's uncle and the Lady in the next days. When she took her leave on the third day, Aididh almost felt sad, without knowing why.

It was only after she had gone that his uncle explained she was the Lady of Erin, the powerful Druidess, who had come from the isle across the sea. He explained that Aididh, upon his tenth birthday, would be sent to Erin to be raised by the Lady and her people.

He would be educated with the knowledge of the great magic men. He would be trained as a warrior and leader of men. He would be taught to read and write and to speak several languages and he would be given the Erin Dal Riata territory.

And from that day until he left Alba on his tenth birthday, Aididh was treated with more respect by his uncle and his clan. His cousins, Ciniodh and Donal, also paid him his due respect, but not without jealousy and spite. They didn't care that they were needed as the future leaders in their homeland, all they knew was that Aididh, their parentless cousin, would be going on some grand adventure and they were not.

Over the years, news of Aididh's exploits as a warrior as well as a Druidh reached Ciniodh on a regular basis. It seemed that Aididh was destined for greatness in body and mind. Aididh was true, and loyal, and fierce in battle, and his powers as a man of magic instilled fear in the new Christians, who had forgotten their pagan past. Aididh didn't deny the rumors of his power; on the contrary, it gave him an air of one not to be trifled with, and that gave him an advantage. Keeping the mystery kept him alive. Those who lived and fought with Aididh knew him as fair and kind. And in two very different ways he earned the respect of people on both Erin and Alba.

United States, Present Day

Aedan smiled, thinking of Ireland, as it is called today. What a beautiful, savage island. He remembered standing on the rocky shore the first time he arrived on the isle, wondering to what barren forsaken place he had been sent. It was only as he moved inland that he beheld the true splendor and wonder of the magic of Erin. It was as if time stood still there and he had arrived at some place so ancient one had to experience it to know. It was green. Everywhere green and lush with trees and brooks, teeming with life and mystery. Everything was old, full of wonder and lost knowledge. He wanted so much to know it all, to experience everything, to become a part of it. And within days of arriving as a youth, he knew he had found where he belonged.

Aedan spent the next twenty years, training and learning the magic of the Druidh. Aedan was at home among the Irish, much more so than in Alba. There was something more magical about Erin, more ancient, more earthbound.

Perhaps it was because this is where most of Aedan's training occurred, or perhaps his connection to the land and the people was stronger because they were more accepting of him and his connection to the old religion.

Perhaps it is where he felt the closest to his Celtic ancestors. Perhaps it was the lack of Roman influence. Whichever it was, he loved the people, he loved the Goddess, and he fought ferociously and aggressively to protect the island from the north invaders.

Chapter Fifteen

THE MORNING BROUGHT more bad weather, but at least the plows had removed most of the previous day's snow, so driving Aislinn home from the hospital wouldn't pose much difficulty.

While Aislinn was waiting for the paperwork to process for her discharge, Aedan ran back to his hotel to shower and pack a bag, knowing he was going to insist on staying with Aislinn until she was well. He smiled, anticipating the battle over that decision, but Aedan would risk her wrath to ensure her safety, especially after the suspicious footprints around her car.

Until Aedan determined her accident was just that, an accident, he would take no risks with her life and leave nothing to chance.

Before arriving at the hospital to pick up Aislinn, he also made arrangements to have her car towed. Once the damages were assessed she could call her insurance company and decide what to do.

As the nurse wheeled Aislinn down to Aedan's car, the pain pill she'd taken a few minutes before was beginning to take effect. Aedan helped her into the passenger side, making sure she was settled before shutting the door. He thanked the nurse and came around to the driver side and climbed in. He glanced over at Aislinn and chuckled. Her head was back, leaning against the window, eyes drooping slowly in a losing battle to stay awake. He smiled and pulled away from the hospital.

By the time they arrived at her home, Aislinn was completely out and Aedan carried her inside. He brought her into her bedroom and gently placed her on the bed, then pulled the covers over her.

He next found a spare room and brought in his bag and tossed it on the bed, grateful he didn't have to try and fit his large frame uncomfortably on a couch.

Aislinn's house wasn't huge, but it was warm and inviting. Two rooms were bedrooms and a third she used as an office and craft room.

Aedan continued his exploration and came upon a photograph of Aislinn and, who he guessed was, her mother. He surmised the picture must have been taken prior to the cancelled wedding. A second photograph was Aislinn standing with an elderly woman Aedan guessed was her grandmother.

Gazing on the pictures, Aedan felt a twinge of sadness he'd buried long ago. He found himself longing for the love of a family. He wanted nothing more than to one day have a family of his own. He stoically pushed the feelings aside. There would be no more longing. He would have the family he dreamed of with Aislinn.

Aedan moved into the living room spying a large fireplace at one end flanked by bookshelves packed to overflowing. The prospect of sitting in front of the warm glow of a fire in the evenings with Aislinn pleased him immensely.

He stepped over to the mantel, running his fingers over the Celtic design on a vase that sat above the fireplace. He liked being surrounded by such images as they reminded him of his homeland.

He noticed three or four books on the coffee table. He picked one up, gazing at the title. He couldn't help but grin. Romance novels. He guessed she had a bit of a romantic side. He would so enjoy getting to know more about this.

Out of the corner of his eye, Aedan noticed something that made his breath catch unexpectedly in his throat. He moved over to the couch and picked up a cloth lying in a heap at one end. He touched the intricate designs reverently. The blanket must have survived all these years because of the magic woven into it. Aedan returned the cloth to the couch, remembering how Aislinn's naked body looked lying upon it on the altar stone in the glen.

He remembered with exquisite clarity the agony of hurriedly wrapping her in the fabric, shoving her away from the battle, watching her being taken away, seeing the pain and confusion on her face. That night haunted him constantly.

Now, as he looked at the cloth, he couldn't help the weighty feeling taking root inside him. For days now, he'd been feeling unsettled as if things were shifting. He suspected the closer it drew toward Beltane, the more he would need all the strength and fierceness of his past to overcome whoever, or whatever, the Lady predicted would threaten he and Aislinn.

AISLINN WOKE NEAR EVENING. She remembered Aedan picking her up from the hospital but didn't remember him driving her home. He had to have been the one who brought her in and put her into her bed. She wondered how he knew where she lived, but figured he probably found her license in her wallet which was in her backpack.

She could hear someone moving about in the kitchen and figured the noise was probably Aedan. She flung back the covers and climbed out of bed, moving slowly as to not aggravate her head. She opened the door and gingerly made her way down the hall.

As Aislinn made her way toward the kitchen to see what he was up to, she happened to glance into the living room and saw a robust fire burning in the fireplace. She was more than a little stunned by how comfortable he'd made himself.

Aedan looked up at her appearance. "Aye, you're up," he greeted, busily taking a pan out of the oven. "I hope you're hungry. I've made a nice roast to help ye regain your strength."

Aislinn rubbed her eyes, unable to believe what she saw. "You've certainly made yourself at home in *my* house," her voice was tinged with annoyance.

"I just wanted to help ye with a few things," he replied in all innocence. The sincerity of his statement caught her off guard.

"Aedan..." She didn't know what to say. "I can take care of myself."

"I ken. I'm just offering a wee bit of help while ye are recuperating."

She threw up her hands in exasperation. "I'm going to take a shower. We'll talk about this after I come out."

Several minutes later, Aislinn strolled into the living room, towel drying her hair. She felt refreshed and a bit stronger than she had in days. She dressed casually in sweatpants and a thermal button shirt. Her feet were bare and she'd tried to tame her hair by pulling the wild locks back into a ponytail. She plopped down on the couch. "Look, Aedan, I appreciate this ..."

"Good. Here. Have some dinner. You're Irish, you can appreciate a good meat and potato meal." Aedan handed her a plate, essentially cutting off any further protest from her.

Aislinn shook her head. The meal smelled delicious, she had to admit, and her stomach rumbled in anticipation.

"Eat. We can argue later," Aedan said nonchalantly as he poured her a glass of wine then sat beside her on the couch.

Aislinn acquiesced and took a bite. "*Ahh.* This is really good, Aedan. I haven't had a meal like this in quite a while."

"The protein will help you get stronger." Aedan took a bite of roast then drank his wine. "I shopped while you slept and stocked your refrigerator. You donnae cook much do you?"

"No. Not really." She took a drink of wine.

"Take it slow, Aislinn," Aedan said in all seriousness.

His comment caused her to pause, not wanting to risk asking to what he referred. Instead, she didn't say anything more while she finished her dinner, which to her delight tasted absolutely delicious.

"My grandmother used to make dinners like this when we would visit her. I remember walking into her house and the whole place would smell so amazing. She would have fresh soda bread just out of the oven, and she would always offer me tea, even when my mother thought I was too young." Aislinn smiled at the memory.

"'Tis a good memory to have."

Aislinn sighed, becoming serious. She turned to face Aedan. "While I appreciate everything you've done, Aedan, I'm fairly certain I can handle things from here on. I think I'll be alright taking care of myself."

"I donnae doubt that you are capable. I am aware of your need for independence. I respect that, I even admire it. But please, donnae confuse someone wanting to help you with sacrificing your independence. You've been injured and all I want to do is help while you heal. I enjoy being with you."

Aislinn reached for the bottle of wine, but Aedan's hand stayed hers. "Not with the pain medicine."

She pulled her hand back.

"I need more in the way of food than you, that's why I bought groceries."

"Aedan you can't stay here."

"Why not?"

"Aedan, this is my home."

"I promised I would look out for you for a few days."

"Promised who?" She countered.

"The doctors, your principal."

Oh God, there he went being all chivalrous. "Aedan, I don't really know you. We've only just met." What did she really know about him, she asked herself. Not much other than he had no family, was from Scotland, but possessed an Irish name, worked at the art institute and had been very kind toward her and her students. Aside from that, she knew nothing else about him. "Don't you find this a bit awkward?"

"Do you?" he responded.

"Well, yes actually." The truth was she felt very disconcerted by his comfort around her.

"I like being with you," he said again.

"You said that."

"I mean it."

His honesty surprised her and rendered her speechless. Still, she admitted, if only to herself, she found his straightforwardness refreshing. He spoke what he thought.

"Have I given ye any reason to distrust me?"

His question jolted her from her thoughts. Aislinn looked away. On the contrary, he'd given her every reason to trust him. He'd been nothing short of kind and helpful. "No," she admitted. "You've been the perfect gentleman."

"So, ask me what ye want to ken."

His offer surprised her. How did he know what she was thinking? She swiftly recovered.

"How long have you worked at the museum?"

"About ten years."

"Where did you go to school?"

"University? Edinburgh."

"Are you an only child or do you have brothers and sisters?"

"There is just me."

Aislinn huffed. "Aedan why do you just give me short answers? You offer nothing else in the way of information about who you are, how you think or feel about things." Her frustration was evident.

"Ye ken more about me than ye think."

"Aedan, you are so cryptic at times."

"Ye are right thinking there is more I could tell you."

Ah-ha. She knew it. "Then why don't you?" Aislinn rose from the couch taking his plate and hers and going into the kitchen.

"Now is not the right time," he called behind her.

She paused. *Right time?*

"You need to rest." Aedan came into the kitchen alongside her. "I'll see to the dishes."

After the big meal and wine, Aislinn did feel drowsy and not up to a sparring match with Aedan. She would let her questions drop for now.

"This conversation is not over."

"I suspected as much," he teased.

"I want you to know, that against my better judgement, I'm agreeing to let you stay here because I'm too worn out to fight with you." *And because weird as it might be, I do trust you.* "I owe you my thanks for helping me."

"You owe me nothing."

"Still, thank you," Aislinn conceded, leaving the room wondering if she'd just made the biggest mistake her life.

He'd had a hundred opportunities already to harm her had he wanted, she reminded herself. If anything, he seemed rather protective of her. Were there really guys out there like this, with noble qualities and true words?

Even though she convinced herself everything would be fine concerning Aedan she locked her bedroom door when she turned in for the night.

Chapter Sixteen

AEDAN DIDN'T TURN OUT to be the axe murderer Aislinn's fears anticipated. Actually, the next few days passed rather quietly while Aislinn rested. Despite her protests Aedan insisted on doing everything for her. Every time she tried to pitch in and help with something, Aedan would remind her there were only a couple of days left of her pampered life and she should enjoy it.

They fell into a comfortable routine of eating dinner by firelight, talking and then retiring to their respective beds. Aislinn noticed how Aedan loved to have a fire in the evenings. He seemed to prefer the serene, gentle glow of the fire rather than the lamps to illuminate the room. The simplicity never bothered Aedan. So many times Aislinn found herself thinking he should be living in some medieval castle full of candles and big fireplaces.

She smiled to herself. Aislinn was growing used to Aedan's presence, even as he still did things to her insides she tried to ignore. She found she actually enjoyed having someone around to talk to. They had a lot in common, especially their love of Celtic art, which she discovered quite by accident the night before in a discussion about the Viking influence on Irish design.

This night, however, Aedan seemed less inclined to engage in a scholarly discussion. While Aislinn finished cleaning up the dinner dishes, Aedan sat, subdued by the fire, sipping a small glass of whiskey, staring into the flames.

"Are you okay, Aedan? You seem a million miles away tonight." Aislinn sat down beside him in front of the fire.

"Something like that." He turned to her. "Aye, I'm fine," he said, smiling a reassuring smile as he finished the remainder of his drink and set aside the glass. He turned back to the fire.

Aislinn thought his smile held just a hint of sadness, and oddly, she found herself curious. Why would a man so self-assured, so together, be so melancholy?

He seemed different tonight, not only because this evening he wore his hair unbound, giving him a more untamed appearance, but because of his pensiveness as well.

Aislinn watched the way the firelight danced over the strong planes of his face, and as she did a funny tingling crept up her spine.

Aedan. One who is fire.

The flames lapped at him with moments of light and deep shadows, intermittently flickering over his body. One moment he looked wild and fierce and in the next, gentle and kind.

Aislinn was mesmerized by the fire's ability to show him in such contradiction and as she studied the way the light played over him, she was reminded of something she just couldn't put her finger on.

"Ask me, Aislinn," he suddenly spoke, looking at her, his dark eyes piercing and deep with a knowledge of something just out of her reach. She wished more than anything she understood what kept skipping away from her. "Ask me to kiss you."

She found herself unable to look away, inexplicably drawn by the unnamed mystery he seemed a part of.

"Who are you?" she whispered, giving voice to her thoughts.

And in answer he turned fully toward her and lowered his face to hers.

"Ask me and I'll show you."

His finger tips lightly stroked her cheek and then slid into her hair gripping the back of her head.

Aislinn swallowed hard, having difficulty ignoring his request. She instinctively tipped her head ever so slightly and murmured "Kiss me."

The moment Aedan's lips touched hers, Aislinn found herself transported to a timeless place where the difference between dreams and reality became indistinguishable. His kiss was so tender and at the same time passionate and erotic, making her believe dreams were possible.

"Remember me," came his whispered plea before he kissed her again. And just like when Aedan kissed her in her classroom, she found herself completely melting against him, moving into his embrace with a natural ease as if it were as familiar to her as the air she breathed.

He tasted like whiskey and male and the feel of his lips dancing across hers was so tantalizing it conjured a longing she only knew in her deepest fantasies. She wanted to remember, she wanted to know those images flirting just on the edge of her memory.

Fire. Aedan was fire. She could almost feel the flames snap and crackle around her as he kissed her so deeply she could swear she could feel him inside the deepest part of her. She marveled at how his kiss made her feel things she'd only imagined. It's a shame dreams weren't real.

That thought was suddenly sobering because dreams weren't actually real. They were either wishes or nightmares. And as much as she longed to hold on to the mystical feeling Aedan elicited, she recalled the previous time her dreams consumed her and the heartache that ensued.

Aislinn abruptly pulled away from Aedan. "I'm sorry."

"Aislinn?"

Aislinn stood, trying to calm her ragged breathing and still her racing heart. She held her head from the dizziness of standing too fast. Aedan reached for her, but she stepped away.

"You don't understand. I can't do this," she stammered.

"Do what?"

"This. Us."

Aedan rose and stepped toward her. "Aislinn?" He reached for her, but she again moved away. "What is it?"

"Nothing." She didn't want to rehash that old wound. "I'm sorry. I think I'll turn in for the night."

Aislinn offered no further explanation.

Aislinn awoke several hours later and after using the restroom, noticed a light coming from the living room. She tiptoed down the hall to see if she needed to close the glass doors of the fireplace or if perhaps Aedan had left a light on.

The glow from the dying flames illuminated Aedan who was still sitting on the floor against her couch.

His eyes were closed, head back, looking blissfully asleep. She didn't dare move another inch, or else he would spring awake. The man had the most uncanny knack for hearing every tiny sound.

She knew she should turn around and walk back down the hall. But she didn't. And despite retreating from him earlier, she couldn't deny the opportunity to look at him, *really* look at him, while he slept.

There was a wildness about him she hadn't noticed before tonight, something a bit feral. His hair wasn't straight as she first thought. His tresses cascaded over his shoulders with slight waves, which for some reason, reminded Aislinn of water tumbling unbridled over a waterfall. In the thick strands of hair were several braids with small beads woven in that were only visible now that his hair was loose.

His eyelashes and brows were the same dark color of his hair, adding to the dangerous quality of his look. His cheekbones were firm, and his face took on a rugged appearance from the shadow of his beard.

He boasted a thick neck and shoulders and his arms were large and strong. She remembered how firm they were when she had gripped them in the throes of the kiss.

She couldn't help thinking that if she ran her fingers over his taut stomach, and torso, it would be equally as hard.

It wasn't hard to imagine him as some ancient prince wielding a heavy sword with little effort.

She swallowed hard, allowing her eyes to drift lower. God, he was huge and hard and that very male part of him strained proudly against his jeans.

Why did she torment herself? Lord, how could she not? He took her breath away. And his kiss...timeless...consuming...and oh so familiar.

She trembled. She tried not to feel these things about him, and yet, here she stood, thinking how very much he looked like the man she had dreamed about.

"I can feel your gaze touching me, Aislinn." His deep husky voice startled her out of her musings. He opened his eyes and captured her gaze through the dimness. "Go to bed, Aislinn, before I take you to bed. I grow weary of being a saint."

That was all the incentive she needed to scamper back to her room.

Chapter Seventeen

THE NEXT TWO WEEKS passed quickly. Aedan drove Aislinn to school and home again, while her car was in the shop. He loved being with her, but more importantly he could keep watch over her. He felt unsettled of late. Something loomed before them and until he knew more about what he was up against, he felt better having her with him as much as possible.

Aislinn's head healed nicely and once the stitches were out, only a small scar remained. Her students loved hearing the story of what happened. They were fascinated with the whole rescue, especially the part of being stranded at school. The kids saw Aedan as some superhero who saved their teacher. Aedan would just smile, letting them think what they would. Little did they know he would let nothing happen to the woman he'd waited an eternity for.

Several days after returning to work, Aislinn presented him with an outline for the project they were to work on. She laid out art themes for each grade level, kindergarten through twelfth grade, cross-referenced by grade, topic, artwork or medium. All that needed to be done was to format it and expand it into a web-based data base. He was sure this is what she'd been working on in the evenings when purposely avoiding him after he'd kissed her. She'd felt something in that kiss, he knew. But she didn't speak of it.

The work she'd accomplished in such a short time surprised Aedan, and he figured she'd thrown herself into the project as a means to hasten his departure. Unbeknownst to her, he wouldn't be leaving any time soon and also unknown to her, the kiss in front of the fire was just the beginning of what was between them.

He could sense the stirrings within her and her denial as well. He knew she didn't understand her sudden and very intense connection to him. She wasn't ready to let go of her perception of the world and entertain the idea of who he was.

He'd felt her pleasure and desire at her visual exploration of him several nights before. Her gaze was so thoroughly erotic, his body ached in a matter of moments. She was surprised when he, aroused and frustrated, had let her know in no uncertain terms what he intended to do if she continued to torment him with her heated look. She was shocked to think he could sense her looking at him and had kept her distance since.

Today began as the previous days had. He picked her up and spent the day at school with her. While she taught, he worked on making adjustments to the project outline she'd given him.

When they were finally on their way home, Aislinn was subdued, preferring to stare out the window rather than engage in conversation.

"When are you going to admit you enjoy our kisses," Aedan suddenly said, attempting to draw her out of her musings.

"Excuse me?" she asked, her brows raised.

"Kissing me. Ye liked it. Both times."

"What are you talking about?"

"I ken ye enjoyed kissing me."

"And you know this because?" she questioned.

"I ken what you're feeling," he suddenly confessed, waiting for her reaction.

Aislinn turned to look at him. "Really?"

"Uh-huh."

"Get real. No one can do that."

"I can."

Aislinn shook her head, eyeing him skeptically.

Aedan just smiled, hoping soon that she connected the little hints he revealed.

Fifteen minutes later, Aedan noticed a relieved look cross her face as he maneuvered the car into her driveway. He watched her glance at her house with furrowed brows while gathering up her things.

"Funny. Why is my door open? I don't remember leaving it open." She shrugged, reaching for the door handle.

Aedan's skin bristled. He reached across and halted her exit. "Stay here, Aislinn," he said in all seriousness. The commanding tone of his voice instantly stopped her. She looked at him apprehensively. "I mean it," he instructed looking at her house. "Donnae leave the car."

Aedan carefully opened the car door, slipped out, and cautiously approached the house. He moved along the front, ducking under the picture window, glancing back to see her nervously watching him.

With the stealth and skill of his battle training Aedan entered the house, moving from room-to-room amidst the destruction that greeted him. He was completely silent while searching every closet, behind every door, and in every conceivable place someone could hide.

Confident whoever had been there was no longer in the house, Aedan started to leave but abruptly stopped when he heard a noise coming from the living room. He moved silently toward the sound, preparing to surprise whoever remained in the house.

He rounded the corner with a fierce roar at the same time a startled scream greeted him. Instinctively, he froze, realizing the noise was Aislinn. The look of sheer terror on her face stalled him in his tracks. She sucked in several large calming breaths, patting her chest.

"You were taking too long."

"I thought I told ye to wait in the car." His voice sounded more agitated than he intended. By the look on her face, she was about to tell him what he could do with his demands, but then he saw her eyes widen in shock at the condition of her house.

"Oh my God." She stood in the middle of her living room, utter disbelief crossing her features.

All around her lay her possessions, broken, scattered, torn to shreds. There was damage to every item, including the furniture. Nothing had been left untouched. Whoever did this was thorough with their destruction... *Or their search for something,* Aedan thought.

Aislinn remained oddly silent, moving from room to room, inspecting the obliterated contents. Aedan watched her pick up the remnants of a picture then set down the broken frame. She stepped over dishes and foodstuffs, moving through the kitchen and dining room.

"I have to call the police," She said with a shaky voice. "I'll get my cell out of the car."

The police spent several hours at Aislinn's house. They dusted for fingerprints, took pictures and made their report which would be available in twenty-four hours for insurance purposes.

The police speculated that whoever broke into her home probably had her confused with someone else since nothing appeared stolen. It looked as if the motive was destruction rather than burglary. The crime scene was clean, and there wasn't any evidence they could collect. Still, the officers were polite in offering some hope for finding the culprit.

Through the entire ordeal, Aislinn remained quiet. "I can't stay here," she finally commented, closing the door behind the police. "Every piece of furniture is ruined." As she looked around the room, she spied something. She moved to a corner of the living room, tossing the rubble out of the way and reached for her grandmother's blanket from under a pile of broken glass and pieces of wood.

She clutched the cloth to her. "Oh God, "she whispered.

Aedan could feel her unraveling. He'd seen this in battle many times. Men who were valiant in the throes of the fighting, only to fall apart when they saw the devastating aftermath.

He took her elbow and led her to her room. "Get some clothes," he instructed. He searched through her belongings until he found a small travel bag, tossing it toward her. "Here. Put what you can salvage in there." Aislinn began sifting through the garments.

He watched her pick a few clothes and place them in the bag, adding a few undergarments and shoes. He also collected some papers and documents he'd found near her small fire safe, and added them to the bag.

"Come on. We can buy anything else you need. Let's get out of here." He tugged her from the room. Aislinn didn't put up a fight.

As he led her through the house toward the door, she wrenched away from him long enough to grab her grandmother's blanket before following him out to his car.

Aislinn anxiously paced the length of the hotel room bedroom after placing her few belongings on the bed and while Aedan let in room service he'd called ahead and ordered on their way over.

Bedroom? Aislinn thought. *This hotel room had a separate bedroom? This was no cheap suite.* Aislinn glanced around at the furnishings, noting the quality of everything. The quirky thought that she'd just become Julia Roberts in Pretty Woman crossed her mind as she wrung her hands nervously.

She watched Aedan hand a tip to the young man who delivered the room service and close the door after he'd left.

"Are you a drug dealer or something?" she asked, strolling through the hotel suite. Aedan handed her a glass of wine he'd poured that had been delivered with their meal.

"Do I look like a drug dealer?" he asked pouring himself a glass.

"Maybe. Just look at this place. It's as big as my house. This suite actually has a separate bedroom and dining area. This must cost a fortune."

Aedan shook his head. "I'm not a drug dealer, Aislinn. I work for the Institute."

"Then how can you afford this?"

"I can afford it," he confirmed, not explaining that he had considerable wealth he'd accumulated over the years he'd been alive.

Aislinn continued to pace, drinking her wine.

"Aislinn, I know you're upset..." Aedan couldn't finish his statement.

"Upset? Of course, I'm upset.. I have absolutely nothing left to my name except some underwear, a few shirts, and a hotel toothbrush. Her voice, took on a shaky quality. She paused near the table while she finished her glass of wine and poured herself another.

"I worked so hard at putting my life back together this past year, and all for what?" Aislinn took several gulps of wine. "Everyone thought I was crazy for leaving Grant. It didn't matter that he only used me, all they could see was Grant's status and the material things that brought."

Aislinn took another large gulp of her wine. "Just when things started to get back to normal ..." She looked over at Aedan. "You know, nothing has been normal since *you* arrived." Her gaze was accusatory.

She finished her wine and poured yet another glass. This time she grabbed the wine bottle off the table. "I think I'd like to be alone." Aislinn left Aedan standing in the living room, retreating to the bedroom and slamming the door after her.

She paced inside the bedroom. The break-in didn't make sense, unless of course it was Grant following through on the threats he'd made that he would ruin her life. *Hadn't he already done that? But why now after all this time?*

Aislinn felt numb, not from the wine so much, but from the devastation and violation of seeing everything she'd worked so hard to obtain, totally destroyed. Her life was out of her control again, and in so many ways. She couldn't help but include Aedan in the list of things that didn't make sense.

He made her so mixed up, turning the comfortable routine she'd strove so hard to achieve completely upside-down. He filled her with desires and yearnings she didn't want to pursue and, not to mention, how he insightfully spoke of her feelings as if privy to them. Things couldn't be any crazier.

She snickered, realizing how irrational her thoughts were. Plain and simple, she was not ready to give her heart again, no matter how much he thought he knew her, and now with losing everything, she really didn't know whether or not she had the strength to start over again.

Aislinn couldn't control the tears filling her eyes, couldn't control the helpless sobs shaking her. She slumped to the floor.

Aislinn didn't know how long she'd been sitting in a heap on the floor until familiar strong arms encircled her and pulled her up. The empty wine bottle that had been on her lap, tumbled to the carpet.

Aedan sat her down on the bed, sitting next to her, wiping her tears. "You are upset with me. It's okay if it makes you feel better."

His tenderness touched her, "I'm sorry. I'm just upset with everything," she explained, struggling to keep focused through the quantity of wine she'd drunk.

Aedan touched her face, brushing a stray lock of hair away from her eyes so she might see him. "You will get through this. You are strong. It's okay to be upset. Anyone would be."

She shook her head.

"You will." He encouraged.

Aislinn lifted her eyes to his. She touched his face, lightly running her fingers over his rugged cheekbone and jaw. The light shadow of his beard bristled under her fingers.

The wine inspired more courage than she normally held, and looking at him she searched his eyes for clues, for answers for the mess her life presently was.

Aislinn longed to feel comfort instead of the chaos. She wanted a few moments of respite from the uncertainties and the heartache. And in searching for this, she leaned into Aedan and tenderly placed a kiss on his lips.

They were warm and inviting and parted ever so slightly when she kissed him. His acceptance of her action surprised her, and she pulled back to look at him. He returned her look with a gaze that held unmistakable hunger in their depths.

She kissed him again, with a boldness she hadn't known she possessed. He cupped her face, entwining his fingers in her hair. His thumb caressed her lips seconds before his mouth descended on hers, claiming her with a full deep kiss that left her breathless and yearning for more.

His lips slid over her face and neck, kissing each place they touched. She held no doubt he wanted her; she could feel the passion emanating from him.

"Stay with me," she pleaded, taking a turn to rain kisses over his face. He kissed her again, before reluctantly pulling his mouth away.

"Aislinn," his voice was thick with regret. She felt him draw a steadying breath.

"Stay."

"I'm nae going to make love to ye tonight, Aislinn," he huskily whispered against her ear.

Aislinn stiffened and sat back, the impact of his words stinging her. "Oh, God." She quickly looked away, as embarrassment filled her.

Aedan turned her face to look at him.

"Ye are beautiful, and lord knows how tempted I am, but you've had too much to drink and you're hurting. Taking advantage of this wouldnae be right."

He picked now to add honorable to his list of qualities? Her inner voice mocked.

"I'm sorry," she stammered.

"Ye have nothing to apologize for. You're a desirable woman." Aedan once again wiped a stray tear that fell from her eye. "Why donnae you rinse your face and join me in the living room. We can talk there if you'd like." He placed a light kiss on her forehead and helped her up.

A FEW MINUTES LATER, Aislinn joined him. Aedan patted the spot next to him on the couch and when she sat, he pulled her against him. Long moments of silence filled the room as Aislinn listened to the steady rhythm of Aedan's heartbeat.

"Aislinn, I can feel the turmoil inside you as if it were another being in the room with us. Ease your worry. Tell me what happened with Grant."

Ease your worry? What a strange thing to say, yet it sounded perfectly natural coming from Aedan. "Aedan, you know ..." Aislinn paused looking for the words, "Sometimes I get the feeling ..." She paused again trying to describe the familiarity she sensed around him. "Oh, never mind."

More long, unsettled moments passed before Aislinn spoke again. "I never told anyone except my grandmother what happened between Grant and me."

"And you carry the hurt with you, still. I can feel the sadness circling your heart."

Aislinn looked at Aedan curiously but decided not to pursue his statement.

"Tell me." He tightened his arm around her reassuringly. "Aislinn I too ken what 'tis like to give yourself to someone and the despair of having it all taken away."

This new awareness about him touched her.

"I know what the emptiness feels like," he added.

"It's difficult to talk about."

"It does help to talk about it," he encouraged.

"It's a long story and it's complicated."

"I'm nae going anywhere."

Aislinn drew a deep breath, steeling herself for the memories and heartache she knew would come with her explanation. "I didn't have it taken away. I let it all go," she began. "Grant was handsome and smooth. I was in my last year of university and quite captivated by his charming manner." Aislinn shifted against Aedan.

"His ambition drew him into politics, even before college, something his family groomed him for from an early age. My uncle was a politician in Washington and through various connections knew Grant's father. It wasn't long before we were introduced. Everything Grant did or said was all part of a calculated plan, but I never knew this. I was pretty enamored with him and the exciting lifestyle he offered." Aislinn sighed. "At first we were happy. Grant tolerated my quirky artistic ways. He often would make excuses for my appearance after I would arrive home from school covered in paint, having spent the whole day in a studio art class. Eventually, he stopped making excuses and asked that I change before arriving home if he had guests. When we would go out to a function, he always chose the outfit he wanted me to wear for the occasion. He wanted me to always look my best, and made no bones about what he wanted my image to be, especially at parties or dinners we attended. After I graduated I began looking for a teaching job, and began planning our wedding. At the same time Grant began working for a senator my uncle introduced him to, and instead of continuing to look for a job, Grant suggested I postpone work in order to travel with him and attend his functions. When I think about it, I hate how blindly I did what he requested, but you know ... hindsight."

"He manipulated you," Aedan acknowledged.

"Yeah. Looking back on it, he controlled everything."

Aedan let out a contempt-filled snort.

"There wasn't a definitive moment when I began questioning my future with Grant. I had what I thought were butterflies and dismissed them as nerves due to the impending wedding. When I tried to talk about my reservations with my mother, she firmly pointed out how perfect my life was and not to embarrass her in front of my father's brother after he so graciously introduced me to Grant. She reminded me how my father didn't provide for her and how she struggled as a result and that I should be happy with Grant. So, I accepted my apprehension as normal and told myself I loved Grant. The closer the wedding got, the more restless I became. I didn't dare voice this to anyone. I put on a good front, but inside I was so confused."

"Aislinn 'tis understandable how torn ye must have been. Your heart was telling ye one thing, but the people around you were telling you another."

"I should have seen it, Aedan."

"Donnae blame yourself." Aedan tenderly touched her cheek. "Never blame yourself."

Aislinn sighed. "As the time passed, I found the nagging little voice in my head becoming quite persistent. I could no longer ignore the sense that something wasn't quite right. Every time I thought of my future with Grant, my stomach did strange flip-flops. Not the 'I'm-so-excited' type, but the kind filled with dread and foreboding.

More and more, a deep-seated loneliness settled inside me. Something was missing."

Aislinn looked up at Aedan who nodded, encouraging her to continue.

"Even the intimate times were not very intimate, or very exciting. Let's just say Grant wasn't very romantic or adventurous. Making love felt more obligatory than romantic. Most times Grant left our bed right after sex or fell asleep immediately after. I found myself making excuses that perhaps he was tired due to his hectic schedule. I kept trying to convince myself this is what love was like."

"Och, that mon couldnae even make love to ye proper!" Aedan huffed, slipping into his thick native accent.

Aedan's sudden remark astonished Aislinn. On any other male his comment would seem amusing, but coming from Aedan, it seemed perfectly natural. She had the uncanny feeling he really believed every man had an obligation to please his woman and do it the right way. He had such an old-fashioned sense of chivalry. She couldn't help but smile.

"I'm sorry Aislinn, please continue."

"When we were stuck at school in the snowstorm, I told you about a dream I've had since a teenager. Well, there is actually much more to the dream than just the battle I spoke of. This isn't the time to go into it, but suffice to say the dream has very sexy parts full of passion- breathtaking, heart-stopping passion, the kind of passion that makes- your- breath- catch- in- your- throat- when- you- look- at- someone. As our wedding date approached, I began having the dream again, over and over, night after night. And each time I woke from the dream I realized I didn't feel that kind of passion when I thought of Grant. Actually, just the opposite.

"When I looked around, I realized how empty my life had become. I had no job, no friends, my creative outlet was gone, and I didn't feel love for Grant. I had nothing. And despite everything I still doubted my feelings. Why would everyone continue to say how perfect my life was? Why couldn't I make myself believe I did have it all?"

"Ye didnae ken."

"No, I didn't know. Looking back, I think the dream was a warning of sorts, maybe my intuition trying to tell me something wasn't right. My grandmother said the voice of my heart and the universe were telling me I was on the wrong path. I had to learn that the hard way."

Aedan gently rubbed her arms.

"My life completely turned upside down in the span of one night. Needing a bit of fresh air and escape from yet another boring dinner party, I snuck out the side door of our house and strolled toward the backyard. I was enjoying the peaceful solitude and the quiet night and by pure chance, I happened upon a conversation between Grant and his father coming from the rear of the house. At first, I thought to join them, and I never intended on eavesdropping, but I stopped and found myself listening anyway ..."

United States, 14 Months Ago

"How's the job going with Morrison?" Grant's father inquired.

"He is anxious to get me to Washington after this damned wedding."

"And what about ... what is her name? Christine? Does Aislinn suspect anything?"

"Her?" Grant laughed. "She is so trusting, and I am ever the diligent husband-to-be. The woman doesn't suspect a thing."

"Be careful," Grant's father reminded him. "We don't want a scandal right now."

Grant chuckled. "She has no clue this is merely a marriage of convenience. She's so naïve. She thinks we are the happy little couple. I'm just waiting for her uncle in Washington."

"Keep her busy. She's good for your image. Your career needs her right now." There was a pause in the conversation in which the tinkling

of ice against a glass either Grant or his father drank from was the only sound breaking the silence.

"A word of advice, son. Get her pregnant right after the wedding. A child will keep her occupied with something else besides you. In a few years, when you are established in Washington, you can divorce her."

"Sometimes it's hard to continue with this charade. I have to tell her everything, what to wear, how to act, what to say. She can be so helpless."

"That is why you have Christine. Aislinn won't notice, she'll be too busy raising your children."

UNITED STATES, PRESENT Day

Aedan tightened his arms around her. "I didn't have to see Grant to recognize the disdain in his voice and his indifference to the prospect of a marriage with me. I was shocked by his blunt declaration and stunned to find his father was also in on the deception. I was equally as shocked to learn he was sleeping with this other woman as well." Aislinn clutched her heart reliving the pain of that night.

"In that one instant my entire world came crashing down. Everything I thought, everything I was told, was a lie. I remember the bile climbing its way up my throat and the urgent need to escape, but I remained frozen to the spot, stunned and unable to make myself move for the longest time. Finally, a moment of clarity broke through and I fled. I bolted from the yard and the house with nothing but my keys, purse, and the stupid dress Grant insisted I wear that night."

Aislinn swiped at tears sliding down her cheeks. Aedan continued to hold her.

"I remember the long numbing ride north to my grandmother's house. I remember how angry I was when I realized what a fool I'd been and that Grant only wanted to get to my uncle through me. I actually believed him when he said he cared for me. Yeah, right. Thinking back, I'm sure he never said he loved me. How many times did I make a fool of myself saying I loved him? God, how he must have laughed at that.

"I was completely crushed that I was nothing more than a pawn in his game, a well-played pawn. And when I told him I was done, he threatened me, said I'd never get a job, that he'd see to it I was ruined. He publicly blamed me, his parents blamed me, hell, even my own mother blamed me for ruining my life and hers. The things the newspapers accused me of were awful. All fabricated by Grant, of course." she scoffed. "I never told anyone what I overheard. I just took all the humiliation and fault and I ran. The only person who knew what had really happened was my grandmother."

Aislinn wiped her nose and sniffed again. "I couldn't even form the words to explain to her why I'd suddenly showed up at her door, hysterical and completely disheveled. Gram just led me into the house, turned off the phone, made tea and sat with me until I could talk.

"Boy when you go against what the universe wants, it sure lets you know in a big way. I wasn't supposed to be with Grant, I know that now. Strangely enough, I eventually felt relieved. At least I didn't have to pretend any longer that I was happy.

"My grandmother never judged me but instead loved and supported me. I spent the remainder of the summer up north at her cottage, healing while I looked for a job and a place to live away from Grant. Now I have a great job doing what I love, students I adore, colleagues I admire and overall, my life is finally settling down."

"You didnae mention Grant to the police," Aedan noted.

"No. And I won't unless I can prove his involvement. Right now, I can't."

No words were spoken for a long while, until Aedan finally spoke. "I donnae want you to compare me to this man," he said poignantly. "Don't close yourself off to possibilities. Have ye ever considered that your dream was not a warning, but maybe a promise?"

Aislinn thought for a moment. "Ha. That some medieval warrior is going to come and sweep me off my feet?" she answered skeptically. "Not likely. I can't do possibilities. I just don't have it in me right now." A yawn escaped Aislinn before she could speak further. The effects of the wine and the stress of her lengthy confession were finally taking their toll.

Aedan lightly kissed her forehead. "Why donnae ye close your eyes and try and get some rest?"

Aislinn snuggled against him and closed her eyes.

"Aislinn?"

"*Hmm?*"

"I'm honored and humbled you trusted me enough to tell me."

"Thank you for listening," she yawned again fighting a losing battle with sleep. "Will you tell me about the person you lost?"

"One day, Aislinn. Soon."

Chapter Eighteen

AEDAN SAT AT THE TABLE, bare feet propped up on the chair beside him. Having just showered and slipped on a denim shirt over his jeans, he decided to have a cup of coffee before Aislinn woke.

Concern etched his brow while sipping the hot brew. He placed his hand on his chest where the stone from her keyring hung beside his. He thought about the condition of Aislinn's house yesterday. It was a good thing she hadn't mentioned Grant to the police. He wasn't convinced Grant was involved. Why would someone so concerned with image and reputation as Grant was, want to create more of a scandal just when the previous one had died down? It didn't make sense. The precise way every single item in her home had been ransacked clearly indicated a search, and a very thorough one at that. No, the destruction of her belongings wasn't due to a vindictive ex as Aislinn suspected, but instead by someone searching for something as *he* suspected.

Aedan took another long sip of coffee, further strengthening his resolve not to let Aislinn out of his sight. If someone was looking for the stones, there was no telling what they might do to find them.

His thoughts strayed to Aislinn. He'd lain awake half the night thinking about her. How tempted he'd been to take her after she offered herself to him. He'd almost given in, but she wanted him for all the wrong reasons. It took all of his self-control to deny what he so desperately longed for, so he settled for holding her as she worked through her demons concerning Grant.

He had to admire her strength in recounting such a difficult time in her life. He now understood her distraught state at the loss of her possessions. They were a symbol of her independence and the decision to follow her heart.

He was sure the fact that Aislinn was once again having her dream was making her cautious around him. No wonder she rejected any romantic inclination toward him. It would explain her reasoning to tell him about Grant.

He smiled. Little did she know he could feel the stirrings inside her regarding him. He felt her curiosity and her desire even as she denied any attraction toward him.

He would not distress her further with the truth. Soon, though, if she didn't remember him on her own, he would have to reveal who he was.

Aislinn came up behind him, jarring Aedan from his thoughts. She flashed him a smile.

"Good morning."

"Good morning. There is coffee and rolls if you'd like something to eat." Aedan rose and pulled out a chair for her.

"Coffee would be great."

Aedan poured her a mug of coffee.

"I've got a sub for today and tomorrow," she explained, sipping the hot drink.

Aedan nodded.

"Could you take me home? The insurance adjuster is going to meet me there at nine, and then I've got a cleaning company coming."

"You've been busy this morning," Aedan commented, sitting down next to her.

"I just want everything back to normal as fast as possible. I may have to go out and look for furniture, depending on what the adjuster says. I will rent a car and pick up a few basic things today with the money in my savings."

Aedan wanted to offer his financial assistance, but knew better. Aislinn harbored a deep need to prove she could take care of herself. If he offered her money, she would resent him. No, he would let her do this on her own.

"I will take you wherever you need to go today." Aedan held up his hand as she began to protest. "I insist and I don't mind."

Aislinn let it drop.

Aislinn sipped her coffee, and a moment passed before she spoke again, changing the subject.

"Aedan, thank you for listening last night and for not ... you know ..." She looked at him with hooded eyes.

He smiled knowingly. "Aye. I ken."

Her gaze moved away from his, and as it did, Aedan touched her arm to bring her attention back to him. "Never be embarrassed with me about anything. Never."

She nodded. "I was just upset ..."

"Ye have every right to be upset by what happened. 'Tis only natural to want comfort."

"Well, I appreciate your discretion."

A little while later, as Aedan and Aislinn pulled into the driveway of Aislinn's house, a car awaited them. Aedan dropped Aislinn off to meet with the insurance agent while he made a quick trip to the grocery store for a few items.

A tall man dressed in a suit stepped out of his car and greeted Aislinn. She unlocked the front door, inviting him in.

"Whew! Someone sure did a number here," the agent said, following Aislinn inside the house. "By the way, I'm Don. You must be Ms. O'Neil." He offered his hand in greeting. Aislinn shook it.

"Hi."

"Pleased to meet you Aislinn," he began. "I'm wondering, did you call the police? I mean do you have a police report?" Don took out a leather binder and fished through his pockets for a pen.

Aislinn rummaged through her bag and pulled out the police report she and Aedan had picked up on their way over. She handed it to him.

"What did the police say?" Don asked, jotting down information in his notebook.

Aislinn kicked some things out of the way with her foot. "They think whoever did this probably mistook my house for someone else's. Nothing was stolen, but they destroyed everything."

"Did you have anything of value in your house?"

"Nothing except the usual. A television, some electronics. My laptop and digital camera were with me at work. I don't have anything else. That's why the police thought this break-in was a mistake."

"Family heirlooms, perhaps?" The man looked at her with raised eyebrows.

"No. Nothing like that."

Don took off his jacket, hanging it on the front door knob. Aislinn saw him sifting through items on the living room floor as he did.

Don spent the next forty-five minutes moving from room to room, inspecting the damage and writing things down in his notebook. Aislinn could hear him moving objects and swiping things out of his way in each room.

"Well, I can see everything is a total loss. I'll just need some information and I'm sure we can help you, Aislinn." Don startled her. He'd moved right up behind her without making a sound. At the same time, Aislinn heard Aedan pulling into the attached garage.

Don stepped back while she cleared a spot at the unbroken end of the dining table for him to lay out his papers. She set a chair upright and placed the seat in the frame, balanced enough to sit on if he didn't wiggle. She offered the makeshift seat to Don. She rigged another for herself.

He flipped over a page in his binder and began asking a series of questions, requesting basic information such as place of employment, phone number, birthday, etc. Aislinn thought the questions he asked in addition to the uncomfortable way he looked at her a bit odd. They should have all that information on file, she thought, but in the next moment thought they needed to verify facts to make sure she was who she said she was.

Partway through the questioning, Aedan came in carrying bags of groceries. Aislinn noticed his gaze intently fixed on Don as he put the groceries away. After he'd finished with the food, Aedan stepped over to Aislinn and stood behind her, legs apart, arms crossed over his broad chest. He made an imposing figure, one Don didn't ignore.

Aislinn watched the unspoken exchange between Aedan and Don with curious scrutiny. Aedan was intentionally intimidating the man, and his tactic worked because Don became fidgety and began quickly wrapping up the interview.

Don rose from the table, glancing briefly at Aedan before offering his hand to Aislinn. "Well Ms. O'Neil. We will be in touch in the next few days, after we process the claim forms."

Aislinn rose with him and shook his hand. "Thank you for coming so quickly." She walked with him to the front door and let him out. After she closed the door she turned to Aedan.

"I donnae like him," he stated.

"Why?"

"I didnae like the way he was looking at you."

"You're being silly." Aislinn shook her head. *God, men could be so primitive.* "What did you get at the store?" Aislinn strolled over to the fridge and peeked inside to see what Aedan bought.

"Why don't ye make a list of what ye need and we can start shopping," he suggested.

Aislinn rummaged through a broken drawer searching for a pen and paper. She found them in a pile of debris.

"Start with the kitchen," Aedan suggested.

Aislinn had just begun writing when a knock at the front door interrupted her.

"Good morning, Ms. O'Neil. I'm Laura Williams from Hendrickson Insurance," came the pleasant greeting as Aislinn opened the door. The woman handed Aislinn her card. "I'm sorry I'm late. Traffic was a bit of a problem. I did try to call your cell, but I only got your voicemail." Aislinn opened the door and let in Ms. Williams.

"Ms. Williams, another agent just left. A Don..." Aislinn realized she didn't know his last name.

"I don't recall someone named Don, but then our office is growing so much these days. I have your policy right here, and by the looks of your house, you're going to need some money right away for clean-up, utility repair, and item replacement. I'm prepared to write you a preliminary check today. Let's take a look, shall we?"

As Aislinn led the second insurance agent toward the dining area they were nearly mowed down by Aedan hurriedly brushing past them, rushing out the front door. Aislinn wondered what had gotten into him, but shrugged apologetically to the woman.

"I can see you will need a total replacement of everything," Ms. Williams said, having paused to survey the destruction before following Aislinn into the dining room. She set her brief case on the table.

"Be careful how you sit." Aislinn warned her about the chair.

"Do you have a police report?"

"Yes." Aislinn showed her the same report she'd shown Don.

Ms. Williams nodded and handed the paper back to Aislinn. "We'll pay for a hotel until you can reoccupy your home."

"She has a place to stay," Aedan said, coming in the front door, stomping the snow from his boots having overheard their conversation. He once again took a stance behind Aislinn. She shot him an angry glance.

"Well, okay then," Ms. Williams agreed. "How about we go over items you'll want to replace."

For the next two hours, Aislinn and the insurance agent made a detailed list of all the items needing replacement, while Aedan made arrangements for the electrical company and cable company to come repair the wiring.

While they were working, the cleaning company also arrived, and Aedan gave them strict instructions to salvage anything they could when they were clearing out Aislinn's house.

Ms. Williams left Aislinn with enough money to start replacing the larger items and promised that in a couple of days the remaining amount would be transferred to Aislinn's bank account.

As Aislinn walked Ms. Williams to the door, she couldn't help notice Aedan following close behind.

Aislinn said goodbye, closed the door and turned, bumping right into Aedan.

"What was that all about?"

"What?"

"You know perfectly well. The 'he-man, Neanderthal' act."

"I'm nae acting."

"Well then, you're scaring me with the whole testosterone thing." She sidestepped Aedan.

"Aislinn, the man who was here earlier was nae an insurance agent," Aedan explained.

"Don't be ridiculous. There was just a mix-up at the office after my phone call this morning. Two agents must have been assigned my case by accident."

Aedan paused. "Then why didn't he leave you with any financial compensation? Why did he become so nervous when I arrived?"

"Because you acted so aggressively," Aislinn said.

"Maybe, but you're staying with me."

"No. I'm not."

"Aye. Ye are."

"I'm perfectly capable of getting my own hotel room."

"I'm through discussing this." Aedan threw up his hands.

"And I'm through with you telling me what to do," Aislinn snapped back.

"Is that what this is about? Me telling ye what to do?"

"You might be used to barking orders back at the museum, but not here."

Aedan ran his fingers through his hair, obviously frustrated. "I'm trying to help you. I donnae think ye should be alone."

"I told you before. I don't need to be taken care of."

Aedan sucked in a breath. "Will you *please* stay in my hotel room?"

"Thank you for asking, but no!"

"*Arrgh*..." Aedan shifted his weight to his other leg digging in for a battle of wills.

Aedan took another deep breath and grew very grim. "Aislinn, I didnae want to mention this, but I'm worried about the man who was here. I donnae trust him. I cannae explain it, only that I have a funny feeling about him. I care about you. I want ye safe. I'm not trying to question your ability to take care of yourself. God knows, you're a might stubborn about that, but I'm bigger and stronger than you and if something were to happen, I could protect you."

Aislinn saw Aedan's humorless expression and began having doubts about her judgement when she recalled suddenly finding Don had soundlessly crept up behind her or never offered his last name. "Do you think he wants to hurt me? Do you think he had something to do with what happened to my house?"

"I donnae ken. I'm nae trying to frighten you, but something is nae quite right about him. You gave him a lot of your personal information."

Aislinn could see something wasn't sitting well with Aedan. He paced nervously and seemed keenly on guard.

"That man looked like he crawled out of bed and threw on a rumpled suit and not like a professional who meets with clients in public every day. His hands looked too rough for someone with a desk job. I donnae ken how he fits into all of this. I just want to be cautious, that's all. I wouldnae ask ye to do something you didnae want to do if I didnae think it important. So, humor me. Please just stay in my suite."

The determined look on Aedan's face concerned Aislinn. He was worried about something, alright. She thought Don's demeanor a little odd, but Aedan had noticed far more than she, and what he'd picked up on made her generally uneasy. Aislinn paused.

"If you really think it's necessary, I will stay at your hotel."

Aedan let out a long breath as his muscles visibly relaxed. "Thank you," he said. "Now, I ken ye need to shop, so I will be your escort and chauffeur."

"You won't find traipsing through stores dreadful like most men?"

"I didnae say that, but your companionship is worth the sacrifice."

"Aedan you don't really have to do this."

"Are we going to start this again? I'm going with you."

"Are you sure?"

"I'm sure."

"Then you really *aren't* like most men."

Aedan just smiled.

When Aislinn and Aedan returned to her house later in the day, they were surprised to find all the debris had been removed and everything was vacuumed and cleaned. One box of items remained for her to go through, mostly personal items, documents, photographs, and some knickknacks.

"It looks so empty, like the day I moved in, except..."

"Except what?" he asked.

"Except it's not a beginning."

"It could be."

Aislinn looked at Aedan recognizing the implication of his statement. "I wish you'd stop doing that."

"Doing what?"

"Never mind. Can we just leave and go back to the hotel? I'm tired and just want a hot bath."

Within minutes of returning to the hotel, Aislinn found herself soaking neck deep in the most luxurious bubble bath she'd ever had. Yep, Julia Roberts or not, she found indulging in the luxurious warm scented water most inviting.

She let out a big yawn, thinking back over the day. She marveled at how attentive Aedan had been throughout the day, and admitted she actually enjoyed his company. He even became a bit playful while they shopped, which she suspected he did for her sake, but she also noticed the tension behind his smile, and the worry lines at the corner of his eyes or across his brow. Something bothered him, something he kept inside, something he did not want her to know. She wondered if the institute was giving him a hard time for being away so long. Whatever it was, Aedan kept it to himself.

She found it perplexing that she'd become so attuned to this man that she could discern such nuances in his demeanor. *Just when did that happen?*

Aislin stretched and slid a bit deeper into the relaxing water, closing her eyes.

He was there, in the quiet place just before sleep, the place where fantasies   danced   through   her   mind. Aedan...quiet...confident...strong and powerful. Her protector. Her warrior. In her half sleep state, she found herself drawn to him, his eyes so dark and full of secrets she longed to know.

She recalled their kiss in front of the fire, the heat, the passion, the way the flames engulfed her, the way Aedan engulfed her. He'd said, 'You know me' and she thought for a brief second he might be right. Everything about him felt familiar. His presence was there, in some deep place inside her ...

Aedan's rapping on the door jolted her awake. "Dinner is ready."

Startled from her sleep, Aislinn sat up much too quickly, splashing water over the side of the tub. She must have dozed off.

"Thanks," she called out, coming fully awake, hurling a towel over the puddle on the floor. She climbed out, dried off and dressed, joining him a short while later.

"I'm sorry I took so long. I was so relaxed, I nearly fell asleep." Aislinn sat with him at the dining table.

"I had a feeling. You seemed pretty tired." Aedan removed the covers from their meals and poured them each a glass of wine.

"I think I'm more emotionally drained than anything"

"You've had a stressful few weeks with the accident and now your house."

"I'll bet you can't wait to get back to Chicago. You never expected any of this."

"I'm not going back yet." He paused to take a bite of food.

"Aedan, you came all this way to complete this project and it seems as though everything is conspiring against us finishing it. We've hardly worked on it."

"We've gotten a good start with the work you've done. We'll finish it," he said confidently.

Aislinn took another bite of her dinner, silently studying him. He was attractive, she couldn't deny that. He was so completely sexual, so completely male, and against her better judgement, she found herself wondering what making love with him would be like.

She caught her thoughts. The last time she dared look at him, really look at him, he said he could feel her touching him. Goose bumps rose on her arms. How he could sense her and know what she'd been thinking was beyond her. She saw him intentionally gazing at her. She hurriedly looked away.

After finishing dinner, they settled in the living area. Aislinn curled up on the couch, sipping her wine. Aedan sat next to her.

"I miss having a fire in the evenings," Aedan confessed. "That is something I've always liked. There is something so elemental about fire, something simple, ancient, even magical." Aedan looked over at Aislinn.

Aislinn liked that he had actually revealed something about himself, even if the information was accompanied by that mysterious look.

"I know what you mean. I love to have a fire as well. When I was looking for a house, I specifically looked for one with a fireplace."

Aedan smiled.

"Aedan?"

"*Hmm?*"

"I want to apologize for being angry with you earlier. I know you had my best interest in mind when you suggested I stay here."

"Aye." Aedan drank his wine. "I'm glad ye are here." He smiled warmly at her.

Aislin gazed at him, relaxed and confident. How could she have ever compared Aedan to Grant? They weren't even remotely alike, she'd discovered. Aedan possessed an earthy ruggedness, a regal stature, commanding and authoritative. Although, a man of few words, what he did speak was honest.

Aedan could be just as demanding as Grant, but in an opposite way. Aedan was used to giving commands and expecting his orders to be obeyed without question because his motives were selfless. Grant on the other hand, flaunted a smooth polished air, lending to phoniness. Grant's authoritativeness was purely selfish in nature. The only person Grant cared about was Grant. Grant always made excuses and explained himself, Aedan on the other hand never needed to explain anything. He was open and honest in both words and actions and she found she admired this.

Aislinn shuddered and told herself to be careful. She found herself entertaining ideas she told herself she wouldn't think about.

"Aedan, do you think that man will come back to my house again?" She changed the direction of her thoughts.

"I donnae ken."

"I can't imagine what he might want or what I've done to provoke this, unless it has something to do with Grant."

"Ye've done nothing," Aedan answered, swiftly jumping to her defense.

"Maybe we are making more out of this than necessary."

"Perhaps."

"Well, I for one will not let him keep me from moving back into my home in a few days."

"Ye willnae be unprotected."

"What does that mean?"

"It means exactly that." Aedan's tone brooked no argument.

The way he'd taken on the role of her protector was at once heartwarming and at the same time disconcerting. He could be quite stubborn. "Aedan..."

He immediately held up his hand to halt the protest about to escape her lips. "Nae tonight, Aislinn. I grow weary of this argument."

"But ... "

"No," he spoke firmly abruptly reaching over and pulling her into his arms.

In a surprising move, he placed his lips on hers, quelling any further complaint. His unexpected action stunned Aislinn and she didn't have time to pull away before realizing what was happening. Her traitorous lips never muttered another word, only a soft, astonished whimper escaped before she felt the slightest curve of a smile cross his lips.

Chapter Nineteen

IRELAND, PRESENT DAY

Brennis stood in the dingy shadows of what used to be a church while Collin paced nervously, raising from the old stone floor a cloud of dust which danced in the sunlight filtering in through the colored windows.

"Well?" Brennis asked, impatiently. "What news do ye have?"

"He has found and spoken to both Aedan and Aislinn. Well, mostly Aislinn."

"And?"

"He said he couldn't get near enough to Aislinn because and I quote 'Aedan hovers around her like a hawk circling its prey.'"

"Me brother is cautious," Brennis confirmed. "Ye can thank yer blunder in the snow for that."

"I don't think he knows everything, but he senses something. As for Aislinn, our man confirms the amulet is not in her house anywhere. They did a complete search for it. So, it must be either on her or with Aedan. But what I found most interesting, and I think you will too, Brennis, is that Aislinn, after being questioned, seemed to have no knowledge of an heirloom or important family artifact."

"Why I wonder? Has my brother nae told her of the stone? Now, this is curious, especially with Beltane fast approaching." Brennis stepped away from the dark corner where he stood and strolled over to one of the dirty windows. He rubbed away the grime from one section of colored glass. "Why would me brother nae want her to ken what the stone is?"

"What if she doesn't know who she is? What if he hasn't told her or she doesn't remember?" Collin offered as explanation. "Twelve hundred years is a long time, and modern people don't readily believe in magic or people from the past just showing up in modern times. What if he's waiting hoping she remembers something? Or what if she doesn't have the stone?"

"She must have it - how else did he find her, you fool. If the two halves didnae meet, I wouldnae be awake." Brennis turned from the window. "Aislinn is a direct descendent of the Lady of Erin. Donnae underestimate the Lady's ability to have seen this far into the future. There could be things in motion we ken nothing about. Aedan was her favorite. The Lady would do all in her power to help him."

Collin scuffed his foot across the floor leaving a dirt trail behind. "Our man said he almost had a hold of her, but Aedan showed up and perched himself right beside her, watching his every move. Getting to her will be difficult if he's around."

"I can do nothing until Aedan comes to this isle. I cannae fight him if he isnae here. I think 'tis time we give my brother a reason to come. He will bring her and the stones. If he thinks her life is in danger ..." Brennis' voice trailed off.

"We can find a reason to hasten his arrival," Collin said.

"Aye. We must. The longer he waits, the less time I have. If he thinks someone is after his woman, he will come to where he knows he can hide her. He will come and bring the stones." Brennis turned to Collin. "Keep him moving toward Erin," Brennis demanded. "I must have the amulet. My remaining time is measured by his. If we fail, you gain nothing and I cease to exist."

"I will contact our man and give him instructions. Give me a few days."

Brennis glared at Collin through the dim light. "The end draws closer. I did not wade through this endless void of time for a mere taste of the future. I want to take that future from my brother as he took my past from me. I cannae do that when I cannae reach him."

"I will also send a couple more men. Together, I'm sure they can devise a way to encourage your brother to expedite his arrival to Ireland."

"Good. There is much to prepare." Brennis said, walking past Collin and exiting the small room.

Chapter Twenty

Aedan found himself humming an upbeat tune while maneuvering his SUV along the highway toward Aislinn's school. He couldn't keep the silly grin from his face thinking back on the way he'd surprised Aislinn by kissing her a little over a week ago and how things had changed since then. He knew he'd completely caught her off guard by his abrupt move because of her stunned expression the instant before his mouth crushed down on hers. Oh, but how quickly his playful diversion turned into a heat-laden kiss, surprising even him.

He'd met his match in stubbornness and tenacity and he found her so exciting and so exhilarating he couldn't help himself. And once he started kissing her, he couldn't keep the act chaste for more than a few seconds before the need to deepen the kiss into a passion-filled exploration of her lips and mouth.

He'd kissed her so near senseless, she actually whimpered when he pulled away. When she'd realized what had happened, she excused herself for the night, which was probably a good thing, considering how aroused he'd become.

She never mentioned the kiss the next day or the rest of the week as she put her home back together, but Aedan knew she thought about it. He could feel her curiosity as she cast guarded glances his way when she thought he wasn't looking. She purposely avoided every argument he tried to goad her into, and even remained quite amenable when he insisted on accompanying her to her house after school to wait for furniture deliveries. She was determined he would not catch her off guard again.

In the midst of this unnamed game between them, a sense of closeness began to blossom. He'd always been honest with her when he said he could feel her, and he knew Aislinn really didn't comprehend exactly what that entailed, but she at least entertained the idea that he was able to read her well.

Still, their relationship was one of close friends rather than lovers, which was exactly why he'd kissed her. He wanted to once again try and jolt her memory which seemed so stubbornly locked away. He wanted to confirm that he thought of her as more than just a friend. He wanted her to remember what they had meant to each other.

Time was running out, spring was fast approaching, and Aislinn didn't remember any more than she had when Aedan first met her. Little snippets of memories here and there caused her to pause and look at him strangely, but nothing more. If Aislinn was caught briefly by some memory, she easily dismissed it.

He really couldn't blame her for being skeptical. It was the way of her world. People of this time knew nothing of magic and mystical things. As much as he wanted to scream, *"Aye, it's real. I am real!"* he didn't because he wanted her to figure it out.

Now, as time ticked away, and every day that passed brought Beltane closer, the very real possibility that he would have to tell Aislinn everything loomed before him. But hope remained for now.

Just yesterday, he'd walked into Aislinn's classroom and found her and her friend Beth huddled together, whispering and giggling quite obviously about him, by the way they hushed immediately upon his arrival. He was flattered that Aislinn was talking about him with her friend.

He stood up a little straighter, lifted his chest a bit higher and perhaps smiled a touch wider. He turned on the charm a bit more because he was so damned delighted Aislinn had taken an interest in him. She watched him for several minutes, believing he wasn't aware she studied him. He could feel her curiosity and och, Christ, he felt as prideful as a puffed-up peacock strutting around a barnyard. In that moment she looked at him as if he were a possibility instead of a pain in her arse and he was delighted and this was the reason for his jovial mood this morning.

As he pulled into the staff parking lot, he noticed Aislinn just arriving as well. He parked alongside her. She was just gathering up her things and hadn't left her car yet.

"Good morning," Aedan said, coming around his SUV and opening her car door for her, the smile still curving his lips.

"My aren't we in a good mood today," Aislinn teased, stepping out of her vehicle.

"Spring is in the air," Aedan stated.

"Ah, Aedan, in case you haven't noticed, there is still snow on the ground."

"It's in the air Aislinn. Take a deep breath. 'Tis not far away."

Aislinn just shook her head and turned in the direction of the school.

As they began walking toward the building, their casual banter kept them both preoccupied and neither paid much attention to the other car pulling into the parking lot. There was nothing out of the ordinary about another car as other staff often arrived early for work and neither Aedan or Aislinn gave the vehicle a second thought.

A sudden alarm cursed through Aedan's veins a split second before the sound of the gun. The hair on his arms stood on end, his body bristled with warning. He glanced over his shoulder and saw the other car hadn't parked but circled instead. He turned toward Aislinn the instant the loud crack split the frigid early morning air.

Aedan lunged toward her and shoved her to the snowy ground, knocking the wind out of her in the process. He covered her, looking in the direction of the shooter who was speeding away.

"Are ye alright?" Aedan jerked Aislinn to a sitting position. She held her arm, coughing, clearly dazed. "Aislinn are ye all right?" He yelled louder, swiftly assessing her. He saw the blood on her hand where she held her arm and hurriedly removed her coat, tearing at her blouse sleeve to see the wound. He sighed in relief. The bullet only grazed her, but left a fairly good gash in her arm.

"Somebody shot at me," she muttered, dumbfounded.

"Listen to me." Aedan grabbed her shoulders and jerked roughly to snap her out of her daze. "Get inside the building," he demanded. "Donnae do anything until I come back, understand?" Aislinn nodded.

"Where are you going?"

Aedan ran back to his SUV and sped off after the retreating car.

Aedan clenched the steering wheel, white knuckled, fighting his rising anger. Rage didn't do a warrior any good, yet he was so blinded with fury by the attempt on Aislinn's life, he couldn't help his anger.

"That man is a dead man," he spoke aloud, pursuing the automobile through the early morning light. He followed the car down deserted, snow-covered back roads, driving dangerously too fast. Several times he got close, but each time the driver of the other car sped out of reach. The icy country roads proved so dangerous, Aedan found maneuvering his SUV difficult and over and over again had to slow to take a turn or pull out of a slide.

As the chase continued, the other driver was becoming more erratic in his desperation to escape Aedan's pursuit. Despite the road conditions, Aedan didn't let up. Minutes passed until finally, the shooter's car lost control and careened off the snowy road.

The car flew several hundred feet before slamming into a tree. A frustrated roar escaped Aedan's throat. He slammed on the brakes of his car, skidding to a stop. Aedan grabbed his sword from under the seat and leapt from his vehicle, approaching the driver, still tangled in the twisted metal.

"Who are you?" He bellowed, jabbing the point of his blade into the man's Adams apple and drawing blood. "Why were you trying to kill Aislinn?"

The driver managed a weak, sinister smile. "Not kill."

"Then what?"

Aedan recognized him instantly as the man who'd posed as the insurance agent at Aislinn's house. Aedan grabbed what he could of the man's shirt and shook him. This obviously caused the man a great deal of pain as he groaned uncontrollably.

"Tell me," Aedan bellowed, yanking the man from the car, allowing no concern for the man's injuries. "You can die easy or I can make your death a most unbearable experience. 'Tis up to you. Now tell me. Why were you shooting at Aislinn?"

The man coughed and closed his eyes. When he opened them, his ominous stare met Aedan's a second before they were filled with a blank emptiness. He no longer lived. Aedan heaved him to the ground in disgust, searching the man's clothes for any clue to his identity.

Aedan next searched what was left of the car, finding the gun and bullets and throwing them off into the woods. There were no clues as to why he would be shooting at Aislinn.

Aislinn paced, nervously wringing her hands. Back and forth, up and down she strode across her classroom, not knowing what to do. Aedan had been gone a long time. Too long.

What if something had happened to him. He told her to do nothing until he came back, but what if he didn't come back. Shouldn't she call the police or something? People were beginning to arrive for work and she wasn't sure what she should do.

Water. I need water. She went to the sink where she filled her mug with water. Her hands were shaking so badly, she could barely hold the mug. After one sip, she set the mug down and instead splashed cool water on her face. *Aedan, where are you?*

Aislinn purposely kept the light off in her room and went into her back storage area, not wanting to face anyone who might pass by and see her in the room. As time ticked by, Aislinn became more and more distraught with the endless waiting. The precise moment she'd hit her limit with waiting, and decided to go to the office, she heard the door to her room open.

"Aedan?"

Aedan came into the storage area, searching her out. Aislinn flung herself against him as he wrapped his huge arms around her. She pounded his chest. "I was so scared. I thought something happened to you."

"Your arm?" He pulled her out of his embrace to inspect the injury. "We need to bandage this."

"It's fine."

"You were lucky."

Aislinn noticed the grave edge to Aedan's voice. It frightened her.

"Aedan, what is going on? Just what are you mixed up in? You said it wasn't drugs. We need to go to the police."

"Aislinn, listen to me. It's not drugs. I'm not mixed up in anything. I can explain what is going on, but not here, not now. No Police!" His demand was firm.

"You're scaring me. Why are people shooting at me?"

He looked at her and let out a long breath. "Because you are my woman."

"What!" she screeched, a second before his hand clamped down over her mouth.

"*Shh.* Keep your voice low."

Aislinn jerked away from him. "Can we cut the he-man bull shit, Aedan?" Aislinn attempted to lower her voice, despite being near hysterics.

"'Tis true."

She started to protest, but he shook his head with a look so stern, so sobering, she instantly halted her verbal assault.

"'Tis too much to discuss here. I have things I must do right away, and then I will tell you everything. Will you trust me?"

Could she? Aislinn looked up into his dark eyes that just this morning were alive with amusement, but now held an ominous foreboding. "But we need to call the po..."

"Nae, Aislinn!" He again demanded.

"But the children, the school. They have to know someone is out there with a gun."

"They are in no danger. The shooter is gone," Aedan confirmed.

"I'm supposed to report this."

"Nae, Aislinn. You cannae report this." He stroked her arm soothingly. "Please, just trust me a bit longer. I promise I will explain everything."

Again, Aislinn found herself assessing him and thinking of all the strange things that had happened since meeting him in Chicago.

"Are you in some sort of trouble?"

"No. But you've got to trust me," he again demanded. "Say you will trust me, please." He again looked agitated at her indecision. "Aislinn this is serious. Please?"

There was something in the somber nature of his request that tugged at Aislinn. He asked her to trust him, but in that request there was so much more. She saw his face, fierce with resolve to protect her and his determination warmed and frightened her.

In this split second of uncertainty, Aislinn took inventory of all the questions, all the unknowns, all the possibilities and desires. She needed to decide whether to trust her instincts or follow logic.

There was a very clear line between the two. So much weighed on her decision, not just from Aedan, but from her. She recalled the last time she ignored her instincts.

Aislinn took a steadying breath. "Yes, I trust you," she finally said.

Aedan let out a long breath, quickly gathering her up into his arms and hugging her. He held her so tightly against him, she could feel his warmth wrap around her as if it were a tangible thing.

"It will be alright. I promise," he whispered against the top of her head, cradling her against him.

Long moments passed before Aislinn stepped out of his arms, and looked up at him.

"You will have a room full of children, soon. They will be safe I promise. Nothing will happen to them. You need to be strong and get through this day. You have to trust me as I asked you to do. Try and push aside what happened this morning and just get into your daily routine. Can you do this until the school day is over?"

"Don't do this, Aedan. Don't keep me waiting. I can't stand not knowing what is happening." Aislinn pleaded, again wringing her hands, nervously.

"It's complicated and will take more time than we have right now to explain."

"Aedan, no, please. I'm so worried."

"Donnae worry. I will always protect you." He took her hands and looked into her eyes. "You *can* do it. You *are* my woman, and you are strong," he reassured her. "Let's get your arm bandaged and you can change your shirt for one you keep here in the closet. Then go and prepare for your students' lessons as you always do." Aedan gave her hand a squeeze. "I'll be right back with the first aid kit."

Aislinn numbly did as Aedan requested, and after he bandaged her arm, he left again. Aislinn busied herself setting out papers for her first class when Aedan returned with a cup of coffee for her.

"Take a deep breath and stay calm. Try to think of something pleasant," he encouraged as he handed her the cup. "Mayhap think of me and my kisses," he teased.

Aislinn smiled bravely, blinking back tears. She appreciated his attempt at distracting her, however arrogant it was. As she sipped her coffee, she grasped that something monumental was happening, something beyond her control, something that was sweeping her up and carrying her down a raging river without the means to change directions or to stop. She felt the outside forces once again manipulating her life, and as before, she felt small and insignificant against it. She remembered her grandmother telling her when the universe wanted something, nothing could stop it. This was one of those times, she knew.

AEDAN WAS PROUD OF Aislinn's show of normalcy. He knew she was anything but calm. He could feel her turmoil tightly gripping him. Several times he moved near enough to touch her or place a reassuring hand on her shoulder. This in turn helped to calm her and refocus on her students.

Her second graders particularly liked Aedan slipping his arm around her waist at one point, as he sensed panic rising in her. The students were so astute, they long ago figured out he cared for their teacher. They loved to *"ooh"* and *"ahh"* and giggle when he touched her. Aedan would wink at them, as if letting them in on his little secret. He earned their affection this way.

Mid-morning, Aedan felt Aislinn had pulled herself together enough for him to slip from the room for a few minutes. The time had arrived to set into motion things he had planned from the day he'd arrived.

He had taken very seriously the Lady's warning of facing obstacles in his quest to find Aislinn and prepared for what he would do. After this morning, he left nothing to chance except perhaps hoping Aislinn would have remembered him. But now it was even too late for that. He hoped her trust extended beyond his protecting her from immediate danger, because what he would ask of her tonight would tear the very fabric of her reality and the essence of who she was.

Aedan wasn't gone long, but noted her sense of relief when he returned a while later. Despite all that had occurred, Aislinn managed to get through the morning.

When lunchtime rolled around, she collapsed in a chair, so drained from the stress and worry and the effort of keeping up a calm appearance, she was exhausted. She waved away anything Aedan offered in the way of food or drink, and instead just closed her eyes and rubbed her forehead.

Aislinn's principal broke the few minutes of quiet with his entrance as he strolled into her room all smiles from ear to ear. "Congratulations, Ms. O'Neil. What an accomplishment."

Aedan noticed Aislinn's confusion.

"Your leave has been approved, unanimously, I might add, by everyone at the district office."

Aislinn shot a questioning look at Aedan.

"Yes, Ms. O'Neil has submitted quite a proposal to the institute. They are anxious for her to begin work," Aedan spoke up, corroborating the story.

"Certainly. We've already arranged a long-term sub to begin tomorrow, so you may gather the necessary paperwork and have ample time to prepare and pack before next week."

Aedan saw the look of shock on Aislinn's face in response to her principal's statement.

"What you'll be doing for our district is monumental. I'm looking forward to the results."

Aislinn looked between Aedan and her principal. "Ah, yes...thank you," she managed, still not fully understanding what was happening.

Aedan reached out to shake the principal's hand, "I really appreciate your expedient attention to this matter. I'm sorry the institute didn't give us a bit more notice," Aedan apologized.

"Quite alright, Mr. MacKendrick." He turned to Aislinn. "Have a great and productive rest of the year. We'll see you in the fall." He shook Aislinn's hand before turning and leaving the room.

Aislinn turned to Aedan, bewilderment on her face, "What just happened?"

"You're going on paid leave to work in Chicago with me."

"I am? When did this happen?"

"Today."

"Aedan, I'm not leaving. I'm not going to Chicago."

"Aislinn, this is part of the trust I'm asking you for."

"How did my principal ever agree to this? That would take an epic magical feat to make that happen," she half-joked. When Aedan didn't respond, but only just looked at her, she threw him a quizzical look. "I don't want to know." She held up her hand to dismiss any further explanation. "This is too much. My head is splitting. I'm going to get some Tylenol." She rose and went toward her bag in the back room.

GETTING THROUGH THE rest of the day was difficult, but to her credit, Aislinn made it. By the time the last class left, Aislinn was moving and talking rather mechanically as if on autopilot, so Aedan helped her collect all the papers and resource materials and anything else she'd thought she'd need. She laid out her curriculum lesson book for her sub and wrote a quick letter explaining where materials were.

The plan was that she would follow him to her house where she would pack a suitcase and then follow him to the hotel. They would then leave from there.

Aislinn remained silent as she packed her belongings and wrote a letter to the mail carrier. She hadn't noticed Aedan had added more clothes to her bag, as well as pulled a few documents from the box the cleaning crew left for her to go through and added them to the suitcase as well.

Once they were at the hotel, and their cars emptied and belongings carried to the room Aedan was able to relax. He ordered them something to eat and drink. Aislinn seemed to have calmed and was eating a little.

Part way through their meal, Aedan rose. "I want to show you something." Aedan went into the living area and retrieved a pad of hotel paper. He brought the tablet back to the table, holding it out for Aislinn. She put down her glass and took the pad, looking at a pencil drawing Aedan had sketched out.

"Have you ever seen this symbol before?" Aedan asked her as he sat again.

"No. Is it Celtic? Looks like it might be."

"Yes, it's Celtic. You don't recognize it?"

"Should I?" Aislinn asked setting down the page. "Aedan why did you go after the guy who shot at me? Did you know him?"

"I didnae ken him. I recognized him as the man who impersonated the insurance agent."

"What? The guy who was in my house? Why would he be shooting at me?" Aislinn dropped her fork and sat back. "Just what are you messed up with, Aedan?"

Aedan sighed, running his fingers through his hair. His heart sank, dreading the conversation he knew was coming. He had hoped to avoid this, hoped she would have recognized and accepted him before this. He wanted more than anything to spare her the pain and uncertainty of what he was about to tell her.

"Aislinn, we have to talk about something." He could feel his intense manner unnerve her. "I have to tell you some things you are going to find difficult to believe, but I want you to keep an open mind." He took her hands in his.

Aislinn nodded slowly, eyes wide with apprehension.

"Remember at school during the snowstorm you told me about a dream you've had for many years about a battle, the same dream that showed you what passion was?"

Aislinn nodded skeptically.

Aedan drew a deep breath. "That battle was an actual event. I was in that battle. You were in that battle. He raised the sleeve of his sweater to reveal a scar on his forearm. "I was struck by an arrow trying to take you to a safe place to hide. Do you remember that part of the dream?"

Aislinn reached out to touch the scar. "How do you know about this? I didn't tell you about that."

"The two people who were being united in the ceremony were you and I. Our union was meant to form an alliance between two tribes to stand against the Norse who were raiding our coasts."

Aedan paused a moment to allow her time to process what he had said. "But there were people who wanted to keep the union from happening; people who would stop at nothing to destroy any plans or attempts at alliances. They wanted to discredit me, to weaken my position."

Aislinn averted her eyes staring out as if seeing the memory in her mind as he spoke. Aedan touched her arm, bringing her attention back. "I believe the people who broke into your home, and caused you to run off the road, and who shot at you are all connected to this somehow."

"What?" she said in disbelief. "This is crazy. That dream takes place a very long time ago."

"Trust your heart, Aislinn."

"The police said the break-in was a mistake; that my house wasn't the real target because they didn't steal anything." Aislinn shook her head, trying to make sense of everything.

Aedan rose and retrieved his coat. He fished something out of the pocket and returned to the table. "They didn't steal anything because they couldn't find what they wanted. They were looking for this." Aedan laid the stone from her key ring on the table.

"My stone. You had this? I thought I lost it."

"I removed it from your key chain."

"Why would you do that? You knew I was looking for it. Why didn't you tell me you had it? My grandmother gave that to me many years ago." Aislin's voice was tinged with anger.

"Aislinn it's not a stone. It's an amulet, and it's very old and very valuable."

"An amulet?"

"One half of a pair needed for a ritual."

"Aedan, do you know how ridiculous this sounds? An amulet? Really?"

"Did your grandmother ever talk about legends? Did she ever tell you old stories?"

Aislinn shook her head then paused as a thought came to her. "Maybe. When I was a little girl, when Gran and I would walk together. She told me a little poem about earth and fire."

Aedan watched Aislinn focus on the memory. "I can't seem to recall it, though. It was a long time ago. I was very young."

Aedan took her hands in his again. "I know what I say sounds incredible, I'm asking you to believe something which has no basis for truth in your world."

"You know as well as I this can't be- "

Aedan cut her off. "What I speak is true."

"So, you want me to believe you're some ancient guy I slept with in order to form a military alliance between two tribes hundreds of years ago?"

"Twelve hundred years ago."

"Oh, my God, Aedan. This is insane." Aislinn jumped up from the table, pulling her hands out of his. She put distance between them. "How can I be from twelve hundred years ago?"

"You are a reincarnate of her."

"And you? How are you alive?"

"Magic. My half of the amulet kept me alive to find you."

"This is utterly crazy." Aislinn spun around and stepped further away.

"How much of the dream do you want me to recount, Aislinn, until you know I'm telling you the truth?" Aedan's voice grew agitated. "I know you wore a thin pale green gown, pinned at the shoulders. I know you were nervous approaching me. I can tell you that as you saw me, you knew me as your mate and that we were fated to be together. Your body was painted with the same ancient symbols as the blanket that has been passed down to you, the very same blanket I wrapped you in when I pulled you away from the fighting. I know you were an innocent when you came to me. Our ceremony was on Beltane, a fertility ceremony. How would I know these things, Aislinn, unless I was there?"

"Oh, my God. Oh, my God. Oh my God ..." Aislinn kept repeating over and over again in utter disbelief, all the while pacing back and forth.

Aedan reached for her but she pushed him away. "Leave me alone."

"I hid you behind a tree until your guards found you. They took you away then and I knew in that instant, I would never see you again. I've been waiting for you for centuries. You are the other half of my soul."

"This is impossible! "

"Aislinn why do you think I unnerve you so much? There's a familiarity you feel, a connection to me you can't explain. Why did you know you were not meant to be with Grant?"

Aislinn watched him with fear in her eyes.

"I am not some crazy person making this up. You know the story. We share the story." Aedan sighed. "Can you imagine knowing your whole life you were meant for someone?" Aedan tried to hide the hurt of her denial, but knew he failed. He spoke quietly. "I have felt you inside me, your feelings, your emotions, and your soul." Aedan ran his fingers through his hair as he continued. "I've held a sense of you since I was ten years old. I have carried the promise of our union in my heart my whole life."

Adean looked deeply at Aislinn. "When our union was broken up, it nearly destroyed me. I spoke of knowing the devastation of losing someone the night you told me about Grant. I was speaking of you. I was given the chance to find you again, and it was this promise that kept me going all those years when things seemed insurmountable and hopeless. I donnae try to understand how this connection works; I accept that it does. It's a rare gift, and it's true. Aislinn, if you open your heart you will find me there. I've always been there as I always will be."

"This can't be." Aislinn paused in her pacing. "People don't live over a thousand years."

"Suspend what you know, and imagine the impossible. It can be."

"No." She shook her head frantically.

"Sometimes there are bigger things out there that defy logic, Aislinn."

Aislinn fled from the living area.

Aislinn paced back and forth, across the length of the bedroom, trying to come to grips with what Aedan had just told her. Short of thinking he was completely insane and had possibly escaped from a mental institution, she didn't know what to think. What Aedan was asking her to believe wasn't possible, was it? How could someone live over a thousand years? She rubbed her head, God, but did she have a headache.

The little nagging inner voice reminded her that he knew things about the dream she'd never told a soul. So much would make sense if everything were true. She laughed a twisted sort of laugh. She couldn't even believe she was entertaining that idea. And yet there were so many things...

A knock sounded on the door interrupting her thoughts. "Aislinn? Can I come in?"

Aislinn didn't answer.

"I'd like to show you something."

Aislinn finally opened the door and let Aedan in. In his hand he cradled Aislinn's stone. He set it down on the bedside table. He reached around the neck of his sweater and tugged out a cord which he pulled over his head. On the end of the cord hung an amulet similar to hers. He laid his stone down beside hers and slid the two pieces together. The instant they touched the hair on her arms bristled, and a fleeting memory of seeing these stones before flashed through her mind. Together, the two halves formed a crescent design, the design Aedan had drawn on the paper earlier. A design she had seen before.

"These were used at the ceremony and will be needed again."

Aislinn didn't say a word as she stared at the amulet and her certainty began to falter. Long moments of silence hung in the air while she struggled with the multitude of conflictions assaulting her.

"Aislinn, please donnae leave this suite. Donnae go out where I can't protect you, do you understand? Regardless of how you feel about what I've told you, there is a very real danger out there. Let me gather and pack my things. We'll go together. We will work this out. Promise me you'll not leave."

She nodded still rather confused and shocked that someone would want to harm them.

"Aislinn?"

"Yes." She agreed much too quickly.

Aedan left Aislinn's room, took a quick shower and packed his belongings. Once done, he threw on his pants and went to check on Aislinn. She wasn't in the bedroom where she'd been. He went into the living area and found her standing near the window, staring at a television news report about the man found dead in the same town as her school. She looked up with disbelief at him as he entered the room.

"Beth texted me to watch," she offered as a means of explanation.

"I didnae kill him if that's what you're wondering." He turned off the television and came up alongside her. "But I would have, to protect you." His stoic gaze conveyed the truth of his words.

"Are you alright?" Her silence genuinely concerned him. She did not answer but stared wide-eyed at his tattooed torso.

Aedan studied her as she hesitantly touched one of the spiral designs on his forearm, running her fingers over the intricate details of the pattern. She followed the design upward to his biceps where the knotwork band circled his upper arm. His skin tensed under her touch.

"I know these," she whispered, seemingly lost in a memory. Her hand glided over his chest where yet another design covered his heart. Her eyes and fingers lowered to the spiral outline beginning just below his navel and intertwined with the dark trail of hair leading beneath the waistband of his trousers.

She turned him slightly to see he bore yet another spiral and crescent pattern on his right shoulder blade. He clamped his hand firmly over hers, halting any further exploration.

She drew back suddenly; the realization of where she'd seen those designs crossed her face.

"Oh, God." She shook her head, looking up at his face then back down his body. Aislinn fought the panic rising inside her. "Something very strange is happening!"

Aedan caught her the instant her legs buckled beneath her.

Aislinn sat up pushing the hair from her eyes. She was surprised she'd fainted. She'd never fainted, never even came close, except once- she glanced in Aedan's direction- that time at the art museum, when Aedan was near.

She gazed through the dimness of the room to where Aedan stood leaning against the window frame, gazing out over the city at some point in the distance.

Aislinn rose and moved to stand next to Aedan. He looked down at her.

"How do you feel?"

"Honestly, I don't know. How would you feel if someone told you everything you just told me? She looked up into Aedan's troubled eyes then lowered her gaze. She reached out her hand and ran her fingers over the woven knotwork designs on Aedan's bare arms "These are connected to magic." Aislinn spoke softly, trying to come to terms with her new reality.

"I am a Druidh."

"Did you use magic on my principal to allow me to leave?"

"Aye."

"And you found me in the snowstorm with magic?"

"Aye."

"Aedan," she paused. "Are you using magic on me ... to make ... you know ... make me feel attracted to you?"

"Nae. I don't need magic for that." He seemed defensive about her accusation, but then sighed, adding, "It's forbidden to use magic for personal gain or pleasure. Ye are attracted to me because we were meant to be together."

"You didn't use it to kill that man?"

"I told you, I didnae kill that man. He slid off the road into a tree."

Aislinn nodded. Silence descended between them while she tried to absorb the truth of his words.

"So, you are really over twelve hundred years old?" Aislinn suddenly asked. Aedan turned to look at her briefly.

"Give or take, but aye."

"Do you know how incredibly unbelievable this all sounds?"

"'Tis true. You ken the dream, Aislinn. You ken our connection. Grant wasnae your first man. I was. "

Aislinn smiled a bittersweet smile at the male pride in Aedan's statement.

She wiped at a tear trickling from her eye.

"You sensed, deep down, you were nae right with Grant. You know you didnae love him, nae really. Because it was me ye loved."

Aislinn swallowed hard, dropping her eyes.

"Aislinn never doubt my love for you. Even if you doubt all else, donnae doubt that."

Aislinn nodded slightly, sighing in resignation. She looked away as he returned his gaze out the window. She didn't doubt his feelings for her.

She lifted her hands to her shirt. Her fingers trembled nervously as they pushed the buttons through the buttonholes. As each one came undone, her resolve weakened and she found herself drawn into a possibility she never considered.

"Aedan," she whispered, drawing his attention to her back. He turned as she faced away from him, slowly lowering her shirt down her arms. She reached one arm around behind her and lifted her hair away from her neck. On her left shoulder blade, hidden beneath the thick curls Aislinn revealed a birthmark in the same crescent shape as the connected amulets, and the design tattooed on Aedan's shoulder blade.

"It seems I may be connected to magic, as well."

He reached his fingers out to stroke her skin. "You have the mark of the Goddess. Aye, I believe ye have magic in you. 'Tis why you reacted so strongly to seeing me the first time in Chicago and then again tonight when seeing my Druidh marks."

"When I was younger, my grandmother told me my birthmark was a special mark given to me by the fairies. She told me all the women in our family bore some mark, but none were in the same shape as mine. She never explained why this shape was important, but she said I would know one day if I was meant to know. I never told anyone what she'd said. As I grew older, I just figured she made up a story so I didn't feel bad about having a birthmark."

Aedan ran his fingers over the mark. He stepped closer to Aislinn's back and replaced his fingers with his lips. His breath warmed her skin and gave her gooseflesh where it caressed her. Aislinn once again experienced a yearning as deep as the yearning she knew from her dream. The desire flared within her and she found herself giving over to the mystery that for years had haunted her slumber.

Aedan ran his hands along her arms, sliding her blouse off and to the floor. He kissed her neck, then her shoulders and back. He tugged her bra strap down her arms, reaching around her to unclasp the hook. Her undergarment joined her blouse at her feet.

He lifted her arms and braced them against the window, holding them with his hand. She shuddered involuntarily. She wanted this man so badly, she ached. Never had she felt such fierce longing as she did for him. She was on fire and Aedan was the source of that heat. Everywhere he touched, she burned.

He cupped his other hand over her breast and pulled her back against his hard body. "I want you," Aedan whispered huskily against her ear, nipping at her earlobe.

Aislinn shivered, feeling him straining against her and she loved the feel of him. His lips continued to blaze a fiery trail down her neck and back as he continued to press against her.

"Aedan," she breathed heavily.

He released his hold on her, allowing his fingers to skim over the silky skin of her arms, down her shoulders, along the sides of her breasts, before he splayed his fingers across her stomach and pulled her back harder against his arousal. Aislinn's knees grew weak as she watched his hands caress her. "Oh, God," she gasped. The feel of him thrusting against her backside made her breath catch in her throat.

"Aedan ..." her voice panting, "I ..." His fingers once again slid upward, pausing briefly on the bandage that circled her upper arm. She found her gaze focused on that white piece of gauze stained with blood. Her blood. From a very real attack.

He nuzzled his face into the curve of her neck, kissing her. His fingers toyed with her nipples. "Say it Aislin. Say you want me as you did that night."

"I want ... I ... Aedan, please. We have to stop."

He froze instantly at her words.

He placed his lips next to her ear, where she could feel his words on her skin. "Ye can ask that? You can deny what is happening between us? It's drawing us together. It's the magic." His body fully aroused, rested, along the length of hers. "It was like this that night, too. You know."

"That was a dream." she choked catching her breath. "But ..."

"You know 'tis nae a dream. How can ye possibly still think that?" He ran his fingers through his hair, obviously frustrated. He stepped away from her.

"I don't know what to think."

Aedan bent down, picked up her blouse and bra, and pushed them at her. She clutched them against her, suddenly self-conscious. She just stood there, frozen, shaking, aroused, confused, looking at him, as her mind tried to reconcile the unbelievable events of the day from being shot at by the man who posed as an insurance agent and then turning up dead to what Aedan had told her about himself. Everything suddenly came rushing over her, completely overwhelming her.

She hadn't intended on crying, but once the tears started, she couldn't stop them.

Aedan gathered her up in his arms and just held her the entire time she sobbed uncontrollably.

A long time passed until, finally, she cried herself out. Aedan led her to the couch. She sat on the edge of the sofa, still clutching her clothes against her.

"Aislinn, get dressed." He pulled her blouse out of her hands and helped her slip it on. She set her bra aside. Her hands trembled attempting to button her top, so much so, Aedan took over finishing the task. He then stood, pacing the length of the living room.

"Aislinn, the kind of passion you dream of does exist. It's what's between us. I know you felt it."

Aislinn remained silent, as a shudder traveled down her spine. She'd felt it all right; she hadn't *stopped* feeling it since first meeting him.

"Aedan, I feel lost again. My whole world is turning upside down. Everything I know isn't what it seems. I'm losing control again."

"Search your heart. I am real, Aislinn."

Aislinn saw the flash of pain in his eyes when she did not answer. It was several long moments before he spoke again.

"We are no longer safe here."

Aislinn didn't miss the double meaning of his words.

"We will leave in the morning."

Chapter Twenty-One

FURY ROSE OFF AEDAN. His thunderous roar reverberated through the entire hotel, upon waking and finding Aislinn had vanished sometime during the night. How in the name of all that was holy could he keep her safe if she took it upon herself to leave?

He ran his fingers through his hair. God's blood the woman could be infuriating. What was she doing?

Aedan spent half the morning in search of Aislinn's friend, only to find Beth was attending a meeting for the day and wouldn't' be available until late afternoon. He hadn't intended to frighten Beth, pounding like a crazy man on her door at dinnertime, breaking the hinges with his zealous fervor, but his patience was gone after waiting an entire day to speak with her while Aislinn was alone and unprotected.

Aedan didn't know any other way to find Aislinn. He knew exactly where she had gone; there was only one place she'd run to feel safe. The problem was Aedan didn't have a clue where her hideaway was or how to get there. But Beth did. Which is why he wasted no time hunting Beth down and scaring her half to death with his frantic request for her to give him directions to Aislinn's grandmother's cottage.

The multitude of apologies Aedan bestowed on Beth wasn't enough to compensate her for beating down her door in his haste, and he promised to make it right. Thank the Gods Beth wisely perceived the seriousness of his request and didn't waste time with too many questions before giving him the directions and agreeing to tell no one where Aislinn was.

He hadn't expected Aislinn to immediately accept everything he'd told her the previous evening, but he hadn't expected her to run away either, especially after she'd showed him the mark she bore and the way the passion flared between them.

Och, Christ, she wanted him as much as he wanted her and for a fleeting moment, she let herself believe in him, but then, just as quickly as her desire rose, he felt the doubt creep back and douse the fire.

She wasn't just fighting painful memories of Grant; she was denying the inevitability of their destiny and a reality she could not accept.

With Beltane so close, Aedan feared the consequences should she never fully accept who he was. She might be inclined to accept his explanation, but if she didn't love him, he would not go through with the ceremony. And that possibility left him with nothing but emptiness in the pit of his stomach. For without the Beltane ceremony, he would cease to exist in her world. If he left her, he knew she would be devastated, full of guilt and reasons never to trust again. He didn't want to condemn her to a life of loneliness, and yet that's exactly what would happen if she didn't realize she was the woman in her dream and he was the man she loved.

He should have anticipated she'd run after talking about feeling lost and her world crumbling down. Her life was coming apart, the same as it had with Grant. She ran away then. Of course, she would again.

Aedan exhaled a long breath. For hours he'd felt her anxiety building. He gripped the steering wheel tighter. Finding her was urgent, especially now there were those who would harm her to keep them apart. Her trepidation grew with each hour that passed, and as night descended, and he was helpless to do anything except get to her as fast as he could. Christ if he had to tie her to a chair to keep her from leaving again by God he would, for her own sake. At least she'd be where he could protect her.

Aislinn nervously peeked out the window for the hundredth time just to make sure she didn't' see anything out of the ordinary. Surely no one would find her up here. However, every little noise made her jump. She was having second thoughts about her decision to flee Aedan's hotel room last night. This seemed to be a pattern with her, fleeing when things got impossible. And impossible they were, and unlikely, and unreal, and unbelievable, and all the other 'un's' she could think of.

She paced across the small living room, stopping to warm her hands by the fire and to turn over her jeans which were hanging over a chair drying out. She hadn't planned this little escape very well, and hadn't prepared for having such rough arrangements in the tiny cottage with no heat and no electricity. All her belongings were still at the hotel except for her wallet which she'd had sense enough to grab knowing she would have to buy food on the way here. God, this was déjà vu.

Thank God the key still resided over the doorjamb where Gram always left it and that there were still a few logs cut and stacked in the back yard she'd trudged through the drifts of snow and brought in for a fire. She placed the leftover food in the snow bank by the back door and hoped the racoons wouldn't discover it. Water trickled from the faucet so the pipes were not totally frozen.

She could make do, she thought.

She chided herself for not seeing to the upkeep of the cottage after her grandmother had passed, but she hadn't the heart. There were too many memories and it was extremely difficult for her to come here.

The small house would have felt more comforting if she had a lantern, or batteries for the flashlight, now, as darkness approached.

Suffice to say, the only light besides the fireplace was the one candle she found in the kitchen.

Making a mental list of everything she could do tomorrow, such as shovel a walkway, bring in more wood, and make sure her car wasn't stuck in the snow-covered driveway, didn't really keep her thoughts from straying to Aedan.

Weird, but she felt much safer when he was present. She wished, as blackness of night approached, that he were here, regardless of who or what he claimed to be.

Aedan was definitely imposing enough to discourage anyone from harming her, but, she reminded herself, that hadn't seemed to stop the man yesterday. But he was dead, right?

She shook her head. Dead guys on the television, a man from the past, fertility ceremonies warriors, battles ...

Aislinn peered out again thinking any sleep tonight was probably out of the question. She hadn't slept at all the previous night as everything played over and over in her mind as her remaining control vanished. She was now functioning on pure adrenalin.

Aislinn picked up the poker from the fireplace and sat on the floor between the couch and the hearth, perched for any would-be attacker.

As night fully descended and Aislinn sat huddled in the darkness, she couldn't keep her thoughts from straying to Aedan. The attraction toward him pulsed so strongly within her, she could swear at times she could hear it. Was this truly because they were connected in the past somehow like he'd explained, or was her libido just working overtime?

God, but she still tingled from their intimate interlude the night before. His whole body covered her, pinning her right against the window with his hard, muscled thighs. Lord knows, she was going to let him take her then and there if it weren't for the sobering glance at her bandage and the *"I'm from the past"* confession creeping into her mind at that very moment.

He was frustrated, she knew, but damn, so was she. So once again, she ran to the one place she felt safe and protected and could think, only her grandmother was no longer here and she didn't feel safe. And now here she sat, with no answers, and no more in control of anything than before, equally as irritated at how her body betrayed her logic. She was scared. Every little noise had her jumpy and gripping the poker tighter.

Even if Aedan was a figment of her dreams, she'd give anything for that figment to be here. She didn't know what to do should someone come after her again, with a gun. She felt so vulnerable, and completely alone.

Aislinn abruptly stiffened at hearing an unfamiliar noise outside the small cottage. Her hold on the poker tightened, her heart raced, as she silently stood, counting the seconds ticking away. She tiptoed toward the small kitchen window where she thought the sound came from and peered out. The darkness prevented her from seeing anything. She heard the noise again, and raised the poker above her head, preparing to attack.

The door to the cottage burst open and Aislinn squeezed her eyes tight and brought the metal rod down with all of her might. The rod halted mid-stroke nearly jolting her arms from their sockets. The poker was yanked from her grasp. Aislinn let out a scream.

"God's blood, woman," Aedan bellowed, easily catching the iron poker in his large hand. "I'm trying to protect you and you're screaming like a banshee."

Relief crossed Aislinn's face at recognizing Aedan's voice. She patted her heart, trying to slow the frantic beating. Aedan pulled her against his chest, wrapping his arms round her. He rested his chin on the top of her head. "Och, 'tis good ye are safe, lass," he whispered into her hair.

Aislinn pulled out of his arms and stepped away. "You scared the shit out of me."

"You looked a mite, fine and brave, screaming and waving that wee stick around."

"Stop teasing me. I can protect myself."

"Och, Christ. Nae that again." He rolled his eyes as Aislinn jerked the poker from his hand, scowling at him.

"Where are your trews?" Aedan's eyes deliberately raked slowly down her long shapely legs, then just as slowly back up, lingering where the juncture of her thighs hid just under the hem of her shirt.

"Trews?"

"Your pants. Why are you running around in your underwear? Nae that I mind- makes the drive up here well worth it- but you'll catch a chill." He smiled smugly.

"Drying by the fire. I spent half the day bringing in the firewood and I got soaked. I didn't bring anything else with me." Aislinn stepped to the couch and grabbed a blanket, wrapping it around her waist.

"I've got your bags in my car," he said, shifting his gaze from her to survey the cottage.

"It's a bit primitive," Aislinn apologized, seeing him scrutinizing their surroundings, making mental notes of the layout.

"'Tis sturdy enough. Is there nae light?" Aedan asked, inspecting the lantern on the table and checking it for fuel.

"No. It's empty."

"'Twill be warm enough by the fireplace tonight." He rubbed her arm reassuringly. "In the morning I'll check the propane tank," Aedan said, at ease with all he noted. "I will get our bags from the car. I think there is enough wood for the night. Tomorrow I will gather more."

Aislinn sat in front of the fire, wrapped in her grandmother's blanket. She held the two amulets in her fingers. She kept her eyes lowered, staring at the stones, turning them over in her hands.

"Can you feel the power in the stones?"

Aislinn clenched her fist around them. "I feel a slight vibration." She sighed and set the stones aside.

"Why did you run from me, lass?" Aedan finally asked.

"I was scared. I felt overwhelmed. I didn't know what to do. I couldn't bear the thought of losing control again," she confessed. "How did you know I'd be here?"

"I knew this was a place you felt safe. This is where you came when you left Grant."

"I wasn't feeling safe before you came here."

"I ken."

"You felt it?"

"Aye, It took me a while to track down your friend Beth to find where the cottage was. I donnae think she'll be wanting to see me any time soon. I nearly scared her half to death."

Aislinn smiled. Beth wasn't daunted by much. She could imagine Aedan all blustery and intimidating. Poor Beth. Aislinn's smile unexpectedly turned to a yawn.

"You havenae slept?"

"No."

Aedan slid closer to Aislinn and pulled her against his chest. "Ye can rest now."

Aislinn could do anything but rest being this close to Aedan. Every nerve became instantly alive and attuned to his nuances. She listened to the steady, comforting beat of his heart; the familiar scent of him wrapped around her with every breath she took, his hand tenderly rubbed her shoulder. No, sleep was out of the question.

"Can you tell me about yourself?"

"What would ye like to know?"

"What was life like back then?"

"It was very different. More barbaric by today's standards, but much simpler, too. We still valued what was important, clan, family, land and we fought to protect those things." Aedan paused a moment. "I have nae spoken of my past to anyone."

Aislinn could see a bewildered look move across his face as he said this, but he continued.

"I told you I lost my mother when I was two. I was fostered with my uncle Alpin in the Del Riada territory in the western part of Scotland. We called it Alba. I donnae remember much about the actual move. Alpin's wife accepted me, but she began having her own children and spent less and less time with me. Her sons were the sons of the high chief of the Dal Riada, so naturally they were the focus of the household.

"It was nae intentional that I was ignored or overlooked in lieu of Ciniodh or Kenneth as you'd say and his brother Donal or Donald. It just happened as a normal progression as their station became different than mine. To be honest, I preferred it that way. I had a lot more freedom to come and go, and to do what I liked without people guarding my every move. In truth, I ken Ciniodh and Donal were envious of my ability to slip in and out as I wished."

"You like your freedom?"

"Verra much. I would spend a lot of time as a young lad outside the walls, roaming the hills or forests. I donnae like the confines of the buildings."

Aislinn could imagine the wild little boy, running through the heather, chasing the wind over the hills. She smiled at the image.

"I received the same battle training as my cousins. We would spend four to five hours each day learning to fight and use weapons, but there were times we were allowed to be boys, too. We performed our share of pranks and mischief.

"Ciniodh and Donal were jealous of me. I was older, larger, more graceful and more skilled, and according to the women, I would be pleasing to gaze upon when grown."

Aedan looked down at her and winked as his voice took on a humorous tone.

Aislinn couldn't help but smile at his smug self-awareness again. *And God bless him,* she thought. Those women were right. He *was* pleasing to look at.

Aedan cleared his throat, seemingly in response to her thought before he continued. "When I turned eight I was pledged to the Great Lady as one of her druidhs. I knew upon first seeing her that our lives would be forever entwined. I felt she always intended me to come with her to Erin. It was a mere formality that she bargained for me with Alpin.

"She foretold that his sons were to be great kings in Alba, and they would need me to hold the Dal Riata territory in Erin for them. I left for Erin...er, Ireland when I reached ten years of age. When I arrived on Erin I learned I had a half-brother, Brennis, and he and I began our magical training.

"I ken ye will find this hard to believe, Aislinn but when I first saw the Lady, she promised me I would ken a love like no other. At the time I dinnae ken what she meant. I thought she meant I would find a sense of belonging or family, which I did with the Irish people, but shortly after, I saw you across the keep. You dinnae see me, but almost immediately I felt the sensation of you inside me. I cannae explain how it filled me with such completeness even at that early age. The whole world seemed right and I knew my purpose in it."

"And did I know you?"

"Aye. You still do." Aedan's surety touched her.

"'Twas my brother who constantly undid what political ties I managed to negotiate. Brennis always thought he was the rightful leader of the Dal Riata in Erin. He resented me when I came across the water with the Lady to claim the chiefdom. Truth be told, I would have been very happy if he were the one who had the burden of trying to secure the land."

"Secure the land?"

"At the time, the Norse were raiding the coasts of Erin, and 'twas in the best interest of all the eastern shores to unite against them. Brennis was so singularly focused on being denied his leadership, he couldnae see the threat arising. I spent many years working with the Lady to secure friendships with the two tribes below my land. Our union, the ceremony you ken, was the culmination of many years of negotiations and sacrifices. The alliance was the first in what I hoped would be more, but my cousin's betrayal of not providing the promised fighters to beat back the raiders, added to Brennis' claim he was the rightful ruler and that I had betrayed them with empty promises. Brennis conspired with a western tribe, the Un'Neills to break up our ceremony. And as you know, he was successful."

"Un'Neill? Like in my last name, O'Neil?"

"Aye."

"My ancestors broke up the ceremony?"

"At the time, ye were nae an Un'Neill. Twelve hundred years is a long time, things change, history changes, people move around, marriages happen, names change."

Aislinn yawned. Her thoughts were spinning so fast, she didn't know what to think about first. Her emotions were all over the place.

"We'll talk more about this later. You need to try and rest."

Aislinn was grateful for Aedan's suggestion. She was feeling the weight of the day beginning to take its toll. She closed her eyes and shifted against him. A few moments of quiet with the crackling of the fire lulled her into much-needed slumber.

Chapter Twenty-Two

SCOTLAND, 9ᵗʰ Century

Brennis boasted proudly the death of his brother. The MacKendrick had not seen the ambush Brennis had prepared.

The news of the warrior's death was celebrated by those on the hilltop, loyal men to Brennis. Now he could reclaim his place as the rightful leader of the Dal Riata.

An ominous feeling crept over those gathered as the ground rumbled with the thunderous sounds of a horse fast approaching the hilltop woods. Further conversation halted as rider and horse approached.

"MacKendrick lives," the rider bellowed, reaching shouting distance. "The warrior is alive!"

Voices that only a moment ago were raised in celebration abruptly fell silent with the rider's news.

The rider pushed a bundle off the horse to land with a thud on the ground before halting to dismount. He grabbed a torch from someone toward the back of the crowd and shoved his way through those gathered and into the center of the circle.

"'Tis as I say. Yer brother yet lives."

"That cannae be. I felled him," Brennis spat.

"Aye, ye did. He did fall with his death wound. 'Twas the Lady. She appeared as if from nowhere. She healed him with her magic and gave him an immortal life."

"Are ye daft? 'Tis nae possible," another spoke.

The rider recounted exactly what he'd seen and heard, despite the skeptical faces of those around him. "'Tis as I say. As MacKendrick lay dying, the lady appeared and brought him back from the very brink of death. She gave him half of a magical talisman and promised he would find the other half in the future. She bade him that Erie was still in need of him." The rider looked at Brennis. "He will nae leave Erie in your lifetime, Brennis. The MacKendrick rules the Dal Riata, still."

"'Tis great magic she possesses if she can promise him that," Brennis said, disbelievingly.

"Aye, 'tis all true." As if to prove a point to a still doubting audience, the rider strode over to the bundle he'd tossed from his horse, bent, and lowered the torch for all to see.

The firelight revealed the figure of a man, dressed in a blood-stained white robe, painted with the mares of a Druidh. He was battered and beaten, but obviously alive.

"One of the Lady's magic priests."

An instant hush fell over those gathered.

The rider continued. "He can make you live as long as the MacKendrick and keep what is rightfully yours."

Brennis shifted uneasily on his horse as a sinister smile crossed his face. Ah, what could be done with such power, he thought. He surveyed those around him with a new sense of purpose. He too felt the possibility stir in his blood. He turned to the men gathered around him.

"Bring the priest. We have work to do."

Ireland, Present Day

Brennis growled tossing aside the parchment he'd been reading. With an angered sweep of his arm, he sent a pile of tomes and scrolls that had been on the table, tumbling across the floor.

There was nothing in the old writings concerning him, the sleep spell, the immortality spell, or even the Lady or Aedan. It was as if everything had been wiped from history ... or ... he thought, too secret to chance being written down. Too many years had passed for an oral version to have survived and there wasn't enough time to scour every depository of ancient manuscripts on this bleedin' isle, so this left Brennis with no means to find the correct spell except for Aedan and he was a half a world away. He needed to get his brother to Ireland as quickly as possible.

Without the immortality spell these men didn't stand a chance in a fight. They were not warriors, he knew. *Och they werenae even the dark priests they thought themselves to be.*

They only dabbled with cheap tricks, not real magic. And, he was sure none of them had ever lifted a blade.

There was one weapon Collin had shown him, a gun, but it was loud and would draw too much attention. Besides, it would kill much too fast. There would be no dying time in which to extract information or for Aedan to watch him take Aislinn.

No, he was on his own to confront his brother, the way he knew, with the blood and force of his sword.

Oh, how he wished his loyal men-at-arms were here with him. They'd obviously remained true, believing he would rise to lead the Dal Riata. They saw to the building of this stead; they saw to passing the commitment of his care to their sons and their sons' sons, anticipating the power they would wield once again.

But history had changed, and the power they craved was now a thing of the past and this coven of fake priests arose from the ancestors of his men. Yet he was the only one who knew the magic and they were expecting him to teach them. And he would teach them some, but not all. There was some magic he would save only for himself.

It wouldn't be much longer before his brother made his way to Erin. He only needed to bide his time a little longer. In the meantime, while he waited for word about his brother's movements, maybe he could train a few of these men to wield a blade with some semblance of skill, at least to cover his back when he began hunting for Aedan. That is, if they could find swords or a blacksmith in this God forsaken land.

In the meantime, he needed a woman, maybe two, to give his thoughts a rest and occupy the empty hours. Brennis left the room in search of Collin.

Chapter Twenty-Three

UNITED STATES, PRESENT Day

Aislinn opened her eyes and looked around, taking a moment to remember she was resting in her grandmother's cabin.

She sat up and pulled the blanket tighter around her shoulders. The cottage was chilly despite the bright sun shining through the windows. She placed a log on the fire. How long would they be safe here, she wondered. She shook her head to dispel the thought.

A faint thud sounded outside, then another. Aislinn's brow furrowed as she stepped to the window to investigate. She pulled the curtain aside and gazed out at Aedan busily chopping wood. He was shirtless despite the cold, his skin glistened with sweat from the effort of his task.

Aislinn watched with fascination as the muscles in his arms and chest rippled with undeniable strength and power as he brought the axe down with such force the ground vibrated. The logs split with such precision and skill, it was as if he willed them apart.

She was undeniably attracted to him. *Just look at him,* she thought as her eyes continued to scan every inch of him. He looked like an ancient God, wielding his weapon with such determination and deadly beauty. There was no denying the fact that her body craved this man from the very moment she'd met him in the giftshop of the museum. He was perfection and Aislinn felt the force of each stroke of the axe deep within her as if it were him deep inside her.

Aedan raised his eyes and sought her out through the window. He winked playfully at her as if he were aware of her thoughts. She quickly dropped the curtains, taking a deep breath to calm her racing heart. Yes, desiring him was one thing. Reconciling everything else that he'd told her was what she couldn't seem to come to terms with. She no longer knew what was true anymore, and this had her feeling disconcerted and vulnerable. She knew the moment she encountered Aedan in the museum gift shop that that was the instant her life had begun spiraling out of control The only thing was, she had no idea how to stop it.

Aedan quickly dunked his head in the lake, flinging back his hair wildly as he withdrew. The frigid water cascaded down his face and chest and he let out a howl from the shock. He dipped his hand in the water and hurriedly washed the sweat from his skin. Heating water and washing in the cottage would have been more convenient, but Aislinn was there, and after the way she'd looked at him through the window moments ago, it was better he clean up this way.

Aedan had risen early, leaving Aislinn to sleep. He'd shoveled the driveway, and left to find a place to order propane. He'd arranged for a delivery later today. At least they'd have hot water, a means for cooking, and to run the old gas converted refrigerator. Still, there was no electricity for lights and heat would have to come from the fireplace, but even so, he found the old cottage rustic and charming.

He was very comfortable with the lack of amenities, having lived many years without them, but he did worry that Aislinn might find the inconvenience too much. He was hoping the simplicity might provide a quiet opportunity for Aislinn to find and feel the power of being a part of him, the land, the magic and their past. But to do this, she would have to let go of everything she'd ever known and accept a new reality that had no basis of truth in her world.

Aedan finished washing, using his shirt to towel off before heading back toward the cottage. Right now, he needed to put on dry clothes and grab a bite to eat.

As he flung open the door to the cabin and stepped inside wet and half undressed, Aislinn sprang to her feet and hurried to close the door behind him.

"What happened?"

"Nothing. I washed up in the lake."

"In the lake? Are you crazy? It's freezing. You'll catch a cold. Let me get you a towel." Aislinn hurried toward the bathroom to fetch a bath towel.

"I donnae get sick."

"Oh."

"But you can still fuss over me if you like."

Aislinn threw the towel at him and strolled back to the living room to sit by the fire.

"Did you start the wood stove in the bedroom?" Aedan called, as he retrieved a sweater from his bag sitting on a kitchen chair and tugged the knit garment over his head.

"Yes."

"Good, it won't be long until it warms that room."

Aedan grabbed a knife and plate filling it with cheese, crackers, and an apple and brought them into the living area, placing them on the coffee table.

"Come eat."

"I'm not hungry, but I'd kill for a cup of coffee."

"Propane is coming and as soon as the gas is delivered, you can perk some in the old pot on the stove. I bought a few more groceries, too. They're out in the snow bank keeping cold. I also purchased oil for the lantern and batteries for the flashlights and a few candles."

"Is there anyone out there? I mean after us?" Aislinn asked, worry tinged her voice.

"Nae. I think we will be safe here for a while, until I can figure out our next move."

Aedan looked over at Aislinn and saw the worried look on her face. "I will not let anything happen to you, Aislinn. I promise." He handed her a piece of apple. "Please eat something."

She reluctantly took the fruit.

"Tonight, I'll cook you a proper meal over the fire," he offered.

"You seem pretty comfortable roughing it," Aislinn noted.

"I lived many years before electricity. A fire in the hearth was the most important thing in a home. We cooked with fire, and used the fire for heat. The hearth was the place to gather and tell stories or plan battles. We sang by the fire, we read by the fire." Aedan looked over at her, and pinned her eyes with his, "We made love by the fire."

Aislinn jerked her gaze away.

"Fire was a central part of our lives."

"That's why you liked having a fire in the evenings at my house."

"Aye. There's something mesmerizing and ancient about sitting around a fire."

Much to Aislinn's relief, the propane delivery truck pulled into the driveway interrupting further conversation. *Perfect timing*, she thought, standing up with a little too much enthusiasm. She wanted no more visions of Aedan making love near a fire.

By late afternoon the refrigerator was running, and the stove was working. Aislinn finally got her cup of coffee, which she had to admit tasted delicious. She sipped the warm liquid leisurely watching Aedan prepare potatoes, onions, and vegetables that he wrapped in aluminum foil. He placed pieces of beef in an old cast iron skillet he found in the kitchen and set it on the hearth.

"Let me know when you are ready for me to put the food on," Aedan instructed, wiping his hands on a rag.

"Where did you learn to do that? I'm guessing you were probably not a Boy Scout."

Aedan chuckled at her humor. "You learn a lot of things being alive as long as I have, but 'tis nae secret how to prepare a meal over a fire. Anyone who has camped knows this."

"I didn't know."

"You dear Aislinn, are neither a camper nor a cook!"

"Hey." She threw a pillow from the couch at him, but he easily dodged her assault.

"A man could starve waiting for you to cook. After Beltane, I will teach you the art of cooking for a warrior."

The lighthearted mood suddenly vanished at the mention of Beltane. *Damn.* She was trying her hardest not to think about any of the implausible things he'd told her. Why did he have to spoil a nice afternoon by bringing that up. She was hoping by not mentioning anything to do with what he'd told her, it would all just go away.

She felt the sudden need for fresh air.

Aislinn set down her cup, rose and went toward the rear door. She slipped her feet into her boots. "I think I'm going to take a little walk," she announced, putting on her coat and mittens. "I won't be long."

Aislinn left the cabin and strolled toward the bluff that overlooked the lake below. The tumultuous waves mirrored her inner turmoil. The cool breeze stung her cheeks as she pulled her jacket tighter around her. There was no hint of spring on cold days such as this, despite what the calendar indicated.

This location, looking out over Lake Michigan, was one of her cherished spots, a place she felt close to her grandmother as she gazed out over the waves. Over the years she'd spent many days swimming and playing along the shore of the lake and just as many days trying to find solace in the familiar view. Today this place brought no comfort.

"I wish you were here, Grams. I sure need someone to talk to," she choked a whispered plea. I want this man. Oh, how I do. But everything else ..." she let her unfinished sentence whisk away on the breeze. She couldn't even sort her feelings enough to complete her thought.

"Gram? Are you here with me?" she called out as the wind seemed to answer her, lifting her hair to caress her face as her grandmother had once done.

The wind, Aislinn thought for a moment. *What was that little saying about the wind her grandmother had told her years ago?* She tried unsuccessfully to piece together bits of the memory she'd long ago forgotten.

She hadn't realized the time that had passed as she stood there staring out over the water. The sun had nearly set and she'd only just noticed. Her thoughts were so jumbled when it came to Aedan. Could he really be who he said he was, she wondered. *There is a very special man out there for you.* Aislinn remembered her grandmother reassuring her after leaving Grant. *You will know him. In your heart, you've always known him.*

"Gram, is it Aedan? Is he who he says he is? Am I part of the bizarre story unfolding? Gram did you know?" Her questions remained unanswered as they drifted away on the breeze.

"I can feel the conflict you wrestle with."

Her thoughts were interrupted by Aedan's approach. She tossed a quick glance at him beside her before turning her gaze back to the lake.

"You are torn between wanting to believe who I am and the improbability," he stated.

Aislinn remained silent, recognizing that was exactly what she struggled with.

"I feel your attraction toward me, Aislinn," Aedan stated.

She remembered looking at him sitting on her living room floor when she thought him asleep, felt the heat at him intimately pressed along her back in his hotel room two days before, and her reaction today when he looked at her through the window. No, there was no use denying that fact any longer.

She again glanced at him and gave a half-cocked smile before once again looking away.

"Your arousal is a palpable thing inside me."

"You can actually feel that?"

"Oh yes."

Aislinn gave a slight nod.

"Magic is very real. This world has just forgotten. Look around this place." Aedan swept his arm over the landscape of her grandmother's property. "It draws you. You're a part of this, ye ken. Ye must feel it, your connection to this." He gestured to the air and the water. "This land is filled with your grandmother's magic and has been protecting you since your arrival."

"You can feel that, too?" she asked skeptically.

"Aye. And I noticed the wards your grandmother carved around the door."

"Now you are saying my grandmother knew magic? Aedan this is ludicrous."

Aedan let out a long breath. "Aislinn, I am who I say I am," he said. "Can't you suspend your disbelief and consider my reality?"

Aislinn remained silent.

"What if I hadn't told you who I was? What if I were just an ordinary man? Would ye accept me into your life more readily?"

"But you're not an ordinary man, are you?" There was something in those dark depths that tugged at her, something unnamed and irrational.

She knew her excuses were weak in light of all the evidence to the contrary, but she couldn't put into words exactly what it was that made her so hesitant to believe what he'd told her.

It was as if she teetered on the precipice of something, looking out into a mysterious void, frightening and at the same time tempting. One step and she would either be swallowed up by the blackness or rewarded.

"You are afraid of finding everything I told you is true and relinquishing your precious control."

Aislinn looked up at him as she turned in the direction of the cottage. "No. I'm afraid of finding out it's not true, because if it's not, it would completely destroy me."

Aedan remained where he stood, watching Aislinn as she retreated to her grandmother's cottage. Before going inside, she paused at the door, inspecting the door frame for the symbols he spoke of and must have found them because she reached out and touched the carvings, then glanced back at him before going inside.

He didn't blame her for being so confused. From the moment he'd entered her life, her world had been turned completely upside down. She fought so hard trying to reconcile everything that seemed too irrational to be real. Her undeniable attraction toward him only added to the list of things that didn't make sense to her. He could feel the times when she wanted to believe, when his truth seemed to wrap around her heart, but then rationality would just as quickly claim her and he would feel the confusion return.

Aedan followed Aislinn to the cottage, stopping to retrieve an armload of firewood before going inside. As he placed the wood near the fireplace, he felt the comfort of sleep come over her as she rested in the other room. He brushed off his hands, reaching for the altar blanket from the couch. He carried it to the bedroom, placing it over her. For long minutes he gazed upon her as she slept. If he could take away all the doubt, all the heartache, he would gladly trade places with her. His only consolation was in knowing when she finally accepted who he was and could love him, she would know him as her true love, the man she was fated for. Until that time her world would remain uncertain.

Aedan left the room and went to the hearth where the dinner he'd prepared earlier sat. He arranged the coals and slid the pan into the fire so that their meal would be ready when Aislinn woke. It worried him by how little she ate when she was nervous or scared. He hoped he could convince her that she needed to keep her strength up without frightening her as to the reason. She needed to be strong and ready should a situation arise with regard to the people who threatened them.

He sat on the couch contemplating the danger lurking so close. He knew the way to discover who hunted them, however he needed to perform the magic on a full moon and it was still a day away. Until then, they would stay close to the cabin where they were safe and where he could protect her.

"Aididh!"

Aedan jumped up from the couch when he heard Aislinn call out to him using his ancient name. He sprinted to the room, only to find her in the throes of a fitful dream, crying out "Aididh."

"Aislinn. Wake up."

Aislinn's eyes shot open at the same instant Aedan approached her.

"Aislinn?"

She sat up and wiped the tears from her eyes. He sat beside her on the bed, brushing an errant tear from her cheek.

"It was the dream," she whispered. "It was so heartbreaking. They were dragging me away…"

He pulled her against the warmth of his body.

She made no attempt to move away from him. "I was so completely lost. I felt as if my heart had been ripped from my chest, in my dream I mean. I kept calling to him, but they were pulling me further and further away. I couldn't reach him. I pleaded for him to find me."

"And I did."

Aislinn looked at him then as the poignancy of his words touched her and the air between them danced with uncertainty and anticipation. She placed her hand gently against his cheek, stroking his lips with her thumb. In a surprising move, she leaned in and placed her lips against his, kissing him long and hard. He rewarded her gesture by returning her kiss with equal fervor and intent.

As she kissed him, he felt the swell of her inside him, as if the flood gates to her pent-up emotions suddenly opened and her acceptance washed over him in wave after wave of tantalizing glory. There was such resolve in her surrender, he felt her letting go as if it were a tangible thing.

She pulled back again and looked deeply into his eyes.

"I'm tired of fighting what I can't control." She again pressed her lips to his, stroking his face and hair.

"Take what you need from me, Aislinn." His voice was low and sultry, and promising. And by her hasty need to taste his mouth again, he knew his statement touched her in the one place that needed him without regard for thought or reason.

"I want you, Aedan," she whispered against his mouth.

In a flash, his arms tightened around her, pulling her against him. His lips devoured hers before the last syllable of his name was spoken.

"Aedan, whether you are real or a fantasy, it doesn't matter. I want you."

"Are ye sure lass? You've struggled so with this."

"I'm sure. Tonight, I want to be with you."

He raised his hands to her face, stroking her cheeks. "Och, ye think 'tis just for tonight? Ye know 'twill be more than that."

"Let's only talk of tonight, Aedan. That's all I can give for now."

His mouth found hers and kissed her hard and fierce. His tongue plundered her mouth possessively, over and over drawing moans of surrender from her. He would bed her well. He would make her feel cherished and loved, but for now there would be no leisurely lovemaking. Her heightened state was near frenzied with abandoned need. She was determined to find fulfillment with him and he'd see her satisfied, in whatever capacity she needed.

"Come, let's go out to the other room."

Aedan grabbed her hand and led her to the living room where he pulled the pan from the fire, before he sat in the middle of the floor and pulled her next to him.

"Ye will know such pleasure in my arms," his voice was thick with passion as he stroked her face. "You will shatter and become reborn a hundred times. You will learn my touch, my scent. You will know me in your very soul as you once did and then we will speak of more than just tonight. I donnae make love without tomorrows."

He could feel his words arousing her, filling her with promise and affection. He could feel her yielding. Too long her desire for him had been repressed, and now, unleashed, it easily consumed her demanding and hot. He would not disappoint her. He would give her everything she craved from him.

"Come here," he whispered, easing her to straddle his lap. She placed her hands on either side of his face and lowered her lips to his, kissing him with intense passion. Her body melted against his, her hips ground against his. He was not impervious to her passion flowing through him like molten lava. His body reacted almost immediately, craving to give her everything she wanted.

His hands moved swiftly over her body, touching, stroking, claiming her even through her clothes. Aislinn was so completely aroused, and he knew she was close to surrendering.

He unzipped the front of her jeans and slid his hand inside stroking her. Aislinn pushed herself onto his hand as a tortured moan escaped her throat.

"I feel what you feel," he reminded her, knowing that in the haze of her oncoming orgasm, how erotic she'd find that truth.

He slid his finger into her, which encouraged her to move more aggressively against his hand which stroked her. Aedan kissed her purposefully and hard, until her lips were swollen and full and she was kissing him back with equal intensity in between breathless pants.

Her body tensed.

"Find it. Find your passion," he whispered, near gasping from his own arousal. She clung to him then, his words sending her over the edge. She moaned with compete abandon, her body finally giving up all the frustrations she'd been harboring. She soared with her climax, shuddering and writhing in his arms, helpless, and completely engulfed by her intimate submission. He held her tight against his body, his hand still buried between her thighs, as she moaned and wiggled and took all he gave her for seemingly endless moments.

"Oh, my God," she stammered, letting her head fall to his shoulder.

"'Tis only the beginning," he murmured, in between his own ragged breaths.

Aislinn lifted her face away from him and looked at him before rising to her knees, moving off his lap to kneel next to him.

He tugged his sweater over his head, tossing it aside, watching her gaze move over him. She ran her fingers over the tattoos adorning his body, smiling when his muscles rippled and his skin prickled under her touch.

"You are a beautiful male," she sighed, and in a moment of brazen confidence, she leaned over and kissed his chest. A moan of pleasure escaped him. She pulled back and smiled.

"Och, Christ, lass."

She lightly caressed the knotwork encircling his biceps. Aedan closed his eyes and raised his face to the heavens, praying for the strength to resist her exploration.

Aislinn's fingers made a trail from his chest to just below his navel, teasing the tendrils of hair on the path leading lower. Her fingers tugged at the snap of his pants and he once again took a deep breath for control before hurriedly shrugging out of his jeans. He reached for Aislinn and tugged her to lie beside him. He kissed her long and hard, hungrily indicating he wasn't finished with what he intended to share with her.

"I've had enough of your clothes between us," he said, pulling her sweater over her head and unclasping the lacy bra she wore. He stared at her for long moments, unable to speak while Aislinn squirmed under his gaze.

Aedan found his voice again. "I remember when I saw you for the first time that night in the glen, the firelight dancing over your skin, like now." He paused briefly and kissed her again, his tongue mingling with hers. "Ye were so nervous with everyone just outside the fires. I swore I would make ye ken only me. I swore you would know nothing but our loving. Christ, how ye burned me. Your touch seared right through me, and I didnae ken how I'd survive the feelings."

He knelt next to her and looked down at her. "Ye looked at me with such resolve. I knew you felt what was between us, the promise of our connection that the Lady had deemed. I knew the rightness in the deepest part of me."

He reached for the waistband of her jeans and pulled them down. She raised her hips up so he could slide them off. Her panties followed.

Aedan knelt between her legs, looking at her laid open before him. "Your body was painted with a design starting here." He reached out and touched her shoulder, drawing the design with his fingers. A second later, the design appeared on her skin.

"Aedan how?"

"*Shh.*"

He bent and kissed her shoulder, running his tongue over the design on her skin. He pulled back slightly. "And the pattern circled here." His fingers skimmed along her shoulder, to her chest, across her breast. Her nipple puckered and hardened from the touch of his fingertip, as once again the design appeared on her skin.

He placed his mouth on her breast, sucking and teasing her taut nipple with his tongue. "And here," his fingers circled her other breast, as the design appeared on the path his fingers took. Once again, Aedan's mouth found the tight bud, licked and teased it, until he felt her shudder beneath him.

"Aedan, I can see it," Aislinn sighed between the touch of his tongue and the arousal coursing through her.

"Aye."

"How is this possible?"

He kissed her lips tenderly. "'Tis magic, I think," he whispered with a twinkle in his eyes. He kissed her again before sliding down her body. "The design fanned out across your stomach..." His fingers drew the wisps of curls of the design, "...as if tempting me to follow where they led." He kissed and nipped the tender skin of her abdomen, inching lower.

Aedan loved watching her flush and squirm when the designs appeared on her skin. He loved being the source of her deepening passion, and loved watching her shiver in anticipation of where he would touch her next.

When he kissed her in her most feminine place, she elicited a moan of utter capitulation, her fingers tangled tightly in his hair and she shattered beneath him. She cried out his name and clutched at him, writhing and trembling with her orgasm.

He pulled away from her then, and turned her over onto her stomach. He ran his hands over her back and each place he stroked, the design appeared.

"The marks continued to circle and spiral onto the small of your back." He kissed her there, gently sliding his hand beneath her. "They beckoned to me." He touched the marks on her skin. Even now they tantalized him, calling him to possess her. He raised her to her knees, kneeling behind her.

"Och, lass, I'm a strong man, but even I donnae possess the strength to resist the magic that is between us."

Aislinn yielded to him as he bent over her, kissing her neck and back, sliding into her, cooing love words in her ear to help her grow accustomed to him.

Once completely inside her, such a sense of possessiveness came over him that it was nearly his undoing. The rightness of being within her overwhelmed him to the point he had to force himself to move slowly, despite the need to hasten his movements.

He reached under her and captured a breast in his hand, rubbing the tight peak until she involuntarily pushed back against him, silently indicating what she needed from him. He ground into her with deliberate steady movements, but increased his thrusts when he felt her body tense.

He moved within her then, giving her what she wanted, and what he needed. As her body helplessly convulsed around him, his control swiftly unraveled as he became lost in the promise of his own release.

With the urgency of his thrusts, he suddenly held the very profound thought that this was everything he'd ever longed for. And with that revelation, he experienced his own release deep within her.

"Aislinn," he moaned between breaths, still caught in the throes of the tremors wracking him. Her name held a myriad of sentiments he could not voice. Instead, he withdrew from her and gathered her in his arms, relying on his actions to convey what his words could not.

He was not fool enough to think Aislinn would have a change of heart about him this soon. This night was merely the satisfying of long ignored needs. But it was a start. And for now, he'd accept that.

Chapter Twenty-Four

AISLINN FELT THE TINY tug on her head as the last remnants of sleep slipped away. She pulled the blanket tighter over her. At some point during the night, she and Aedan had moved to the bedroom. He'd carried her to the bed and continued to make love to her all night until they both were completely exhausted and well satiated.

Aedan made it easy to feel no guilt or regrets about sleeping with him because after the initial time he'd made it more than clear he wanted her just as much, if not more, than she wanted him.

She felt another tug on her head. "What are you doing?" she asked, her voice still husky with sleep. She stretched languidly, still basking in the afterglow of their lovemaking.

Aedan sat next to her. "I'm putting a braid in your hair."

"Why are you braiding my hair?"

"Because I'm claiming you."

"Claiming me?" Aislinn was perplexed.

"Wearing a braid signifies you belong to someone. 'Tis a custom."

"You've always had a braid in your hair."

"Since I was first given a sense of you by the great lady. My heart was given to you then."

The sincerity of his words and gesture touched her. How easily he could speak of commitment and forever. For her it was not that easy.

He let her hair drop, and instead trailed his fingers down the underside of her arms, lifting them over her head as he snuggled down beside her.

"I will nae tire of hearing my name as you come, sweet Aislinn."

She smiled, closing her eyes to the warmth coiling inside her belly. He wanted her. No pretense, no hesitating, just the basic need to mate with the one he loved. Yes, he needed her as much as the air that filled his lungs and his want of her aroused her so thoroughly it was but a few moments before she was once again calling out his name.

AISLINN LAY SPRAWLED across Aedan's chest, quietly listening to the steady beat of his heart. "Yer a good fit, Aislinn O'Neil" Aedan whispered against her ear, "but if I stay in you any longer, lass. I will be needing more." He slid her off of him and positioned her in his arms. "Ye need to rest a wee while now. You're going to be a bit sore, I'm afraid."

Aislinn was warmed by his words. She felt empowered knowing he wanted her so much. And, she admitted, he was an incredible lover. Never had she been reduced to such a primal state as to be so bold or so completely out of control, so willing to do or say anything, even beg for release from the sweet torment he wrought in her.

She freely gave herself to him. Even now, she tingled and craved him in that deepest place between her thighs, and she knew she would never be the same. She would always ache to have this man, and the knowledge of this was at once disconcerting and so very erotic. With a sense of bitter sweetness, she wondered if things might be easier if she had not tasted heaven.

She looked at the man she lay entwined with. He seemed so completely undaunted by their intense intimacy. He was completely natural and comfortable lying with her. Aislinn envied his easy assurance. She on the other hand fought a barrage of emotions, none of which were peace.

He looked down at her then, the knowing look in his eyes, the crease of his brows indicating he knew of the turmoil inside her.

"Even now ye find you cannae sort your feelings for me."

Aislinn looked away, unable to meet his gaze.

"Ye still cannae accept who I am. Ye ken I love you, lass."

"You're so sure."

"Aye."

Aislinn felt guilty for the insecurity she still harbored about him. He surely read the doubt in her expression before she looked away.

"Ye have given me your body, but I donnae have your heart," he said, sadly.

"Aedan," she began, but didn't know what to say.

"'Tis alright for now." He breathed a resigned sigh. "But you'll be needing to love me." Aedan kissed her forehead and tightened his arms around her. "Your body already knows me well. 'Tis only a matter of time before your heart does, too."

Aislinn shifted and stretched. She could get used to lying around all day making love and then napping, but her stomach rumbled. She glanced over at Aedan. He was awake watching her.

"Ye snore."

"I do not."

"Like a banshee. And ye steal the blankets."

Aislinn looked down at herself all wrapped up, and he barely covered. "Oh my gosh, I'm sorry," she said, attempting to disentangle herself from the covers.

Aedan roared with a deep, husky laughter, taking her by surprise. She halted at the sound. She loved the sound of his hearty laugh. He didn't laugh enough.

"Aislinn, I donnae care if you bring down the rafters, as long as you are by my side."

She smiled. His declaration was so honest it was painful to see how much he loved her.

"I'm hungry," she stated.

"Aye, I hate to admit it when I have such bonny legs wrapped around me, but I'm hungry, too."

Aislinn wiggled away from him, slipping from the bed. Separating from him was the jolt of reality she'd wanted to avoid. She stood and turned to face Aedan. She was suddenly very sobered as the implications of sleeping with this man struck her. How could she have been so reckless as to not take precautions against getting pregnant? Last night had been so damn exciting, she effortlessly disregarded any thought of consequences. They'd been thoroughly negligent, not just once, but countless times and now she was regretting her indiscretion.

"Aedan, what if I become pregnant? We didn't do anything to prevent it." Aislinn looked at him for reassurance that he would be responsible should the unthinkable happen.

"Would having my child be that bad?" Aedan studied her face.

Aislinn couldn't hide the doubt clouding her thoughts.

"You doubt my commitment to you?" He ran his fingers through his hair. "I wouldnae have come inside you if I didnae accept the possibility of a child, Aislinn."

His words were terse, and edged with irritation. He was disturbed that she thought he would be so reckless about lovemaking. Aislinn remained silent. The look on his face conveyed that he was aware of her uncertainty.

Aedan sat up on the edge of the bed and reached his hand out to place it on her abdomen. Her skin warmed beneath his touch. "Aye, I gave you enough of my seed to make a hundred babes." Aedan was quiet for a moment, before he whispered something in a language she could not decipher. The words sounded sad as he spoke them.

"Ease your fear, Aislinn. You'll nae be pregnant." He rose and kissed her forehead, his playful demeanor now gone.

Silence filled the room after his departure. Aedan's words tugged at her so. He still planned on them having a future together. Just a moment ago that prospect seemed very frightening but now, oddly, felt very disappointing.

Aislinn was grateful for the few minutes alone to pull herself together. Last night had been wonderful, a night she would remember always. Sex with Aedan would become that by which all else would be measured. She never thought it possible to be so intimately made love to that the act became a spiritual experience. However, it was time to face their situation. What had occurred between them didn't change the fact that she was locked in a cabin in the north with a man who wove fanciful tales of being from the past and waiting through time to find her and her life being in jeopardy because of this man.

All the fixings for sandwiches were laid out when Aislinn entered the kitchen. She joined Aedan at the small table, watching him while he ate. After professing how hungry she was, she barely nibbled at her sandwich.

"Are ye at a loss for words?"

"I don't know what to say."

"Cannae ye love me just a wee bit, Aislinn? After what we shared?"

"Aedan, you are a great lover ..."

"I ken I please ye in our bed, but ye still guard yourself from me."

"I have all these thoughts, these memories of something I thought was just a dream my whole life. I want to believe, I do more than anything but it's hard."

"I donnae understand how you can continue to deny it. Your indecision has gone on too long. I grow weary of it. I donnae ken what else I can do." Aedan was frustrated. "I've told you things I would have no way of knowing."

"How do I know I didn't talk about them when I was hurt?" Aislinn snapped back.

"How do you explain the mark on your back, Aislinn? How do you explain that you possess the other half of the amulet? How do explain the magic in this place? How do you explain the intensity of our lovemaking and the symbols appearing on your body?" Aedan's voice was tinged with indignation. "Do you not recognize them from your dream?"

Aislinn had reached her breaking point with her pent-up emotions and fears. Her voice became loud and harsh. "I can't explain my birthmark. I don't know about the amulet. I don't feel the power you keep speaking of. I don't know what to think about the marks. I don't know what to think about anything!" she yelled, taking a deep breath to calm herself upon seeing Aedan's increased agitation. "I do feel something when I'm with you. Something I can't explain."

He raised his eyes to hers.

"A sense of familiarity, a sense of longing. Aedan I don't know. Maybe it's just good sex." She threw down her sandwich.

"'Tis more than just good sex." Aedan was visibly hurt by her words.

Aislinn regretted her statement knowing full well there was more than simply casual sex between them.

"Ye still compare me to your ex." Aedan ran his fingers through his hair. "The difference, Aislinn is my words are true." Aedan rose from the table looking down at her. His eyes held the pain of her indecision. "I've waited an eternity to find you and now my time is almost over. I'd hoped you would love me or at the very least grant me a small place in your heart." He paused. "Even with all the magic in my power, I cannae make you love me Aislinn. 'Tis only your love that will save me." Aedan turned, walked into the kitchen lifting his coat from the hook near the door. He pulled open the door and quietly left the cottage.

Aislinn dropped her head in her hands.

Aislinn paced nervously. The night was descending and Aedan had not returned to the cabin. She was worried. All afternoon she thought about what he'd said, *"Now my time is almost over"* and her heart constricted.

She knew there were things he withheld from her, things that had to do with her ability to love him. Yes, maybe she did hesitate because of Grant. That wound was still very raw. Maybe Aedan was right that she was unfairly comparing him to Grant.

Aislinn knew she'd hurt him. Her words were so unkind. Perhaps she was trying to push him away. She really wouldn't blame him if he'd left. If he did leave then she wouldn't have to admit her feelings and she could go back to her perfect little quiet life, a life, she admitted, that no longer appealed to her.

Aislinn looked at her watch again. Where could he be? She stepped over to the front window and looked out over the lake as the last remnants of color streaked across the sky. The trees were black silhouettes against the deepening hues. As the woods behind her became eerily void of light, Aislinn noticed a slight amber glow coming from the beach beneath the bluff. She instantly knew what it was.

When she was younger, she and her grandmother often lit a fire on the beach and roasted marshmallows. Aedan must have built a fire from stray driftwood to keep himself warm while he stubbornly stayed away.

"He's going to freeze his ass off," Aislinn huffed, going to the back door and slipping her feet into her boots. She put on her mittens and wrapped a scarf around her neck but passed on putting on her coat, trusting that her bulky sweater would keep her warm enough for the few moments it would take to call him back.

Aislinn grabbed her flashlight, just in case, but from the looks of it, Aedan had a good fire going. She made the short walk across the lawn to the embankment, stood on the bluff, and gazed down at the beach. She spied Aedan surrounded by the fire.

She shook her head finding the path leading down the hill and quickly traversed the icy sandy slope to the beach. Reaching the bottom, a disquieting feeling that something wasn't right came over her. Aislinn made her way toward the fire.

"Oh, my God." Aislinn's mouth fell open. There in front of her stood Aedan, dressed only in his pants, coat tossed aside, thigh deep in the frigid lake. The hilt of a sword stuck out of the water in front of him. A circle of fire floated on the water surrounding him. He held his arms toward the sky flames dancing in each one of his palms, his head thrown back, his eyes closed tightly.

Every tattoo on his body glowed red hot, as if they were being branded on his skin at this very moment; though he seemed unaware that any of this was taking place. Aedan chanted something in the same language he'd used earlier. Gaelic, maybe, but she wasn't sure.

He repeated the words over and over in a forceful tone, every muscle taut and strained from the enormous effort of whatever he was doing. His chest heaved with each gulp of air.

Aislinn was deathly afraid to move or say anything. She stood very still, with her heart pounding and her hand over her mouth to keep from screaming.

Aedan suddenly lowered his head, staring into the lake around him. The water took on an eerie blue hue, swirling around his legs. A thick mist suddenly formed within the ring of fire, rising from the water like hands clawing their way up from the depths of someplace

Aislinn didn't want to think about. They pawed and reached and surrounded Aedan, obstructing him from Aislinn's view.

As Aedan's body jolted forcibly against the mist engulfing him Aislinn sank down to sit on the icy sand. She felt horribly frightened of the power Aedan was wielding.

A cool breeze brushed past Aislinn, stunning her momentarily with its sting. The wind felt like a reprimanding slap, cautioning her not to watch what she didn't believe. The wind blew and floated as if it were a serpent slithering through the sky, circling around her, whipping her hair in one final gesture of warning before floating away and wrapping itself around Aedan, rocking him where he stood. His hair flew in wild disarray from the gust coiling around him. His body shook violently.

Aislinn closed her eyes, unable to watch. She covered her ears to try to block out the agonizing cry escaping from Aedan's throat as tears rolled down her face. With the last trace of Aedan's cry fading into the night Aislinn dared to open her eyes and looked. He lowered his hands and brought them out in front of him, cupping them as if holding something. Slowly, a ball of moving light formed, not fire, not mist, but a combination of both.

Aedan stared at the globe of light, seeing something in its core not visible to Aislinn. She swiped at the tears on her cheeks. *He's making magic.* Not silly hocus pocus bar tricks but real mystical magic. Magic drawn on ancient wisdom and knowledge of the earth; magic lost to the modern world since people had stopped listening to nature and its rhythms; magic which had vanished into history. Aislinn knew without a doubt *that* was what she saw. She knew with a certainty the man standing in the water a few feet from her carried out a long-forgotten ritual. No wonder the wind admonished her for witnessing his secrets.

Suddenly every nerve sprang alert with heightened awareness. Inside her something awoke and restlessly stirred. She looked up at the stars dotting the sky and the full moon rising as an ancient sensation blossomed inside her. The night sharpened all of her senses, and she shivered. Reason abandoned her as the night unfolded its mysteries and splendor and she reached to comprehend the knowledge offered her.

Aislinn closed her eyes, realizing the only way to know the mystery was to accept the truth of Aedan. A profound presence of him filled her, and in one defining moment, Aislinn cast aside all the doubts, all the fear, and found him there, mighty and tender, and she surrendered to the belief he was real.

Her spirit stirred, yearning to soar with the new realization caressing her heart. The power that possessed her and filled her to overflowing was at once intoxicating and liberating. Her heart floated toward some unnamed pinnacle she couldn't define, and in doing so, she knew the magic. Fire. One who is fire.

Aedan.

He'd been with her always, tucked away in the deepest place of her soul, waiting for her to find him. Her soul rose with the marvel of the night and the new consciousness of the man inside her. Somehow, some way, he'd defied time to find her and Aislinn was struck with awe and admiration.

Aedan wasn't from this time, she knew this now, with every fiber of her being. He came from a time when the world was steeped in magic and mystery, when hills and the trees were alive, and ancient voices *did* whisper on the breeze, when offerings were given, rituals were performed and ceremonies were carried out in wooded groves with fires and drums. "Oh, my God," Aislinn cried softly, so as not to disturb him. "You." She began shaking uncontrollably as the revelation washed over her. "It ... *is* ... you."

The blue light faded from Aedan's hands and once again, lifting them to the sky, he invoked the flames in his palms. Speaking again, he closed his eyes and Aislinn saw the wind spring forth and leave the circle swirling around Aedan once before disappearing into the night. Aedan's hair stilled. The mist surrounding his legs faded, and the tendrils slipped back into the stillness of the water.

He continued with his words. The fire in Aedan's palms seemed to take on weight, pushing down on his hands. The weight became so great that Aedan buckled in the water and fell to his knees.

Aislinn stiffened, watching some unseen force push Aedan's hands under the water. He let out another tortured cry, collapsing.

Everything suddenly became very still. The fire vanished and with it, the light. It took Aislinn a moment to realize that whatever had been happening was over. She scrambled to her feet. She fumbled to find the flashlight. Something wasn't right. No movement came from the water.

"Aedan?" she called, still searching the ground. "Aedan?" Her foot kicked the flashlight. "God, Aedan, wake up!" She found the flashlight and clicked it on, running toward the water. She shone the light in the direction she'd last seen him. The sword rising from the water gleamed ominously when the flashlight beam struck it. "Aedan? Where are you?" She swung the light back and forth over the water, frantic to find him. The water was freezing and he wouldn't live long in it.

Finally, she spied him, and without thought, plunged into the painfully frigid water. She cried in anguish as the icy water soaking her sweater weighed her down. She tripped on the rocks under the surface and tumbled into the water. Aislinn quickly regained her footing, reaching Aedan. She pulled at his head, turning him over and dragged him toward the shore.

"Oh, God, I can't do this." She slapped his face. "Aedan, you have to wake up. You're too big. I can't get you out of the water. Oh please." She began to cry in earnest. "Somebody, please help," she called out, but she knew there was no one for miles around. She pulled and tugged and managed to get him partly out of the water. "Gram if you can hear me, help me."

Aislinn's strength began to fail as she started to stiffen from the cold. "Aedan, please," she cried, trying to roll him the rest of the way out of the water. "I can't do this." She slipped on the icy sand, and fell on top of Aedan's lifeless body. She found getting up difficult because her muscles were cramping from being wet and frozen. She could no longer bend her fingers.

With her last ounce of energy, Aislinn rolled Aedan one more time, finally getting him totally out of the water. The force of rolling him onto his stomach over the uneven ground pushed enough of the water from his lungs that he began coughing.

"Aedan?" Aislinn wiped his face, and pushed back his hair. He continued to choke and cough.

"You have to try to get up. We're wet and we're going to freeze. Can you hear me, Aedan?" He collapsed again, but at least he breathed. "Come on you're the warrior. Get up!" she screamed at him.

He managed to get to his knees and stumbled to his feet. Aislinn grabbed his arm and led him toward the path. He buckled to his knees again. "Aedan, I can't do this. Please. Try. I'm so cold. I can't last much longer."

Aislinn's teeth chattered uncontrollably. Aislinn leaned into him, wanting so bad to just sit, but knowing if she did, she'd never get up. "Aedan I can't lose you again. I know it was you in my dream. I know. Aedan we're so close. Just up the hill, come on. You can do it." She cried out her command. "Aedan!" she yelled at him again. That seemed to rouse him enough so he was able to pull himself up again. "Just ... a ... little ... more." Aislinn's chattering teeth kept her from talking.

The door to the cottage burst open as they both stumbled in. Aedan clutched at a chair to remain upright. He leaned and stumbled his way to the living room, tearing his wet pants from his body. He collapsed in front of the fireplace.

Aislinn tugged and tore at her wet clothes frantic to remove them, shivering and shaking uncontrollably. Her muscles screamed with pain as they began to thaw. Her whole body shook with pain as she trudged to the fireplace and the warmth of the fire.

Aedan was sprawled on the floor unnaturally exhausted. She tucked a blanket around him and wrapped another around her own shoulders. In a moment of lucidity, she added more wood to the fire. She finally fell then, collapsing on the floor, hugging her knees, rocking back and forth and trying to get warmth into her body.

A long while passed before she could move, and her first thought was of Aedan as he hadn't moved at all. She knew she needed to get his blood circulating, so pulling the blanket from him she began drying him, while massaging his arms and legs.

What Aedan did at the water, whatever was revealed to him in the globe of blue light, was something he was paying dearly for. His legs were swollen from being immersed in the water for so long, and he was completely drained of strength. He could have died had she not been there.

Aislinn continued to rub over him with comforting strokes, feeling the warmth come back into him. She ran her hands over the smooth planes of his chest and down his abdomen. She vigorously rubbed his thighs where she knew his muscles were tight and aching and as she did, he moaned from the pain.

Aislinn shifted herself so she sat beside him, once again tucking the blanket around him. "Aedan? Are you awake? How do you feel?"

"You'll be finding out if you donnae stop stroking me."

Aislinn smiled.

Aedan tried to sit up but gave up after his muscles protested. He closed his eyes and sank back down. "Never mind, lass. I will have to settle for dreaming of ye for now." He instantly drifted off to sleep.

Aislinn left Aedan to rest while she showered and dressed in dry clothes. She should offer him something warm to drink, but wasn't sure what. Maybe she should make a pot of coffee, if not for him, then for her. He would probably need something more. Broth? She knew that would offer him the most nutrition, but how to make it? She went to the kitchen and opened and closed the cupboards looking for a pot. She'd seen her mom make soup many times. Didn't you just cut up everything, toss it into a big kettle and cook it? She opened the refrigerator and spied the chicken and carrots left from the other night. She might add some potatoes and celery and most definitely onions. She could do this. A little salt and pepper, too. Easy, right?

As the hours ticked by and the soup simmered while Aedan slept, Aislinn found a small first aid kit tucked away in the bathroom closet. She rubbed cream on the burns on his hands and wrapped a gauze bandage around them. She re-tucked the blanket around him and brushed a lock of hair off his face. She stared at him sleeping. How could she have not known him? How many men were built as big or as commanding as he, not to mention that ageless look which made her jittery the moment she'd seen him in Chicago. How many men carried swords or spoke with phrases "*Would be honored*" or "*Ease your worry*?"

From the first moment she'd looked into his eyes, she'd seen the secrets there. He said to her "*I know you*," but she dismissed it, afraid to believe what her heart knew. He'd been hidden there, inside her, just as he said and it took the fear of losing him to recognize him and believe in him. *And now what?* She wondered sadly, yawning and placing her head on his chest in the early hours of the morning as the cottage filled with the aroma of simmering soup.

After a restless night, Aedan stirred and woke. "Aedan? You're awake." Aislinn touched his face. "How do you feel? I made soup. Would you like a cup?"

"Ye made soup?" Aedan looked surprised.

"You are ever full of surprises, Ms. O'Neil." Aedan leaned back against the couch, obviously exhausted from the small effort sitting and talking to her took.

"I've got to get my strength back," he moaned.

Aislinn scrambled to her feet. "I'll get you something to eat."

Aislinn brought out a mug of hot chicken soup and handed the cup to him.

"I didn't know what to do. I was sick with worry and you were there sleeping for hours so I made soup."

Aedan took a sip. "Hm. I'd say you're learning. 'Tis hearty and good."

Aislinn smiled, relieved by his returning strength. She knelt beside him.

"And ye bandaged my hands?" Aedan set down the mug and unwrapped his hands.

"They were burned. Aedan I was so afraid. You could have died." She wrung her hands and her voice became a bit shaky. "You frightened me so much." Tears gathered in her eyes.

Aedan pulled off the last remaining gauze and flexed his hands. No burns remained on his palms.

"How can that be? Aedan, your hands were raw and blistered."

"I heal fast." He picked up the mug and continued to sip his soup watching her.

"You *did* hurt your hands when you pulled me from the car," she realized. "All this time I thought I imagined the bruises."

"No, you didn't imagine it. I healed then, too." He drank his soup again. "Ye are a courageous and strong woman with the way ye helped me." His pride in her showed not only in his voice but in his expression as well.

"Aedan, I saw. I saw everything."

Aedan remained quiet as the unrest surfaced within her. "You were on fire, and then you were glowing. Well, you weren't glowing, but all around you glowed, and the wind and mist. You screamed from something painful and ..." Aislinn took a deep breath remembering the pain he'd experienced.

Aislinn looked away, recalling what she herself had experienced on the beach and her revelation of who he was. She felt she was part of the night, a connection to something she couldn't name.

"I think I heard my grandmother's voice on the breeze," she confessed. "The wind stung my face." She touched her cheek. "Like a slap."

"Aw, so you did experience something."

"Yes. It was powerful," she admitted.

Aedan finished his soup and set down the mug. "Lass, I find I am still weary. When I am stronger, we will speak more. I need to rest." Aedan stretched out on the floor near the fire. "Let me hold you while I sleep." He held out his arms to her.

Aislinn slipped easily into his embrace. She could lend comfort to his battered body. She snuggled up against him, her head resting against his chest, her leg draped over his. She placed her palm on his chest as he kissed the top of her head. She hugged him tighter. "Don't leave me."

"Och, lass, I donnae intend to."

Chapter Twenty-Five

Four days after Aedan's foray into his magic, he felt better. His body held no scars or any indication he'd been hurt.

Aislinn rose early, showered, dressed, and busied herself scrambling eggs for their breakfast. From the kitchen she could hear Aedan get up, and a moment later he joined her at the table.

Aislinn dished up the eggs, adding toast and coffee to the table before she sat down. Quiet moments passed until Aedan finally reached over and put his hand out to stop her from toying with her food. She hadn't even noticed she was doing it.

"I feel your unrest. What is bothering you?"

Aislinn put down her fork and drew in a long breath to steady herself for what she wanted to say.

"Aedan, as much as I would like to do nothing but stay here, I'm growing restless. We have jobs and responsibilities and remember someone who is shooting at me?"

Aedan nodded. "Aye. I know who wants to hurt you. That's why I performed the magic." He stroked the hand he touched.

"To find that out nearly killed you. What if it had?"

"It has been a long while since I have performed magic of that magnitude."

Aislinn turned her hand and absently interlocked her fingers with his. "What if I hadn't come looking for you?"

"I counted on your grandmother's protection. She is the one who brought you to me."

Aislinn suddenly pulled her hand away from Aedan. "Aedan, I went to the beach because I thought you were stubbornly going to stay away and I knew you'd freeze if you did."

"Ah, ever practical again, I see. Did ye not feel *something* as you said when you came for me?" he asked her.

Aislinn abruptly pushed back her chair and stood, stepping away from the table. She pinned Aedan with a steely glance. "I have never been so frightened in my life. I could tell you were in pain and I couldn't do anything. And then you were face down in the water, not breathing and I couldn't lift you."

Aedan leaned back in his chair and crossed his arms over his chest. "I did not intend to frighten you, only to gain information."

"You act as if it were nothing. You take chances. What if you'd died? What would I do then?"

"But I didnae."

Aislinn just shook her head and looked away, not understanding his nonchalant attitude.

Aedan straightened the chair, firmly planting his legs on the floor.

"Aislinn do you know who I am? Truly?"

Aislinn turned around and looked at him sitting stiffly in the chair. Her eyes clearly mirrored her emotional turmoil, remembering the thousands of dreams of him. She'd seen every muscle, every strand of hair, every tattoo with absolute clarity, now. She'd felt his body take hers in a union so magical she would often wake and feel as if it had really happened. Aislinn moved back to the table and slipped back onto her chair.

She knew him then and she knew him now. "Yes."

Aedan's expression visibly eased, feeling the sincerity of her words. Reaching across the table, he took her hand once more in his.

"Aislinn, I know you find me attractive."

Oh yes. She felt her cheeks blush. That was undeniable. He melted her insides every time he looked at her. They were both in a constant state of arousal around each other. She couldn't lie about that. "Yes."

Aedan smiled a sad smile "But do ye love me?"

"You are wonderful. You're an incredible lover. I feel free and open with you. I enjoy our intimacy immensely. When I thought I was going to lose you, I felt devastated. Is that love? This is all happening so fast." Aislinn saw the sadness fill his gaze. "Why do you keep asking me that? Am I supposed to love you? Aedan, I think there is more to this than what you've told me," she said.

Aedan sighed. "Aye. There is. 'Tis very complicated." He rose from the table, went to the pocket of his coat, and began fishing for something. He pulled out the two amulets and brought them back to the table. He dangled the stones in front of her. "I told you they were to be used for a ceremony. That ceremony is for you and me, to be held in two weeks on Beltane."

"Two weeks?"

"Aye. On the night of April thirtieth to May first. It's a time of year when ... "

"I know about the whole spring, fertility, have sex all night, thing," Aislinn spoke up.

"'Tis more than that. 'Tis a time for unions. A time to honor the God and Goddess. You and I must go to Ireland and in the same ancient grove as your dream, we have to unite, to make love and perform the ritual. 'Tis the only way I can stay in your time." His eyes found hers and held them. "There is one who will try and stop us. He has already tried."

"And what happens if we don't go to Ireland and perform this ritual?"

Aedan let the stones drop flatly on the table in front of her. "Then I will disappear back to my time, perhaps to another dimension, I'm nae sure, but wherever I end up ..." Aedan ran his fingers through his hair sitting across from Aislinn once again. "I will be cursed to live forever without you."

"What happens to me?"

Aedan's gaze dropped to the stones lying between them on the table. "Ye resume your life. Ye go back to work, live your life and forget me."

Forget? How could she forget Aedan? Aislinn suddenly felt sick. Could she live her life without him? Could she forget his kisses, his caresses?

Aedan slowly raised his eyes to hers. "Aislinn, I willnae ask you to perform the ritual if you do not love me, as the spell will bind your soul to mine."

"After everything, you would sacrifice that? You would condemn yourself?"

"For ye. If ye couldnae love me, then yes."

Having eaten very little, Aislinn rose from the table and absently cleared the mess from breakfast. She toyed with scraping the dishes.

Aedan's last words had stung. He would sacrifice everything for her, and she selfishly questioned how she felt about him. Loving him meant everything to him, but in the end, he would think only of her.

The silence between them grew unbearable, and once again, after some time passed, Aislinn sat down across from him ready with more questions.

"Is everything about the Chicago project a lie?" She looked at him with eyes that pleaded for him to tell her 'no.'

"I was desperate, Aislinn. I didnae ken how to be with you. I wanted so badly for ye to remember me, and remember how much ye loved me. Twelve hundred years is a long time, and there ye were walking out of my life as ye walked out of the museum, with no memory of who I was or what we were to each other."

"So, you lied to me?"

"At first I thought up the project as a way to see you, but I quickly realized how the institute would appreciate the work. I faxed them the outline, and as you know, they did like it."

"And you really work for the art institute?" she asked.

"Aye, in acquisitions."

"Who wants to hurt me?"

"What do you remember about the ceremony long ago?" he inquired.

"The people, the fires, the drums."

"Do ye ken why we were being united?"

"You said to unite two tribes."

Aedan continued to explain. "They were the two most powerful on Erin. One, the Dal Riata, my tribe, from the very northeastern portion of Ireland. The other was your tribe in the southern part of what is Northern Ireland, the Dal n'Araide of the Kingdom of Ulidia. Beneath these two tribes, a third resided called the Dal Fiatach. For many years, in between wars, I negotiated a peace between these three tribes along with the Lady, the great Druidess, your aunt. Our unification was imperative because the Norse were raiding our coasts and it was only a matter of time before an all-out assault happened."

Aedan shifted but continued. "Peace was precarious at best, so to help maintain it, the Lady arranged a marriage between us. Secretly she gave each of us a gift, a sense of the other so we would know each other and know we were mates.

"Hopefully, with our two clans united the Dal Fiatach would see the wisdom in joining us. Up until then, they held no interest and were actually encouraging the Norse to form settlements in their territory. All the while we were trying to keep them out.

"Their joining with the Dal Riata and the Dal n'Araide meant I would become extremely powerful, controlling all of the eastern part of Ireland."

Aedan ran his hands through his hair. "And to add to the already complicated politics, I had a half-brother, Brennis who was bitter that I ruled the Dal Riata. He was none too pleased. He felt he should be the one to rule, and there were many who agreed with him." Aedan took a drink of his now cold coffee.

"When we were young, Brennis showed early signs of jealousy through malicious use of magic. His cruelty extended to animals and people alike. Because of this, he was nae allowed to continue with his Druidh training. His hatred only grew greater over the years.

"He saw how the Lady befriended me, how the other tribes welcomed me, how our own people backed me, how willing I was to fight and die for them. Brennis spent his whole life undermining anything I did for the Dal Riata. He felt he had the right to everything, including you, and he wasnae going to let me have you."

Aislinn toyed with the stones on the table while Aedan's words sank in.

"Do you remember much of the battle?"

Aislinn thought for a moment. "I remember the pain and the blood."

"Do you remember the men fighting?"

"I remember the battle but not very many specific details about the men."

Aedan pursed his lips. "As I have previously explained, my brother very carefully courted another tribe to our west, the Un'Neills.

"Brennis promised them he would get rid of me, rule the Dal Riata and allow them their campaign for High Kingship. He conspired with the Un'Neills to break up our ceremony, knowing full well most of our men were across the sea fighting against the Pics with my cousin, Kenneth, leaving us vulnerable and unable to defend any attack.

"This battle succeeded in planting mistrust against me and my efforts to keep the Dal Riata whole. Your clan wanted to trust in our union but still they had a back-up plan to wed you away to the Dal Fiatach if something should go wrong, and as ye know something did go wrong. Brennis and his men attacked the night of our ceremony. My brother thought he should be the one marrying you and had every intention of kidnapping you had your clan not secreted you away. I should be grateful the old chief did have the wisdom to recognize Brennis's vindictive nature and keep ye as far from him as possible. However, the cost of his wisdom was our separation.

"I left Erin right after and journeyed to Alba…er… Scotland to explain to Ciniodh what his lack of support cost. By the time I arrived in Alba, Ciniodh had already made up his mind to dissolve ties with Erin. He would no longer support the fight on Erin against the Norse when the raiders already occupied his own western shores. Kenneth had decided to move his seat further east into Alba and arranged the marriage of his daughter to one of the Un'Neill chiefs.

"It was devastating news and a betrayal that weighed heavily. My territory was left divided and the clans I worked so hard to unite broke ties with me and Kenneth after supporting Alba for many years in fights against the Picts.

"I was heartsick at losing ye, and at the news Ciniodh conveyed, so I was distracted on the return trip to Erin and didnae see the ambush my brother and his men laid for me. That is when Brennis killed me or would have if nae for the Lady intervening."

Aedan looked up at the ceiling. "It was a time of such unrest. Clans fought against each other and the north men were trying desperately to establish themselves in Ireland. The lady was desperate to keep her island, her people, her way of life, out of foreign hands. There were so few lands the Romans or Saxons hadn't conquered. It isnae my place to pass judgement on the right or wrong of her decisions. 'Twas the way of things at the time. Ireland wouldnae be the Ireland of today if anything had been different."

"Who was the man shooting at us, Aedan? How is he connected to this?"

Aedan hesitated a moment letting out a sigh. "Someone I suspect is working for my brother. I donnae ken how, but Brennis is here, in this time. He continues to plague me, continues his vengeance against me. He knows the magic. Shortly after he tried to kill me, he disappeared. I thought he'd died. And surely after fifty or sixty years I was certain he was gone. Now I am nae so sure. Perhaps he knew what the Lady had done for me. Perhaps he found his own way to traverse time.

"I donnae ken why he is here, but I suspect he still bears his hatred for me and will see me undone until the very end. He will try to come between us."

Aislinn rose from the table and began pacing nervously. The grim reality of the situation became clear. "Aedan, I don't understand why this should matter to him after all this time."

"Jealousy, is a powerful thing. I was ... I am a very powerful Druidh. Brennis wants the stones, I'm sure. He wants the power and magic they hold when together. I was warned by the Lady all those years ago there would be someone who would come after the stones. Brennis was so intent on destroying me and getting his hands on the amulets, he has followed me through time to accomplish it. I fear he knows how to use the stones to stay in this time and with the magic and immortality in his grasp he would become very powerful and very dangerous."

Aislinn continued to pace, holding her stomach, sick over everything Aedan had explained. She didn't want to hear more, but she had so many questions needing answers.

"And what will Brennis do to me if he kills you?" Aislinn didn't wait for an answer, the look of utter despair that filled Aedan's gaze was telling enough.

"He willnae kill me, and I will not let him harm ye. I swear Aislinn." Aedan's reply was determined and true.

Aislinn sat back down and put her head in her hands. Her head was near splitting with a headache. Aedan stood up behind her, massaging her shoulders.

"'Tis hard to accept, I know. 'Tis a lot." Aedan came around and knelt in front of her and took her hand.

"Aislinn, I grow weary of this eternal existence. All I ever wanted is what other men have; a good woman, a family, and the chance to grown old. I ken the moment I saw you in the glen you were my soul mate. I've waited through eternity to find ye again. There is no prize at the end of this, only me and my pledge to love ye always, to the end of our days."

Aedan sighed. "I just want to get through Beltane. I just want all this to be over and for us to be together." He placed her hands against his cheek. "Aislinn, search your heart. Try to remember how ye felt about me on that night so long ago. Try to remember the promise of me the Lady granted ye."

Aislinn heard the desperation in his words and his melancholy tore at her. She could no longer stand seeing the pain etched on his face and rose to move away from him to escape it.

How ironic the twists and turns her life had taken. When she pleaded for something to distract her from the winter doldrums, never did she expect anything like this. She wanted to laugh hysterically at the absurdity. There was a very real threat to her life, and things could get much worse before it would be over. And then what?

What if Aedan didn't make it? What if she didn't make it? There was a very distinct possibility that even if she committed to Aedan and tried to go to Ireland with him, one of them would be killed.

She rubbed the pain in her temples. Her head was spinning. She just didn't know what to do. She needed fresh air, needed to clear her head, needed the time to sort this all out. But according to Aedan, time was what she didn't have. Aislinn suddenly felt closed in by everything. Panic began to rise inside her. She wanted to flee, just like she had when her world with Grant crumbled. She needed to go out.

"I think I need to go for a walk," she suddenly announced, moving hurriedly to the door and lifting her coat off the hook. She swiftly left Aedan and the confines of the cottage, pausing a moment to take in deep breaths to still the fear climbing its way up inside her. She attempted to concentrate on her surroundings, using the tangible things such as the trees, the remaining patches of snow, the birds she could hear, to anchor her thoughts.

The day was beautiful for April, crisp and clear and Aislinn hoped the biting fresh air would clear her mind of all the conflicting emotions overwhelming her.

She wished she could avoid this. She wanted to pretend nothing else existed, but she and Aedan and that everything he'd told her wasn't true. But she knew the truth and she could no longer deny it.

Decisions. She needed to make decisions. Why was her heart so reluctant to let Aedan in? Because, she admitted there was the very real possibility this wouldn't turn out well, and she could lose him after giving him her heart. With the intensity with which she would love him, she would never survive a hurt that deep. Grant had been devastating enough; losing Aedan would kill her.

Despite all her protests and denials, Aedan had managed to slip into the very place she had tried to keep him out of. She could feel him there, in her heart, where he'd always been.

Aislinn continued to walk deeper into the woods, stepping over the snow-covered brush. She'd walked these woods a thousand times, knew how dense they were, knew where each deer path led, where the swampy area started and where the best place mushrooms grew was.

Today, the forest seemed as foreign to her as her life did. The seeds of despair which took root in her stomach days ago, now curled and clawed their way through her growing apprehension. This was happening too fast and was too complicated and Aislinn again felt as if everything was unraveling.

"'Tis not safe to wander from your grandmother's property."

Aislinn was startled to hear Aedan's voice behind her and stopped and looked over her shoulder to see him approaching. Aedan came up alongside her and took her hand helping her step over a fallen log buried in the snow.

She took a sidelong glance at him. Right now, Aedan was the only thing real in her life. He was everything she'd ever dreamed about. Everything about him was wonderful and magical and her heart did flip-flops every time he looked at her. His long hair shimmered in the sunlight, hinting at just a trace of auburn hiding amidst the black. His eyes were dark and deep and spoke of the enormous burden he carried, yet sparkled in amusement when he could, just for a moment, forget everything weighing so heavily on him. His kind and caring nature proved uncomplicated and she loved the way he enjoyed simple things such as sitting by a fire or walking with her.

Remarkably graceful for his size Aedan held her hand and arm gently as he helped her through the rough terrain. But Aislinn knew he was a force to be reckoned with in battle. She remembered him in her dream, fierce and powerful, swinging his sword as if the blade were little more than a twig. He would protect her with his life because he loved her.

Her heart skipped a beat. He loved her so much and suffered so much to find her and yet would give up everything if she asked. Her throat tightened and tears threatened. His selflessness tore her up inside. To love so unconditionally...

Aislinn stopped suddenly, turning toward Aedan. She raised her hand to his face and gently touched him with a sad caress. She sought the dark depths of his eyes for the answers she longed to find.

"Aislinn," he whispered.

"Make love to me," her request was born from the anguish swelling inside her. "Now. Here."

She kissed him, not trying to hide the turmoil in her passion. More than anything she wanted him to ease her unrest and be the one real thing in her life.

Aedan kissed her long and hard, backing her against a tree. He kissed her face and neck finding his way back to her mouth where he kissed her so intensely her lips swelled full and lush. He discarded his gloves, shoving them in his pocket before tearing at the zipper of her jacket.

"Aedan I need you," she stammered between breaths. Tears snaked from the corners of her eyes.

There was nothing leisurely or tender in the way she wanted Aedan. Aislinn's need of him was hot and lustful and desperate for the connection with him that grounded her, that made everything all right.

Aedan lifted her shirt, unclasping her bra. Her breasts spilled out gloriously peaked from the cold. He licked and sucked the tightened buds until she squirmed against the tree, yearning for so much more. He easily pinned her to the trunk with his hard body, but she strained and arched into him indicating her rising need.

She wiggled pushing down her pants, as he continued to kiss and caress her. She tore her mouth away from his, panting feverishly. Again, tears trickled from the corners of her eyes and he kissed them away.

"Donnae cry," he reassured her between kisses. "I ken ye are letting go. 'Twill be alright." He pulled away just enough to tug at the zipper of his jeans and position himself.

She cupped his face with her hands, looking deep into his eyes as he entered her. Tears trickled from her eyes as she became lost in the very real act of loving him. She wept with the absolute reality of feeling him deep inside her, not just physically but in her heart as well.

Aedan made love to her fast and hard, as he too was caught up in the frenzied need consuming them.

She shattered into a thousand tiny pieces in his arms, as he held her tightly against him. She felt him shudder and quake and drive deeper into her. With a final powerful thrust that crushed her against the tree, he came deep inside her.

"Look at him rutting like an animal in heat," the man dressed in black whispered, stepping from behind a tree and lowering a pair of binoculars. "Too bad Brennis isn't here to witness this. He would be delighted at finding them in their intimate embrace and then killing the woman."

"Give me the binoculars," a second man spoke, jerking them from the hand of his cohort. "Yep, It's them," he confirmed, lowering the glasses, nonplussed by what he saw.

"They are protected by the magic."

"Brennis taught us how to get around that. Besides, all we need to do is get them moving toward Ireland and Brennis." The first man said, restating their plan. "Come on, it's time."

Aislinn clung to Aedan's jacket, holding him close as she sought to calm her ragged breathing. Aedan slid his hand to her bottom and pulled her tighter against him. He was reluctant to break their connection.

"Sweet Aislinn. 'Tis so good with us." He nestled his face next to hers and kissed her. "I feel your acceptance. Please donnae cry." He wiped the tears from her cheek, cupping her head with one hand while the other continued to hold her against him. "It will be ok." His lips covered hers once again, only now, with tenderness.

"I do love you, Aedan. I do," she confessed between his kisses and her tears. "I tried so hard not to. But I can't, not any more, no matter what happens."

"Ah, Aislinn how I've longed to hear those words." He sighed, kissing her cheeks where the tears touched her. "I ken the risk ye take to love me, but there is no other way. We were always meant to be together. Admitting you love me is giving up everything you thought you knew. I feel your pain of letting go of that reality. But I'm here."

Aislinn sighed and sucked in a shaky breath. He knew what she couldn't put into words. The consequence of loving him meant starting over and accepting things she never believed possible. In a way it felt good to let go of all her apprehensions, all her fears, but now loving him not only would mean boundless joy, but along with it came the risk of equally as much sorrow. Still, she knew she had no choice. Loving him was her destiny, one she'd dreamed about for years.

After many long moments, Aedan finally withdrew from her. He lovingly wiped what remained of the tears on her cheeks with his thumb, and kissed her once again before releasing her.

"Come here. You're going to freeze if we donnae get ye covered. He clasped her bra together and pulled down her shirt, placing a kiss on her nose. As Aedan helped her with her pants, he paused and looked over his shoulder, somewhat warily. Aislinn watched his keen eyes scan the woods. She could see his concern.

Aedan finished helping her pull up her pants. "What is it, Aedan?"

"I'm not sure." He became uneasy, zipping up his jeans. He turned to her and smiled reassuringly. "'Tis alright, but let's go back. I'd like to get my sword from the lake on the way. A warrior is not whole without his blade."

"That is such a medieval thing to say."

"Perhaps, but 'tis the truth of it."

Aedan very carefully led her back the same route they'd taken from the cottage, deviating only when they reached the lake. He became alert, his body tightened. He muttered only a few words on the return walk, always polite and loving, but with heightened awareness. He became guarded and watchful, not relaxing until they reached the edge of the protected property. Aislinn was reminded that this strikingly beautiful, deadly powerful man was above all else, a warrior.

Aedan's sword stood suspended in the water, as if it were King Arthur's Excalibur. When the sun hit the metal just right, the glare was blinding. Embedded in the hilt resided a blood red jewel Aislinn guessed was a ruby. This was the same sword he'd shown her student, Devin. She remembered at the time how odd she thought it was that he brought a sword with him from Chicago. Now, she understood, his sword was an extension of himself.

Aedan stepped into the frigid water and gripped the hilt, easily lifting the blade from its icy confines. He looked elegantly agile as he swung the sword over his head, swiping and slashing the air around him, stepping from the water as if he were a god coming forth from the depths.

He stretched and twirled and thrust at an invisible foe, obviously very comfortable with the blade. The ease with which he moved spoke of years of training. His concentration and calculation were instinctive within him.

"Feels good in my hand." He glanced up and winked at Aislinn. "As good as ye do."

He gripped the hilt, testing the weight and balance of the sword. Aislinn watched him, enthralled by this ancient man. His hair whipped wildly about his face, giving him a riotously fierce appearance. He would kill to protect her.

There was something very primal about Aedan, something very basic, she noted. He expressed deep loyalty, a need to love and protect and to do the right thing at all costs. Life was simple for him because of his security in his priorities. She envied his surety and commitment.

He came over and slipped his arm around her waist, tightening his hold just enough to show off his muscles in his arm. "Ye like to watch your man."

Her man? Aislinn glanced up at him and smiled. *Yes, her man.* His comment was ruthlessly male, but the absolute truth.

Aislinn reached for his sword and surprisingly, could barely lift it. She dropped the heavy blade with a thud. He moved to help.

"Wow, this is heavy! You make it look so easy."

"You're supposed to hold the blade like this." He stood behind her, reaching around to help her lift it.

"It's surprising how commanding this feels in your hand." The sense of power she felt holding the sword amazed Aislinn. She spread her legs, bracing herself as Aedan slowly let go of her arms.

"Now point the tip straight out from you. Feel the weight, the balance." Her arms shook a little and Aedan stood ready to help if needed. Bring the blade around to one side, like this, as if you are slashing." He guided her arms to the left. "And then to the right." She sliced the air to the right, a bit wobbly, though.

Aislinn couldn't hold the weight of the sword longer than a few moments, and eventually lowered it, relinquishing the weapon to Aedan.

"Thank you. I've only seen the ones at the museum. To think I actually held a real weapon, and an ancient one at that."

"You'd make a great warrior, Aislinn," Aedan praised.

"I'm not so sure about that. I'm getting cold and I'd like to clean up."

Aedan smiled. "I could pamper ye a bit. Maybe give you a massage, rub your shoulders and other places, and make you scream in delight..."

Aislinn looked at Aedan, laughing. She couldn't help but be amused by his attempt at a joke, however his humor didn't belie the grim disposition just behind his words.

"You are trying to hide your worry from me."

He drew in a long breath. "Something is coming. I can feel it."

"Something bad?"

"Aye." He patted his shirt where underneath the cords that held the two stone pieces rested. "The time for Beltane draws near. I fear Brennis will try everything in his power to see we do nae unite and I am sent back in time. He shot a quick glance at her.

"This scares me." She stroked his arm, seeking reassuring comfort in touching him.

"Ye havenae changed your mind about loving me?"

"No. I couldn't even if I wanted to."

"I like to hear that."

"Why don't you finish practicing while I go clean up," Aislinn suggested.

"Aye," he agreed.

Aislinn turned and climbed the embankment but spun around again.

"Aedan?" she called out.

"Aye?" he answered turning toward her.

"I love you."

"Ye always did, my Irish princess. Ye always did."

Chapter Twenty-Six

AISLINN EMERGED FROM her shower, clean, refreshed, toenails polished and generally well primped. She called out to Aedan but when he didn't answer, she figured he was still down at the lake.

Aislinn made herself a cup of tea and sat down at the table. She only took one sip when the door to the cabin suddenly burst open, startling her. Aislinn stumbled to her feet, knocking over her chair in an attempt to rise. Two men rushed in.

"Ah. What do we have here. The warrior's woman. She's even lovelier than Brennis described," one of the men mocked with a thick snarl. He stood tall and erect, sneering at her with cold, empty eyes. He loomed over her, much too large for her to attempt to fight him. His face was rugged and covered in beard stubble giving him a sinister appearance. His brown hair was tied back. His clothing extremely tight strained against his muscles. His whole demeanor spoke of one purpose. *Her*. He lifted a gun and pointed the barrel directly at her.

Aislinn gasped and recoiled from him.

The second man stepped closer to her. Slightly smaller than the first, but equally as menacing. This man's eyes held a crazed look as if he would be just as comfortable killing her as eating dinner.

Aislinn stepped back and frantically scanned the room for any possible way to flee.

"You think to escape? Not likely. I'm surprised you have the strength after your little morning fuck session."

Aedan's intuition was correct when he'd sensed something earlier today in the woods. Aislinn stepped cautiously to one side, but both men countered, stalking her. She didn't know what to do. She needed to find a way out. She needed to warn Aedan.

Aislinn took another step backward, trapping her against the counter. She reached for the nearby dishes and hurled them at the intruders.

Glass crashed everywhere, silverware clattered to the floor, but they easily dodged everything she threw at them. She was cornered with no way to escape.

The first man fired a warning shot. She froze, but an instant later, she desperately tried to dash around them. She kicked at the man with the gun and he staggered back momentarily but lunged for her. He hit her square in the face. Stunned by the impact, Aislinn slumped forward.

Suddenly and without warning Aislinn felt anger so strong it completely immobilized her. Her breath caught in her throat and her body shuddered at the foreign sensation. The intensity of fury she felt stifled her. Somewhere in the haze of pain and the frenzied storm inside her, she knew the feelings were not hers. *Aedan*. She felt Aedan. She was consumed by the rage coming from him.

The men easily caught her, wrenching her arms behind her back. Aislinn screamed Aedan's name with all her might before a fist slammed into her face. She slumped into her captor's arms.

"GET YE HANDS OFF MY WOMAN!" Aedan bellowed, bursting through the open door. He stopped instantly, seeing the knife at Aislinn's breast and the gun pointed at her head.

"You donnae want her. "'Tis me ye are after," he seethed. "Let her go."

"Actually, MacKendrick, maybe I do want her, and then after I'm done, she'll be waiting for your brother. He has big plans for her, if you know what I mean."

Aislinn tried to focus on the man speaking as Aedan began advancing toward the man at the door. The click of the cocking gun halted him.

"He will never have Aislinn."

"We know we cannot kill you, but we also know without her, you'll be a distant memory come Beltane. So, either you give us the stones, and you can have what short time remains until Beltane, or we kill her now."

The second assailant moved toward Aislinn. He grabbed roughly at her and she cried out and kicked at him. He answered her attack by punching her in the stomach which had her doubling over and gasping for breath.

"She's a feisty one, MacKendrick, I'll give you that."

Aislinn could see, no Aislinn could *feel* Aedan's pent-up furry. He was near exploding and let out a roar that reverberated through the rafters. Aedan's gaze fixed on the knife lowered to Aislinn's neck. She tried to squirm away from the cold blade on her skin. The man sneered at her feeble attempt.

"I don't have the stones," Aedan lied in the hope of stalling them. "Neither does she."

"Nice try, MacKendrick. Without the stones, your brother would still be sleeping in the bowels of our, *um*... church."

Aedan took in the bit of information. Brennis must have used a sleep spell that woke him when the two stones met. But how ...

He looked at the assailants furiously. "At one time she had it, but when one of your buddies ran her off the road in the snowstorm, it became lost in the snow."

A quizzical look passed between the two men while they contemplated the possibility that Aedan may have told the truth.

Aislinn glanced at Aedan through her swollen eyes. He never told her he suspected her accident wasn't an accident.

"How did ye breech the magic of the cabin."

"You're not the only one who knows the Druidh arts, MacKendrick. Your brother taught us what to do. A simple spell. He will teach us more after he has the stones."

"You are a fool if you believe that," Aedan growled.

The attacker pulled Aislinn tighter against him but lowered the knife, looking at the other in response to Aedan's statement concerning Brennis' intent. Aedan moved forward, but paused, seeing the blade rise to Aislinn's throat once more.

"It's too bad she has to go. She looks delicious, MacKendrick." The man nuzzled his face into her neck, licking the blood that trickled from where the knife had nicked her flesh.

Aislinn swallowed hard, turning her head, her gaze meeting Aedan's. In the momentary glance she read his thoughts.

"You weren't so coy this morning fucking the warrior." The assailant grabbed hold of her hair and yanked her head back making her look at him. She groaned with pain. He wound his hand tightly in her tangled mass of curls, dragged her to the table and slammed her against it. With quite a bit of force, he shoved her back and attempted to part her legs.

Aislinn still found the strength to resist him. In one last attempt, she kicked him with all her might as Aedan lunged forward at the men.

"RUN!" Aedan shouted.

Aislinn bolted for the open door, Brennis' men close behind.

She ran frantically for the woods, daring to look back. Aedan followed the men with his sword raised closing the distance between him and the man with the gun. The man turned at the last second, just as Aedan's blade pierced him. The gun went off, flying out of his hand. At the same instant, the second man reached for Aislinn and knocked her to the ground. Aedan leapt on top of him before he could raise the knife to her and the two rolled off Aislinn, locked in combat.

The man raised his arm thinking he would plunge the knife into Aedan's heart, but instead, Aedan grabbed his arm and doubled it back on the assailant. Aislinn heard the sickening sound of a rib cracking as Aedan rammed the hand holding the knife into the chest of the man.

It was over within seconds. The man went lifeless under Aedan. He dropped him to the ground, scrambled to his feet and hurriedly moved to Aislinn. She stared wide-eyed, horrified.

"Aislinn." He gathered her up and wrapped his arms round her, rocking her gently against his strong body. "'Tis over. You're safe now." Aislinn looked down at his blood-soaked hands then up to his face before slumping against him.

"*Shh*, don't try and move." Aedan watched Aislinn struggle to open her swollen eyes. She looked around as best she could. He sat next to her on her grandmother's bed, holding ice to her head. She nervously glanced at his hands, now devoid of all blood.

"You killed those men."

"I'll not apologize." Aedan ran his hand through his hair. "Aislinn, I am a man of another world, one where the rules are very different than yours. One either lives or dies by those rules. Tonight, we live."

There could be more attempts as Beltane drew near. He didn't voice this fear. He'd drawn her into his world of magic, immortality, and evil and expected her to love him, at the same time diminishing all the codes she lived by. He knew it would be hard for her to reconcile what she'd witnessed.

"Did you bring me to the bed?" Aislinn's voice interrupted Aedan's thoughts, drawing his attention back to her.

"Aye."

"Aedan you're hurt," Aislinn said, seeing the stain of blood on his shirt.

"I have a bullet in my shoulder ye will need to remove when you can."

"I'll get the first aid kit." Aislinn tried to sit up but her injuries prevented movement.

"I'll be fine for now. You need to rest."

Aislinn lay back down.

"I cannae tell you how proud I am of you. You fought well. You're a feisty Irish lass."

"I was so scared. I know he wouldn't have stopped if you hadn't ... I know he would have killed me." Aislinn sighed and looked away for a moment. "Aedan what about the bodies?"

"They are gone. I took care of them. 'Tis a good thing your grandmother's cottage is in such a remote location. No one will be the wiser as to today's occurrence." Aedan pulled the blanket over her, tucking it around her. "Rest. We can talk more later." He kissed her forehead ending further conversation.

Aedan turned hearing Aislinn come into the living room where he stoked the fire and waited while she showered. "I made us a spot by the fire where you'll be warm and ye can rest on me. If you'll let me, I'll brush your hair."

"Aedan, you don't ..."

"Let me, please Aislinn." He knew how important it was she not reject his touch. "I know you are hurting and not just on the outside. Don't shut me out. I can't stand to see ye feeling this way."

He led her to the fire, sat down, then sat her between his outstretched legs. He handed her a mug of steaming tea, and took the brush out of her hand. He ran it through her damp hair.

"I love the way ye smell after ye come out of the bath."

She relaxed from the soothing strokes of the brush. Her eyes began to fall, heavy-lidded. She set down the mug and leaned back against Aedan.

He lowered his face next to her, whispering softly. "Did ye ken red haired women are sacred to the Goddess? 'Tis true. Red is the color of life blood, and women's blood, and the blood of childbirth. You symbolize all that is feminine, Aislinn. You hold a special place among women. That is why you were chosen for me. Ye are my equal, my other half, and today you proved that with your strength and cunning. No one can ever take that away from you. You are a fierce little thing and you make my blood boil. As soon as you're feeling better, I'm going to love ye like never before. I will banish all thoughts of today from your mind." He placed a kiss on her temple.

His strong arms came around her, cradling her against him. She snuggled in tighter, leaning her head on his shoulder.

"I felt you today, Aedan. Inside me. Just briefly, but I knew the feelings were yours, not mine."

"Ye did?" He turned her to look at him a bit puzzled.

"I felt your anger. At first I didn't know what the sensation was, the feeling was so strong and sudden, and it took my breath away. By the time I realized what was happening, it was already subsiding, but I was comforted, in a strange way. It made sense for me to feel you. I felt empty when you vanished, sad, as if I were missing something." She snuggled against him once again, closing her eyes.

"'Tis strange you felt me now, and before Beltane. 'Tis the connection I spoke of. 'Tis the way I feel you inside me. 'Tis how I know you."

"Is the connection there all the time?"

"Aye. Since I saw you in the gift shop."

"Is that why I felt faint?"

"Aye. You felt the sudden jolt of your connection to me."

"Is this how you felt connected to me in the past?

"Aye. And how empty I was when ye were gone."

Aislinn reached up and stroked his rugged face. "Do my feelings ever frighten you?"

"Aye, like earlier. I could feel how scared ye were. That's how I ken something was wrong."

She gently brushed aside a strand of his hair. "How do you live with it?"

"Aislinn, it gets easier, I promise." He kissed her again. "Rest now, my feisty princess, and heal. Beltane fast approaches. I willnae let anyone stop us, this time."

Aislinn turned her face into Aedan's chest. The moment before she slipped into slumber Aedan could feel his place within her heart and he breathed the sigh of a man who had waited a hundred lifetimes to once again know that feeling.

Chapter Twenty-Seven

AISLINN ROLLED HERSELF up in the blanket, not wanting to wake. She reached for Aedan, but patted empty space. She sat up, startled. Her muscles screamed in protest. God, she hurt everywhere.

"Aedan?"

"I'm here, in the bedroom getting dressed."

Aislinn wrapped the blanket around her and stepped into the bedroom. Aedan busily packed his bag. Naked and still dripping from his shower, he gathered his clothes.

Aislinn curled up on the bed and snuggled back into the pillow to watch him. He smiled at her obviously loving the hungry look she gave him.

"God, you're beautiful, Aedan," Aislinn purred, eying his tight firm body from head to toe, pausing a second to linger on his rear; the same rear she remembered thinking was perfect when she first saw him at the museum. She smiled at the memory.

He chuckled quietly and paused in his dressing to stand full and proud in his regal stature.

"'Tis nice ye find me so pleasing, Aislinn."

Aislinn smiled. "I thought you knew how I felt."

"Sometimes 'tis nice to hear the words from your lips," he coaxed her.

"I find you extremely pleasing. I could watch you all day."

"Ah, if we had all day. I'd like nothing more than for ye to show me how pleasing you find me."

Aislinn smiled. "How is your shoulder?"

"Hardly a mark. You did well." Aedan retrieved several shirts and stuffed them into one of the bags. "We must be on our way. Please rise and ready yourself to leave."

Aislinn nodded, understanding the urgency of his request.

When Aislinn joined Aedan in the living area, she could see him pacing nervously, all humor gone from his expression. He was frighteningly grim.

"Are you done with your things? Can I put them in the car?"

"What's wrong?"

"We must leave before others are sent."

Aislinn hurriedly threw the last few things into her backpack. She grabbed her coat and boots, and met Aedan in the driveway. She gave one last longing glance at the cottage.

"We can come back here for a while, after 'tis all over." He came up alongside her. "I ken ye are feeling a bit hesitant right now. I will nae lie and tell you it will be easy, but I will protect you. We have to go. It's no longer safe here."

Aedan held open the door for her. This tiny cottage already held so many memories for them. "Thanks, Gram," she whispered as the car pulled away.

After traveling on the road for a while, Aislinn noticed Aedan's shoulders relax. He hadn't spoken at all.

"Aedan, where are we going?"

"To Ireland, via Canada. Toronto to be precise."

"What? How? I don't have a passport with me."

Aedan reached into his jacket and pulled out two passports, one of which was hers.

"Where did you get this?"

"From your house in the rubble after the break-in."

"You took it? You knew I'd go with you?"

"I hoped."

"Do you sense any danger right now?"

"Nae right now. I'm nae sure they ken where we are headed. They would expect us to depart from Chicago or Detroit. I donnae think they would expect us to take the long way through Canada. They ken we will end up in Ireland for Beltane. Brennis knows where the grove is. He will track our movements. There is a place, a cave actually, that is close to the grove and is well hidden. We will hide there."

"A cave?" Aislinn's voice expressed her doubts.

"Aislinn, what's left of the grove is out in the middle of an ancient forest, in what is now a large county park. The way to access the site is by foot, and it's a long hike. No one today knows what the area used to be, though throughout history, stories of those woods being sacred have been handed down. Sometime ago someone had the foresight to preserve the area as a park.

"The only way to hide from Brennis is in the cave. He willnae be able to find it. It's been there for centuries, but is very secret. I know a cave isn't the most comfortable accommodation, but it will have what we need. I have stored a few necessities over the years. It's only for a couple days, until Beltane and then 'twill be all over."

Aislinn nodded, a bit bewildered. "Are you sure the supplies will still be there? Someone could have found..."

"Aye. The supplies will still be there. The entrance is hidden."

By magic, she thought. "You've had this planned?"

"I've had a long time to prepare, and many centuries to keep it stocked."

Aislinn didn't say anything. She believed he knew exactly what he was doing.

"We will enter Canada and head to Sudbury today. That will be a good place to rest."

"I feel like a fugitive," Aislinn remarked.

"Aye."

Canada, Present Day

Late in the evening, Aedan and Aislinn arrived at their destination. What normally would have been a beautiful trip through the Georgian Bay area became a hurried escape. She was extremely uncomfortable; her already sore muscles were stiff from the long car ride. She was grateful when Aedan finally pulled into a hotel and rented them a room.

Aislinn followed Aedan's lead. When he was quiet, she became quiet, When he seemed extra alert, she too became alert. She admired his awareness of everything around them but she felt completely inadequate against a foe she didn't understand.

They put their bags in the hotel room.

"Are you hungry, lass? We could get a bite to eat." He pointed across the street to a small restaurant.

"I'd like something to drink."

"I ken ye are nae feeling your best, but maybe eat a sandwich too?"

Aislinn forced a brave smile.

He took her hand and squeezed it. "I feel your fear, too. It will be okay."

She looked up at him. "I know." Still, she couldn't seem to shake the foreboding feeling taking root deep inside her.

They walked across the street to the restaurant, taking a quiet booth in the back where they would be less conspicuous, but also so Aedan could see the whole restaurant and whoever came and went.

Aislinn absently picked at her sandwich, trying very hard to hide her turmoil from Aedan. But how could she not be worried about what would happen once they reached Ireland? She knew their journey also concerned him, even though he would not voice this to her. She could see his worry in the lines on his brow and the rigidness of his body.

"Can ye nae eat just a wee bit?"

Aislinn put aside her thoughts and looked from Aedan to her plate before taking a bite of her sandwich. She envied Aedan's ability to stay calm and focused and not to let his anxiety get in the way of his base necessities. He'd finished a huge plate of food and a large glass of beer, and looked mildly satisfied.

"I envy how you live in the moment," Aislinn remarked, taking another bite of her food.

"You learn, when you've been around as long as I have, the simple things are the most important. Family, friends, food, drink, shelter"- he winked at her- "a good woman. Everything else comes and goes."

"Are you going to miss being immortal?"

"Nae. I only ever wanted a normal life, a family, a chance to grow old and have grandchildren. I donnae want to live forever. 'Tis nae natural. 'Tis the curse I accepted to find you. I'm tired of watching the world change, Aislinn. I long for simplicity again, like we found at your grandmother's cottage. We could make a home there, one day. You could do your art. I could build you a studio and you could teach classes. Would ye like that?"

"Very much."

"Would you have my children, then?"

Aislinn looked at him and her heart swelled with love. She nodded to him shyly, loving his satisfied look. She realized she'd like nothing more than to make a home and family with Aedan, but her nagging feeling made her joy short-lived. She dared not voice the ominous thoughts, though. She was afraid to plan a future with Aedan.

He smiled at her. "We'll be needing a bigger bathtub, though. I'll be wanting to join ye once in a while."

Aislinn smiled. She never stopped marveling at how much he wanted her. Sharing a bath did sound tempting. "That would be nice."

"Maybe even a hot tub." He raised his eyebrows in a smirk.

"You are truly evil," Aislinn laughed. "But that would be wonderful."

"Och, you've never been taken in the water, have you? Oh, such pleasure you have yet to enjoy."

"Okay, enough, enough. You're embarrassing me."

Aedan laughed. "I havenae begun." He reached across the table and squeezed her hand. "Aislinn, you're a good woman. I sure do love you, lass."

She touched the hand holding hers. "And you're a good man, Aedan. The man of my dreams, literally. How many women can say that?"

"Probably nae many."

"Then I am lucky."

"'Tis a beautiful clear night. Would you care to take a walk. I think 'twould be safe enough for a wee bit."

"I would like that."

Aedan paid for their dinner and they gathered up their coats and left the restaurant. Aedan, ever vigilant, constantly scanned for anything unusual while they walked. He tried very hard to dispel her fears and kept a positive façade around her, but Aislinn, already becoming attuned to him, sensed his unsettled feelings. He slipped his arm around her, pulling her close as they walked.

"I will always keep you safe," he said again.

She looked up at him and smiled, hoping he knew she believed him with all of her heart. They walked for several hours, making small talk and enjoying the relative anonymity of the city.

Aedan led Aislinn to a bridge overlooking a small river. They were surprisingly alone in the dark shadow of the bridge and he paused to rest against the rail.

"Are you cold?" He turned up her collar for her.

"No. I'm fine."

"Are you sure ye donnae need me to warm you up?"

Aislinn smiled, "I'm okay, but *um*, you can kiss me."

"I donnae ken. 'Tis a lot you ask of me."

"Okay, then..." Aislinn began stepping away, but found herself swiftly wrapped in Aedan's arms, his mouth coming down on hers. She loved the way his kiss started so innocently, sweet and simple, but quickly turned hungry and devouring. A very sexual man, Aedan wasn't the least bit timid about experiencing passion to the fullest. Mindful of her lip and bruises, he kissed her fully, to near breathlessness.

Her hands slid down to his backside and pulled him against her. How she loved the way he felt against her, solid and safe, and she knew by the growl escaping his lips, he loved it, too. She never knew it possible to be so loved, so cared for, so worshipped, so complete, until she'd met Aedan. Now, she couldn't imagine her life without him and the security he instilled in her. And yet, a dark cloud hung over her head and invaded her senses.

"What is it?? Aedan asked.

"I don't know For a moment.." She looked up into his concerned face. "I don't know if I could ever live without you. I'm finding I need you so much."

"Aye. 'Tis the way ye make me feel, too, lass. 'Tis the connection growing."

"Aedan, I'm so afraid of what's going to happen in Ireland." She circled her arms around him.

"Aye, lass, I worry, too."

Aislinn laid her head against Aedan's chest. "I love you."

"Ah, lass, 'tis so good to hear those words after twelve hundred years. I will never tire of them." He kissed the top of her head. "Come on. Let's go back. You can show me just how much ye love me."

Aislinn rolled over, aware even in slumber, Aedan was not lying beside her. She woke instantly and opened her eyes, letting them get used to the dark. She could see Aedan's silhouette at the window; he sat peering through the parted curtains.

"Is everything alright?"

"Aye."

"Come back to bed, then." Aislinn slipped from between the covers and approached Aedan where he sat on the back of a stuffed chair, staring out over the city.

"In a while."

"Aedan, what's wrong?"

"Nothing. I was just thinking."

Aislinn moved into his arms, in a squatting position on the chair, and snuggled against his bare chest. She pulled her t-shirt over her bare legs. She reached up and stroked his face and chin, rough from a day's growth. He appeared quite rugged with the beard shadow and the light of the city shining on him.

"I don't think I've ever seen you so pensive."

"I was thinking about ye."

"Me?"

"Aye. How much I have asked of you. How much you have gone through." He touched the bruise on her forehead. "I wonder how fair I've been putting you through all this. If I hadnae come to your school, you would be in your bed right now resting for another busy day with your students, oblivious to me and all this." He motioned outside.

"And I would still be lonely, only dreaming of my handsome warrior but never knowing him." She touched the tattoos encircling his arms. "I'd never really know his touch or his kiss, and you would have lived forever for nothing. You didn't know all this would happen."

"But I did. I was warned someone would try to stop us. Ye deserve so much more than to be on the run, hiding in hotels. Ye deserve more than a hurried ceremony to unite us. Don't ye wish for a wedding with all the trimmings?"

"Aedan, I think all girls dream of a knight coming to sweep them off their feet and a big white wedding, but it's not the reality. It's not important. What's important is our being together, not the ceremony. I've got my knight." She kissed his chest. "And that's all I need."

"Aislinn ye have been strong and brave, even when your life was in danger. You trusted me and accepted all I asked ye to believe, where I hailed from, why I was here, the magic, our bond and union, the ceremony... A lesser woman wouldnae have so willingly accepted all of that. And you ask for nothing. You should have so much more. When this is all over I pledge to ye we will have the kind of ceremony you've dreamed of, with all the trimmings."

"Aedan, the kind of ceremony I've dreamed of takes place in a sacred grove with drums and fire and this guy full of tattoos."

"Ye ken what I mean." His smile was troubled. "A ceremony that is proper for this century."

"Are you asking me to marry you?"

"Was nae the way I intended, but yes I am."

"Aedan, I don't care about all that. I just want to be with you."

He tightened his arms around her,

"Come back to bed with me. I need you."

"Aye." He turned her face and kissed her. "I'm going to love ye good and full till you're senseless."

"Oh, promises, promises, warrior," she teased, right before he scooped her up and carried her to the bed. She squealed from his quick actions.

"You will be begging for mercy before I'm through with you." Aedan laid her down and pulled off her shirt in one fluid movement. He raised her arms over her head, pinning them down with his large hand. He positioned himself to her, gaining total access to her body, not allowing her to move.

"Now, I will show you what a warrior can do."

Aislinn woke to the sunlight pushing its way through the parted curtains. Aedan slept beside her. She loved the way he looked in the morning after a night of intense lovemaking, all rugged and untamed, with his hair loose and in disarray. She could easily picture him back in his day, riding through the forest on horseback, or sitting in a great hall with other clansmen, drinking or talking of battle.

She loved the marks on his body, signifying the mystery and knowledge he was privy to. God, she loved his body, strong and powerful and commanding. She loved the way he could make her squirm and writhe and beg him to take her. She loved the way he claimed her, possessed her, and wasn't the least bit shy about proclaiming she was his or taking what was his.

Aislinn felt empowered by this, and she loved all of it. She loved Aedan's good heart. She loved his honesty, and the way he always spoke his heart. He cared deeply for what was closest to him, and she knew without a doubt he would protect her with his life. This is also what she was most afraid of.

Aedan's kind of fairness and nobility had long been forgotten in her world, and he was completely comfortable with who he was, even in today's world. How did she deserve such a man. Was she worthy of loving such a person?

"Oh yes, Aislinn," she heard him whisper. "Ye are."

"You're awake."

"I have been. You cannae take your eyes away from me."

Aislinn smiled.

"I ken ye love me, lass. I can feel your heart. I am your man, always, and ye can look at me all ye want. I love seeing such hunger in your eyes. I love that I know how to satisfy you and love knowing how you love being loved. Och, I am filled with such manly pride to know I'm the one you open to and share your most intimate moments with. I'm near bursting," Aedan paused, kissing her. "And oftentimes humbled."

"Do you think the connection will always be this way?"

"Aye. It cannot be any other way. 'Tis our fate, a gift the Lady gave to us long ago."

"I wish I could thank her."

Aedan smiled. "I think she knows, and you will honor her on Beltane."

Aislinn placed a kiss on Aedan's brow before slipping from the bed and going to the bathroom. She started a shower and stepped under the warm spray. As she turned to close the shower door, Aedan stepped in behind her.

"Ye think after all those love words you can just leave our bed?"

"I just wanted to clean up."

Aedan reached behind her and picked up a bar of soap. "I think I can take care of that."

He stood behind her and turned her to face the spray of water. He lathered up his hands, sliding them over her shoulders and neck, smoothing the soap over her skin. He raised her arms over her head and ran the bar of soap along the underside of them, down her sides, just skimming her breasts with his fingers.

When he was done, he lifted her arms around his neck, before sliding his hands over her breasts, using the soap to tease her nipples into tight peaks. He lathered his hands again, reaching around her to cup her breasts again, squeezing and stroking them until they were full and aching. She arched into his hands closing her eyes and leaning her head back against his chest.

"Ye like that."

"*Hmm.*" She wiggled against him, feeling his arousal against her backside.

"Hang onto my neck. I can feel you going all weak-kneed. I'm nae done washing you yet."

"Oh God."

Aedan soaped his hands over again and slid them over her midriff and back, stroking and sliding over her slippery skin. He flattened his palm against her belly and tugged her against his hardness jutting between their bodies, stiff and probing. Aislinn couldn't think of anything except her need to have him inside her. A small moan escaped her lips.

"Nae yet," he teased, rubbing the soap between her legs then followed with his fingers, stroking her flesh, sliding between her thighs. She pushed against his hand, straining for the completion he was determined to prolong. He removed his hand despite her whimper of protest.

Aedan ran the soap down the length of one leg, then back up again, returning his hand to the heated juncture between her thighs. He stroked her again before removing his hand. She moaned her disappointment. He smiled at her displeasure. He slid the soap down her other leg, prolonging the journey upward. The anticipation of Aedan's fingers reaching their destination caused Aislinn to squirm against him.

"You are truly evil," she groaned when he purposely avoided touching her. His only reply was a throaty chuckle.

"You're enjoying this aren't you?"

"Very much."

She released her arms from around his neck, turning to face him, pressing her body against his while seeking his lips with hers.

"Two can play this game," she whispered against his mouth, pushing the damp hair away from her face. Her hands roamed and touched his wet warm flesh, caressing and exciting him. Her arms encircled his waist, hands sliding downward where she squeezed the firm muscles of his rear and pulled him toward her. She kissed and licked his chest, lightly nipping his nipples, trailing her tongue over each mark adorning his body. His abdominal muscles tightened as her kisses traveled lower, her tongue continuing to trace the spiral design that ended just below his navel. Like him, she kissed and touched every place except the one place she knew he wanted her to be.

"I donnae like this game very much," he protested, bringing her face back to precisely where he wanted it. He let out a loud growl as she took him in her mouth then, teasing and sucking until he was nearly bucking beneath her.

Aislinn moved back and looked at Aedan. His eyes were filled with such raw hunger, flames rose and danced within them. Even the water spilling over them could not quell the heat building between them.

Aedan pulled her up and pressed her back against the cool tile wall, pinning her with his hard demanding body.

"Enough games." He crushed his lips against hers, hotly plunging his tongue into her with long suggestive strokes. He ground his hips against her with the same intensity he plundered her mouth. He shoved eagerly at her thighs, encouraging her to shift to accommodate him.

"I will make you come so hard you will forget everything except me. Aislinn, I will brand you with my very soul. Christ if anything happens on Beltane, I will make you remember me and this fire raging between us. I will burn my memory into your very depths."

His words were honest and desperate. "The next few hours I will take all I can from you. I will have you over and over, loving you in every way imaginable until you drop from sheer exhaustion. I will make sure ye will ken me always, nae matter what comes. I will always be a part of you."

He blazed fiery kisses down her neck and shoulders as her chest heaved from panting. His mouth captured her breast, scorching her where he sucked and nipped her. His other hand thumbed and teased her other breast, relinquishing the flesh to his hungry mouth. He greedily sucked her nipples until they were rock hard and straining against his tongue. He lapped the water trickling between her breasts, licking his way back up her neck to her mouth where he continued to ravish her.

His hands skimmed over her sleek, wet skin, eliciting a need curling so deep inside her it was almost painful.

"Aedan, please," she begged.

He answered her plea by sliding his fingers deep between her thighs, causing her to gasp at the intimate caress. He slowly withdrew, then easily pushed in again. She shuddered helplessly.

Aedan dropped to his knees, bracing her with his free arm, knowing he was all that held her up. His tongue licked her with tantalizing strokes as sweet moans of surrender escaped Aislinn.

He rose to his full height, lifting her leg up around his hip. He braced her against the wall and with one deep thrust, joined their bodies together. He remained motionless, as she squirmed against him and begged him to move. He lifted her other leg so she rode his waist, allowing him the sweet pleasure of burying himself within her. He plunged and ground against her, making her gasp with each thrust.

His wet hair cascaded around his face, obscuring him from her as she felt the tightening begin deep within her belly. She frantically pushed the strands aside, wanting to look at him as he moved inside her.

Her climax came sudden and powerful, and seemingly never-ending. She clutched at Aedan as she trembled and quaked and constricted around him, compelling him to quicken his thrusts. He drove feverishly into her, erupting with a roar, thrusting the very essence of heat and fire into her.

Composure was long in coming. Aedan lay his forehead on Aislinn's shoulder. She fell limp against him, utterly spent. The water continued to beat steadily on their heaving bodies as Aedan continued to stir within her.

Eventually, he gently slid her legs from around him and helped her to stand. He held onto her while she regained her footing. Once able to stand, he ran the soap over her body one last time then carried her from the shower to the bed.

"I'm going to bed you well, Aislinn. This whole day you will know nothing but me making love to you."

"But ... "

He placed his fingers on her lips. "*Shh*. I'm meaning to have you lass, a hundred times over. I'm hard and aching for ye even now, and I want to hear ye screaming my name until ye can scream no more. Aislinn, love me, touch me, know me to the fullest..."

Because it might be all we have, hung in the silence between them.

"I have nae burned for anyone like this, Aislinn. You consume me. I feel such a need to possess ye, as I did that night."

"Then take me," she whispered.

Aedan spun her around in his arms, placed his hand on her neck and bent her over the bed. He spread her legs with his own and swiftly buried himself deep within her. He moaned his pleasure at being joined with her and immediately began a hurried rhythm.

Her orgasm climbed from the very depths of her, sudden and deep. He groaned with male satisfaction as he too, found his release.

"Heavens, lass, ye take all I give you." His voice cracked with emotion as he gathered her in his arms and moved to lay with her on the bed. Several moments of silence passed before Aedan kissed her forehead lightly. He trailed his fingertips lovingly over Aislinn's arm.

"So many times, I watched men go to their woman before a battle, not just for obvious reasons, but for more than that, I think." He paused a moment to gently run his fingers down the side of

Aislinn's face. "I think they sought affirmation someone cared for them, and would miss them and mourn them if they didnae return."

Aislinn leaned up on her elbows and looked down at Aedan. He toyed with her hair, brushing the locks away from her face.

"I watched them, even as they mounted up, how they would steal a kiss or touch right up until the second they rode away. I saw the longing in their eyes, as they looked back over their shoulder one last time before steeling themselves for what they had to do. Some couldnae even look back. Until now, I never really thought about what they must have been feeling. 'Tis the same uncertainty that makes me near desperate in my need of you. A man knows when he has a good woman, and Aislinn ye are a good woman. I love you so much. Och, Christ, lass, I donnae want to leave you."

The sadness in Aedan's voice tore at Aislinn. She leaned up and kissed him. "I never knew I could love someone so much, either. You've become a part of me."

Aedan tightened his hold around her.

"We have to keep believing that all will go well on Beltane."

"Aye we do."

Chapter Twenty-Eight

Aedan finished signing his name and slipped the paper back into the envelope. He tucked the envelope into his backpack alongside several other documents. He glanced at Aislinn, sound asleep, sprawled deliciously across the bed. He was ever amazed how well she matched his stamina and insatiable sexual appetite.

His heart constricted with fear of the unspeakable possibility they might be prevented from completing the ceremony. The possibility tore at his insides and fueled his fierce, essential nature to protect her. He scrawled the final lines of the institute's address on a larger yellow envelope and placed inside it the curriculum work they'd completed. He knew the institute would be interested in what they'd done, and if the worst should happen...well, submitting their work was the least he could do for her.

His throat tightened, making swallowing difficult. He watched the steady rise and fall of her breasts while she slept. Her acceptance was unwavering, once she found him in her heart, once she loved him, she felt the stirrings of their mingled souls and, despite the risks, gracefully and completely took him in.

He sealed the envelope and placed it near his backpack. He then rose and strode over to the bed, looking down upon her sleeping form. He wanted her again, and his body drew taut and firm with anticipation. He knew she would never deny him, as she craved him as much as he craved her.

They were acutely aware their desires fueled each other and they were powerless to deny the fire dancing between them. If truth be told, they reveled in the passion that connected them.

Aedan slid over her, holding himself above her. "Open for me Aislinn," he whispered into her ear, into her dreams. She shifted languidly, yielding to him even in slumber. He nestled himself tenderly between her thighs slipping into her warm heat with a soft moan. He fought a fierce longing to plant a babe deep within her womb, wanting so desperately to leave a part of him with her should he not survive.

He moved against her and felt more than heard, her intake of breath.

"Keep dreaming, Aislinn," he whispered in his intimate seduction. "Just feel me."

She arched against him as he withdrew and entered her in long, slow, strokes, lifting her with his movements.

"*Mmm.* This is quite the way to wake up." Her body erupted helplessly from the delicious pleasure of him moving within her.

Aedan joined her with his own quick climax moments later, then ruthlessly followed their orgasms by a thorough ravishing of her mouth and body by his tongue, eliciting yet another helpless surrender from her.

Aislinn glanced over at the darkening sky through the window. Aedan knew the sense of dread flowing through her. Their time together in their own little world within the hotel room had drawn to an end. He gently stroked her back as she lay sprawled over his chest, their bodies still lovingly joined, claiming every second they could.

"Lass."

"Don't say it, Aedan."

"I wish I didnae have to."

"Then don't"

"I'm sorry. I must." He kissed her forehead. "We have to get to Toronto by morning."

He slid Aislinn off him, pulling her against his side. Her protest didn't go unnoticed. "Have I not bedded ye well, as I promised?"

"You have."

"Hold the memories of these past few hours in your heart, Aislinn." He tightened his hold and kissed her forehead.

As was customary after their love making, Aedan placed his hand on her abdomen in anticipation of saying the magic that would prevent Aislinn from conceiving. This time he hesitated, struggling with indecision. She would easily conceive if he allowed it. Her body was ripe with the need for a babe, he could feel it, even if she could not.

It was selfish of him, he knew, to want her to carry his child when the possibility existed he would not be here to be a part of it. The need was so strong, it took all of his willpower to finally whisper the magical words that would negate the possibility of a child from their union.

As he spoke the words, he couldn't keep the sadness from his voice, nor stop the lump forming in his throat. He looked down at Aislinn. She softly wept.

Chapter Twenty-Nine

AEDAN INSTANTLY SENSED the danger they were in as they approached Pearson International Airport in Toronto. He had purchased the tickets to Dublin ahead of time, and had any papers he needed to complete faxed to the hotel. He wanted to avoid as many lines as possible.

He paid to keep his car in long-term parking for several weeks, and he and Aislinn packed only necessary items in their carry-on backpacks. They would travel with no luggage other than Aedan's sword which would accompany them in its case. Aedan carried the necessary paperwork from the Art Institute declaring its value, antiquity status, the fabricated explanation of research on the sword being done at Trinity College, and made arrangements to meet a broker he had worked with numerous times in the past. If he needed, Aedan could resort to other less conventional methods for convincing customs to allow his sword.

As they moved between cars, preparing to enter the airport, Aedan's whole demeanor once again became vigilant. He didn't speak, except for quick, short comments. He became extremely alert and observant and his movements were minimal and precise.

Aedan placed a hand on or around Aislinn at all times, and his eyes constantly scanned their surroundings. His sense of urgency wasn't lost on Aislinn. He could feel her insides knotting with fear as she carefully followed him.

Skillfully, he snuck them inside the building without being noticed. He could have easily used a protection spell, but if others knew the magic, as he suspected, the power would have been easily detected. Aedan counted on finding them first, not the other way around. He knew they did not want to cause a commotion in the airport and this was his advantage.

Aedan and Aislinn moved toward the counter to claim their tickets. "Act naturally as if you've done this a hundred times. He took hold of Aislinn's elbow as they approached the counter. Aedan presented his sword and papers and requested the broker he'd arranged to meet.

He and Aislinn and the sword were immediately escorted into a waiting room specifically designed for elite circumstances. There they were interrogated, their paperwork scrutinized. In the end, they were detained only a few minutes before they were allowed to pass through to the waiting area.

Aedan's skin bristled. He could feel them close. He knew they would attempt to go after Aislinn, and this made him more cautious. Aislinn was near breaking, Aedan knew, but they made a good show of being a happy, easygoing couple.

"I really need to use the restroom, Aedan."

Aedan looked at her warily.

"Please, I'll only be a second, I promise." She stood on her tiptoes and kissed him reassuringly.

"Aislinn, here, take your ticket." He pulled a pen from his pocket. "No matter what happens, get on the plane. Wait for me in Dublin at this hotel." Aedan swiftly wrote the name of the hotel on her ticket envelope.

"Aedan," she took the ticket, slipping it into the front of her backpack. "I'm just going to the bathroom. I'll be out in a second." She turned and went in.

Aedan paced nervously. Every second seemed an eternity until she finally reappeared.

He looked down at her. "I meant what I said, Aislinn. No matter what happens, get on that plane."

Aislinn sobered at his seriousness. Just as the instructions left his lips, the hair on Aedan's arm stood up. "Get behind me," he shoved her back just as someone whizzed passed them flashing a knife. The man disappeared into the crowd.

"Go! Run for the plane!" He grabbed her arm and shoved her toward their departure gate.

Aedan wasn't fooled for a moment. The first man was a decoy. He instead turned toward the man he knew must be behind them.

"Are you alright?" Aedan asked, finding Aislinn about to board the plane and pulling her aside. Aedan leaned his head toward Aislinn and spoke low.

"I donnae ken if I caught them before they contacted anyone in Ireland. We will get a head start if they didn't make a call."

"Did you kill them?"

"Aislinn, I am a warrior, a fighter, a Druidh. I swore an oath to protect you."

"Did you kill them?"

Her question held the edgy tone of panic. Aedan stared at her, but he didn't lie.

"Aye."

"So, you are leaving a trail of dead bodies for the authorities to find us?"

"Not exactly."

"What does that mean? Magic?"

"Yes. It will appear as if they fought each other."

"Oh God." She turned away, looking for an empty seat in the waiting area.

Aedan sat beside her.

"It's like at the cottage. I know what you are. I've seen you a thousand times in my dream, in the heat of battle, but..."

"But now it's real." Aedan completed her thought.

Aislinn nodded, but was prohibited from continuing the conversation due to the boarding announcement coming over the loud speaker.

"Come on. Let's get on the plane."

Ireland, Present Day

Eight and a half hours later, Aedan and Aislinn were disembarking from the plane in Dublin.

Once again, Aedan cautiously moved them through the airport, but without the sense of urgency he'd felt in Toronto. He hoped it was due to their arrival not being anticipated as they feared.

Aedan rented a car and hurriedly got them on the road. Once they left the city, Aedan chose smaller, less-traveled roads to take them south. Aislinn just stared out the window.

"You have been quiet." Aedan finally broke the silence.

"I'm just thinking how surreal this all is."

"Are you having second thoughts?"

"It's a little late for that, don't you think?"

"They would have killed you."

Aislinn pulled her gaze from the window and looked at Aedan. "You killed those men without thought, without hesitation. Doesn't killing bother you?" she asked.

He didn't tell her how at first he loathed it. He never got used to the sick feeling that plagued him for days after a battle, but years of familiarity hardened him to where he could bear it.

"Aye. It bothers me. Taking a life is always serious. But 'twas necessary."

"But- "Aislinn protested.

"What would you have me do, Aislinn? Would you rather I let them kill you?"

She looked away. "It's all so barbaric. Geez, this is the twenty-first century."

"And people continue to kill one another, Aislinn. Wars, famine, political unrest. What has truly changed?"

Aislinn returned her gaze out her window. "There are a lot of people in my world who go through life untouched by those things you mentioned. That's my reality. So, excuse me if the killings bother me just a little."

Aedan reached over and took her hand in his. "Aislinn I wish I could take away all the heartache, all the pain. I ken your life has been turned upside down, and it bothers me to see what you're going through. Despite the obstacles, ye know we are meant to be together."

He took his eyes off the road momentarily to glance at Aislinn. She met his look briefly before pulling her gaze away. "Och, lass. Donnae ye think I wish Beltane could be over? We are so close now. Donnae give up on me now."

"I'm not giving up. Just trying to process everything."

"That's my Irish princess."

Chapter Thirty

AEDAN TOOK THEM TO the hotel in Dublin that he'd booked and left the car in the parking lot. He packed a small provision of food and water and they made the trek deep into the woods under the cover of night.

Aislinn didn't remember all the details, but they hiked for several hours through thick trees and brush. Aedan moved through the forest as if he had done it hundreds of times. He was familiar with every twist and turn and foothold. Still, his ease didn't lessen her apprehension.

Eventually, they reached the entrance of the cave, and just as Aedan had said, all the supplies were untouched and stacked neatly in preparation for the day he would need them.

"We have food and water," he explained, helping her off with her back pack. "There are blankets in the trunk and a small stream further back into the cave if you'd like to wash. The water will be cold, but I will build a fire."

Aedan fished around in one of the wooden boxes, and a few minutes later Aislinn heard the click of a lighter and saw the flicker of a candle suddenly illuminate the dark.

Aedan showed her the way to the stream. Aislinn clung to him, following behind, more than a little spooked by the eerie shadows the candle cast on the wall.

"Have you always known about this place?"

"Aye. I hid her many years ago. I then realized this would be a place I could come and go throughout the years, when I needed to hide or lay low for a while until I could reappear. I keep the entrance hidden with magic."

Aedan stopped at the edge of a small stream flowing between cracks in the rocks. He set the candle down and looked at Aislinn. He seemed to have more to say, but instead pulled his eyes away. "I will go and start a fire."

She rejoined him a while later, where he had small fire going and their beds made up.

Aislinn wrapped herself inside the warmth of a blanket, facing the fire hoping to alleviate the chill she felt. Aedan lay down behind her.

"You're shivering."

"I'm cold."

"Come here." Aedan pulled her closer and leaned over her, pulling her against him and tucking his blanket round them both. He kissed her cheek. "Daylight is still several hours away. Why don't you try to get some sleep."

Aislinn yawned. "I know you were just trying to protect me," she said, referring to him killing the men at the airport. "I know why you did it, and although I don't necessarily like it, I accept it."

"Those men were warriors in their own way. They died the way they knew," Aedan explained.

Aislinn nodded and snuggled closer into him.

"Get some sleep. There is something I'd like to talk to ye about tomorrow."

Aislinn yawned again. "Is it important? We can talk now..."

"It can wait."

Any answer Aislinn would have given was lost as she drifted off to sleep.

United States, Twenty-Three Years Ago

Aislinn skipped through the tall grass alongside her grandmother as a butterfly fluttered just out of reach. They often took walks through the fields surrounding the cottage when she would visit, especially if it were too chilly to go down to the beach. Today the sun was shining brightly, promising a warm day. Her small hand felt good encased within her grandmother's.

"Aislinn," her grandmother paused and looked down at her. "I'd like to teach you something.

"Yes, Grams?"

"It is something that you may one day need to know."

"I'm good at remembering."

Her grandmother smiled down at her. "Of course, you are, that is why I'm going to teach you this little poem."

"Ok."

"I call on the wind for my breath, and the water to quell my thirst. I join my body with the earth and share my passion with fire."

Aislinn looked at her grandmother. "That's it?"

Her grandmother smiled. "Yes. Now repeat it after me."

Aislinn did as requested and repeated it over and over, until her grandmother was satisfied she would retain the passage.

"What is this for?" Aislinn asked her grandmother.

"It's a magical verse for something very special. You will know if and when you are to use it."

"I call on the wind for my breath, and the water to quell my thirst. I join my body with the earth and share my passion with fire ..."

Ireland, Present Day

Aislinn's eyes shot open and she abruptly sat up. *Share my passion with fire...Aedan...One who is fire.*

"Aislinn?" Aedan came awake as sudden as she. "Are ye alright?"

"I remember." She looked over at Aedan. "I recalled the little saying my grandmother wanted me to memorize."

"Ye dreamed it?"

"Yes. I was walking with her one day and she made me repeat it over and over. I promised her I would remember it, but of course, I completely forgot."

"Not completely if it has come to you. What is it?"

"I call on the wind for my breath, and the water to quell my thirst. I join my body with the earth and share my passion with fire." Aislinn paused, looking at Aedan. "*You* are the fire."

Aedan pulled her into his arms and lay back, snuggling with Aislinn.

"It is a magical invocation to the four elements," Aedan explained. "Your grandmother knew there was something special in your future, and she wanted to prepare you for magical things. She was a magical woman, Aislinn, and she believed you would be as well. She wanted you to be aware of how the elements would guide you."

Aislinn thought for a moment before speaking. "I remember when I saw you on the beach in the water, how the wind swirled around me and how it seemed to slap my cheek. I think perhaps the waves helped me push you to the shore, and the rocks and sand were rough enough to cause you to cough and breathe. Do you think I caused that just by pleading for help when I was trying to get you out of the water?"

Aedan smiled. "I have no doubt. I also have no doubt we are to invoke the elements on Beltane eve, as the Lady did just before you joined me in the stones."

"I am her ancestor after all."

"Aye, ye are."

"I wonder how many of my ancestors were born with a birthmark. I wonder how many females the blanket and amulet were given to. Were they given any more information than I was? If Gram knew these things, why didn't she just come out and tell me?"

"Did your mother know?"

"She never spoke of any of this. She always said my grandmother was different, a little off. I don't think she bought into any of it."

"Then your grandmother told ye just enough to help you find out for yourself if the events unfolded. "'Twould be a bit awkward if throughout history every female thought they were the one to find the warrior. They would live for nothing except that. In the process, they would forget to live. You have a very good life and career. You told me numerous times how content you were. If ye had known what the future held for you, you would be simply sitting around waiting for me. Ye wouldn't be the person you are, have the experiences you had, or touch the lives you've touched."

"So, I was told just enough that if things began falling into place, I would know what to do."

"Your grandmother was wise."

"I'm surprised the little saying came back to me. It was a long time ago. I was very young when she taught them to me."

"And you will teach the poem to our daughter one day."

Aislinn smiled, warmed by his thought of their future together.

"Aedan, why is everything with the Goddess so sexual? I mean, why do we need to make love on Beltane?"

"What is more instinctive in human nature than sexual desire? What is more primitive? More spiritual? When are we at our most vulnerable or accepting? You must remember, Aislinn, people thought of sex a bit differently back then. Sex and procreation were as much a part of life as was death. Mating is part of being human. 'Tis natural. 'Tis a renewal of life. To use sex in a ritual is as natural as the wind or rain or the sun or anything else of the earth. Beltane is the time to be without shame before the Goddess. A time to give oneself and embrace the passion of life, of spring, of renewal. There is nothing sinful about being human. 'Tis a time to celebrate life."

"Was your Aislinn beautiful?"

"Aye. Ye look just like her."

"How did you know you'd love me?"

"Ye are the same as Aislinn in all ways. I cannot explain because I really hadnae spent time with her...er...you until that night, but I felt ye inside me my whole life. My connection to ye was strong from the time I was a young man. There were ways in which I ken ye, more than things like your favorite food or favorite color. It was deeper things. I knew your heart. I knew what made ye happy or sad. I knew how strong ye were and how you loved. The smaller things like food or colors are what I am learning about you now."

"Will I feel you inside me?"

"Aye. I'm there. My feelings will grow stronger. Remember at the cabin when you felt me?"

Aislinn nodded, recalling the intense emotion she knew was Aedan. "What if you had discovered you didn't like me?"

"There was no way that could happen."

"Aedan, you are thinking of a girl twelve hundred years in the past. The world was vastly different then."

"Are ye doubting my love for ye now?"

"I don't want you to be disappointed about being stuck with me."

"I'm not disappointed. Just the opposite. I'm ever intrigued by you."

"No regrets?"

"None."

"I'm pretty lucky, too."

"How so?"

"You are quite the catch. I see the way other girls look at you and then me. You're extremely good looking, you know."

Aedan laughed. "Let them look. I only have eyes for you. I'm glad you find my appearance pleasant."

"Aedan, you are wonderful, not just because of your looks, but because of who you are. You're genuine and honest, and say what you feel. I even like the whole warrior thing."

"I'm glad I please you, Aislinn."

Aislinn knew his sentiment was heart-felt. She snuggled into him closer, closing her eyes. She felt so safe in his embrace. She wished she could remain like this forever.

Aislinn woke later in the morning and found herself alone on the cave floor, covered with the blanket. She sat up, spying Aedan a few feet away. He busily yanked off his clothes, changing into an old tattered kilt he'd stored in the cave.

Kilts, she knew, were worn much later in history, but the by looks of it, Aislinn suspected he'd adopted the garment sometime during his long life as it looked to have seen many fights. Aedan wore his hair loose and hanging free. He belted his waist with a leather band he slipped his sword into. Leather pads protected his forearms and leather boots adorned his feet. He looked untamed and wild, and Aislinn was sure this is what he must have looked like hundreds of years ago as he readied for battle.

He bent and retrieved two knives from a pack and tucked one into his boot and the other into his belt.

"Aedan?"

"He's out there. I can feel him moving through the forest."

"No." Aislinn sat up, suddenly very frightened. "Don't go."

"I have to, Aislinn. If we are to have Beltane without threats."

"Aedan, no."

"I must." Aedan lifted her hand and placed within her palm the two halves of the amulets which he'd removed from around his neck.

"Guard these."

"What if…"

"I'm coming back to ye lass. Donnae ye worry. I didn't wait all this time to die now. "He bent and kissed her forehead. "Please stay in the cave where you will be safe." He instructed as he rose and exited full of determination and confidence.

Aislinn busied herself with folding Aedan's clothes and tidying up the blankets and makeshift sleeping area. She stoked the fire, making the air surprisingly warm. She ate a little food, drank a little water, and washed up in the stream.

When she ran out of things to keep her busy, she sat down near the fire. She found herself staring into the dancing flames. Did she really possess the bit of magic her grandmother thought she did? She didn't feel very magical at the moment. Actually, she felt scared and fearful of what might happen to Aedan. Fighting her uncertainty, Aislinn looked deep into the flames and spoke the first words that came to mind.

"If Aedan is fire as I suspect, then please guide and watch over him today." Even to her, her plea sounded a bit unconventional and silly, however there was honest sentiment behind her request. And as if in response, the flames flickered and momentarily became brighter. In her heart, she chose to believe the fire actually acknowledged what she asked.

Brennis slinked cautiously through the brush, circling the general vicinity of the ancient stones that were once the sacred altar. The dense woods were thick with the scent of damp earth and the eerie stillness only a forest could provide. The towering trees cast long gnarled shadows that lent to the ancientness of this place reminding Brennis of the past with every step he took. Every second he stalked this glen was another second his anger and resentment toward Aedan festered and grew.

He knew Aedan was close. With just over two days until Beltane, there was no way Aedan wasn't here. He also knew his brother was using magic to keep he and the woman hidden. His lips drew into a tight snarl. His brother could use whatever means he could conjure to stay hidden and it wouldn't matter. He would find him. Time hadn't diminished the few magical tricks he knew.

Brennis whispered words in a long-forgotten language, scanning the brush. "I ken ye are there, Aididh. Come out and face me like a mon."

Aedan stepped from the shadow of a copse of trees like a god emerging from a forgotten land. "Brother." He simply stated, his stare never wavering from Brennis.

"Ah, so ye decided to show yourself at last."

"So, destiny has brought us together once again." Aedan said, emotionless.

"'Twould seem," Brennis answered, locking his eyes in a deadly unrelenting gaze.

"What is this folly, Brennis. Why have ye followed me through time?"

"Revenge."

"Does it really matter at this point, Brennis? History doesnae ken or care of our deeds."

"I want retribution for everything ye took from me."

"It is long over, Brennis."

"Ye were handed everything that was mine. Ye stole my land and kingdom, had the support of the chiefs, the magic of the old ones, all because of your backstabbing, lying cousin across the sea. Now 'tis my turn to covet the power from you. Now 'tis my time to become greater than ye ever were. With the stones I will live on, and you will become nothing."

"You will never have the amulet."

"Donnae be so sure of that. I will kill you and your last image as you turn to dust will be me fucking your woman. Aye, I will take her from you, too."

"She is nae for you. She never was."

Brennis drew in a sharp breath and answered Aedan's reply with an evil chuckle. "Ye have spent your whole life harboring a false sense of security about your future with your woman." Brennis glared at

Aedan. "I want the stones." He simply stated, pausing before adding, "and the woman," he sneered.

"And ye will have neither." Aedan answered.

Brennis raised his sword. Aedan countered, repeating the gesture. Two warriors stood facing each other, conflict inevitable.

"We will see, Aididh. Ye ken I am the better fighter."

"Aye, but I've had years to practice," Aedan mocked.

Brennis bristled at this, not admitting the potential disadvantage this posed.

Brennis initiated the first move, lunging at Aedan with sword swinging at him. Aedan easily deflected Brennis' blade, moving to circle him like a predator stalking his prey. Aedan's tactic of moving around his brother kept Brennis constantly shifting to avoid his brother's blade and gave Aedan the opportunity to strike.

Aedan lunged at his brother. Brennis quickly parried his attack and countered with a powerful blow that reverberated the ground as his sword struck Aedan's. Aedan easily deflected the blade, countering with his own powerful swing.

Their heavy footfalls and the clashing of metal upon metal echoed through the forest, silencing even the birds in the trees. Brennis charged forward with a powerful thrust, catching Aedan's upper arm, slicing his flesh with the sharpened blade.

Aedan ignored the blood spurting from his arm and returned Brennis' attack with one of his own, giving no quarter with blow after blow until Brennis was forced to step back.

Again, Brennis came at Aedan, maneuvering around him to catch him from behind, however Aedan was quick to spin, keeping him one step ahead of his brother and allowing him to pierce the flesh of Brennis' abdomen.

Brennis drew in a breath, clutching his side as his shirt stained with the blood seeping from the wound. He stared at Aedan with a fiery gaze. The injury only enraged Brennis more. Despite the pain, he mustered his strength and came at Aedan, sword slicing through the air as blow after blow was given and deflected by Aedan.

Each parry and strike Brennis made was a reminder of the past, a time when the conflict had its birth, and the bitterness and hatred Brennis harbored toward Aedan became as deep-rooted as the very trees they stood amongst. Every blow was a culmination of a lifetime of resentment and jealousy, a reflection of a fractured relationship that had been forged in their youth. Hatred had consumed him to the point that only killing Aedan would give him the justice he longed for. All these years had led to this single moment when he would finally have what he was due.

Once again they lunged at each other, their swords clashing with violence and determination. The sound of metal against metal carried away on the wind. Swords clashed and recoiled, over and over again.

As the fight continued, both Brennis and Aedan were bruised and bleeding and fatigue began to take its toll. Both Aedan and Brennis were breathing heavily, ignoring the multitude of wounds gracing their flesh. In this fight, they were equally matched and Brennis knew the only way he would win against Aedan was by cunning instead of strength.

Brennis seethed with hatred. "I cannae wait to taste your woman," he called out in an attempt to unman Aedan with his threat, but Aedan remained steadfast in his strength and ability and offered no response to Brennis' statement. The battle continued, a brutal dance of death and fury.

Suddenly without warning, voices were heard approaching. Nearby a group of hikers drew close, carrying their backpacks and gear, heading directly for Brennis and Aedan.

Brennis and Aedan, both realizing they were no longer alone, halted their duel and slipped into the shadows of the trees. Silence enveloped the grove, except for the excited voices of the hikers nearly upon them.

Brennis seethed with unspent fury. "This is nae over," he hissed between gritted teeth, glaring at Aedan, as he stepped back further into the trees, reluctantly disappearing into the forest.

It was evening before Aislinn heard the rustling at the cave entrance and the tell-tale sign that Aedan had returned. She spied him tearing away the kilt he'd worn. "Aedan?"

"Aye, 'tis me."

As she approached, she noticed he looked rather disheveled and dirty, covered in sweat and grime and blood.

"I've been so worried." She spied the gash on his arm as well as the numerous other smaller cuts. "You're hurt."

"Nae too bad. You can fuss over me after I wash." His reply was brisk and he spoke no more, leaving to make his way further into the cave were the stream ran.

During his absence, Aislinn rummaged through the trunk of supplies Aedan had stashed in the cave in hopes of finding a first aid kit. Her search was rewarded with a small supply of bandages, gauze and a jar containing some kind of ointment.

She waited by the fire for Aedan, becoming apprehensive by how stoic he was upon his return.

He sat down next to her, still damp and smelling of soap. His skin prickled as the fire began to warm him. He took her hand and squeezed it momentarily before releasing it.

"You are quiet, Aedan." Aislinn noted his weariness.

"Aye, I'm not in much mood for conversation."

"Your arm is still bleeding. I found these in the trunk." Aislinn held up the dressings and ointment she'd found. "Can I bandage it?"

Aedan nodded.

Aislinn proceeded to put the salve on the slice in his upper arm, then wrapped it tightly in gauze, noting that he should have had stitches to repair the wound.

When she had finished, she surveyed her handiwork.

"Thank you."

"I take it you found Brennis?"

"Aye."

"And did you kill ...."

"Nae. But I did wound him. We were interrupted by hikers."

Aislinn just nodded, not asking any more questions. She could see that fighting his brother weighed heavily on him and rendered him reluctant to speak. She worried that with Brennis still around the threat against them continued to be very real. She suspected he was thinking the same.

Aedan lay on his make-shift bed, pulling Aislinn to lay down beside him, spooning against her back. He snuggled his face next to hers and sighed deeply as his arm came around to hold her. Within minutes he stilled and became quiet. She could hear the rhythmic inhale and exhale of his breath. He slept. He must have been exhausted. Aislinn, too, closed her eyes, languishing in the thought that he was here and they were safe, for now.

Feather light kisses on her eyelids woke Aislinn from sleep. She smiled and snuggled closer to Aedan, turning slightly to face him. She let him continue to kiss her face, loving the dreamy way he woke her. She sighed against him.

"I love waking beside you," she whispered against his throat. "A girl could get used to having mornings like this."

"I can feel your love, Aislinn. It warms me and gives me the courage to do what I must do today."

Aislinn sobered at his mention of looking for his brother. She wanted to remember this moment. Aedan so beautiful, lying next to her, strong, virile and protective. She knew in her heart he loved her. She could feel it.

"Your connection to me is growing. You're beginning to sense it, even now."

"I love you, my warrior." Aislinn leaned up and kissed him deeply.

"Aye, my Irish princess." He kissed her in return.

"And I adore the kilt, by the way."

Aedan let out an unexpected laugh.

"A girl can have her fantasy," Aislinn confessed.

"Can she now? I guess the fifteenth century was good for something. I will most assuredly remember to bring the plaid home when this is all over." He kissed her tenderly, before propping himself up on his elbow, looking down at her.

"I want to teach you something," he spoke, all evidence of jest gone. "Something you need to know for the ceremony."

Aedan toyed with a strand of Aislinn's hair. "In this time, we unite as one. In this grove, 'twill be done. To give a soul to share a heart. To come together, never to part. Oak and May and Beltane fire, on this night we find desire. Fill us with the ancient's call. Goddess blessing to one and all."

"That's beautiful, Aedan."

"Aye. 'Tis what we must recite. I wanted to give you a chance to memorize it.

Aislinn repeated what he had spoken, briefly paused, then added: "We call the wind as our breath, the water to quell our thirst. We join our bodies with the earth and share our passion with the fire."

Aedan looked at her curiously.

"I think we are supposed to say that, too. I don't know how I know that, but those magical callings my grandmother taught me were important. I think it was for this."

"Aye. Ye were the Lady's niece, after all, magic is in your blood."

Aislinn was quiet for a bit before finally speaking up. "Aedan, I'm concerned about Beltane," she confessed with profound seriousness.

"Aye."

"Brennis is still out there."

"Aye. 'Tis why I'm going out in a bit to look for him. I'd like to believe I rendered him unable to fight, but I cannae be sure. "

Aedan looked at Aislinn and grew somber. "I willnae lie to you, lass. If I donnae find Brennis today, there is a chance he will find us on Beltane. I'm hoping the magic will hold long enough for us to do what we need to do, after that he will no longer exist and be a threat." Aedan took her hand and explained everything the ceremony involved.

"It will be as I remember from my dream, or at least the part before we are interrupted."

"Aye. Remember, above all else, we must keep making love. Donnae stop no matter what. We must bless the Goddess with our union, all of it, including our releases."

"Kind of kinky, don't you think?"

Aedan's lips pulled into a tight smile. "'Tis what will make us truly part of everything. We will bare our souls and give the deepest, most intimate, thing we can offer to her."

Aedan saw the look of fear cross Aislinn's face. "I will protect you at all costs. Nothing will happen to you, I promise."

"I know." She leaned into him and kissed him.

"Let's wash up and get something to eat. There is more we should talk about." Aedan took her hand and helped her up.

Aislinn became concerned by the sullen mood falling over Aedan as they cleaned up and dressed. He became quiet and distant as she sat by the fire watching him don his kilt and accessories.

"I wish I could see you wear this more often. You look very handsome."

"'Tis a comfortable, practical piece of clothing."

"Well, it's pretty darn sexy." Aislinn sighed.

Aedan looked up while strapping on the leather arm bands and smiled sadly.

Aislinn felt the very long moment of silence descending between them. The stillness was thick and settled in the pit of her stomach.

Aedan slipped a knife into his belt and looked down at Aislinn. He swallowed hard, moving closer to her and kneeling beside her. His expression was somber and resolute.

"Aislinn, if something goes wrong," his voice cracked. "if I am sent back to my time, there are papers in my backpack." He touched her arm, having difficulty speaking.

"I've added your name to everything, all my bank accounts and land. You willnae have to worry about money or work. 'Tis all yours. There is the name of a trusted man in Chicago. Ye must contact him. He knows of you, and will know what to do."

Aedan quickly went over a few more details as Aislinn unraveled. He wiped at the tears sliding from her eyes.

"Aislinn, go to Chicago and empty my apartment. There are some very valuable antiques there. My lease is good for six months, so there will be time." He looked away, swallowing hard.

Aislinn shook her head. His words making her more distraught by the minute. "No. I don't want you talking about this. Please. This is scaring me."

"Aislinn, 'tis just in case." Aedan ran his fingers through his hair. "I donnae ken what will happen, but I want ye taken care of. I want to ken ye will be all right. I couldnae live knowing ye were not taken care of. Everything I have is yours. Please keep my sword to remember me. There are papers from the Art Institute in my bag that will allow you to transport my blade home. The name and number for the broker is there, too. He also knows what to do. Passports, keys, the hotel info, 'tis all in my backpack."

"I don't want your money, Aedan."

"I ken, but I donnae want ye to ever worry about anything." Aedan reached over and took her hands. Aislinn lifted her tear-streaked face to his. "I told ye I would always take care of you."

Aislinn's stomach twisted in knots. She tried to look away from Aedan but he turned her face back to him, forcing her to look at him.

"Donnae ye think this is killing me to have to tell you this?" he spoke through gritted teeth. "It feels like a knife plunging into my heart to hurt you. I would give anything if I didnae have to think about this, but I must."

Aislinn noticed how tightly the muscles in his jaw clenched as he forced himself to continue.

"I want you to ken, nae matter what happens, I love you and I loved you well, and I will cherish the memories of our time together." Aedan swallowed hard.

More tears trickled down Aislinn's cheeks as she reached out and touched Aedan's face. She saw the unshed tears in his eyes.

"Ye are my only love, Aislinn."

"Aedan," she sobbed. "Don't leave me!" She threw her arms around him.

"If all goes well, I willnae have to." He wrapped his arms around her.

"And if the ceremony doesn't happen? How can I live without you? Aedan, my heart is breaking."

"As is mine, Aislinn." He kissed the salty tears staining her cheeks.

"Be strong and live for the both of us." Aedan looked away. "Marry, Aislinn, and have babes. Lots of babes. Name one of them after me." His voice was etched with the heartache of his request.

"I couldn't marry anyone."

"Ye must," Aedan said firmly, holding her shoulders. "I want ye to be happy. I want ye to live."

"I want *your* baby." Another tear trickled down her cheek as she struggled with the impossible thought of never seeing Aedan again.

He kissed her full and deep, bushing the tears from her eyes. "Be brave for me, my Irish princess. Ye must." Aedan gave her hands a squeeze, then rose silently, picked up his sword and exited the cave.

Aislinn buried her face in her hands. "I can't," she choked, sobbing helplessly.

Chapter Thirty-One

"AISLINN," AEDAN WHISPERED, brushing the hair away from her tear-stained cheek. "Aislinn, wake up."

Aedan saw how Aislinn once again had cried herself to sleep, waiting for him while he attempted to locate his brother.

Unsuccessful in finding Brennis, Aedan hoped the wound he'd given him was the reason for his absence. It was a serious wound, one that would most assuredly prevent his pursuit of he and Aislinn, but he just couldn't be sure. After searching for nearly the entire day, Aedan returned to the cave, having no choice but to prepare for Beltane eve. The night was nearly upon them and there were things that had to be done.

Aedan gently touched Aislinn's shoulder. "Aislinn?"

Aislinn opened her eyes. They were red and swollen. Aedan's heart ached at the sight. "'Tis time."

She sat up. I must have fallen asleep."

Aedan nodded. "Aye. Ye did."

"Brennis?"

"I didnae find him."

Aislinn looked away from him. A moment of panic crossed her face as she returned her gaze to Aedan. "Aedan, what if...what if I can't...you know...finish? I don't know if I will be able to think of anything else except Brennis finding us."

Aedan tried to make her feel better with his attempt at humor. "I can always make ye think of me." He teased, his lips pulling to a forced smile.

"I'm serious, Aedan."

"I ken ye are," he conceded. "I've made ye something to drink that will help you." He motioned to a mug sitting near the fire.

Aedan took her hand. "Come. I have something for you." Aedan lifted her to stand and led her over to a smaller chest that sat on the dirt floor further from the main supplies. Several candles burned allowing her to clearly see what he was doing.

Aedan opened the chest, reverently running his fingers over the fabric laying inside, before picking up the bundle. He turned toward her holding out a folded cloth of the palest green material.

"This is the gown ye wore."

"Oh Aedan." She looked at him in amazement. "How?" But before he could answer, she provided the answer to her own question. "The magic. The same as my grandmother's blanket. I should have known." Aislinn accepted the gown from him, clutching it to her heart.

Aedan next removed the blanket from his pack.

"You brought it?"

"Aye. It should cover our bed now, as it did in the past."

Aislinn fought back tears. "You thought of everything."

"And there's one more thing." Aedan strode over to where Aislinn had laid the stones near their belongings and picked them up. He placed one around his neck and placed the other in the palm of her hand, closing her fingers around it. "Put this around your neck."

Aislinn's fingers trembled as she clasped the stone. This didn't go unnoticed by him. He took her hand in his, giving a reassuring squeeze.

Aedan lowered his face to hers and whispered. "I am going to light the fires and prepare the circle. When ye are ready, come join me. Ye will ken the way. I will be waiting for you. 'Tis almost over." He kissed her cheek then turned and left the cave.

The night greeted Aedan with familiarity. The cool breeze was arousing with its soft caress against his bare skin. Every nerve ending came alive with heightened sensation. Somewhere off in the distance he could hear the rhythm of this place beckoning him with its tempting pulse. He closed his eyes and drew a deep breath. He could smell the moss, feel the trees, the vibration of every living creature surrounding him. The very life of this grove seeped into him.

He could feel Aislinn as clearly now as he ever had, as if the night were a part of her, too. His heightened awareness mystified and excited him. He welcomed it.

Aedan waited, standing in the center of the grove, near the large flat stone draped with the blanket. The fires burned brightly all around the perimeter, casting light and warmth on the altar area.

Although well aware of what might be outside the magic circle, he could not think on that. He'd spoken all the magic he could, set all the spells he knew to protect this sacred space. He'd done all within his power to assure this time would be theirs. He hoped that Brennis was either too injured or couldn't breech the magic surrounding this sacred area. He whispered a silent plea to the Goddess for her protection.

His concern now was that Aislinn see only him and could put aside any worries for this night and allow her sensual need of him to guide her. He raised his eyes in the direction of the cave.

Aislinn emerged from the cave and made her way through the fires along the path toward him. His breath caught in his throat and his heart skipped a beat. She looked so ethereal, dressed as he remembered. Her gown billowed out around her as she approached him. It revealed just enough of her curves to entice him. His body responded instantly.

As Aislinn drew close her eyes met his and he could feel her strength and resolve. He noticed the slight change in her gait as she sensed his pride in her. Her acceptance amazed him. He wanted more than anything to make this night everything it was meant to be. He wanted Aislinn to lose herself in him, to become part of him.

He would take part of her soul tonight and in return give her a part of his. Tonight, they would truly become one.

"Ye look breathtaking." He gazed at her. "I have waited so long to see ye like this. I cannae take my eyes from you." He slid his hands over her bare arms until he reached her hands and clasped them. "Ye are shaking."

Aislinn looked up into his eyes and nodded.

"Donnae be frightened. Tonight is for us. 'Tis meant to be a blessed occasion." He lowered his lips to hers and kissed her tenderly. "Ye are so beautiful. You make my blood hot already." He wasn't surprised by her instant reaction to his words. He splayed his hands across her bottom pulling her tight to him, grinding his pelvis against hers to prove the truth of his words.

"Touch me, Aislinn. Touch me as if you've nae known me. Let my heat and scent fill ye, arouse ye, and make you mindless for naught but me." The corner of his mouth lifted in a faint smile.

Aislinn gazed hungrily upon him. He loved knowing how much he pleased her, and enjoyed how her eyes explored him.

He watched her lush green eyes begin a journey over him. Her gaze started at his chest, then his arms, which he gave an extra flex or two, proudly demonstrating the power they possessed. Next her gaze traveled downward along his abdomen. His belly tightened in anticipation. The feather light touch of her gaze followed every tattoo.

He stood taller, swelling with male virility as her gaze traveled downward, resting briefly on the loin covering he wore. The meager cloth could not hide the way her scrutiny affected him. He saw her involuntary shudder as she wordlessly devoured him, moving around him, taking in his backside and sturdy thighs.

Och, Christ! He didn't know how much longer he would be able to stand being the recipient of such heated looks without touching her. He felt her satisfaction as clearly as he did on their first night and he felt honored and even a little smug with the knowledge he was the one who would make love to her this night.

She slid around him, touching the strands of braided and beaded hair falling over his shoulders and when she met his gaze he felt her unwavering acceptance of him through her eyes moist with unshed tears.

"God's breath, lass, ye can make me hard with just your hungry look." He drew in a deep breath to cool the hot blood coursing through his veins.

"It's very strange to feel your emotions inside me, to not know which feelings are yours and which are mine," she whispered.

"Aye. Just feel them. Don't try to sort them. There is no 'yours' and 'mine.' It's just 'us.'"

Aislinn touched his face, running her fingers over his cheekbones and square jaw. She touched his lips a moment before she stood on her tiptoes and pulled him down to kiss her. She pulled back a bit, whispering against his mouth.

"I feel how you want me."

"Aye," he moaned, more than willing to play this seduction game as she kissed him, deeper this time. He wanted nothing more than to grab her and thrust his tongue into her mouth, but he held himself in check, letting her continue.

She pulled away, a bit breathless, before lowering her mouth to his chest. Her tongue caressed his nipples. He couldn't help the moan escaping his lips as she kissed and sucked at him. Her fingers roamed and caressed him while her tongue continued to tease.

He felt her tongue glide down toward his abdomen, tracing the spiral design on his skin. He sucked in a breath anticipating where her kisses were headed. Her hand snuck under the cloth and cupped him, pressing into him. Her fingers stroked his length, pausing only long enough to tug away the cloth covering him. Her hands clamped onto his thighs as her warm mouth descended on him. He closed his eyes, desperately trying to hang onto his control, which was quickly ebbing away. Aedan moaned with the sheer pleasure of her intimate kiss, but knew if he allowed her to continue he would become totally helpless and give in to her ministrations.

He lifted her up by her arms and slammed his mouth against hers, despite her protests. He drove his tongue deep into her, as she melted against him.

"Now it is my turn," he growled against her. "And I will nae be so leisurely. I ken ye are ready. I can taste the heat coming off you."

He kissed her deep and hard once again, making her oblivious to anything but the feel of the wild erotic rhythm of his tongue, and the way his passion danced in her veins. He pinned her against his body with just enough room to allow his hand to slip between them to caress her breasts through the sheer material.

She moaned and tried to squirm against him, but he kept her locked precisely where he wanted her. He squeezed the tightened buds of her nipples and reveled in the way she pushed into his hands, wanting more. She tore her mouth away from him, gasping for breath. He buried his face in her neck, trailing kisses down her throat. She threaded her fingers in his hair, holding his head as he kissed her.

Aedan seized the fabric of her gown and tugged upward. He raised the dress above her legs, pressing himself against her belly with a promising thrust. She answered his movement by rubbing against him, indicating in a most female way, her need.

Weary of the gown's hindrance, Aedan yanked it completely up and off. In one swift move he scooped Aislinn up into his arms, carried her to the large flat stone and laid her upon the blanket. He sat on his knees staring at her.

He loved the way the ancient designs magically appeared on her body, circling her breasts, like fingers straining to caress her. He bent over her and took one breast in his mouth, licking and sucking, while gently toying with the other. She arched up off the blanket in response.

He moved away again, sitting back on his heels, looking down at her, flushed and ripe with passion. Aedan caressed her, slowly drawing the magical designs on her body, knowing they would become a permanent reminder of their connection. He watched Aislinn squirm and close her eyes, succumbing to the heat rising from his touch

"Aedan please," she begged him in helpless frustration, writhing and twisting against his fingers that teased and aroused her.

He bent and kissed her navel and belly, finally kissing her in the place yearning for his attention. He licked and stroked her until she was hot and panting beneath him, begging for release.

His body burned with the aching need join with her and Aedan understood another moment could not go by without being inside her. He rose up, positioning himself between her thighs.

"Aislinn, do ye accept me as your life mate?"

Aislinn closed her eyes as the profound meaning of his question settled within her depths.

"I accept you as my life mate, Aedan." She kissed him deeply. "Will you accept me as yours?"

"Aye, Aislinn. I do now as I did then."

Aislinn reached up and lifted the half of the amulet that hung around Aedan's neck. She held her half in her other hand, ready to unite them.

When he entered her, Aedan felt a million bright stars explode inside him. The endless years of longing washed through him. The fear, the loneliness, the hope and the love. Always the love. She knew his thoughts now, his feelings, with each star shimmering and burning between them.

And as she opened to him physically, she opened herself to his soul. She took him in as the other part of herself. As his body joined perfectly with hers, so did his heart. He sighed, allowing the sensation to sweep him away.

Everything outside the circle no longer mattered. It didn't register that there might have been the glint of something reflected in the firelight. Aedan was so completely lost in their lovemaking, it commanded all his attention.

He ground his hips into hers at a fevered pace, his thrusts nearly lifting her from the blanket. He was so consumed by the exquisite orgasm building within him, he was heedless of naught but the erotic rhythm of their bodies.

"Let me feel you come Aislinn," he whispered in her ear, knowing how his love words aroused her. In response, he could feel the tightening of her body around him, the tremors moving through her and sweeping her into the brief void of oblivion.

As Aislinn's orgasm claimed her, the ancient words left Aedan's lips. "In this time, unite as one. In this grove, 'twill be done. To give a soul, to share a heart. We come together, never to part. Oak and May and Beltane fire. On this night we find desire. Fill us with the ancient's call, Goddess' blessing one and all."

Aedan, too let out a moan signaling his oncoming orgasm. "Connect the amulets, Aislinn," Aedan moaned nearing his own release.

Aislinn pushed the two pieces of stone together as Aedan experienced the familiar tightening in his loins. His thrusts increased.

Out of the corner of his eye, he caught the flash of steel beyond the fire. With no time to react, Aedan instinctively covered Aislinn's body with his. Aedan froze. He saw the glint of metal from the blade as it came down on him. The slick steel pierced his flesh before he could react.

At first Aedan thought nothing of the gasp of air leaving his lungs, as the quickening of his climax took hold. A long, surreal moment occurred before Aedan recognized his gasp was the result of being struck. Momentarily dazed by the impact, he moved once again inside Aislinn, not noticing the blood splattering everywhere.

He took refuge in being joined with Aislinn, and the way her body demanded his fulfillment. And blissfully he felt his body yielding. He felt his muscles tense, felt the shudders claiming him as his essence spilled forth into her. In that moment, he realized the line between ecstasy and dying had blurred.

He lifted his head and looked outside the circle.

"Brother," Brennis mocked. "Quite noble how ye protect your woman. Or maybe ye just wanted to finish what ye couldnae finish all those years ago." Brennis moved back from Aedan. "She makes ye vulnerable. I killed ye once before because of your woman. Now, ye will die again, because of her."

Aedan looked down at the blood seeping from his side.

"No!" Came the agonizing cry from Aedan's throat as he tore himself away from Aislinn and the pain of his wound took hold and his mind cleared.

Aislinn.

His first thought was only of protecting her. He shoved her in the opposite direction, sliding from the altar and stumbling to reach for his sword that he had at the ready lying near the base of the stone.

Reaching deep inside himself and finding the place where instinct and adrenaline overshadowed pain, Aedan let out another loud roar and rose to his full height, lunging at Brennis, slicing him across the shoulder

"And ye dear brother should never assume you've killed me," Aedan bellowed, again, fiercely swinging at Brennis.

The air was heavy with tension as Aedan and Brennis circled each other, both covered in blood. Brennis' eyes blazed with a fiery determination, as Aedan stalked him, purposely maneuvering him away from Aislinn.

Their swords met in a thunderous clash of steel against steel that had each of them stumbling back from the impact. Their eyes locked in an unrelenting gaze as blow after blow they fought on, each strike punctuating a lifetime of grievances and jealousy. Bloodied and battered, they both fought with the unspoken resolve that they would fight to the bitter end.

Aedan's muscles screamed, as he drew up to his full height and brought his sword down on Brennis. Brennis staggered but was quick to recover and in turn swung his sword wide as Aedan again moved forward only to suffer the impact of another deadly blow to his body. He was met with searing pain as Brennis' blade slid deep inside him. Aedan knew instantly that this wound would be his end. Aedan faltered and dropped to his knees.

Brennis moved toward Aislinn.

"Aedan!"

From somewhere behind him, Aedan heard Aislinn's scream. The anguish and fear in her voice was like fuel to the fire that still burned within him. Rage filled him thinking of what Brennis would do to her if he did not stop him. And it was this fury that kept his heart beating and his lungs gasping for air. Drawing a ragged breath, Aedan manifested a strength he didn't know he possessed. He mustered every ounce of his remaining energy, rose up, and dove at Brennis from behind him. Brennis turned at the last second, the same instant Aedan's blade caught him unexpectedly across his abdomen, cutting a wide, deep gash from side to side. Blood and innards spurted from the injury.

Brennis stumbled, gazing in bewilderment at the slice across his body that would be his death wound. The look of shock on Brennis's face spoke that he never thought he'd lose this fight. A moment later, a hideous laugh escaped his throat.

"It seems we shall both die this night. 'Tis a fitting end, donnae ye think? To just disappear into dust, all those years ye waited- now for nothing. At least I took everything from you, just like ye took from me."

Brennis dropped to his knees, his strength waning, his blood pooling on the ground beneath him. Aedan swayed, equally as unsteady, but remaining upright.

"You didnae care for our people. You only cared about your cousin on Alba and his causes." Brennis spat with his fading breath.

"Uniting the coast is what kept the Norse off Erin's shores," Aedan bellowed. "Didnae ye learn your history while in this time? 'Twas nae the Un'Neills that saved Erin." Aedan pressed his hand over the seeping wound in his side. "Brennis, ye spent your whole life hating me for faults nae of my own. Your jealousy and greed blinded you to my intentions. I never wanted to rule. I would have gladly given Erin to ye if ye would have heeded the Lady's predictions."

Brennis collapsed to the ground, any argument he might have spoken was unmercifully caught in his throat.

As Aislinn cowered near the alter, her gaze happened upon Brennis. His stare was fixed on her, and for a fleeting moment as death claimed him, his gaze belied the hardened warrior.

Aedan threw down his sword and stumbled toward Aislinn, nearly reaching her before collapsing. She ran over to him, pulling him against her, fumbling for his half of the amulet around his neck. He heard her quickly choke out the words, "In this time we unite as one. In this grove' twill be done. To give a soul, to share a heart, to come together, and never part. Oak and May and Beltane fire, on this night we find desire. Fill us with the ancient's call. Goddess blessings one and all." She took a hastened breath, still holding the two halves of the amulet together. "Oh Aedan. It's done."

Aedan didn't realize she held him, covered in his blood. He never saw the look of terror and utter helplessness on her face at finding his body pierced by Brennis' sword. He didn't know she held his head in her lap, rocking him, crying to the heavens. His only thought was to protect her.

"Are ye hurt?" his words choked in his throat, as he gazed upon her with the realization that his life was slipping away.

"No," she reassured him.

"I am mortal now," he rasped, with the last of his strength, his face a mask of the anguish at what that meant.

Aislinn's tears stung his skin every place they fell. Of all the emotions that churned and faded within him, one remained: regret.

"I love ye so," his words were barely a whisper as he struggled to remain coherent. In this one last moment as the warm blanket of death seeped through him, and his connection to Aislinn waned, he experienced the tiny touch of something not there before. A little spark of life danced within her. He tried to reach for it, but the flicker slipped away as the veil of darkness descended over him.

Aislinn watched in horror as the life faded from Aedan's eyes and her magnificent warrior fell limp in her arms.

"Oh, God, no!" she screamed, shaking Aedan, desperate to wake him. "No...no...no...Oh, Goddess, help him. Don't let him die. Take him, please. I will gladly give him to you if I must, but don't let him die. Oh Aedan..."

She brushed the blood-soaked hair from his face as she rocked him in her arms. So much blood covered his lifeless body. The gash in his side was the one he took as he covered her, a testament to his oath to protect her at all costs. The second wound he had suffered trying to move Brennis away from her.

Aislinn glanced outside the circle and saw the man who had taken Aedan from her, lifeless on the ground. She blinked and looked again at Aedan, then back to where Brennis lay. Within a second blink of her eye, Brennis was gone. The confusion of the last moments was replaced by silence. Only the crackling of the fire hammered in her ears and the blackness of the night greeted her gaze.

"Please, Lady. I freely give him back to you so Aedan may live."

She leaned over Aedan, still not willing to believe he was gone. Aislinn watched the circle of fire dance and spring to life around them. As the flames flickered higher, she saw the fire inching closer. She knew it would be only minutes before the flames reached her.

Tears poured down her face as she continued rocking his lifeless body. "I love you. Oh, God. We did everything right. Oh Aedan...She kissed his cold lips one last time as the fire crept forward.

"It wasn't supposed to happen like this." She could feel the heat from the fire on her skin and in those last moments before it totally engulfed her, Aislinn saw the image of a woman standing just outside the flames, strangely familiar, silently watching. Odd, she thought, how beautiful the Lady was amidst the death surrounding her.

"Say the words," came the gentle voice.

As the flames rose higher around her, a memory came to Aislinn. An image of long ago and long forgotten of a little girl with wild red hair, walking in the damp aftermath of a summer rain, with her grandmother as she frolicked and danced in the wet grass.

"Aislinn, I want to teach you something that you will need to know. One day you will teach the poem to a special man."

And with her dying breath, Aislinn whispered the words her grandmother taught her. "I call the wind as my breath, water to quell my thirst. I join my body with the earth and share my passion with fire."

Aislinn closed her eyes and placed her head on Aedan's chest. She could feel her life ending in the blaze as the flames rose and consumed her. The roar became deafening in her ears just before everything faded in silence.

Chapter Thirty-Two

AISLINN'S EYES FLUTTERED open. She instantly squinted against the brilliant sunshine. The brightness assaulted her, making her head ache even more. A moan escaped her lips as she closed her eyes again, praying the pounding in her brain would stop. It didn't. Again, she opened her eyes, this time more carefully. She was completely and utterly disoriented.

She slowly looked from side to side, mindful of the incessant throbbing persisting in her head. She studied her surroundings, trying desperately to shake the confusion muddling her brain.

Why was she in the woods? And for that matter, she thought sitting up, why was she naked and near freezing? Her teeth chattered uncontrollably. She rubbed her arms to get the blood circulating. She suspected, by the blueish tinge of her skin and the ache in her limbs, she'd been lying out in the cold for some time. Her legs screamed in protest as she awkwardly stood.

She glanced down, seeing for the first time the crimson stains and strange tattoos marking her skin. *Blood.* Her mind took a moment to register exactly what she was seeing, but then the memories returned. They flooded her with such force, she staggered back against the stone she was near.

"Aedan," she cried, her breath billowing out in a white vapor around her. She reached for the blanket draped over the alter stone and wrapped herself in it. In doing so, she absently touched her half of the amulet hanging around her neck. She took a step forward.

"Aedan?" she called, looking around. No answer came. "Aedan?" she called again, but only silence greeted her.

He was gone. Everything was gone. No Brennis, no fire. Nothing. Nothing remained except the frozen stillness of the grove.

They'd failed.

The grief was so physically overwhelming, Aislinn had to reach for the rock for support. She collapsed against it, unable to stand. The sorrow was all-consuming. The emptiness paralyzed her.

There was nothing within her. Nothing remained where his heart had briefly resided. Aedan's very essence was gone. Emptiness filled her with such heart-wrenching despair, she fell to her knees, her body heaving unmercifully, as she proceeded to be sick.

In between bouts of retching, Aislinn screamed in protest at Aedan's disappearance, but to no end. She found no relief. The grief assaulting her was unbearable.

On the ground, a few feet from her she glimpsed the gown she'd worn. The beautiful pale green dress that just hours ago had caressed her skin, now lay where Aedan had tossed it hastily aside in his blinding need to have her. It was covered with blood and grime. Resting on top of the gown was Aedan's blood-covered sword.

She scrambled to pick them up, hugging the dress to her breast reverently. The tears erupted; great helpless sobs wracked her body, shaking her to her very soul. Her grief tore her in two. Losing Aedan was like losing half of herself and she knew with a certainty she would never be whole again. Her tortured cries filled the grove where only hours ago he'd stood so strong, so vibrant and alive.

Aislinn didn't know how long she wept. Her sense of time was skewed, but she was certain hours had passed. She sat lifelessly staring at the trees. She knew she should get to someplace warm, but deep down she didn't care if she did or not. She wanted to die. If she sat here long enough she would stop feeling the biting chill settling into her bones, making her shiver uncontrollably. Surely, once she became numb, she would blissfully fall into slumber, then into death. Only a few minutes more.

Ye must live. She looked up through her swollen eyes, thinking to find Aedan standing beside her. How cruel memories could be. He'd known all along. Aedan knew how great the possibility was the ceremony would not be completed.

"I can't go on without you." She lowered her head once again, wearily fighting a losing battle with the cold.

Ye must. Aislinn's head snapped up. "Are you here?" she whispered, rising to her feet looking around. No. The wind played tricks on her; the wind that had once caressed her now cruelly taunted her.

She crumbled to the ground again, still clutching the gown tightly in her fingers. She teetered precariously between reason and oblivion, fighting the inner struggle between the voice in her brain and her broken heart. She fleetingly thought the cold was beginning to affect her.

But there was something just on the edge of complete surrender that wouldn't let her give in. Aislinn found one fragment of strength keeping her grasping at life, and despite her heart's protest, the instinctive will to survive was strong. Not understanding how, she managed to pull herself up. *The cave*, she thought. She needed to get to the cave.

Unsteady on her feet, she managed to drag the sword toward the cave. What had been only a short walk the night before, now seemed an endless trek. Her legs felt heavy, and each step took enormous effort, but onward she moved toward the hidden entrance.

The only light in the cave was the dying embers of the fire Aedan had started the day before. Aislinn paused just inside, allowing her eyes to adjust before stepping further in. She dropped the blanket, sword and dress, retrieved a couple of logs, and placed them on the fire. She blew on the coals until a small flame erupted and caught one of the logs. At least she would have some light and heat. She rubbed her hands and glanced around. With the light, however, came the stark reminders of what she'd lost. Aedan's belongings were scattered around the cave, vivid tokens of the deep sorrow clinging to her.

Aedan's plaid lay beneath the sword she had dropped. Tears misted in her eyes as she thought about how sexy he'd looked draped in his kilt, and how she would never see him like that again.

He can't be gone. Her heart refused to believe what her brain screamed at her. "Aedan, damn you. How could you leave me alone? So alone."

Aislinn spied his leather coat laying atop his jeans and picked it up. She held the jacket to her face and inhaled deeply. The leather smelled of him, heather and the sea - the scent she knew from her dreams; the scent that had comforted her when she was hurt, the scent that aroused her beyond reason and wrapped around her like her grandmother's blanket.

She held the jacket next to her face and sank to the floor by the fire cradling the garment. God, she wanted to hold him, wanted to be wrapped in his arms once again, wanted this all to be a bad dream. The tears poured uncontrollably from her eyes as she rubbed her cheek against the soft leather. She just wanted to touch him again, to hear the deep resonating sound of his laughter, to see the playful twinkle in his eyes as he teased her. "Oh, God," she cried, wracked once again with irrepressible sobs. How would she ever go on without him?

Hours later or maybe days - Aislinn had no sense of time - she woke. She didn't know how long she'd slept, except the fire had burned out and she shivered from the cold.

She found a candle and some matches. She was afraid of the dark. If truth be told, she didn't want to die in the dark. She lit the candle with shaky fingers, physically weak and emotionally exhausted. Aislinn quietly surrendered to her grief.

She looked down, absently watching the candle light flicker over her skin. The shadows danced and licked at the red patches of dried blood still coating her. Aedan's blood. The blood he'd shed while he covered her to keep her from harm. She touched the magical designs covering her flesh. They would forever be a heartbreaking reminder of the magic and the failed Beltane ceremony. The cold amulet hung around her neck, feeling heavier than before, the weight nearly unbearable.

She slid her fingers lower to where Aedan's seed remained on her thighs. How merciless fate was, forcing her to experience such bliss and then to witness the life drain from the magnificent warrior.

She knew with a surety Aedan was dead. He'd died in her arms. He'd died protecting her. He'd died making sure she lived, and despite the fact that she lived, she had no desire to live without him. Aislinn collapsed to the ground again, waiting and praying for sweet oblivion to take her.

Aislinn could feel Aedan's fingers gently stroke her cheek. *Ye must wake,* his voice whispered in her ear. *Ye must open your eyes, Aislinn.*

I can't. I don't want to. An agonizing groan escaped Aislinn's throat as she fought to remain in the void between life and death, but the touch of Aedan's fingers, the lull of his voice calling to her, a lifeline, pulling her from the depths of absolute despair. Her eyes fluttered open, and, despite her protests, she came painfully awake amidst the cold and dark.

"Aedan? Are you there?" her voice cracked with dryness; the words barely audible. She placed her hand on her cheek where he had touched her. Her skin felt warm. How could that be?

"I feel you, Aedan." She didn't know what was happening, but she knew with a certainty Aedan was willing her to live. She pulled Aedan's coat around her, needing the comfort and security the smooth leather provided.

Perhaps she'd become delusional, she thought in a moment of lucid reflection, imagining what her heart longed to hear. Her strength kept her alive, nothing more. She began sobbing, crying for the loss, crying from the pain, crying because there would be no relief from the torment tearing her up inside.

Sometime later, Aislinn woke again. She managed to put a log on the fire and coax a small flame to life before sitting beside it, resting her head on her knees and rocking gently. She felt so lost, so completely alone. Her heart now held a gaping hole that Aedan once filled.

The heartache gnawed at her insides. She missed him. She missed him with every fiber of her being. She knew the feeling would never lessen, she would never stop missing him, and she would be empty forever. Once again the tears flowed from her eyes and she helplessly surrendered to them. This is the way her life would be then. She would always be thinking of him. There would always be a picture of him in her mind, always be the soft lilt of his voice whispering in her ear, always be the space where his heart resided. She hugged her knees tighter as the utter hopelessness engulfed her once more.

Chapter Thirty-Three

AISLINN CAREFULLY FOLDED Aedan's plaid and placed it with the rest of his clothes in his backpack. She managed to get cleaned up and dressed, but even small chores took enormous effort. She tried to eat a bit of dry bread, but her stomach continued to protest. She was so physically weak from exhaustion and hunger she wasn't sure how she was able to move.

She'd gone over the ceremony in her mind a hundred times. What did they do wrong? What should they have done differently? Everything they'd done was exactly as Aedan instructed.

"Damn you!" she said. "You weren't supposed to die." Angry tears gathered in her eyes.

I will always protect you, Aislinn, Aedan had said, and he did—with his very life. And now Aislinn was plagued with this endless suffering. It would have been better had she died with him rather than carry the burden of this ceaseless torment.

She fished in his pack for the hotel keys, but unable to find them, she dumped the contents out onto the ground. Out of the pack fell the envelopes addressed to her. She touched them reverently. She knew what they were. Damn his noble, self-sacrificing nature. He made sure she would be taken care of at all costs. Aedan had more of a sense of his impending fate than he'd let on.

Aislinn placed the papers back in the bag. She could not deal with this right now. She put the hotel and car keys in her pocket. She picked up his passport and opened it, touching the photo lovingly.

The photo was of him as he looked at the art institute the first day she saw him, with his hair pulled back and that arrogant, knowing look in his eyes.

She held the picture to her breast, the tears falling once again. She thought to leave the passport on a rock shelf in the cave, but at the last minute, selfishly couldn't bring herself to part with it.

Aislinn stepped out of the cave, squinting as her eyes adjusted to the daylight. The day wasn't bright, actually just the opposite, a gray, dreary, dismal day precisely matching her mood. She'd emptied the cave of her and Aedan's belongings. Not willing to part with any reminders of him just yet, she stuffed everything in the two backpacks and sword-case. With her waning strength, she knew carrying them would be tiring and wondered how she would manage, but she would not leave anything behind.

She tossed the two backpacks over her shoulder, stumbling with the effort to lift them. She adjusted the sword-case in her hand and stood straighter. She took a step forward and paused, unsure if she could or wanted to leave.

She hesitated only briefly however, because she reluctantly acknowledged there was nothing left for her here. She closed her eyes momentarily, praying for strength then turned and with a heavy, empty heart walked away.

She dared look back only once. The entrance to the cave disappeared. The entrance had always been hidden by magic from everyone except Aedan, and her for a brief time. Now the cave and the magic was lost to even her. Pain gripped her heart as she sadly acknowledged she could never go back.

Chapter Thirty-Four

UNITED STATES, PRESENT Day

Aislinn stared out over the water of the big lake, as she had done for countless days, silently wishing every day for Aedan to come back to her. Once again she'd come to her grandmother's cottage seeking solace. She needed a place where the memories of Aedan were the strongest, where she could feel his presence and imagine he was here with her.

The return trip from Ireland and Canada seemed nothing more than a big blur to her, eventless days of retracing the trip home, fighting all the memories and heartache assaulting her at every turn.

Nights were the worst. They were endlessly long and dark, and Aislinn gave up the idea of ever sleeping the night through again. She would never find peace.

She couldn't accept that she would never see his cocky smile, or see him raise his eyebrows teasingly when she did something he found amusing. She would never again know the touch of his lips or the feel of his hand on her cheek. Never again would he pull her into his embrace after they made love.

She never wanted to need anyone, determined to be content on her own. Then ever so cautiously, she'd opened herself to Aedan, accepting all the magic and dreams as if they were as natural as the air she breathed. He dared her to love him, knowing all along she would. He had felt something in her she hadn't known was there. He'd made her believe, he'd made her vulnerable, he'd made her whole. Finally, she'd let him into her heart, realizing her destiny was entwined with his.

Aislinn couldn't swallow the lump in her throat. The anguish was still so deep, so raw, and the tears continued to spill from her eyes. She needed him so very much. She was lost to herself and didn't know how she would go on, when the very essence of who she was, the other half of her soul, was gone.

Each day she watched the waves lapping the shore, asking herself the same questions over and over. What was the purpose of experiencing something so fantastic, so impossible? Why was she given this glimpse of perfect love only to have the perfection snatched away? What role did she play in the bigger cosmos?

Because that's what she knew now, that she was only a small part of some bigger thing, a brief flash in endless time. But why was she destined to live with such heartache for the rest of her days? Was Aedan alive? Had the Lady taken him? Aedan had said he was mortal, is that why he died? Was there a chance Aedan could come back?

No, she knew. She had begged the Lady to take him, to heal him. By doing so, she gave him up as well. She sighed. He had been certain if he went back to his time he would not come back to her. That was why he'd left the papers and instructions for her. She had hoped he'd been wrong.

Aislinn was not ready to believe their life together was gone. She lowered her head in her hands. She'd known him for such a short time.

"Oh, Aedan ..." came her voice between the tears. Wherever he was, whatever time, did he remember her? She wanted him to remember her. She couldn't dare think he remembered nothing of her.

Each day she prayed this would be the day he would come back to her, and each day her hopes were dashed as she struggled to make sense of the aloneness. The days passed one by one from spring to the end of summer without a hint of Aedan, and Aislinn knew she needed to accept the reality that he was truly gone.

The cottage and the lake held little comfort for her now, even the sense of her grandmother had vanished. She felt restless these days in her attempt to hold on to the memories. Everything was slipping away from her, as if the cosmos or fate was putting distance between her and all she held dear. They were letting her go, as she let go of the hope of Aedan's return. There was nothing left for her here.

Today would be the last time she gazed out over the water and made her wish. Aislinn knew the time for decisions was at hand. The lease on Aedan's apartment in Chicago would expire in a month, and she wanted his belongings moved to her home. She still needed to see Aedan's attorney; she had let the matter of the money Aedan left her unresolved. The beginning of the school year was just around the corner, and she needed to decide if she would return to teaching. There were other decisions she needed to make as well, concerning the future she would make without him.

And as much as she could hardly deal with any of it, she knew the time for her self-imposed exile had come to an end. It was time to leave the cottage and its memories. Tears gathered in her eyes once more. Leaving tore her in two, but she knew she must. She glanced one last time at the place where she saw Aedan standing in the water, where she realized he was the man she'd dreamed about for most of her life.

He was so much a part of this place now, she wondered if she would ever be able to return. His presence was strong here, as if the elements themselves clung to his memory.

"Goodbye," she whispered, to the wind, to Aedan.

Chapter Thirty-Five

THE BIZARRE TURN OF events in just the short span of a couple of hours staggered Aislinn. Gazing out the tinted window of the limousine at the passing Chicago skyline, she couldn't help feel that the world was yet again spinning out of her control.

Only moments ago, she'd stood in the leather and book-filled office of Aedan's attorney. She'd spent all morning debating whether she should even see him, but the necessity of what to do with the items in Aedan's apartment prompted her to keep the appointment.

The ride to Chicago was heartbreaking. Three long hours of time to think about Aedan, to bring up the pain of losing him all over again, to see his cocky smile, hear his deep brogue. She still hadn't come to terms with his absence and seeing the lawyer would only succeed in cementing the truth she fought so hard against accepting.

Upon arriving at the law offices, she was immediately escorted to a private office on the top floor and was pleasantly greeted by an older gentleman, presumably the lawyer, who seemed much too familiar with her.

She presented the letter to him and within a couple of minutes of her arrival she was assured the first installment of one million dollars would be in her bank by lunch time. She tried to tell him she didn't want the money, that she came for other reasons , but she could only stand there, speechless.

If just being handed one million dollars wasn't enough to cause her head to spin, the lawyer, with a very pleased expression, informed her he had additional news. She was completely unprepared for the shock that came next.

Aedan was alive.

It took several long, surreal moments before his statement sank in, and while she digested the news, she was quickly ushered to a chair and handed a glass of water before she fainted.

Aislinn spent the hour trying to grasp what the lawyer told her. Aedan had been found outside the museum on the first of May, badly wounded by what appeared to be stab wounds of some kind. He'd been taken to the hospital and was in a coma. He'd only awoken the day before.

The lawyer must have known precisely how she would react, because he informed her that a limo was at her disposal and arrangements were being made for a hotel suite for her stay in Chicago.

Now, as the limo wound its way through the city toward the hospital, everything seemed like a dream. Her only thought was of Aedan. God, how she longed to see him, to hold him. Was it possible the ceremony did work and they did what they were supposed to do? How did Aedan end up in Chicago? Why was he not with her in Ireland? For now, though, the questions would have to wait. All she craved was one glimpse of his face.

By the time she arrived at the hospital, she could barely pull herself together, and by the time she'd taken the elevator to his floor, she was shaking and practically ran down the hall toward his room.

She burst through the door, pausing only a second to gaze on those dark eyes looking up at her before throwing herself at him.

"Oh, Aedan. It's you. It's really you," she cried, kissing him frantically. "Oh, God, Aedan, I've missed you so much. I thought you'd died." Tears slid down her cheek as she continued to kiss him, running her fingers gently over his face and through his hair, mindful of the tubes and IV's.

She sniffed back her tears. "I'm so sorry you're hurt, but you're here now. How can this be?" She continued to stroke his face and shoulders lovingly, but abruptly froze. Something wasn't right. Aedan hadn't reacted to her in any manner. She pulled back to look at him. "Aedan?"

He gazed at her with such a perplexed look, she couldn't help the sinking feeling taking root in her stomach. "Aedan?"

"I dare say there is not a better way to get all me parts working again than to be greeted by such a bonny lass tossing herself at me." Aedan put his hands around her upper arms, setting her away from him. "But, lass, who might you be?"

Chapter Thirty-Six

SO SHOCKED BY HIS QUESTION, the red-haired woman actually grabbed hold of the bed to keep herself from falling down. She stared at him as if he were joking, but quickly realized the seriousness of his question. His brows furrowed in confusion, as he silently studied her, trying to decide if he knew her or not.

"Aedan, it's me, Aislinn," she stammered, wiping the tears from her cheeks.

"Aislinn?"

"Aislinn O'Neil. You don't remember me?" Her voice choked in panic, as her hand flew to her mouth. "Oh, God."

Aedan reached out and caught her the best he could as she stumbled back. She was utterly shocked that he didn't know her.

"Easy, lass."

"You don't remember, do you?"

"And just what am I supposed to be remembering?"

"Me. Us."

"I dare say, with looks like yours, If I knew ye, I'd not be forgetting."

"Aedan MacKendrick. You work at the Art Institute in acquisitions. You are from Scotland."

"Aye." He continued to watch her, stunned by his inability to recognize her.

"How can you remember that and not me?"

"Lass, I just woke up from a verra long sleep. Perhaps my mind isn't quite awake yet." He didn't let on that he found her knowledge of him very disconcerting.

"You have tattoos, not just on your arms." She pointed to his biceps. "They are on your chest, abdomen, thighs and back too."

"And ye have seen these?" He raised his eyebrows questioningly. He watched her shyly look away as she nodded. "Are we lovers?"

"Yes," she whispered, tears once again brimming in her eyes.

Well, that would account for the fact his friggin' cock had sprung to life the instant she'd kissed him. Even if he hadn't remembered her, his body obviously did.

"And how was it ye thought I was dead?" He watched her hesitate with her answer. He watched the way her eyes avoided his. She either lied or was withholding something from him.

"The accident."

"And what about the accident?" His curiosity was piqued now.

"You were stabbed with a sword."

Aedan drew a breath. No one knew about the wounds found on his body. The doctors identified his injuries as those consistent with being pierced by a large blade. He instantly wondered about her involvement in his attack.

She reached out and touched a scar on his forearm. "This is an old wound." The tears she'd bravely held in check, once again spilled from her eyes, slipping down her cheeks. He watched her spin away from him and hurriedly swipe at them. "I'm sorry. I was so excited to see you again. I didn't expect this. It's a lot to take in." She awkwardly tried to apologize. Aedan unexpectedly found a lump forming in his throat by her distraught appearance.

She suddenly turned around, pinning him with those deep green eyes, which for a flash, seemed familiar.

"Aedan, I spent the summer believing you were dead, trying to get over you, trying to let you go, trying to go on living after half my heart had been ripped away. I prayed over and over for you to come back to me. As painful as it was to lose you, seeing you here, right before me and finding you don't remember what we shared is more than I can handle."

Aedan was conflicted. One part of him continued to be skeptical, extremely leery of this woman who knew too much; the other part of him couldn't help but be deeply moved by her painful confession and obvious connection to him.

Damn, why didn't he remember her if he was as close to her as she suggested. Why would his mind block her out? It didn't make sense.

He rubbed his head. Christ, but he felt weary. His head ached and now there was this to contend with.

Surprisingly, she must have sensed how he felt despite not outwardly showing his discomfort because she looked at him with such sadness, he was sure he'd never forget.

'I'd better go," she choked, glancing down and then back up, as if hoping he would stop her. Instead, he said nothing, so she turned and walked out the door.

"Come tomorrow," he bellowed a second later, positive his voice reached her in the hallway.

Chapter Thirty-Seven

AEDAN SPENT A FITFUL night, tossing and turning and dreaming of a red-haired witch tormenting him in what little sleep he managed to covet. Even the drugs didn't' help. He was sick of the damned needles, IV's, and constant noise of the vitals machine that kept him up every night since waking from the coma. He was ready to leave this place.

He propped himself up. He was restless, and frustrated and he knew precisely why.

Her.

Damn her and her warm lips. His cock had been hard ever since tasting them. He even embarrassed the nurse who came to help him take a shower.

He'd always been rather proud of his male parts, but not today. Today the little smile and snicker from the nurse as she attempted to ignore his affliction, annoyed him tremendously and did nothing but add to his sour mood.

He was sure she would come. If she knew him as well as she insinuated, then she would come. Lovers indeed. He would have remembered making love to that little witch.

Och, Christ, but she was a beautiful woman. But beautiful and trustworthy...*hmm*...they were two different things. He'd seen her look away, withholding some bit of information from him. He would be willing to stake everything that she knew more than what she'd shared. She was so very easy to read and among other things, he was intrigued.

As the morning turned to afternoon, and she still hadn't come, he found he was actually disappointed. Aedan looked forward to talking with her, more so than he admitted. He tried to convince himself his need to talk to her stemmed from the mystery surrounding her. He wanted to find out more about her and what she knew about his attack. However, deep down there was more he wanted to know.

He hadn't stopped thinking about her since she'd showed up in his room yesterday. He hadn't stopped seeing the passion that, for a brief span of time, lit those green eyes.

Christ, but he needed to get out of this place; he was going stir crazy. He picked up the television remote and turned on the TV. He turned it off. He turned it on again then off. Finally, he threw the remote across the room, where it crashed and shattered on the floor.

"Just grrreat," he roared, in his most Scottish accent, flinging back the covers and tangled in the wires and tubes, bent to retrieve the remaining pieces of the remote. It was at that precise moment, when his arse was bare to the world, she entered the room.

"Oh."

He stood slowly, not the least concerned about his gaping hospital gown. If she were going to pick this second to finally show up, then Christ, she would get a show worthy of being late. When he finally did turn around, he was the one who received the surprise. She looked upon him with such a sense of longing, his breath caught in his throat. Christ, she looked at his arse with longing? What was the matter with this woman?

"Are you done gaping at me, woman?"

She just shook her head.

"I'm sorry, Aedan. It's just that ... that ... never mind," she said sadly, obviously remembering something she wouldn't speak of.

Aedan climbed back into bed, pulling the covers back over him, purposely bunching them in his lap.

"I brought you your favorite burger. I'm guessing they are not feeding you as much meat as you like."

She handed him the bag and watched him open it. She had indeed brought his favorite.

"You were nae going to come today," he stated, not questioned, in between bites.

"No. I wasn't. I wasn't sure what to do. Whether you realize it or not, this is very difficult for me."

"Because we were lovers?" He watched for her reaction.

"We were more than lovers."

"How much more?"

"More."

"*Hmm.*" He continued to eat, as if the conversation were as nonchalant as one about baseball.

"and Ms.?"

"O'Neil."

"And Ms. O'Neil, do you live in the city? How did I meet you?"

"I do not live in the city, and how we met, well that's a long and difficult story."

"Where do you live?"

"Michigan."

"And what do you do in Michigan?"

"I'm a teacher."

"And we met in Michigan?"

"No, Actually we met in Chicago, at the museum."

"Ah-huh. And are you going to tell me how?" He prodded.

"Aedan, do you remember anything?"

Aedan thought for a moment. Her question held such a tone of desperation. He truly tried to catch hold of his fleeting thoughts.

There were memories of something, snippets here and there, images that made no sense. Nothing he could articulate.

"Nae."

"I don't know what to do, Aedan. Help me."

"Tell me," he demanded, a little rougher than he intended.

"I can't. Not yet, anyway."

"Do ye ken who attacked me?"

Aislinn didn't answer. Ah, so she did know something. He watched her nervously fidget with a cord around her neck that disappeared under the collar of her shirt.

"Do ye ken them?" he asked again, louder this time.

"No. I mean yes. I mean, I know *of* him."

"Him, not they? But you willnae tell me?"

"I can't."

"Ah, dear Aislinn, for professing we had a ..." Aedan cleared his throat, "a close relationship, I find your reluctance to come forth with information a bit disappointing."

"It's complicated."

"Ye have already made that clear."

"I came today to bring you something." She fished inside a large manila envelope she'd carried in with her. "The keys to your apartment and the keys to your SUV. I left the vehicle in your carport."

"And how did ye come to have these?"

"You don't remember leaving them for me, along with the keys to the hotel in Ireland?"

"We went to Ireland?" he bellowed. "This just gets more and more complicated by the minute." Aedan scratched his head. What the hell was going on.

He looked pointedly at her. "How long have we known each other?"

"Do you want me to be honest, even if you will find my answer hard to believe?"

"Aye."

"Aedan, we met last January ... in this lifetime."

She spoke the last part of her explanation so quietly, he couldn't be sure what she'd said. It sounded like she'd said, 'in this lifetime.'

She sighed, biting her lip. She seemed to want to say more, but didn't. Instead, she changed the subject. "I have to get back to the hotel to pack now. I'm leaving tomorrow."

"Because school is starting?"

"Yes."

"Is that the only reason?"

"No."

"Are you upset because I donnae remember you?" He knew the answer before he even asked it. Still, the hurt crossing her features wasn't any easier to watch.

"You need to rest and heal and regain your strength."

Was this supposed to be the excuse for not being forthcoming with information. Was she afraid he'd have a setback in his recovery?

"Will you come by tomorrow?"

"Do you want me to?"

Of course, he did. She was beautiful, mysterious, and he needed to get to the bottom of what she was withholding, no matter how long it took.

"Aye."

"Then I will stop by before I leave."

Again, she hesitated before turning. It was obvious she desperately wanted to tell him something, but again she remained silent.

"Can you bring two burgers tomorrow?"

She flashed him a half-hearted smile before stepping out the door.

Chapter Thirty-Eight

OCH, WHERE WAS SHE? Aedan looked up from the magazine he'd spent the last hour covering the margins with doodles and scribbles. He'd been trying to keep busy while he waited for her.

He set the pen on the bed table and pushed the whole tray aside. Maybe he should bend over and stick his arse in the air. She'd be sure to come then, he snorted. He never expected her to react the way she had upon seeing his bare person. A screech, maybe even a blush, but just standing there looking at him with such love and adoration in her gaze ... and hunger? Well, it was unsettling to say the least.

And last night he'd dreamed of her. Not the fragmented bits and pieces haunting his dreams of late, but her on a winter beach, wind in her hair, looking out over the water. Then her in a very sexy gown walking through the woods toward him. He didn't recognize either location, but he knew she was clearly with him.

He shook his head. Maybe he was just fantasizing. She could make a man dream such things.

"Hello, Aedan. How are you feeling today?" she greeted him rather generically for someone claiming to know him intimately. "You look better, a bit stronger. You'll be up swinging your swor ..." she caught herself, "You'll be up and around in no time." She handed him the paper bag containing the burgers he'd requested.

"I thought you were going to be here earlier."

"I had some business to take care of on the way here. I also wanted to make sure everything got loaded into the limo."

"Limo? You're taking a limo?"

"It's on loan to me while I'm in the city, to get to the hotel and hospital and then to the train station."

"Pretty swanky for a teacher, wouldnae ye say?" He deliberately tried to goad her into giving him more information.

Aislin sat down on the edge of the bed. Although she did her best to try and keep her conversation formal and polite, her actions spoke of a familiarity around him that went without saying.

"Are you angry with me about something, Aedan?"

"Nae...yes. Och, Christ lass, I donnae even ken ye. I know there's more you willnae speak about."

She acknowledged his statement with a slight nod of her head. "Our worlds have been reversed." She murmured more to herself, but he heard her. "What's that supposed to mean?"

"Right now, you need to heal."

"That's nae an answer."

At that instant, Aislinn happened to glance at the bedside table he'd pulled closer in order to place the bags of burgers down. He followed her gaze to the magazine sitting under the bag.

"Did you draw these?" she inquired.

He looked at her from under hooded eyes, wary of answering her.

"Aye."

Again, she only nodded, but as she did, he watched her trembling fingers begin to unbutton her blouse.

"Are ye thinking to seduce me, lass?" She just looked over, with serious intent, her gaze fixed on him as she slipped each button through its hole. He reached out and stilled her hand as the last button slipped out of its place. "Ye donnae want to embarrass yourself."

"The designs you drew on the page." She pointed to the magazine.

"They are just scribbles while I waited for ye this morn."

Aislinn stood up from the bed and faced him. "They are more than just mere scribbles, Aedan." Aislinn opened her shirt to reveal the tattooed designs adorning her body.

"You are so convinced you do not remember, yet somewhere a part of you does. You gave me these designs."

Aedan's hand fell away from her arm as he examined her painted skin. Flashes appeared in his mind of touching those designs, of making those marks on her flesh. He closed his eyes and rubbed his temple, trying to sort through the myriad of images assaulting him. When he finally opened his eyes and raised his gaze to her, his brows furrowed with a hundred questions. He spoke only one.

"How?"

The rest of his words failed him. His gaze lowered from hers and instead focused on the strange shaped stone hanging on a cord between her breasts. Just days before, he'd been given the personal items found on him when he was discovered unconscious and brought to the hospital. Among his belongings was an odd shaped stone similar to the one she wore.

"I've got to go." her words jolted him out of his thoughts. He grabbed her wrist as she started doing up her blouse again. Her hands were trembling. He released her arm.

"Aislinn?"

"I will miss the train if I don't leave."

"You cannae just show me this and then walk out."

"I have to go," she repeated as she finished putting herself back together physically. However, Aedan could see she was emotionally near falling apart by the way she bit her trembling lip, he suspected to keep from crying.

She paused at the door to his room, looking back at him one last time before exiting.

"This isnae over," he hollered after her.

Chapter Thirty-Nine

Aedan had been ready for the confrontation all day. As a matter of fact, he'd had over a month in which to prepare for it - ever since he'd discovered the money being taken from his accounts. So *that* was the "business" she had been taking care of when she was in Chicago.

Hmm. Even his attorney was very closed-mouthed about the legality of the withdrawal and behaved very suspiciously about the whole affair. He would only say that Miss O'Neil provided the correct papers, perfectly legal and signed by his own hand. The only problem was he didn't remember signing any damned papers.

Och, but this didn't make sense. If his instincts hadn't been screaming to be patient, he would have turned her over to the police who were investigating his attack. He didn't understand why he felt a mite sympathetic for the woman who, by all accounts, he should be extremely leery of.

He waited in her driveway, leaning against his SUV, arms folded in body language indicating he meant business. He watched as she pulled up to the front of her house, straightened her clothes, and pulled her long sweater tighter around her. She glanced at him while tugging shopping bags from the backseat of her car.

As she strode up her front walkway, she appeared completely nonplussed by his presence, breezing past him and climbing her porch steps. She put her key in the door and never looked back to see if he followed or not.

Damn her. She was totally undaunted by him, and of course, he followed her straight into the house. She'd just put her bags in a room down the hall and he heard the door close a moment before she appeared. She looked tired, he noted as she sighed deeply as he approached her.

"Do you remember anything yet, Aedan?"

His reluctance to answer was not because he hadn't remembered anything, which he hadn't, but because he couldn't stand to see the sadness in her eyes when he told her no. So, he said nothing, which was answer enough.

"I need to use the restroom for a moment," she announced, leaving him alone.

While she was gone he took the opportunity to explore her home. He keenly eyed photos, knick-knacks and the usual trivial things, but what caught his attention was the medieval claymore laid out across the mantel of her fireplace. He reached out and picked up the sword in his hands. It was almost as if the blade had been crafted for him, the balance, the weight, were perfect. He didn't work all those years with the weapons at the museum without learning a thing or two about swords and swordsmanship. He tested the swing, but placed the blade down when he heard her coming.

"Pretty expensive bauble, wouldn't ye say?"

"Someone I knew gave this to me."

"You know people who give gifts like that?"

She didn't answer.

"Are ye a thief? Did ye have me attacked to get at this or something else at the museum?" The look on her face was not what he expected at all. She was amused by his question. She actually laughed.

"When I first met you I thought you were a drug dealer, wearing your black coat, driving your big black car and staying at expensive hotel suites."

"But I wasnae, was I? And I donnae have a black coat."

"No, you were not a drug dealer, but you were so mysterious. And ..." she paused. "I have your coat."

Aislinn moved past him, stepping to the front closet and taking out a black leather coat. She handed the garment to him with reluctance and hesitation as if giving up a treasured object.

He lifted the coat from her hands, inspecting the garment.

"But am I wrong about ye being a thief?"

"What's that supposed to mean?"

She walked away from him and sat down at the kitchen table, pulling her sweater around her.

He followed. "Funny thing," he began, circling her, reminding himself why he'd come. "Each month there is a fairly hefty amount being dispensed from my accounts and put into a bank right here in this verra town."

"You gave me the money."

"I did, did I? That's exactly what my lawyer said too." He pierced her with a steely look. "And why exactly did I do that?"

"Because you wanted to make sure I was taken care of in case you didn't come back."

"What proof do you have I did this? Where are the papers from my lawyer? And, come back? From where?" His voice was perhaps louder than he intended, but och, she was so frustrating.

Aislinn looked down and tugged at the hem of her baggie sweater. "I don't have them. I don't know where they are."

He threw his hands in the air. "Ah. How convenient. This is quite an elaborate story you've concocted."

"It's not a story," Aislinn sighed. "Aedan, I didn't want your money. I still don't. I haven't touched it. I was in such shock being told you were alive; I didn't even think about what the lawyer was arranging. All I could think about was seeing you."

"Is that why ye were in Chicago?"

"Yes, and because you asked me to do something."

"In case I died? And what was that?"

"To clear out your apartment, to take care of your belongings."

"Did you get the sword from my apartment?" He nodded toward her fireplace. He was positive the claymore belonged to him. "How about the stone you wear around your neck? Was that mine as well?"

She looked up at him suddenly, hope flashing in her eyes. "Do you have yours?" she blurted out, then caught herself. "I never went to your apartment. I found out you were alive before that. I came right to the hospital."

Aedan stopped his pacing, halting right in front of her, pinning her with his stare. "Ye have got to give me more to go on than this, because from where I am sitting, ye look verra suspicious."

"What did you mean when you said our roles are reversed?"

Aislinn didn't answer.

Aedan resumed pacing nervously, running his hands through his hair. "Your refusal to explain could be mistaken as guilt, ye ken. Who attacked me? Why were we in Ireland? Ms. O'Neil, what are you hiding?"

"Aedan," Aislinn choked. "I loved you with all my heart. You loved me with all of yours. When I lost you, I was devastated. I wanted to die. You knew right from the beginning there was a possibility something would happen, and you'd be taken from me." Tears rolled down her cheeks. "It was always your intent to make sure I was taken care of, whether by you or your estate. That's just the way you were."

"Don't you mean 'Are?'"

"You were different then." Aislinn rose and wiped at her cheeks, notably agitated. "I would give anything to have you back. Every day I wait and hope you'll return to me. My love for you is so deep, I can never love another, Aedan. It's heartbreaking to have you standing before me, knowing what we meant to each other, accusing me of things you know nothing about; so, stuff your accusations up your Scottish ass and leave, please."

Aislinn stood tall, facing him proudly.

"Would that be the ass ye were practically drooling over in the hospital? My aren't ye the feisty Irish princess."

Aislinn's expression suddenly became wide-eyed with shock. "Don't call me that."

"Why not? It's the truth," he said defiantly.

"Because you used to call me that."

"Then, I think I shall continue."

"No!" She was quick with her hand, he'd give her that, but he was quicker. He grabbed her wrist and halted her slap before it reached his face. He forced her hand down.

Perhaps he'd leaned in a bit too close to her then, or perhaps it was the faintest aroma of roses rising from her skin, perhaps he itched for relief from his aching groin, or perhaps it was that his wrath dissipated instantly when he looked at her, leaving him frustrated by his inability to think clearly and be angry with her.

Whatever the reason, his lips slammed down on hers hard and demanding, capturing the protest leaving her throat.

And then the funniest thing happened; he experienced the most bizarre feeling that he'd kissed her like this before. There was something completely right about kissing her and he wasn't about to stop. And och, Christ, she kissed him back, hard and full.

He ravaged her mouth so thoroughly even he could not deny a kiss like that could only happen between two people very familiar with each other.

It wasn't until she pushed him away that he pulled his lips from hers, but he didn't remove his arms from around her right away. He did that when he saw the distressed look on her face.

"I think you'd better go," she stammered.

Aedan hurried out the door in a flash, without an apology, without even an explanation grateful for the cooling effect of the brisk autumn evening breeze on his skin.

Christ, what happened back there? He thought to himself as he maneuvered the car onto the highway. What had come over him? One minute he was telling her she was a thief, the next he was kissing her as if he couldn't get enough of her. He ran his fingers through his hair. *Och*, but that woman was trouble.

He hadn't even gotten the money issue resolved, and frankly, he didn't give a shite about the money; he had so much, it didn't matter.

It was just an excuse to see her anyway, to try and understand why she'd plagued his thoughts every day since visiting him in the hospital. What he really intended on finding out about were the marks on her body. She told him he gave them to her, and he wanted to know how and why. Now he'd have to wait until next time to confront her about that.

Next time.

Oh, aye, there would definitely be a next time.

Chapter Forty

IT WAS THE DAY BEFORE the long Thanksgiving weekend, and Aedan had no plans for the holiday. As he had learned, he lived a solitary lifestyle, without family or friends to speak of. Despite this, he found he wanted the companionship of one fiery Irish lass. Maybe it was the sentiment of the season, or merely that he felt more amicable toward her since kissing her, but he thought he'd pay her a visit and maybe take her out to dinner as a way to apologize and make amends. He hoped she didn't have plans either.

After the kiss they'd shared when he'd confronted her, he found it more and more difficult to ignore the feeling that perhaps they had shared something he'd blocked out of his mind. After all he had very large pieces of his life missing.

He felt guilty at the thought that he could be the reason she seemed so sad when he saw her. She was so secretive about revealing anything of their relationship, which he'd recently learned was doctor's orders. He was told that he had to regain his memories slowly, and on his terms. Flooding him with months of memories would not be in his best interest and could even cause him to regress and never regain his memories.

Still, he hung onto every little detail she'd let slip about him. He left her some way. *Died?* He recalled she said he knew he possibly wouldn't return, from where? Ireland? If what she said were true, and they really had been lovers, it *was* in his nature to see her taken care of.

She indicated in the hospital that he was strong enough to lift a sword. Yes, he caught her slip and the wistful look on her face when she told him someone she knew gave her the sword. He'd given it to her, sure as the sword was his to give. The weapon fit him too perfectly for it not to be his. Where had he acquired a medieval sword?

What puzzled him the most were her tattoos. She so defiantly showed them to him but wouldn't say anything more about them. Maybe she regretted showing him something as important as this. Maybe she decided it was too much, too soon. Christ, he hated not being able to remember whatever she expected him to remember.

It had occurred to him that she was making it all up. He'd even convinced himself that was the case until he recalled the genuinely ecstatic way she'd come running into the hospital, so elated at finding him alive, and then how completely devastated she became when he did not remember her. No one could have faked that. And what about the little things like knowing his favorite burger and having his car and apartment keys, having papers signed by him?

No, he was convinced there was so much more. So, after a month and a half of anger and guilt and frustration and just plain wanting to know what the hell was going on. He admitted, despite his lack of memory, he was drawn to her and that they should at least be friends. And if truth be told, ever since capturing those tempting lips with his, he hadn't stopped thinking of Aislinn.

He wanted to see her smile this time. Mainly because every other time they'd been together it had been contentious, thanks to him. He hadn't made their meetings easy for her, accusing her of all sorts of things. He was a painful reminder of what she'd lost and lord only knew the heartache she suffered each time she looked at him. He hadn't made any attempt to understand her suffering.

No, he needed to make things right with her. He glanced at the large bouquet of flowers on the seat next to him. He would apologize and maybe, just maybe, they could begin to unravel some of his memories.

Upon entering the main door of Aislinn's school building, things went from odd to completely alarming.

The school secretaries greeted him with open familiarity when he checked in at the main office. One even commented how Aislinn would love the flowers. Odd, but he hadn't mentioned who he was there to visit, yet.

On the way to her classroom, another staff member told him the website looked great and asked if it was nearly finished. Apparently he and Aislinn had done a wonderful job.

A quick call to the museum before entering her room confirmed that he and Aislinn had indeed developed the new layout and design for the online resource portion of the museum's website during last winter and spring.

Aedan was completely flabbergasted upon learning the details. And, to add insult to injury a moment later he was met in the hall by several students who waved and gave him a "Hi ya, Mr. Mac" greeting.

Aislinn hadn't lied when she said they had a history, apparently the whole damned world knew. The only person who didn't know was him.

"Oh, Aedan you're back. How wonderful," a woman called to him as she stopped to talk.

He quickly glanced to her I.D. hanging around her neck. *Beth Peterson.*

"Aislinn will be so excited you're here. Oh, she's been so sad during your absence. I'll bet she's glad you're back from Ireland." She glanced down at the flowers. "Aw, you're surprising her. She doesn't know you're back yet. My, aren't you the romantic. No wonder she loves you."

Aedan actually found himself smiling and nodding like a fool, pretending she'd guessed his motive for coming to the school.

"I'll bet you are so excited. It's getting close. I'm sure she could use help getting ready. Boy, she was so sick in the beginning. Oh, but she's going to be so thrilled you are back." The woman winked and patted his arm before bustling on her way.

Excited? Sick? Needing help?

Aedan stood there a moment, too shocked to do anything and definitely too stunned to think about what Beth Peterson was babbling on about. He shook his head, absolutely perplexed by this totally other life he'd lived that he knew nothing about.

When he eventually stepped into Aislinn's classroom, several students gasped and waved and greeted him as a longtime friend. Aislinn's back was to him as she helped a student.

One little boy came up to him. "Hey, Mr. Mac. How's it going? Did you bring anymore swords?"

"Afraid not Devin. Maybe next time." Aedan paused, trying to disguise his sudden bewilderment at knowing the young boy's name. And, as if all the strange coincidences weren't enough to completely disorient him, when he glanced up, there stood Aislinn, in complete shock by his unexpected arrival and very, *very* pregnant.

Aedan recovered quickly, more so than Aislinn, when he realized all eyes were on the two of them. He could feel the anticipation in the air, so he politely bent down and lightly kissed her cheek, and handed her the flowers.

"Mr. MacKendrick. What a surprise." She raised the flowers to her face to inhale their fragrance, trying unsuccessfully to use the gesture to hide her astonishment.

"I should say the same." He glanced at her swollen belly.

So, this is what she'd hesitated in telling him. He didn't have to question the obvious. She would tell him the child was his.

Apparently, with the welcome he'd received within her workplace, everyone else knew the baby was his, too.

It was hard to ignore the signs that he and she had been a couple, when everyone continued to think they still were. Damn, if he had been sleeping with this woman, he wanted to remember it!

And if all that transpired thus far wasn't enough, the proverbial icing on the cake, after calculating it, was that ten months of his life was missing.

"How are you feeling? I mean aside from the obvious," Aedan asked, once he was alone with Aislinn at the end of the day. This is what Beth Peterson referred to when she'd mentioned Aislinn being ill. Come to think of it, he remembered her looking very tired the last time he saw her.

"I'm fine. What are you doing here?"

Christ, this was awkward enough without the nondescript answers from her. He watched her gather up her things and wave off his offer of a chair.

"Aw, lass, when were ye going to tell me?"

She stopped what she was doing and looked pointedly at him. "I didn't know if I would," she said solemnly "because you are a different person now."

Aedan was momentarily taken aback. Her comment hurt more than he let on.

Aislinn looked away and continued to shove things in her bag. "I'm sorry, I'm still surprised by your appearance. I didn't mean it to sound the way it came out, but you know what I meant."

"I'm still physically the same man, Aislinn."

She looked up at him.

"So, ye just happened to think this isnae important enough to mention?" Aedan ran his fingers through his hair, his frustration apparent. "This wasnae something ye should have kept from me."

"Would you have believed me? You don't even remember who you are, you don't remember me, how could you think about being a father?"

Aedan paced. "True. I'll admit, when I first woke and learned about you I was skeptical, even about the money and all. But there have been ... well, even you couldnae have fabricated all I witnessed today." Aedan stopped pacing and helped her when she began putting on her coat.

"Aedan ..."

He caught her before she could say anything further. "We need to talk, lass, but not here. Aislinn, I came here to spend Thanksgiving with you. Will you at least let me take you to dinner?"

Aislinn closed her eyes, and then slowly opened them with a weary sigh. "Alright" she agreed.

"You remembered Devin's name," Aislinn commented, once they were seated at the restaurant. She sipped her water.

"Aye. Surprised even me, but I donnae remember more."

Aislinn recounted what he'd done for Devin and his relationship with the other students she saw every day. She paused once in her explanation to give the waiter her order, but jumped right back into the story as soon as the waiter left. Aedan was glad she willingly spoke of her time with him.

"Of course, they are another grade older since you last saw them, but they haven't forgotten you."

"'Tis because I was important to you." He watched her shift her gaze to the table and fidget with the table cloth.

Good timing, Aedan thought, as the waiter chose this moment to bring their food.

"I didnae want you to be alone for the holiday, I guess."

"You were sure I would be?"

"*I* didnae want to be alone," he confessed.

She nodded, taking a bit of her meal.

"So, are we going to talk about the baby?"

"No."

"Nae?" His raised voice attracted a few curious glances from the people at nearby tables. "Nae?" he said again, in a more hushed, but equally agitated tone. "Donnae ye think I should at least know when I'm going to be a father?"

"February."

"February," he repeated, swiftly calculating backwards. *May*

"The date?"

"The first."

"Ye got pregnant the day I was attacked?"

"Aedan," Aislinn began, becoming more and more upset by the conversation and he suspected by the memories he was dredging up for her. "I appreciate your attempt at interest, but we both know you neither expected or wanted this."

"I never said that."

"You didn't have to. The shocked look on your face said it."

"That's nae exactly..."

"That's exactly what it was."

"You dinnae give me a chance to get used to the idea. Christ, Aislinn, this changes everything."

"This changes nothing. You don't remember me, you don't love me, Aedan."

Aislinn briefly closed her eyes drawing a breath, fighting down her emotions.

"But I have a responsibility, an obligation."

Aislinn abruptly dropped her fork. The loud clink echoed through the restaurant. She rose suddenly, tossing her napkin on the table.

"I do not want to be a *responsibility*, an *obligation*." She looked up at the ceiling, blinking back tears. "Take me home please."

"Aislinn?"

She held up her hand, clearly putting an end to any further words from him. "Just take me home."

When Aislinn opened her door, Aedan could tell she was not having a good morning. His chest tightened. "Och, lass, ye have been crying."

She wiped her eyes and lifted her head defiantly, pulling her robe closed the best she could over her protruding stomach.

"Aedan, what are you doing here?"

"Well, now ye see, 'tis the strangest thing. I donnae ken. It's Thanksgiving day." He'd blurted the first thing that came to his mind.

He'd driven halfway back to Chicago after their disastrous dinner the previous night, when he was suddenly compelled to turn around. He didn't know why, or what made him feel that way, but an hour and a half into his trip he spun the car around and headed back the way he'd just come. The hotel clerk thought he was crazy checking in shortly after checking out.

"I couldnae leave it unfinished between us. I couldnae leave without apologizing."

Aislinn hesitated a very long time before finally opening the door and reluctantly letting him in. He stepped past her, going to the dining table, setting down the bags he'd brought in with him.

"Are ye hungry, lass? I have every kind of breakfast food imaginable. I ken ye donnae eat much, but with the babe and all - "He stopped midsentence realizing what he'd just said. He looked over to her and saw her shocked expression.

"I donnae ken how I know that," he admitted, completely baffled.

Her escape from him couldn't have been hastier. He didn't know if she was upset or happy. She just mumbled something about getting dressed, rushing down the hall.

When she appeared a while later, she seemed more composed. He handed her a cup of coffee, then started to take it back. "Can ye have it?"

She nodded, "Yes." She lifted the cup from his hands. "Although I don't drink as much as I used to." Aislinn eyed the array of food on the table Aedan had laid out. "*Hmm*...not the healthiest."

"Aw, donnae ye think the lad would like a sweet now and again?" Aedan saw her smile then, actually smile. He'd never felt such warmth that went all the way to his toes.

"I *am* hungry." She looked over the rolls, donuts, bagels and fruit. "It seems I'm hungry all the time these days."

Aedan pulled out a chair for her, and sat next to her.

"Aislinn, I was telling the truth when I said I didnae ken why I came back. I just knew I needed to be with you. I cannae explain it." He couldn't put into words what compelled him to change his mind. Christ, he couldn't even figure it out himself. "I just needed to talk to you. I wanted ye to know I understand the heartache ye must feel when you look at me, to know I'm the same and yet nae the same. Still, I must have cared deeply for you if we were having a family together."

"You didn't know about the baby."

"So, then my reaction was genuine."

Aislinn shot him a skeptical glance.

"I'm trying, Aislinn. At least give me that. I ken I am missing a lot of memories." The strangest look crossed her face right then. Her hand paused midway putting a bit of food in her mouth.

"Those memories define who you are, Aedan."

"Then tell them to me," he pleaded. He could see her struggle between wanting to blurt everything out to him and following the suggestions of the medical professionals at not revealing too much too fast. Finally, she spoke.

"What do you remember of your past?"

"My past, as when I was a wee lad? Nothing."

"*The* past."

Aedan hesitated when she put the emphasis on "The."

"And what am I supposed to remember?"

"Us. But, it wouldn't make a difference if I told you. The feelings, the connections won't be there unless you remember."

"I could try." He genuinely meant that.

"Aedan, you can't force yourself to love me just because I told you that you did."

"But there is something Aislinn. I ken it's hard for ye to look at me and ken what you had once is not there, but something is ... a familiarity of sorts. I cannae explain it. It's like when I look at you, you belong - in my thoughts, in my head. Maybe spending time together will help me remember it." He hadn't intended on sounding so desperate, but her understanding suddenly became so very important.

"Aislinn, you are having my child, surely that must count for something?" Aedan touched her hand. "I want to be a part of your life, of our babe's life. I mean that."

Aislinn looked torn. He could see her weighing his argument, calculating the emotional toll having him near and yet not being the same person who loved her would have on her.

Then Aislinn did something so unexpected, tears welled in his eyes. After shifting to get comfortable, she lifted his hand, placing it on her stomach. He felt the tiny flutter of a kick on his palm. The breath left his lungs; his mouth slacked in awe. He was rendered speechless.

After a few wonderous moments, he raised his eyes to Aislinn and saw she was crying. He leaned over and tenderly brushed a tear from her cheek.

"He's going to be a strapping lad, like his da."

Aislinn laughed as she cried, and for a moment, Aedan saw a flash of hope in her eyes. "I think it's from all the sugar."

And this time, Aedan laughed.

Chapter Forty-One

AEDAN SHUT OFF THE computer and checked his watch. Was it this late already? Christ, but he'd been using work as a distraction lately. His plan was to stop by the museum this evening to pick up some paperwork that needed to be faxed in the morning, but ended up staying most of the night. Still, working was better than being reminded that he'd been a total jerk to the first woman in years who had interested him. He corrected himself. Maybe it hadn't been years.

Thanksgiving weekend had started a disaster, going nothing like he planned. He genuinely wanted to spend time with Aislinn, to get to know her. Och but she was beautiful and mysterious and stirred his blood like he'd never known. But the realization of having another life he could not remember and then finding Aislinn pregnant proved a shock he hadn't anticipated. To learn that such a long period of time was missing from his memory was disconcerting enough but to witness evidence that there more to his relationship with Aislinn than he'd ever anticipated caught him totally off guard.

He'd been less than articulate at dinner. Och, Christ, he hadn't expressed the immediate surge of pride he'd felt at seeing her with his child, how she brought out all his male instincts to protect and care for her.

He should have made his intentions clear; that he wouldn't leave her alone. He wanted to be with her and the baby. He wouldn't run away from their past or her. But he hadn't voiced these things to her, afraid he'd scare her with his confession, afraid she would think he was being too aggressive. No, instead he made her sound as if she were a burden he would tolerate.

He ran his fingers through his hair. Christ, he couldn't imagine how his cruel words must have hurt her. She never said another word to him on the drive from the restaurant to her house. She simply stepped out from his car, went inside her house, and shut the door.

If she hadn't let him in the next morning, he really wouldn't have blamed her. Still, he was more than desperate for her to know his awkward attempt at an apology was sincere, and he wanted very much to spend time with her.

They came to an unspoken truce Thanksgiving morning over donuts and a kicking baby. Aislinn accepted his apology and his plea to be involved as genuine, and although she continued to keep her memories to herself, at least it was a start.

It was only since returning to Chicago after that weekend and throwing himself into work that he became preoccupied with wanting to know more about Aislinn. Keeping busy was the only way he could focus on something other than trying to dissect every conversation, every clue she let slip, to piece together the puzzle of his missing life.

He was sure, more than ever, by the way he caught her looking at him, that she continued to harbor deep feelings for him. She was so guarded when he would ask about their relationship, or want clarification about something he remembered. She would even avoid his questions or offer very little in the way of an answer or explanation, and this frustrated the hell out of him. Why was she so reluctant to offer information? How was he supposed to remember if she wouldn't talk about it? When he once again brought up the designs on her body she very firmly told him she would not speak of them. Och, but he was running out of patience with this whole thing.

Aedan turned off the light and locked his office door, leaving by the back exit of the museum, and thus avoiding the cheery holiday decorations adorning the museum and the surrounding street. He wasn't in a very celebratory mood these days, having so much occupying his thoughts. There just wasn't much room left for feeling festive. He had decisions to make concerning Aislinn and his child, his job and pretty much his whole life.

He made his way through the snowy parking lot to his SUV, climbed inside, and proceeded to drop his keys down between the seat and the console.

"Christ," came his disgusted grunt. He shoved his large hand uncomfortably between the seat and plastic frame fishing for the elusive keyring.

As he felt around, he happened to touch something. Annoyed it wasn't the keyring, he brought up a stack of papers and tossed them on the seat before stuffing his hand back down searching for the keys.

Finally, he managed to get a hold of them and pulled the keys, immediately inserting them into the ignition before he could chance dropping them again. As he started the car, he happened to glance at the seat next to him, at the papers he'd extracted. Lying in the pile was an open envelope, thick with folded papers.

Curious, he opened it, sorting through the myriad of papers. There were receipts from a hotel in Sudbury, Ontario and another one from Ireland. The rest were the papers Aislinn must have brought to Chicago with her, legalizing her name on his accounts.

He quickly looked through each one of them, seeing his signature at the bottom of every page. She'd been telling the truth about having them and losing them. They must have slipped between the seat and floor when she first visited him in the hospital and returned his car to him. He folded the papers and slipped them back into the envelope, taking out another set of folded papers. He opened them, seeing the very familiar script of his hand. He began to read..

"My dearest Aislinn, my dearest love,

Centuries of heartache and suffering doesnae begin to compare to the agony I am facing writing this letter to you. I find 'tis one of the most difficult things I must do, and despite the power I possess as a warrior, I am defeated by the thought of living without you.

As I write, I gaze at ye, sleeping peacefully in our bed, and I am moved by the intensity at which I crave you. Even now, my body greedily stirs for you and will ken nae satisfaction until I am inside you. It warms and thrills me how you give yourself to me, although it can be no other way for us.

I have loved you more deeply, more purely, than any man should be allowed to love. If we had a hundred lifetimes together, it would not be enough time to love you. Ye are my love, my life, the other half of my soul.

Aislinn, my only solace is perhaps ye willnae read this letter, and all shall go well on Beltane, and we will be together. But if the fates have other plans for us, and I must leave you, then ye must live for the both of us. Ye must be strong, as I ken you are. Donnae forget me, Aislinn, for time and years will never diminish my memories of you.

I ken ye will nae feel complete again. You will carry the emptiness in your heart where I once was. Imagine I am there, as I will with you, and perhaps across time, our souls may find each other again.

If I cannae be there for you, then ye must make life easy for yourself. Seek out whatever will make you happy. Everything I have is yours, Aislinn. Ye will have nae financial worries, so please seize life and live it for the both of us.

All I ever wanted was to have a lifetime with you, one lifetime in which to love you as we were meant to. Christ, Aislinn, it pains me imagining what you will go through, what heartache you will suffer.

What we have is unique, Aislinn, the sharing of souls. We have lived and loved more in the short time we were together than most people ever do in a lifetime, and 'tis this thought I want you to hold in your heart when the emptiness becomes overwhelming.

I wish more than anything we were granted our time together, but if it is nae to be, then, my love, ken how very much ye will always mean to me.

I love ye now and always, for all eternity,

Aedan

Aedan looked up from the letter. He gazed out the windshield while he digested the words he'd just read. A very remarkable moment seized him as he realized he envied the man in the letter, and then acknowledged that these were his words. To have such a love, a life so intense with someone and not know, well fate was cruel. To learn of the pain and sadness Aislinn carried, that was more than he could stand as well.

No wonder she wouldn't talk about it. She couldn't. He never wanted to hurt her. Christ, he was attracted to her. From the first moment she'd flung her arms around him in the hospital, he had the strangest hunch she held a place inside him. At first he chalked the feeling up to pure physical attraction, but as he grew to know her, the sense of familiarity grew stronger each time he was with her. Seeing her carrying his child intensified the feelings of rightness growing inside him.

It was well past time for secrets, he thought as he glanced at the letter in his hand. *Warrior? Beltane? Soul sharing?* He was ready to know the truth no matter what it might be.

Chapter Forty-Two

AS AEDAN PULLED UP to the tiny cottage, he saw Aislinn outside, carefully stepping over snowdrifts, carrying firewood toward the house. He watched her with intense fascination. She wasn't the least bit awkward or uncoordinated with her pregnancy. Actually, she carried herself like a queen, graceful and proud.

Aedan immediately jumped out of his car, ran over to her and lifted the wood from her arms. "Ye shouldnae be doing this."

"Why? I've got to have wood for the fire."

"Ye might hurt yourself."

"Aedan, I'm pregnant, not helpless."

"Ye go inside. I'll finish this."

But she didn't go inside. She stubbornly bent to pick up more wood, before he once again swiped the logs out of her arms, and escorted her to the house.

She followed him back outside.

"What are ye doing, way up here in this Godforsaken place, in the middle of winter?"

Aislinn paused in mid-reach toward another log, giving him an odd look. "I love to come here."

"Oh? I just wish ye hadn't come by yourself."

"Well, apparently I won't be by myself."

Aedan just threw her a look. "Ye should have told me ye were coming here."

"Are you my keeper, now?"

"Well, nae but..."

"I wanted to be someplace quiet and special for the holidays."

"Alone?"

Aislinn didn't answer him, only let out a grunt while lifting another log. He yanked this one out of her hands as well, adding it to the pile in his arms. He moved past her and into the cottage.

Aislinn stepped over to the wood again, but this time, as Aedan returned, he lifted her off her feet and swept her up into his strong arms.

"Hey!" she protested.

"I told ye I'd finish this."

"Aedan, put me down."

"Lass, I donnae want ye or the baby getting injured. We're a long way from a hospital."

"I'm fine."

Aedan brought her inside the cottage and set her down on the couch. "Stay put. I'll be done in a moment." His voice was firm, but he followed his order with a playful wink.

"How did you know where I'd be?" Aislinn asked as he brought in the next load of wood.

"When ye were nae home, I went up to your school and happened to find your friend Beth working. She told me ye were going to spend the holidays up here. She was more than a wee bit curious why I didnae ken that. She also acted very odd when I asked for directions."

"That's because you destroyed the door to her house, once, trying to find out how to get here."

"Really?"

"Yes."

"*Hmm.*"

Aedan carried in several more arm loads of wood from the stack in the back of the cottage before he carried in his duffle bag and tossed it in the same room as Aislinn's belongings.

He tended to the fire, then sat down on the couch next to Aislinn. He touched her stomach in a loving gesture. There was something about a woman swollen with a babe that touched the most male part of him. He always gave up his place in a line, or carried a package, or any little assistance he could offer as a token of respect for a mother-to-be. But knowing this was his baby, well, this made it all the more profound.

"The lad grows big."

"Is that your polite way of saying I'm getting large?"

"Nae. Ye are the loveliest pregnant woman I have ever seen." Aedan stroked her cheek with his knuckles and watched her blush and then look away. Aedan smiled, but his smile faded as he saw the sadness behind her smile.

"Lass, I do want to apologize to you for being such a fool. Ye tried to tell me." Aedan reached into his pocket and pulled out the envelope he'd found in the car.

He watched as Aislinn's expression changed from distant to nearly distraught as she recognized what he held. She swiped the envelope from his fingers, clutching it to her chest. "I thought I'd lost this. Oh God, I thought I'd never see this again." She closed her eyes, sighing, clinging to the papers reverently. "These words mean everything to me," she confessed. "These were your words."

Aedan sighed and ran his hand through his hair. "I loved ye verra much."

Aislinn opened her eyes and looked at him, nodding. "Yes."

"Why didnae ye tell me?"

"I was hoping you'd remember."

"Aislinn, I am attracted to you. Ye have to see that. I do care about ye, lass."

Aislinn just looked at him.

"Attraction and love are two different things," she finally whispered, pulling her gaze away.

He nodded. In that one statement, he understood the sadness he saw in her eyes just a moment ago. She was missing the man she knew, the man who loved her more than life itself and wrote of his love for her in the letter she still clutched to her heart.

But he was that man.

Now more than ever, he needed to know all the details of his life that he was missing.

"Aislinn, I ken 'twill be difficult, but ye must tell me everything. What did the letter mean when I wrote that I was a warrior? Why do I ken the sword you possess belonged to me? What is all this talk of magic and Beltane? How were we connected?"

Her gaze once again darted to him, this time revealing trepidation and uncertainty.

"Who am I? I always thought I knew, but I find I cannae recall anything before my life in Chicago. I thought at first it was due to the attack, but now I'm nae so sure." He took her hands in his. "What is the purpose of the marks on our bodies?"

"You are a Druidh," she suddenly said.

"What?" He was truly stunned. "A Druidh?"

"Those marks, those tattoos, were given to you long ago."

"When I was young?" If he wasn't confused before, he was really confused now.

"Are you truly ready to hear everything?" She shifted on the couch to face him, placing the letter in her lap, she took his hands in hers.

"Aye. I have to know. Even if ye think I willnae believe you. You've got to tell me everything. Donnae leave anything out."

Aislinn lowered her gaze. He could see her indecision.

"Please. I think 'tis past time for secrets, donnae you?"

Aislinn sighed and again raised her eyes to his. "I will tell you."

Aedan squeezed her hands, offering his support for what he knew would be an extremely difficult task for her.

Aislinn recounted everything, from the day she arrived to work early and witnessed the full moon and unknowingly made her wish, to fainting upon meeting him at the museum. Aedan listened intently as she recounted how she grew to love and trust him, and how they first made love here in this cottage. She told him everything about the magic and his brother, Brennis, pointing out the scars on his body from their fight. She recounted everything he'd told her about his time and how he came to be in this century. She recalled every day they were together, amidst tears and some laughter. She told him every word he ever said to her, every touch he caressed her with, every dream and every fear they shared.

Aedan said nothing as the missing details of his life unfolded before him. He was stunned.

"Wow." He felt like an idiot sitting in front of her, with nothing else to say except that one word. What could he say? How could he digest and process everything she'd just told him.

"Aedan, say something," she finally said after long moments of uncomfortable silence.

"I donnae ken what to say."

She huffed. "Those were my sentiments as well when you first told me who you were."

"How can it be true?"

"It's true. You told me to search my heart. What does your heart tell you, Aedan?"

Her expression spoke that she expected denial and disbelief. He felt neither. He surprised even himself as he just quietly took in all that she'd told him.

As fantastical as the explanation was, as hard as it was to comprehend mystical events, and twelve hundred years of living, every detail she conveyed strangely made sense. All the odd coincidences suddenly fell into place. The evidence was everywhere, and the pull toward Aislinn he'd felt ever since first meeting her, was indisputable. He believed every word.

Yes, deep inside, he just knew every word was true. Aedan looked at Aislinn, who nervously bit her lip. They were supposed to be together, that's why it felt so right when he was with her. That's why he felt so protective toward her and the babe. That's why his body remained in a constant state of arousal around her and why he couldn't stay away.

"Aw, lass." He drew her into his arms. "I'm so sorry for everything you've gone through. I donnae doubt what ye told me." He kissed her forehead then placed his hand on her stomach lovingly. "No wonder I sensed a connection to you."

When he pulled back and looked at her, he remembered reading what he'd written in the letter to her...

I know you will nae feel complete again. You will carry the emptiness in your heart where I once was. Imagine I am there, as I will with you, and perhaps across time, our souls may find each other again.

Aedan drew a deep breath. Knowing about his life wasn't the same as experiencing it. Although physically he was the Aedan she knew, at the same time, he wasn't. Although she genuinely seemed pleased he'd accepted what she'd told him. He knew there was a part of her that ached for the connection that was once their bond, the tiny thread of magic that united her soul with his.

"I want to mean all things to ye again, as I once did. I want to be that man for ye, Aislinn. I want to love ye as before. I want to make love to ye with all the passion and heat that was once between us, but I donnae ken if I can be that man. I donnae ken if I am ever meant to be him again. If all I ever wanted was to be mortal and live a normal life, then perhaps my wish was granted, after all. Perhaps I am only meant to love ye like a man, not an immortal favored by a Goddess. Perhaps we were not meant to love beyond mortal limits."

Aislinn was quiet for a long time before she finally spoke up "Aedan, to feel you inside me, as a part of me, even for the shortest span of time is something I can't forget." Aislinn reached up and touched his face, gazing deep into his eyes. "I'm trying Aedan, but I don't know how to look at you and not see the past."

"Then what shall we do, Aislinn? Should we deny ourselves anything that could grow between us just because it isn't the same? "

Aedan leaned forward and placing his lips on hers, kissed her tenderly. When he pulled back, he saw the unmistakable look of longing in her eyes. God, but he wanted to vanish that from her heart. Right there and then he silently made the commitment to her and their future.

Chapter Forty-Three

AIDIDH MACKENDRICK announced his arrival, early February, wailing loudly like a screaming banshee. But to Aedan, the cry was a most welcome sound after fourteen hours of watching and helping Aislinn bring him into the world. Although he was the warrior, Aedan had never seen such strength and courage as Aislinn exhibited throughout the entire birth ordeal. The tears he shed as they placed tiny Aididh in Aislinn's arms were tears of joy, but also tears of relief that she and the babe were both healthy and perfect. He told her he loved her, then, as he snuggled his face next to hers and kissed her, then kissed his son. She cried with him, but he suspected her tears held heartache with the happiness.

It took several weeks, but they eventually fell into a quiet routine. Aedan cared for Aididh during the day while Aislinn worked, and Aislinn took him under her care as soon as she arrived home.

Sometimes he would surprise her and bring Aididh to her school under the pretense of showing him off to the staff, but secretly knowing Aislinn missed the bonding time when feeding him. This gave her the opportunity during her lunch for some quiet time with Aididh.

Aislinn decided she would finish the school year and then make up her mind about whether to continue teaching or stay home with Aididh. Whatever she decided, he would support her decision.

One night, in mid-March, shortly after Aislinn had returned to work, Aedan found himself standing in the doorway of Aididh's nursery, gazing upon Aislinn silently standing by the crib watching their son sleep. Aedan stepped up behind Aislinn and looked over her at Aididh sleeping peacefully.

"He has grown so much in just a few weeks," she whispered, touching the tiny fingers of his hand. "He is so beautiful, Aedan."

"That he is," Aedan agreed, reaching up and moving aside Aislinn's hair. He snuggled his face into the curve of her neck, lightly placing kisses along her soft skin. "But nae as beautiful as his mother," he whispered moving downward toward her shoulder. He felt the subtle shudder go through her as he kissed her.

"Ah, lass. I want to love ye as a man should love his woman." Aedan slid his hands around her waist, moving his lips back up the length of her neck. "For so long ye have denied my touch. Ye cannae keep ignoring what's between us. I know ye feel it. I feel ye tremble as I kiss you."

"Aedan."

"*Shh*, Let me love you. Permit yourself the chance for passion once again, Aislinn." Aedan pressed himself against her. "We are as intimate as two people could be without making love. 'Tis only natural to want that as well. And I want you, Aislinn. I have for a very long time. I ken ye know that."

"I know."

"Are you all healed from having the babe?"

"Yes."

"Good. I want nothing between us this night." Aedan saw her glance flick over to the sleeping baby. "We will have time before he wakes again. Come."

He scooped Aislinn easily up into his arms and carried her to the bedroom, lit only by several candles he'd placed earlier. He set her on her feet and stood behind her, again burying his face in the curve of her neck. His hands came around to her front, undoing the buttons of her shirt.

"I'm greedy in my need to have ye naked before you change your mind."

Aislinn turned around to face him. She touched his cheek. "I'm not going to change my mind."

"Ah, lass, I like to hear that," Aedan whispered, tugging her shirt down her arms, tossing it to the floor. He grasped the snap at the waist of her jeans and with a determined yank, pulled them open. With a hand on each side of her hips, he slid down her jeans, kneeling before her to pull them off.

He paused a moment, placing a kiss on her abdomen, just above the edge of her panties before he hooked his finger under the sides and pulled them off as well. He stood once again, and unclasped her bra, tossing it with all the other clothing on the floor. He just stood there and stared at her. He'd seen her naked several times before, Christ, he'd watched her give birth to their son, but that was nothing like the desire flooding his veins now.

He let his gaze travel from her head to her toes, near overwhelmed knowing he was going to touch and make love to every inch of her.

"Och, Aislinn ye are a beautiful woman."

She looked away, before he touched her face, bringing her gaze back to his.

"I am glad ye can love me." He picked her up and placed her on the bed, and after hurriedly shedding his own clothes, joined her, lying next to her on his side. He kissed her full and deep, hearing … no, feeling, her sigh as his mouth claimed hers. He smiled. "Och, you like that? It's been a while since I've kissed you like that." Aedan froze and pulled back, realizing what he'd said.

Aislinn grasped his face and pulled it to hers, kissing him with all the passion she'd hidden away for so long. Her kisses were hot and desperate and tinged with tears.

He traced the tattoo designs that adorned her body. It was almost as if they beckoned his fingers to follow them as they circled her full breasts, trailed over her abdomen and around to her back side. They were tantalizing and mysterious with their secrets and as he touched and kissed every design, he was filled with a glimpse of his past. Flashes of a memory, of making love to Aislinn came to him then, and he paused.

The candlelight dancing over her skin, over the designs, reminded him of something just on the edge of his memory. He ran his fingers over her, as if touching the fire itself. Her skin warmed and prickled under his hand and she trembled tellingly as he stroked her intimately.

Something was happening to him, something moved through him then, powerful and ancient, drawing his mind away from this place. As he continued to love her, off in the distance he could hear the unmistakable sound of drums. He felt himself being pulled closer and closer toward the sound, toward a clearing in the woods. He could feel the cool mist of the night on his skin tingling and tantalizing, as if it were fingers caressing him. He could hear the sounds of the creatures, the breeze, and the crackle of the fire. His body throbbed with the pulse of the night, full and heavy with a need as fevered and primal as he'd ever experienced.

He was consumed with this need and his only thought was in seeking release from the sweet torment.

You are the fire. He looked around for the source of those words, but knew they weren't spoken aloud.

The drums beckoned, the blood pounded through his veins, his body matched the rhythm of the night.

A triumphant cry of surrender tore from his throat as he gave himself over to the pleasure moving through him. Aislinn's voice mingled with his as together they fell into oblivion.

Aedan flung himself over onto his back, clutching his heaving chest. He clenched his eyes tight as he sucked in large breaths of air.

"I'm burning, Aislinn. I felt the night, I heard the drums, felt the flames."

Aislinn too attempted to calm her ragged breathing. "Yes."

"'Tis slipping away and I donnae want to lose it." Aedan reached for Aislinn and pulled her to him. "Donnae hold back. Love me with all that was between us. I want to know. I want to remember."

Aedan woke to fussing sounds coming from Aididh through the baby monitor. His gaze settled on the empty space beside him before rising and going to his son.

"Hey, wee one." Aedan said, approaching Aididh's crib. Aididh stopped crying immediately upon hearing his father's voice. Aedan reached in and picked up the child.

"Och, but ye are a strong lad."

Aididh fussed once again. "Let's change your diaper before I take ye to your Mum." Aedan carried the baby over to the changing table. 'I want to thank ye for sleeping so long and giving me time with your Mum." Aedan continued to change Aididh, who seemingly listened intently to his dad. "You'll learn someday that 'tis important to have time with your woman."

Aididh, having enough of the man-to-man talk, began crying.

"Just a second more and I'll take ye to eat. I ken you're hungry, and I'm sure your Mum will gain some relief from your hearty appetite. There."

Aedan picked up his son. "Och, but you're a bonny lad, Aididh." He kissed his son's forehead. "And perhaps you'll have a brother just as bonny as you verra soon." He left the room with the baby.

Aedan found Aislinn lying on the couch, cocooned in the plaid, his plaid, she'd carried back from Ireland. His heart broke. Everything they'd shared during the night only served in bringing back the past and the heartbreaking memories she tried so hard to push away.

Aididh fussed again, obviously hungry and voicing his displeasure. Aislinn woke and sat up as Aedan handed Aididh to her. He sat beside her and watched his son greedily sate his hunger.

Aislinn looked up at him and forced a smile, but he saw the truth behind her eyes.

"I will find a way, Aislinn. I promise."

Chapter Forty-Four

"GET UP, AISLINN, LASS. Hurry." Aedan roused her from sleep.

"What's the matter?" Aislinn suddenly jumped up wide awake. "Aididh?"

"He's fine."

"Then what?" She laid back down.

"Get dressed. We're leaving. We have to go," Aedan tugged her up.

"Aedan, we don't have to go anywhere. It's Saturday, remember?"

Aedan continued to bustle around the room, plopping a backpack on the bed next to Aislinn.

"What are you doing?"

"Packing."

"What? What for?" She threw back the covers and sat on the edge of the bed. "Aedan?"

Aedan stopped and looked at her. His beautiful Aislinn. *Och,* but as Beltane approached, she'd become more and more distracted. Aedan had hoped their continued intimacy would ease her remaining loneliness, but making love only seemed to deepen the emptiness she carried.

He knew she thought about the man he used to be a lot more than she admitted. She tried very hard to hide it, but he saw it each time he looked into her eyes. He saw the hint of longing behind her smile. The letter he'd written to her as his former self said she would always ache for what was lost, and she did. Constantly.

But lately, as spring approached, the emptiness began to consume her. Tonight, as they made love, he could feel the sorrow in her heart more deeply than he'd ever felt it before and it tore him apart knowing how she suffered. Christ, but what he wouldn't give to make everything right between them.

He had gone over every aspect of what she had told him of their ceremony. Day after day, he mentally noted and listed every detail as he tried to determine what they'd missed. The answer unexpectedly came to him this morning as he lay awake looking at her, and he bolted from the bed.

"Where are you going?" Aislinn asked through her groggy state.

"Nae me. We."

"What?"

"Aislinn, I think I figured it out. I think I ken what I have to do, but we've got to get to Ireland before tomorrow so we can try it." He threw a few clothes in his backpack as he continued. "I've gone over and over what ye told me. Ye told me about the night of the ceremony where you saw the visage of the Lady and she beckoned you to say the words your grandmother taught you. When ye first told me the poem you thought it was meant for me as well as you, to say the words. I never did. I never let that magical essence into me or the Beltane ritual that night. I think I need to say them to complete the ceremony."

Aislinn jolted upright, stunned. "Do you really think? Could it be that simple?"

"I donnae think there is anything simple about words that evoke magical elements, but, aye, 'tis possible. 'Tis worth a try. Get up, get dressed. Let's catch the next plane we can. Call Beth and see if she'll watch Aididh for a couple of days."

"What should I tell her?"

"Only that we have to go out of town unexpectedly."

"Oh, my God," Aislinn screeched, hurriedly climbing out of bed.

For the first time since awakening in the hospital, Aedan noticed the flicker of hope in her eyes, and he prayed he was right. "Make sure to pack the amulets."

Chapter Forty-Five

IRELAND, PRESENT DAY

"Och, I cannae remember," Aedan bellowed, pushing farther and faster into the woods, knocking branches out of his way as he went.

"Aedan, it will be dark, soon."

"Donnae ye think I ken that?" he snapped, not hiding his frustration at not knowing where the glen was. He paused, looking over at Aislinn. "I'm sorry. I just thought I'd hold some memory of this place." He scanned the woods, running his fingers through his hair.

Aislinn turned her head, trying to discern something as a sudden breeze ruffled her hair. "*Shh*, listen."

Aedan's skin bristled, watching Aislinn turn toward the wind, her eyes following the movement of the trees as the breeze whipped past them. Something stirred inside him, something deep and powerful. Ancient. He was momentarily stunned by the sensation. Aislinn's voice shook the feeling from him.

"That way." Aislinn pointed in the direction of the swaying branches. "The wind is showing us where to go."

Aedan's feet remained rooted to the ground. "How do ye ken that, Aislinn?" He saw the perplexed look cross her face.

"I don't know. I just do." She looked at Aedan. "I wished I could help you, and then suddenly my thoughts were out there." She motioned to the air around them. "Then I heard something, like a very soft whisper."

403

"Och, I think ye have more magic in ye than you ken." Aedan reached for her hand. "Come. We must hurry."

True to Aislinn's premonition, they found the glen, and the stone just before nightfall. Together they scavenged enough dry brush and wood to start a small fire. They huddled around it, keeping warm in the hours before midnight.

The silence was awkward, both lost in their own thoughts. Aislinn spoke, breaking the quiet. "Aedan, I want you to know, no matter what happens, It means a lot to me that you came here."

Aedan took her hand in his, lovingly stroking it with his fingers. "I ken there was something extraordinary between us, Aislinn. I wish more than anything that I could recapture it, but I do love ye, lass, as much as I possibly can."

Aislinn smiled a sad smile.

"I donnae ken how to make the pain go away for you. I see it each time we make love. You love me, but there are things I am not. Things I may never be. I fear losing you if things donnae go as planned tonight." Aedan sighed. He'd bared his soul to her, his deepest fear and regret.

Aislinn squeezed his hand. "I do love you. Although the loss of who you once were remains deep inside me, it doesn't change my love for you. If the ceremony doesn't work tonight, my life is still with you and Aididh. I am so lucky for the both of you, and I'm so sorry for the pain I have caused you. I promise, Aedan, you will have my heart, no matter what happens."

Aedan searched Aislinn's face and her eyes and knew the truth of her words. "'Tis so good to know. I am fortunate in all things." He told her, touching her cheek tenderly.

Aedan stood solemnly at the sacred stone, draped with the familiar cloth they'd brought from home. Aislinn stood next to him, shivering in her nakedness.

"One moment more, Aislinn while I stoke the fire, then I will warm ye up." He watched as she smiled at his feeble attempt at humor. He hurried to place the wood on the fire.

As soon as the fire burned bright and warm, he pulled Aislinn into his arms and placed a kiss on her forehead. He swung her up into his arms and carried her over to the blanket covered stone and laid her upon it. He easily slid above her, wrapping his arms around her.

"I'm already hard with need, anticipating how sweet being inside you feels," he whispered against her lips.

She smiled sweetly at him. "You always talked to me like that because you could feel how aroused it made me."

He kissed her again. "I can feel ye growing warm." His hand slipped between their bodies, moving to the source of her heat. "And that arouses *me*."

"You don't feel awkward about being out here?" Aislinn asked, closing her eyes in response to his caresses.

"Nae." He took her hand and drew it to his body to prove his point. "I've seen this place in my mind while making love to you. I've been here before, bare before the Goddess, pledging my heart to you." He closed his eyes, momentarily giving into the gentle stroking of Aislinn's hand. "As I will once again." He kissed her long and hard. "Open for me, Aislinn. Say the words as ye take me inside."

Aislinn lifted her eyes to his as Aedan drew himself over her, shifting her legs to wrap around him as he entered her. The fire rose around them as Aislinn lifted the two halves of the amulets and slid them together. Flames burned brighter and hotter with each thrust of his body against hers. He saw the tendrils reach for her, saw the way the firelight danced over her glistening skin. He felt the shudder of her body as she shattered beneath him. He whispered the words a moment later.

"In this time, we unite as one. In this grove, 'twill be done. To give a soul, to share a heart, to come together, never to part. Oak and

May and Beltane fire. On this night we find desire. Fill us with the ancient's call. Goddess' blessing one and all."

So much pleasure washed through him at this moment, a desperation so intense it took his breath. He wanted this woman with more than his body, more than his heart. His soul reached for hers, and he wanted so badly to touch hers. He was near blinded by the brilliance.

His body claimed hers with a need so fierce, he was sure he was being torn asunder in his attempt to grasp the elusive thread of her soul just out of his reach. He strained with every fiber of his being toward her as his body blissfully erupted within her, and the flames engulfed him. The words from her lips reached his ears.

"In this time, we unite as one. In this grove, 'twill be done. To give a soul, to share a heart. To come together, never to part. Oak and May and Beltane fire. On this night we find desire. Fill us with the ancient's call. Goddess' blessing one and all."

Over the roar of the flames, he heard her continue, "I call the wind as my breath, the water to quell my thirst. I join my body with the earth, and share my passion with fire."

He felt something he'd not felt before as he listened to her words, something new and yet so familiar - a connection of sorts. He knew with a certainty it was Aislinn he felt inside him. Aedan felt such jubilation at finding what had been lost.

Aedan looked up for a split second at the flames dancing round them. In their tantalizing depths, he saw the Lady. *Say the words*. He gave a reverent nod to the magnificent visage before lowering his gaze to Aislinn and began to speak.

"I call the wind as my breath, water to quell my thirst. I join my body with the earth and share my passion with fire. My love, Aislinn."

In her fingertips, the two amulets became one, fused together by the magic that had rent them apart in the first place. Within seconds of becoming whole, the amulet disintegrated to dust, blowing away with the wind. Aislinn looked up at Aedan as her eyelids gently closed.

Chapter Forty-Six

AISLINN BLINKED ONCE and blinked again, trying to focus on her surroundings. She sat up suddenly.

"Och, lass, you're awake." Aedan came and knelt beside her.

"Aedan?"

"Aye."

"You're here?"

"Aye, lass." Aislinn threw her arms around him, burying her face against his strong chest. She deeply inhaled the scent that was so familiar to her.

"Where are we?"

"The cave, remember? Where we hid before the ceremony."

"How'd we get here?"

"I brought you. I was afraid to wake you. Yer sleep was, *er*, unnatural," he explained.

Aislinn watched Aedan eye her disorientation with suspicion. Aislinn looked down at herself, naked except for his plaid. She was covered with blood, Aedan's blood.

"Oh, my God, Aedan. Brennis. He killed you."

"Nae, lass. He wounded me, but I killed him. I'm sorry if my blood frightens ye. I'll help you wash."

"I saw Brennis. I saw him stab you. I saw you die, Aedan."

"Just a wee scratch, but I will need medical attention once we return to Dublin." He turned and Aislinn saw the large wound in his side under a makeshift dressing.

"Aedan, can you feel me?"

"Aye. And ye are frightened and confused, but I donnae ken why."

"The ceremony—Is it over? Did we ...? Did it work?"

"Aye. As far as I can tell. I brought ye here after and lit the fire to keep you warm."

"What day is it, Aedan?"

"May second. You slept the whole day, yesterday."

Aislinn's hand flew to her neck. "The amulets. Where are the amulets?"

"They turned to dust. Their magic was through."

"The blanket?"

"Also vanished to the wind."

"The magic is gone. Do you still have your magic, Aedan?"

"Aye. I suspect I will be able to convince a doctor in Dublin to stitch me up with verra few questions."

Aislinn shook her head, stood, and began pacing.

"What is it, Aislinn? Why do I feel such fear in you?"

Aislinn looked down again at her body. Despite the blood, she was whole and in remarkable shape. She looked carefully at her breasts. They were not breasts that just three days ago fed her child.

"Oh my God. Aididh. Where is Aididh?"

Aedan moved up alongside her. "Aislinn?"

"Aididh. Where is he?"

"Who is Aididh, lass?"

"Our child. Our son."

Aedan laid a hand on her abdomen. "I just felt the tiny sparks of possibility a moment ago."

"I'm just now pregnant?"

"I believe so."

"How can that be? He was three months old when we left yesterday."

"Aislinn, sit, please, have a drink of water." Aedan placed his arm around her and led her closer to the small fire. He seated her on a blanket and wrapped another around her shoulders, then retrieved a bottle of water.

"He was our life. Little Aididh. He's gone?" A pang of longing filled her. She touched her stomach.

Aedan sat beside her, concern etching his face. She could feel his love wrapping around her heart. He willed his strength into her.

"I can feel you, Aedan."

He smiled. "'Tis wonderful, is it nae?"

"'Tis wonderful," she repeated in a halfhearted jest.

"Aididh? 'Tis the name you want to call our son?"

"He was beautiful, Aedan, all round and baby plump, and he loved you so much." Aislinn looked over at Aedan, confusion creasing her brows. What was this weird *It's a Wonderful Life* scenario unfolding before her? She didn't understand what had happened.

"Aedan, while I slept, here, I lived a year. You awakened in Chicago and didn't remember anything. We had a son."

"'Tis a dream?"

"I'm not sure, but I don't think it was a dream." Aedan shifted, pulling her back against his chest, placing her in between his open legs, wrapping the plaid and his arms around her.

"Tell me then."

Aislinn took a deep breath, and for a second time in just a few months, she again found herself describing in full detail a life Aedan knew nothing about. She very honestly described the devastation of seeing him for the first time after finding out he was alive and learning he didn't know her. She relived the heartache of being alone and finding out she carried their child and the way he'd come to her, somehow drawn to her by things he didn't understand. She explained how he figured out what had gone wrong at the ceremony and encouraged her to return to Ireland this Beltane.

"And now 'tis as if that life dinnae exist and you are back to where you started."

"I don't know what to think, Aedan. I can tell you exactly what you wrote in the letter you left for me in the backpack over there." Aislinn gestured toward the other side of the cave. "I can tell you the name of the man in Chicago you told me to see. I know all of it, and yet it never happened? It doesn't make sense."

"I knew you, Aislinn, even in a different reality, our lives were still connected. I think the Lady's magic 'tis strong, and our destinies so entwined, our souls would find each other always. I cannae think of any other reason why we could defy time in such a manner."

"I was so heartbroken. I couldn't feel you at all. A piece inside me was missing."

"You can feel me now and verra soon you will feel our son."

"How do I know this is the reality that's supposed to be? How do I know this isn't some strange cosmic loop my life will keep playing over and over?"

"The magic is gone, the amulets, the blanket. I am mortal. The pain in my side 'tis proof of that."

"We were given a second chance to make it right." Aislinn closed her eyes briefly. "Thanks, Gram."

Chapter Forty-Seven

UNITED STATES, PRESENT Day

All morning something strange filled the air. Aislinn was discomfited by it. She could feel Aedan, but his emotions were tempered and still. Maybe she was a little nervous about the assembly this morning. Her students were excited about it. Each year, at the beginning of the school year, the students and staff gathered in the gym for the "Rah-rah let's-have-a-great-year" pep assembly; the school's way to get everyone fired up for the new school year and to start things out on a positive note.

This year, Aislinn would be receiving an award, along with Aedan from the Art Institute, in recognition of their work on the website. Usually, Aislinn wasn't much on big formal accolades, but Aedan had asked her to go along with it just this once. She agreed, knowing this would be her last year teaching.

She and Aedan had decided she would teach this year, and then she, Aedan, and Aididh would move up north to the cottage. Aedan saw to the renovations and modernizations the tiny cottage needed for their growing family. She would miss teaching, she knew, but with the studio Aedan planned to build for her, she'd have plenty to keep her busy.

Aislinn checked her watch. She knew Aedan would be here somewhere. The assembly was due to begin shortly. He was probably waiting in the lounge having a cup of coffee not wanting to disrupt her class.

At 10:30 a.m., Aislinn returned the kids to their homeroom teacher so he could take them to the gym. Aislinn followed the students. There were four chairs set in the middle of the gym floor, one for the principal, one for the person from the Art Institute, one for Aedan and the fourth was for her. The assemblage seemed a bit daunting to Aislinn as she made her way to the chairs. She shook hands with the person from the Institute, looking around for Aedan.

She watched the remainder of the students and staff, file in and fill the bleachers.

The students waved and called to her, and she politely waved back, perplexed as to where Aedan was. Beth and her class were the last to arrive, and because they were younger, the bottom rows of the bleachers were for them. Aislinn looked up at her, shrugged, and raised her brows with a confused expression.

Where was Aedan?

The principal stepped to the front and raised his hand for the kids to settle down so he could begin. After a moment, the gym grew quiet.

He gave the usual welcome back speech, citing how this year would be the best ever. The kids cheered for the upcoming year's events the principal outlined as well as for the new playground equipment that had been installed over the summer. Overall, the students were excited to be back in school.

"And now we have a special presentation for our art teacher, Ms. O'Neil." The principal motioned for the representative from the Institute to step forward, along with Aislinn.

Where was Aedan?

Aislinn stood, and joined the others. She looked out over the sea of faces and thought to herself she would kill Aedan for making her do this alone.

"On behalf of the Art Institute of Chicago, I would like to present to Ms. Aislinn O'Neil the very first Art Educator Award for her outstanding contribution to the Art Institute's Teacher Resource Department. Ms. O'Neil, along with our staff member, Mr. MacKendrick, developed and designed our new interactive, on-line educator resource program."

Aislinn bit the inside of her lip to keep her attention focused. Should she be worried Aedan wasn't here? The next thing she knew she was being handed a plaque and was shaking hands and being asked if she'd like to say something.

What would she say? She wasn't prepared to say anything. Her principal took the plaque from her while she spoke.

"Thank you. I really hadn't planned on speaking much other than to say this has been an incredible experience and—" She stopped, her voice catching. *Where was Aedan?* "And I really appreciate the Institute's willingness to expand their online resource department to make it easier, not only for art educators, but for all educators to enhance their students' visit to the museum with informative and fun material now available on line."

What did she say? Did she even make sense? She stepped back, indicating she'd finished. The gym erupted in applause. The kids were clapping and cheering for her.

Aislinn didn't know how much time had passed before the sudden look of shock and excitement on the faces in the audience registered. She had been recounting the speech she'd made, but for some reason happened to glance at Beth and her students. It was then that she noticed the look on the faces in the crowd. Even Beth couldn't keep from grinning from ear to ear, and putting her hand on her mouth in surprise.

Aislinn glanced over her shoulder to see what all the excitement was about and instantly froze, moving only to put her hand on her chest to still her frantically beating heart. Aislinn couldn't believe her eyes.

She blinked, thinking her mind must be playing tricks on her. But no, there was Aedan in full Scottish regalia strolling toward her.

He was breathtakingly dressed, head to foot, like the Scot he was. He wore a white, cotton shirt, covered by a perfectly fitted suit jacket. He wore his kilt with the plaid, pleated longer in the back, billowing behind him as he walked. The fabric was held in place by a thick leather strap belted at his waist.

Around his waist, he also wore his sword belt complete with sword, as well as his sporran. On his bare legs, he wore the traditional knee-high stockings and dress shoes. His hair was wild and unbound, braided with beads. He carried a large bouquet of white roses and smiled at her with that knowing look he displayed when he knew he had caught her off guard.

Aislinn stood, shocked. She felt as if for all the world she was going to faint. She heard the kids cheer, and she trembled, her hands flying to cover her mouth. She watched him walking toward her, sure she was dreaming. She shook her head, and his smile broadened.

Aedan handed her the flowers. Aislinn looked up at him, still confused, but took them with shaky hands. The kids continued to cheer. They were so caught up in the moment and anticipation.

Aedan suddenly dropped to one knee in front of her and reached into his sporran. Aislinn could hear the gasps and squeals from the audience, but remained confused as to what Aedan was doing.

With everyone as a witness, Aedan pulled out a ring, a beautiful deep red ruby circled with diamonds, much like the stone in the hilt of his sword. She'd no doubt the ring was as old as he was. Like a warrior prince of old, he reached out and took Aislinn's hand.

"Aislinn, will ye have me as your husband?"

He held out the ring for her.

The look on Aislinn's face was one of absolute shock. She was speechless.

"Weel, lass?" He smiled with the familiar twinkle in his eyes that she loved so much. He managed to sweep her off her feet, as he'd promised.

"Yes ... Oh yes."

She flung her arms around him as he stood. He took the ring and slipped the band on her trembling finger as he held her hand over his heart. He kissed her long and good, wrapping his other arm around her to pull her close.

There wasn't a dry eye in the place. Everyone present was moved beyond words, especially Aislinn.

She looked up at him.

"Ye *will* have yer proper wedding as I promised. How's this for a start?"

"You're unbelievable. How did you manage this? I wanted to wring your neck for leaving me up here."

Aedan laughed a deep throaty laugh. "I am nae a knight, but can I sweep ye off your feet, lass?" He scooped her up into his arms and planted a kiss full on her lips amidst the roar of thunderous applause.

The principal stepped over and cleared his throat. "Go home," he winked at Aedan.

Aedan needed no more incentive.

Aedan carried her out of the auditorium straight to her classroom so she might retrieve her belongings.

"How did you manage to keep this secret?"

He placed his fingers on her lips. "I'll tell you everything soon enough."

"Did you have something to do with me being allowed to take the day off?" she asked, picking up her bag.

Aedan just smiled. "'Tis good some of the magic remained, aye?"

He took her hand and led her toward the door.

"Is it true what they say about what a Scotsman wears under his kilt?"

He smiled. "Ye will be finding out as soon as we get home."

Epilogue

UNITED STATES, SIX Years Later

"On your mark, get set, go!" Aedan called, racing for the top of the hill. He purposely stumbled, rolled and pretended to fall so the others would beat him in the climb.

"Da, I beat you. I won!" Six-year-old Aididh called from the top.

"Me too. Me too!" Cheered his younger brother Sean.

"You can't win, too," Aididh argued. "I was first."

"Yes I can, can't I Da?"

Aedan crested the hill, toting the youngest MacKendrick under his arm.

"Aye. Ye are both winners, right wee Robbie?"

"Da," the youngest cooed in seeming agreement.

"Hey, what about me? I could use a little help here," Aislinn's voice came from the beach below.

"Aididh, hold onto your brother while I help your Mum." Aedan passed little Robbie to his older sibling. "She's feeling a bit awkward these days."

"That's because she's fat," Sean piped in.

"She's not fat. She's going to have another baby, right Da?"

"Aye, and this one's giving her a bit of trouble. I suspect it's a girl, but donnae go telling your Mum. She doesnae ken yet." He winked at his boys and disappeared back down the hill, reappearing moments later with Aislinn on his arm.

"Hey, Mum." Aididh called, taking her hand when he could reach it safely, while holding Robbie. Aedan was proud how protective Aididh was of his mother. *The lad takes after his Da.*

"I think it's bath time for ye boys," Aislinn instructed as they walked toward the cottage. Despite the grumbles from the children, Aedan glanced impishly over at Aislinn and raised his eyebrows. Aislinn smiled as the sparks ignited between them.

"*Aww*, Mum."

"Nae arguing about it tonight. Warriors donnae complain," Aedan instructed his sons. "Your Mum's tired, so we're going to go right in and clean up and get to bed. You've had a busy day fighting the sea serpents."

Aedan didn't miss the difficulty Aislinn was experiencing on the walk back. At eight months pregnant, she was larger than she'd been with her previous three and extremely uncomfortable.

"I'll put the boys down," he said leaning over and kissing her. "You go take a bath. I'll join you shortly." He gave Aislinn a wink before following the boys.

After reading the boys a bedtime story and kissing them all goodnight, Aedan made his way to the bathroom, stripping off his clothes as he went. As he sank into the oversized bathtub behind her, he immediately wrapped his arms around her and pulled her against him. She rested her head back on his chest. Aedan ran his hand over her swollen belly. He could feel the bursts of little feet kicking from the inside and smiled. He traced his fingers over the spiral designs on Aislinn's skin, relaxing her. He knew Aislinn was exhausted with this child She'd not felt well for most of the pregnancy. He knew it was her body telling her it was her last.

"This one's a mite feisty." He nestled his face next to hers and kissed her. "She's going to be strong willed and red-haired like her Mum."

Aislinn smiled. "A girl. Oh, how wonderful to have a girl," she sighed. "Aedan, I miss our intimate times," she confessed after a few quiet moments.

"Aye. 'Tis been a long while with this babe. I miss it too."

"I've been pregnant long enough. After this baby, I want you back. It's time for us again."

"Aye. Ye have given me three, nearly four beautiful children, Aislinn. 'Tis enough." Aedan continued to rub her belly. "Besides, I think we will have our hands full especially with this one."

Aislinn smiled and touched his hands, as he kissed her cheek again. "'Twill nae be long before I'll be loving ye right and proper again," he whispered in his most seductive husky voice. "I'll even wear the kilt," he added in a teasing tone.

Aislinn's laugh warmed his heart.

"You'll make me all weak-kneed and willing wearing that," she admitted.

He placed another tender kiss on her cheek. "Ah. Just the way I like you, my Irish princess."

"Then, my warrior, I'm all yours."

~The End~

If you enjoyed Aedan and Aislin's love story, then get swept away once more with three new magical romances by Angela Aaron.

The Guardian, The Ghost and The Fae. Experience the secrets, surprises, and sacrifices of the Shadowstone Legend Trilogy. Contemporary romances filled with magic, mystery, and sizzling passion that provide the perfect fantasy escape.

See below for more information on these and other Angela Aaron books.

If you enjoyed The Fire of Beltane please thank your author by leaving a review.

About The Author

ANGELA AARON IS A WRITER of contemporary romance with a fantasy twist. Her stories have stormy

courtships, intriguing secrets, magic, mystery, enough steam to curl your toes, and plenty of romance to warm your heart. Angela loves to write stories that will suck you in and make you believe every word of it is true. Angela lives in the Midwest with her dogs and loves to camp in the summer and travel to warmer places during the winter.

Pleasure Island was first released in 2011, with the second edition rereleased in 2013. Angie's second book, **The Fire of Beltane** was released in 2012, with the rerelease in 2024. In 2014 Angie released her third book, **A Mediterranean Affair. The Guardian Shadowstone Legend** was released in 2015. **The Ghost ~ Shadowstone Legend 2** was released in 2017. The final book of the Shadowstone Legend series, **The Fae ~ Shadowstone Legend 3** was released in 2023.

ANGIE LOVES TO CONNECT with her readers.

You can reach her at msangieaaron@gmail.com

Facebook: https://www.facebook.com/profile.php?id=100089510231706

Webpage: http://angelaaaronauthor.com/

YouTube: https://www.youtube.com/@AngelaAaronAuthor
Instagram: https://www.instagram.com/angelaaaronauthor/
TikTok: https://www.tiktok.com/@angieaaronauthor

Also Available from Angela Aaron

THE GUARDIAN ~ SHADOWSTONE Legend

CAILEN IS THRUST INTO the mystical role of guardian by an ancient pledge. Sworn to protect the bearer of the enigmatic Shadowstone, he must unravel the magic and power of the sacred Fae object before the Fae can reclaim the stone and the one who bears it.

Rebecca never believed in the Fae or Faerie legends, let alone considered she was descended from one. On the hunt for her missing mother, she becomes embroiled in a dangerous quest with an invisible foe and has no choice but to rely on the assistance of the cocky Scottish laird to stay alive.

As the talisman's secrets are revealed and passion ignites, Cailen and Rebecca must confront the looming heartache threatening their future.

THE GHOST ~ SHADOWSTONE Legend 2

WRACKED WITH UNENDING guilt and torment, Brynn must find a way back into the shadowy realm of Fae to rescue his imprisoned comrades. Only one person can help him undertake this dangerous mission, a witch named Fenora. His love. However, Brynn must set aside his feelings for the exotic sorceress and follow his sense of duty, knowing he will not survive.

Fenora thought her dealings with the Fae were finished. However, the arrival of Brynn and the Shadowstone, as well as the unexpected voice calling to her from her garden, was evidence her dealings with the other worldly creatures were far from over. Torn between her sense of duty as a witch and her love for the tortured ancient warrior, Fenora must, once again, unravel the mystery and magic of her destiny.

Together Brynn and Fenora must bring home those trapped in the unearthly realm, despite a shocking revelation that will threaten their future together.

The Fae ~ Shadowstone Legend 3

ONE STONE, ONE PROPHECY, two worlds collide. The magic, mystery, and passion continue in this final installment of the Shadowstone Legend.

Torn between her love for the warrior, Brynn, and her destiny, Fenora aligns with the Fae, Amae'n, not only with her magic, but with her surrender as well.

Called from history to fulfill his role as protector of the witch Fenora, Brynn must confront his memories of the past and fight for a future with the woman he loves.

As the final confrontation with the Fae approaches, will the sacrifices Brynn, Fenora, and the others have made be enough to triumph? Or will Amae'n find the magic he needs to destroy both Fae and the human realm?

Shadowstone Legend eBook Box Set

Alpha warriors, enchanting witches, and mystical Fae weave a wonderfully magical adventure that provides the perfect fantasy escape.

Imagine a world full of mystery, passion, and danger. Where warriors from the past, modern day witches, and ancient Fae are very real. Their lives become tangled in a web of love, magic, and deceit set into motion by the discovery of a spell-bound talisman and prophetic poem. Events that span the past and present reveal a destiny fraught with sacrifice and heartache, that must be fulfilled no matter the cost.

The Shadowstone Legend series follows the fate of two warrior brothers, Cailen and Brynn along with their lovers, a beautiful Fae descendant, Rebecca, and a tantalizing witch, Fenora. They, along with their companions, must face unseen danger and unexpected conflicts while unraveling the clues hidden throughout an ancient poem. Their future as well as the fate of the Fae and human realms hinges on defeating the evil that threatens them at every turn. What started in the past, ends in the present.

The Shadowstone Legend series (The Guardian, The Ghost, and The Fae) is an adult contemporary fantasy romance with mature content.

A destiny of magic and intrigue unfolds all because he dared to love a Fae

.Pleasure Island

When Cassie Douglas unknowingly arrives at a sultry tropical island resort where the sole business is to provide the perfect pleasure fantasy, Cassie finds it difficult to overcome her inhibitions and join in the fun. When she mees the sexy resort owner, Cassie must decide what is real when it comes to matters of the heart.

Ryan MacKenna isn't about to let the feisty redhead disrupt his life or his business. He lives firmly by his set of self-imposed rules, which keep business and pleasure very separate. However, from the first moment he meets Ms. Douglas, he is in danger of breaking every rule.

The Fire of Beltane

When Aedan is denied his soulmate one fateful Beltane night, he is given the gift of immortality, permitting him to wait for her prophesied return. Reunited after eleven-hundred years, he is disheartened to learn his true love holds no memory of him.

Wishing for a distraction from the winter doldrums, Aislinn never expects to be caught up in a whirlwind of magic and danger with a man she has spent her whole life dreaming about. What he asks of her tests the very reality she holds dear.

Now as Beltane approaches, and with time running out, Aedan and Aislinn must reach Ireland to pledge their love to one another. But in order to live out their destinies, they must overcome an ancient foe determined to see an end to their fated love.

Eleven hundred years he waited for her. He could lose her in a single moment.

A Mediterranean Affair

When Andrea's boyfriend presents her with a romantic cruise through the Mediterranean on Cupid Cruise Lines, it seems just the inspirational backdrop needed for him to finally pop the question. However, when her boyfriend is a no-show and sends yet another consolation gift to make up for his absence Andrea knows any hope for romance is extinguished.

Lorenzo has better things to do than play delivery boy to a spoiled cruise ship passenger.

Returning to his native Italy, after swearing off love, he spends his time in solitude working at the vineyard. Nevertheless, when his grandfather asks him to make the special delivery, he can't refuse. From the moment he walks in on the scantily clad American woman he knows his life is about to take an unexpected turn.

Now Andrea and Lorenzo must each let go of their past to make room for each other. Can they accept the lure of Cupid's arrow despite the miles that separate them?